Blood & Thunder

Blood & Thunder
The Life & Art of Robert E. Howard

MARK FINN
INTRODUCTION BY JOE R. LANSDALE

Blood & Thunder: The Life and Art of Robert E. Howard
Copyright © 2006 Mark Finn

Introduction © 2006 Joe R. Lansdale

Cover illustration and design © 2006 John Picacio

A MonkeyBrain Books Publication
www.monkeybrainbooks.com

No part of this book may be reproduced or transmitted in any form or by any means, graphic, electronic, or mechanical, including photocopying, recording, taping, or by any information storage or retrieval system, without the permission in writing from the publisher.

MonkeyBrain Books
11204 Crossland Drive
Austin, TX 78726
info@monkeybrainbooks.com

ISBN: 1-932265-21-X
ISBN: 978-1-932265-21-7

Printed in the United States of America
10 9 8 7 6 5 4 3 2 1

Table of Contents

Introduction by Joe R. Lansdale	1
Part 1	5
The Oil Boom	9
Isaac and Hester	21
The Traveling Howards	29
Post Oak Country	37
Part 2	53
Authentic Liars	57
The Tattler	73
Soda Jerk	91
The Deal	103
Part 3	123
The Fighting Costigans	127
Lovecraft	145
Conan	165
Part 4	177
Novalyne	179
Vultures and Grizzlies	197
All Fled, All Done	213
Mythology	229
Afterword	249
Bibliography	251
Index	256

Dedication

This book is dedicated to anyone who ever drove to Cross Plains, Texas, stood in the doorway of Robert E. Howard's room and felt a perceptible chill at the thought of being so close to where he created his blood and thunder.

The lamp expires, but the fire remains.

Acknowledgements

A number of people helped me with this daunting project in many ways; it feels like a collaborative effort as much as it does anything else. For invaluable assistance with materials, loaned rarities, photographs, and the sharing of years' worth of personal research, Leo Grin, Dennis McHaney, Brian Leno, Rob Roehm, Richard Bleiler, Margaret McNeel, Dennis Lien, Joe Marek, Jim Keegan, Chris Gruber, Rusty Burke, Patrice Louinet, and Paul Herman were exceptionally generous.

Several folks volunteered their time and efforts to proof-read, fact-check, and act as a peer review for the book, including Rusty Burke, Patrice Louinet, Paul Herman, Steve Trout, Steve Tompkins, Don Herron, Morgan Holmes, and Danny Street.

I enjoyed talking about Texas history, local and otherwise, and Texas writers, forgotten and otherwise, with Charlotte Laughlin, Bill Crider, Joe Lansdale, Scott Cupp, and Michael Moorcock.

I received timely library assistance from Joe White (The Petroleum Museum Library and Hall of Fame, Midland, Texas), Patrice Fox (The Harry Ransom Center, University of Texas, Austin, Texas), Hal Hall (Cushing Memorial Library, A&M University, College Station, Texas), and Andy Sawyer (curator of the Science Fiction Foundation Collection, Liverpool, England).

Many people had to endure endless readings, rants, late-night theories, musings, and explosions of frustration and euphoria. My sincere thanks to Rick Klaw, Peggy Hailey, Cathy Day, Jess Nevins, Jenna Martin, Paul and Sharon Nash, the various members of The Robert E. Howard United Press Association that I sent barrages of emails to, and again to Rusty Burke, Steve Tompkins, and Paul Herman, for not throttling me into submission on more than one occasion.

Throughout this project, Jack and Barbara Baum were extremely supportive of my efforts and their friendship and encouragement was a godsend.

Finally, thanks to comrades-in-arms Chris Roberson for making me do this, John Picacio for making me look good, and of course, to Robert E. Howard for initially getting under my twelve year-old skin and making me want to write.

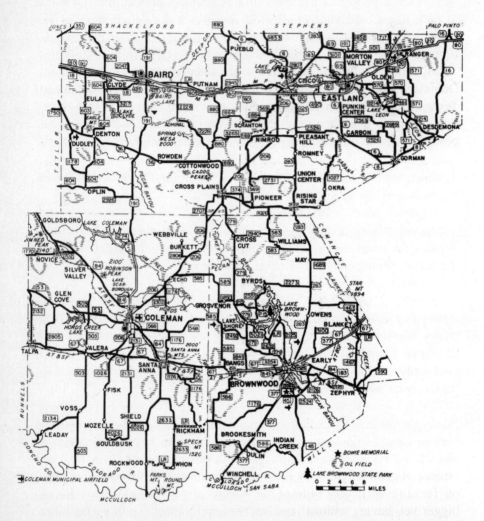

West Central Texas, circa late 1930s, showing geography, farm-to-market roads, and other major features. Clockwise from top left: Callahan County (Cross Plains), Eastland County (Ranger), Brown County (Brownwood and Cross Cut), and Coleman County (Burket).

INTRODUCTION
ROBERT E. HOWARD:
THE TEXAS TORNADO

Robert E. Howard is one of the most important writers ever to come out of Texas, and deserves a place beside such valued Texas writers as J. Frank Dobie and *Old Yeller*'s Fred Gipson. He, like they, helped build a place in Texas literature, though his position is somewhat to one side of the others. Examining his work in a brighter light, however, we would find that his position, as far as influence, should perhaps place him central to the others and broaden his title well beyond that of "Texas writer."

Dobie and Gipson influenced Texas literature—and in fact, gave Texas a literature of its own which had been long and woefully absent—but their impact, though larger than Texas alone, has primarily been noted as regional. Certainly, when the two writers are mentioned—and truthfully, those mentions are becoming fewer and fewer as time marches on—they are spoken of as Texans, and as Texas writers, and therefore they wear only the Texas brand.

Being a Texan myself, I can't say as I find this an absolute negative. But in the case of Howard, few associate him with Texas because so little of his output was directly about Texas—though in another sense, Texas and Texas attitudes, especially the Texas of his time, permeate his work. His creation Conan is a combination of oil field worker, rambling cowboy, and roguish card shark, even if he wears a lot less clothing and carries a sword instead of a pistol.

Howard was a contemporary of the aforementioned Texas writers, but I've never read of him in a literature or history book as having had any impact on Texas literature. In fact, I've never seen him mentioned at all outside of genre circles. My case is simple. Howard's impact is not only on Texas (even if very little of his work is directly about Texas), but is bigger yet, having national and international impact. Truth is, far more people know the work of Howard, and he has entertained far more readers and influenced far more writers, than the works of Dobie and Gipson combined. And you could toss in at least a dozen more popular Texas writers and find that Howard's impact would still measure up.

Actually, comparing Howard with other writers is next to impossible, as he was a genre unto himself. Certainly, he didn't have the style of a Hemingway or a Fitzgerald. But, in many things for which Hemingway is noted—masculine prose, action, and manly adventure—Howard is easily the equivalent, if not the superior. He didn't have the fine mood and texturing of a Fitzgerald, but he certainly had color and pageantry and could create atmosphere with the best of them.

And where often better-known, better-respected writers can dip into dullness in their attempts to steer clear of blood and thunder and the slings of literary critics, Howard waded into this messy end of the literary pool wearing hip boots and a smile. True, he had a number of irritating pulp habits; then again, that was his market, and he was the king of that market. And had he not been cursed with the worm of darkness writhing about in his electric-sparked brain, the worm that whispered to him and bit at him until he took a pistol to his head, there is little doubt in my mind that he would have continued to create and to have impacted Texas and American and international letters—if not as a great writer of literature, then as a writer of tales that readers want to read, and will continue to read long after Howard's bones and the actual works of many currently well-respected writers are dust.

Howard's special ability was to tap into the subconscious, into the true and often not-so-polite desires of what Freud called the Id. He did this best with the male Id, no doubt. The twelve-year-old male, being open to all the repressed desires that Howard displays, was perhaps his most obvious mark, but readers of all ages have fallen under his spell. His characters, like most characters of that era, were primarily male, and when they were not, the view was unquestionably a masculine, and often a chauvinistic, one. Then again, Hemingway would have to bow guilty to this as well, and where Papa Hemingway could become overly precious and even embarrassing in his attempts to present male and female discourse, Howard at least knew what he could do and what he could not.

But again, comparisons fall weakly and silently aside. Howard was Howard, and the situation is this: Howard should be better known not only as a creator of blood and thunder, but as a writer of importance and impact. It may be on the dirty corner of literature where he has had his greatest impact, but alas, it's a corner where he is more than a little evident. His Conan and other characters have been read by millions, and continue to be. His impact on writers, primarily of fantasy, is legion. There should be a Penguin edition of his best work, in the same way Lovecraft's work was recently presented. Hell, he, like Lovecraft—a writer of whom I'm not overly fond, but whose impact, like Howard's, is undeniable—should be on a postage stamp, grinning back at us from the left-hand corner of envelopes.

Like it or not, Howard is a writer of worth, working with dirty hands and a snotty nose sometimes, but flexing strong muscles that even hardcore literature fanatics ought to take note of. There is power in Howard's best work (and certainly some of his writing was awful), a rawness, a wet-bone, visceral relentlessness missing from so many bestsellers, and even from more respected works of literature. It's high time someone took serious note of him.

I haven't known Mark Finn long, and we have yet to have the time to really become tight friends, but I have known him long enough to respect his intent and dedication to this project. This book kicks so many old myths about Howard in the ass, tosses out the shade tree psychiatry, runs over with wide tires and heavy frame the seen-from-afar views of non-Texans, and gets into the real Robert E. Howard. It is the best piece of work ever written about this giant of Texas, and popular, literature. It comes from the inside out. Meaning right out of the bloody, sometimes dark, beating heart of Texas.

But enough. It is time for me to go. Time for me to leave you with Mark Finn, and he in turn to leave you with Robert E. Howard, and with a greater understanding of this Texas maverick's impact on genre literature. And I hope he will leave you, as he did me, with a greater respect for Howard and for his importance as a writer of worth in the broader arena, a scribbler due the respect of such masters of gut-level tales as Jack London (the writer he most resembles, providing one has no other alternative but to play the comparison game). But enough.

I present to you, Ladies and Gentlemen, Mark Finn.

And Mark will in turn present to you, Ladies and Gentlemen—as well as the less gentle and the less ladylike amongst you—the marvelous Tall Tale Spinner of Cross Plains, The Texas Tornado of Pulp, the flesh and blood man of the hour: Robert E. Howard.

Joe R. Lansdale

Part 1

The fifteen-year-old boy stood on the broad sidewalk outside the drugstore and watched the spectacle on the streets. Farming trucks, loaded with men and machinery, trundled by, grinding and coughing as the men laughed and jeered. Horse-drawn wagons followed, carrying pipes and large, interlocking drill bits. The farmers on the streets spoke with rueful envy of so-and-so's good luck. *He's set for life*, they assured one another.

Strangers walked up and down the sidewalks, hurrying to and from the bank, the diner, the feed store. They wore suits, despite the ungodly heat, and small-crowned hats that did not originate in John B. Stetson's workshop. One of the strangers brushed by the fifteen-year-old boy, absently knocking him on the shoulder. "Excuse me," said the boy, quietly. The stranger didn't reply, and his stride quickly carried him out of sight.

Harder, rougher men walked beside these captains of industry. These hard men wore more traditional frontier outfits: denim jeans and high boots, work shirts stained tobacco brown, and crushed straw hats. They didn't tip their hats as the women of the town walked by, but instead let their gaze linger in the women's wake.

The roughnecks on the trucks called out to the farmers, who waved automatically in reply. Large wagons full of men traveling in the other direction pulled up at the hitching post outside of Higginbotham's, and the men piled out, reeking of crude oil and mud. They bellowed and stamped, pushing each other out of the way in their haste to spend their pay. The men fanned out through the town, running toward their boarding houses, the public showers, the icehouse, the drugstore, or the barbershop.

Somewhere, a woman shrieked at the appearance of a roughneck. Other raised voices floated across the street, an argument about money. Glass shattered in one of the stores. Two men staggered out of the diner, swinging furious fists as a crowd of cheering onlookers poured out of the door to watch them. Someone hollered, "He's got a knife!" before the crowd encircled the combatants completely, their frenzied shouts drowning out the sounds of combat.

The fifteen-year-old boy walked past the lean-tos, where men in suits sat on wooden pallets, cooking food over a small fire, with women and children huddled around them. Further down the alley, a larger fire burned in an empty oil drum. A small clutch of men passed a bottle around, swilling generously.

More cars zigzagged around the wagons and trucks going out to the oil field and parking recklessly along the same hitching posts that had held horses last week. The packed dirt road was awash in thick mud from the summer rains and constant traffic. More women appeared on the sidewalks, gazing openly at the men, their eyes cutting under heavy lashes. A gunshot broke through the general din. The sun had just started to dip behind the low buildings. The night was young.

The fifteen-year-old boy watched it all, his furrowed brow darkening his blue eyes as he burned the images into his brain. The magazine he'd bought, the latest issue of *Adventure*, was folded in half and tucked carefully into his back pocket. Tonight, he would read it in the dim glow of an electric bulb, out on the sleeping porch, and dream himself to the other side of the world; far away from the roughnecks, the oil field bullies, and the women of low character.

His name was Robert E. Howard. His life was half over.

Cross Plains, Texas, during Trades Day, January 3rd, 1925 (photo courtesy Margaret McNeel).

THE OIL BOOM

Boomtown Saloon Keeper: How long have you been here, friend?
Gambler: About a week, I should think.
Boomtown Saloon Keeper: And what do you think of our little town?
Gambler: I do not say that everyone here is a son of a bitch, but I do say that every son of a bitch is here that could get here.

Robert E. Howard lived for only thirty years, but they were among the most violent and turbulent years in the history of Texas. It's hard for most modern people to conceptualize Texas as wild and untamed, especially when their only exposure to the state comes from living in or visiting major urban centers like Houston or Dallas, where one can find big box retail stores on every corner and every modern convenience in all of the suburban homes. But in truth, one hundred years before, Texas was virtually uninhabited. Most of the large-scale urbanization occurred in the early part of the twentieth century—during the same span of time that Robert E. Howard was alive.

Texas historian T. R. Fehrenbach estimated that at the beginning of the twentieth century, Texas was developmentally sixty years behind the rest of the United States. Texas had successfully made the transition from farming to agriculture, from cotton to cattle. The fierce battles for land with the Native Americans were still a recent memory. Ranchers and horses, cowboys and steers, were the order of the day for all but the most developed cities in East Texas, where the trappings of civilization were clearly seen and felt through the expansion of the railroads and shipping. Draw a more or less straight line from Fort Worth to Bandera, and everything west of that imaginary line was a vast expanse of ranching land sandwich between lonesome stretches of wilderness.

Large-scale farming soon returned to these areas, and d of the century much of the open range had been dissecte growing wheat, corn, and the king of cash crops, codes of the great deal of tension between the farmers and ranch rural areas, by countless B-grade westerns, but still not with in rural areas, Texas, however, was certainly large enough to the urban areas, cotton industries. which was based around

The population of Texas explo twentieth century. Two-thirds o spreading out to the west. T stimulated by the developm increasing agrarian production. One of the most important industries was the railroad and its expansion not only from north to south, but from east to west as well. As local spurs connected to larger, national lines, farmers and ranchers were able to move their products to buyers in other parts of the country.

For the last time in the history of Texas, the farmers and ranchers were kings. Even as the agricultural community was extremely wary of this modern progress, they had to contend with the emergence of the oil industry, initially developed by outside (non-Texan) interests. Texas reacted to these interlopers in much the same way that the South had responded to the carpetbaggers during the Reconstruction. But those who rushed into Texas to develop the oil industry did so with the same pioneering spirit that nearly every one of the early immigrants to Texas shared.

At the turn of the century, there were only four dominant urban centers in Texas: San Antonio, Dallas, Houston, and Fort Worth. San Antonio was the oldest city and the most cosmopolitan, with a wide distribution of ethnicities, including a large, integrated Chinese population. Despite the economic prosperity of white, Anglo-Saxon farmers, the black and Mexican populations had to contend with sharecropping, itinerant farming practices, and, in South Texas, corrupt politics as the local governments dealt with the flood of immigration from Mexico, a by-product of the Mexican Revolution. Overzealous Texas Rangers, employing the same tactics they had used on the Native Americans thirty years prior, only complicated the situation further as they instigated and suppressed gunplay with equal vigor.

From all of this chaotic swirl came the Progressive movement, an
... reform party that was an offshoot of the Southern Democrats.
... primarily from farmers and ranchers of all ethnicities, the
...med to abolish the purchase of land by parties outside of
...ncreased regulation of the railroads, and to increase the
...y. Progressives also campaigned for tax reform and
...ogressive Party was extremely popular, and a great
...s latched onto it, most notably the Temperance
...ements would wax and wane in the teens
... the fray or old groups were ousted
...ux Klan reentered the scene in the
...ts, helping to elect sympathetic
...ing their tried and true scare
...nchings.
...ng that Texas history is
... Most native Texans
...h of the six flags

and twen...
by scandal a...
early 1920s, they...
Klansmen to govern...
tactics of cross burnings, ...
All of the above is hardly...
built entirely on a foundation of...
are proud of that fact to an unquesti...

that have at one point flown over the state represent a break with the existing government (usually through armed conflict) or a reinvention of government (following the cessation of hostilities). The battle prowess of Texans became legendary, and their conflicts even more so. The Alamo is an internationally recognized shrine, a symbol of courage in the face of overwhelming odds. The Texas Rangers, formed to confront the "Indian problem," engaged in ethnic cleansing to encourage the indigenous people to relocate. Robert E. Howard was particularly fascinated by the Comanche, one of the last tribes to fall under the heel of Civilized Progress as they fought the encroaching settlers to a standstill. The Texas Rangers were celebrated for their bravery, their ferocity, and their independence: what Calvin Coolidge would have mistakenly termed "Rugged Individualism." Texas has always appealed to people who wanted to either make their own way in the world or go down swinging. As romantic as that environment was to the tall-in-the-saddle kind of person, it was hard living for the average folks who just wanted to get by.

One of the longest-running tensions in Texas history came to a head during the Progressive era, as Mexico's Civil War spilled over the Texas border. In 1910, the dictator Porfirio Díaz, in power since 1876, was challenged by Francisco Madero for the presidency. Madero was imprisoned by Díaz, but supporters posted bail for him and he fled to San Antonio, where he issued a call to arms. For the next decade, the tensions between the United States and Mexico would periodically erupt in violence along the Texas–Mexico border. The death toll was high on both sides, with thousands of innocent farmers and workers caught in the crossfire of the revolution. As the struggle for control of Mexico progressed, various factions formed bandit kingdoms amidst the border towns. The most famous of these politicos was Francisco "Pancho" Villa, who, with some backing by the Prussians, actually attacked El Paso in 1916. For the next four years, Villa played cat-and-mouse games with the U.S. Cavalry before retreating to the foothills of Mexico (where he later retired in 1920). During this time, hatred for both Mexico and Germany ran high in the United States, but was exceptionally concentrated in Texas, who urged the rest of the country to draw sabers and clash with the foreign powers.

The combination of immigration, politics, and the rapidly changing modern society made a lot of old-time Texans dig in their heels. They retreated back to the things they understood. Personal honor. Isolation. Self-governed actions. Despite the old guard's efforts to fight it down, the twentieth century came to Texas and the farmers and ranchers had no choice but to try to keep up with the swift changes. But nothing would bring so much turmoil and so completely change the destiny of Texas as the discovery of oil.

During this time of political upheaval, when competing groups battled tooth and nail for control of the state, social changes occurred at a dizzying pace. Pioneers from all over the country arrived daily in Texas, which had already assumed a mythic status as the place to start a new life or restart an old one. Families moved to find fortunes, speculating wildly with their life savings to buy land. The terrific infusion of multiple cultures into essentially barren areas, coupled with the pioneer spirit of taking what was useful and leaving what wasn't, produced a number of unique and indigenous Texas institutions.

In Vernon, Texas, Weldon "Jack" Teagarden, the son of an oil field worker, would combine the sounds of New Orleans Jazz and East Texas Blues to turn his trombone into a liquid, melancholy instrument much like his own laconic singing voice. Utilizing his own slide positions and water mutes, Teagarden made his music an elusive thing, nearly impossible to duplicate. Bob Wills, too, would combine western music and lyrics with a four-on-the-floor swing beat, a horn section, and an unmistakable vocal inflection to create the ubiquitous Texas swing sound. Just as these men made art from music, so too did Howard Hughes combine his love of flying with his skill in invention to revolutionize the aviation industry, an endeavor he bankrolled with his family's fortune (made on his father's inventions in the oil industry, in fact).

These men were all known as pioneers, but there was another pioneer in Texas, born not more than six months apart from Teagarden, Wills, and Hughes, who also blazed a trail in his industry by combining seemingly unrelated ideas to create something new, innovative, and completely unique. His name was Robert E. Howard, and he was the greatest pulp writer who ever lived. Howard wrote stories of action and adventure, violence and warfare. His characters were larger-than-life amalgamations of himself, legendary gunfighters, and other personalities pulled from the pages of recent Texas history. Steeped in blood and thunder, a signature of his writing style, Howard's stories comprise a series of grim snapshots, wildly distorted, through which can be seen the landscape of Texas; but *his* Texas, the way he saw and reacted to it.

Robert wrote to Farnsworth Wright, the editor of *Weird Tales* magazine, in the summer of 1931, "I'll say one thing about an oil boom; it will teach a kid that Life's a pretty rotten thing as quick as anything I can think of." Clearly, he would have been in a position to know best about that, having grown up in boomtowns, surrounded by the kind of people and activities that encompass such a thing.

And yet, the thing that Robert hated most was also one of the most powerful influences on his life and his art. Without the development of the petroleum industry in Texas, there would have been no Robert E. Howard, not as we know him. So much of his personal philosophy, which found its way into his fiction, poetry, and letters, was a by-product of, and a reaction to, the changes in Texas brought on by the oil booms. Robert E. Howard grew up with oil, and it was a hard-knock childhood.

Prior to the twentieth century, there wasn't much use for oil. Machinery needed lubrication, of course, and lamps utilized oil for burning, but that was about it. For example, in 1879, Martin Meichinger struck oil while drilling for water in Brownwood, Texas. At the time, water was far more precious a commodity, as Brownwood had no city water supply. At the shallow depth of fifty feet, Meichinger struck the first oil well in Texas. He harvested the oil in buckets from the limestone shelf, bottled it, and sold it as "Meichinger's Natural Rock Oil." Advertised as a cure for wounds, bruises, sores, cuts, burns, scalds, and "all eruptions on man or beast caused by impurities in the blood," it sold for the princely sum of fifty cents per half-pint bottle and, outside of its use as a liniment, aroused no special interest.

All of that changed dramatically in 1901 when Spindletop exploded at Beaumont, Texas, along the Gulf Coast. The well shot several tons of drilling pipe straight up into the air, followed by a hundred-foot-tall spew of oil that took nine days to cap. Oil was struck, and it irrevocably altered Texas forever and dragged the state, kicking and screaming, into the twentieth century. The timing couldn't have been more perfect. The United States was hungry for oil in the swell of the Industrial Revolution. More oil meant more things that could run on oil, like the newly-developed internal combustion engine. The extraction and refining of oil became an industry that would make Texas the richest state in the Union by 1928.

In fact, Texas changed so rapidly that the rest of the country couldn't readily perceive it, either. The dominant image of "miles and miles of Texas," unbroken save a lone cowboy on his horse overlooking a herd of cattle, is a cultural cliché even to this day. Prior to the television show *Dallas*, which debuted in 1978, a large percentage of the country believed that Texas was still unapologetically agrarian. As early as 1961, those who did understand the economic power that Texas generated wrote snarky books like former *New Yorker* writer John Bainbridge's overly wordy *The Super-Americans: A Picture of Life in the United States as Brought into Focus, Bigger Than Life, in the Land of Millionaires—Texas*. Bainbridge charged that the Texas lifestyle was a combination of "bravado, zest, optimism, ebullience, and swaggering self-confidence," and he didn't mean any of that in a good way.

Workers from Pennsylvania, the oilmen, the roughnecks, and the drillers stampeded into Texas after the Spindletop discovery. Within a year's time, there were five hundred corporations operating in the city of Beaumont alone. Geologists, entrepreneurs, and wildcatters scoured Texas looking for the next gusher; they were followed closely by con men selling fake leases to the rubes. Other boomtowns followed as oil was struck again and again.

The oil fields demanded a certain type of worker. Like miners, lumberjacks, and other organized labor forces, they brought their own language, tall tales, and devil-may-care manners wherever they found themselves working. It was dangerous work; fingers, limbs, and lives were routinely lost in the pursuit and acquisition of oil. Death occurred from any number of mishaps, accidents, or unplanned disasters. The men learned to laugh at—or at least live with—the danger, and it made them carefree and callous at the same time.

The rough work and tough talk were not unlike those found on a farm or ranch. Consequently, many young men with a need to leave the family farm found themselves building derricks in boomtowns like Desdemona or Burkburnett. It took a crew of five rig builders a little less than a week to set up a cable-tool rig. Roustabouts and roughnecks were the brute muscle, able to fetch, tote, and pull as needed. Teamsters made sure that pipe and lumber were in good supply. Wildcatters, independent contractors who speculated on where to drill, were able to hire such crews at the drop of a hat—for a price, of course. Money changed hands freely, and the men who worked the industry followed it across Texas and back again. There was always a new well spudding in, a new field opening up.

A drifting community formed around these roughnecks, consisting of services catering specifically to the oilman's lifestyle: chili parlors, Laundromats, temporary housing, textiles, clothing, and, of course, bootleg beer and whisky, con men, prostitutes, gamblers, and loan sharks for those who got in over their heads. These men played as hard and as dangerously as they worked. Each new boomtown found new faces to add to the roaming city—speculators, local toughs, businessmen, and the like all threw in their lot, trying their hardest to get rich.

The largest single field in the history of Texas was the Ranger Field, which came into full bloom in 1917 when a well on the McClesky farm about two miles southwest of town erupted. Ranger was in the middle of a drought, and several residents encouraged the Texas Pacific Coal and Oil Company to test for oil in the hopes of stimulating the local economy. McClesky #1 was the second well drilled, and its output drew national attention and galvanized the oil-producing outfits that were spread across Texas. The population of Ranger, Texas swelled from 1,000 people to over 25,000. In less than two years, over three hundred wells in the immediate area were pumping in excess of two million barrels of oil a month. The town was completely ill-equipped to handle so many people, and Ranger became one of the most infamous oil boomtowns in history as typhoid, influenza, and fellow roughnecks killed many of the citizens. Gambling, prostitution, and violence were the order of the day, and many times, the

Texas Rangers were called in to administer the law and keep the peace.

Such interest in the Ranger oil field spread to the neighboring counties, as was the norm. Ranger was in the middle of nowhere, but there were two nearby towns that had access to the railroad and a population base that could supply labor, goods, and services: Brownwood, in Brown County, and Cross Plains, in Callahan County. Cross Plains was closer to Ranger, and at the time was enjoying prosperity as new businesses buttressed up against the newly constructed Texas Central Railroad line. Chief among them was Higginbotham's general store, erected in 1915.

By 1917, a local doctor and his family moved to the nearby town of Burkett, from the equally nearby town of Cross Cut. Dr. Isaac Mordecai Howard had been chasing various kinds of oil, land, railroad, and cattle booms since he had graduated from medical school in 1905. The Howards seldom stayed in any one place for more than a year. Living and working in Central West Texas, close to Cross Plains, was as stable as their life had been since their son, Robert, had been born in 1906. And while the boom was going on in Ranger, it would be several years before it would touch the Howard family again.

Oil finally came to Cross Plains, not at once, like in most of the boomtowns in Texas, but gradually, as if it needed coaxing. The *Cross Plains Review*, the oldest business establishment in Cross Plains, reported on November 9, 1917:

> Ranger in Eastland County is suffering an oil boom, a gusher having been brought in near town. Brownwood has developed a paying oil business from shallow wells. The field is said to be unusual in that a number of wells are being drilled with common well-drilling outfits and that the usual derrick is not to be found. Brownwood promises to enjoy a sure enough oil boom. The town of Coleman is in about the same position with reference to the developing of oil. Paying wells have been brought in on the Morris lands and drilling is being pushed on a well on the Gray Ranch. Certainly if all these fields surrounding us are developed, Cross Plains can not be left out entirely. On with the work.

The *Cross Plains Review* did its level best to promote the oil boom as a positive thing. For the next three years, the paper gleefully reported on any oil activity in Eastland, Callahan, and Brown counties. Frequently, the editor, L. P. Henslee, would urge the citizenry to invest in land, build houses, and develop their business to take advantage of the people who would undoubtedly be coming to Cross Plains.

It is not known whether Dr. Isaac Howard was chasing or anticipating the impending boom, or merely making an effort to settle down after so many years of wandering, when he moved his family into a house in Cross Plains in October 1919. His son, Robert, was now 13 and able to attend

Cross Plains High School with his friends from Burkett and Cross Cut. This was the longest the Howard family had stayed in any one place, and the buying of the house signified that Dr. Howard was at last putting down roots. Cross Plains was a small community, but it was well-positioned on the railroad line, and the proximity to the oil boom ensured that certain amenities such as electricity and natural gas would be available to houses and businesses.

By 1920, Cross Plains had over a dozen oil wells drilling as close as six miles from the edge of town. Then, on February 17, 1920, the Vestal Well, owned jointly by Dr. Rumph and Southland Oil, came in a gusher. This well was within the city limits, and it created a sensation as everyone began scrambling around for leases and deeds. The *Cross Plains Review* said, on February 20, "However, to briefly report the matter, Cross Plains has got her oil well—a good one, that no other town or locality can lay claim to and is in reality an oil town. The usual excitement prevails and the erstwhile quiet town is now the scene of everything characteristic of an oil boom."

Whether or not any of the local folks took the advice or heeded the warnings, the town-site oil boom had struck. What had been merely a profitable side business for the merchants could now no longer be ignored. Shallow testing occurred in people's backyards and business lots. The Cross Plains Chamber of Commerce formed. Cross Plains had become an oil field, not as big or productive as the Ranger Field, but certainly productive enough that many diverse groups watched with eagerness. After two decades of doing business in Texas, the oil industry was well-versed in the ways and means of boomtowns. Ranger, and now Cross Plains, were nothing new to the hordes of people who followed oilmen across the country. The people crowded into town with casual indifference, no doubt grateful only for the fact that Cross Plains was already a town and the itinerants wouldn't be required to build up the place from scratch. Cross Plains swelled, just like every other Texas boomtown caught up in the rush of black gold. New businesses sprang up overnight. Thousands of people descended on the sleepy, God-fearing community. The crime that the *Cross Plains Review* had been reporting on in towns like Ranger, Desdemona, and Coleman suddenly became a Cross Plains problem.

Not everyone was excited about the oil boom, however. Years later, in 1928, Robert E. Howard, now a working professional writer, would attempt to write a slice-of-life chronicle set in a small Texas town visited by the oil boom. The book, loosely based on his own experiences, saw print decades later as *Post Oaks and Sand Roughs*. Here's what Howard wrote about the colorful and turbulent times:

> The oil boom struck Lost Plains overnight... the town was deluged with oil workers and magnates. Abstracts flew like

leaves in the wind. It was shallow "town-site stuff" and derricks sprang up in every backyard—standard rigs, built solidly of heavy timbers, spudders which moved on wheels and were an innovation in the Lost Plains country, which was used to "deep tests," and Star machines, which were merely glorified spudders, taller and able to go to a greater depth.

Here was drama, swift-moving action, and great material for story, but Steve moved among it untouched, despising oil and everything connected with it, hating the roughnecks who swaggered and jostled their way through life, and detesting the loud-mouthed, steely-eyed promoters, the keenest of whom had never opened any book in their lives, except some book dealing with the oil industry. Steve spoke the truth when he said he hated them all too much to write about them.

Howard had a good reason to hate the oil boom. His father, Isaac Howard, had chased prosperity, dragging Robert and his mother, who was suffering from tuberculosis, all over the state, for the first eleven years of his life. Each new town was close to new development, be it oil, land, or cattle. Every year or two, the Howards would pick up stakes and move to a new area of Texas, sometimes hundreds of miles away, to start over again. Robert E. Howard wrote to H.P. Lovecraft in October 1930:

> I've seen towns leap into being overnight and become deserted almost as quick. I've seen old farmers, bent with toil, and ignorant of the feel of ten dollars at a time, become millionaires in a week, by the way of oil gushers. And I've seen them blow in every cent of it and die paupers. I've seen whole towns debauched by an oil boom and boys and girls go to the devil whole-sale. I've seen promising youths turn from respectable citizens to dope-fiends, drunkards, gamblers and gangsters in a matter of months.

Even a cursory examination of Robert E. Howard's body of work reveals several recurring themes. The rise and fall of civilizations and their ascent from and descent into barbarism, the corruption of said civilizations, and a singular, moral man against a horde of immoral adversaries can be found in the stories of Conan the Cimmerian, Bran Mak Morn, Solomon Kane, King Kull, and even in lesser characters like Francis X. Gordon, Turlogh O'Brien, and Cormac Fitzgeoffrey. Howard's westerns, his fantasies, and especially his historicals repeat these same messages. It's a philosophy cobbled together from a precocious and voluminous amount of reading and from shrewd firsthand observation of the tension between the old Texans of the frontier and the new Texans with oil, and sometimes blood, on their hands.

Robert E. Howard's intelligence set him apart from his peers in many ways. While he grew into a physically imposing man through rigorous exercise, he earned his money by staying at home, typing stories for the pulps. Cross Plains was a city in transition, with horses tethered to hitching posts right next to parked automobiles and trucks, but it was hardly a modern city. Men were expected to work, if not on a farm or ranch, then in the oil fields. Those who were educated, as Robert was, were expected to have some sort of trade. A lack of education or physical ability meant a position in one of the many service jobs that catered to oil, farming, and ranching. This was not to be Robert's fate. Through sheer force of will and an indomitable need to prove himself, he built a career for himself as a professional writer in an intellectual vacuum, surrounded by a town's indifference to his efforts.

Doing so placed him at odds with his friends and neighbors, and his predicament wasn't helped by his father's standing in the community. At a time of extreme civic progress, when his father was one of the more visible and important men in town, Robert spent twelve or more hours a day typing furiously, creating stories instinctively, and coping with constant rejection, struggling to find formulas that worked and stories that made him proud. Anything to keep him from having to take orders from people he didn't respect, working in an environment that he came to hate.

Despite Robert's wish to avoid the oil boom, it was a part of his identity. His reaction formed a moral stance that he would transfer to his fictitious heroes, a stance that he would strike over and over again in the wood pulp pages of *Weird Tales* magazine and its many competitors. A sensitive man who felt things deeply, he couldn't help but be affected by the constant chaos, violence, and corruption that came with the oil booms. These thoughts, opinions, and characters would find their way to the page through the refracted lens of Robert's inner eye, where they would eventually become some of the most influential fantasy writing of the twentieth century, second only to J.R.R. Tolkien's *Lord of the Rings* saga.

As absorbing as Kull's Atlantis and as detailed as Conan's Hyborian Age are for modern readers, the roots of these fantastic places are in Texas. Howard fictionalized his home state, drawing from its history and geography, and reconfiguring events and places with a masterful eye for action, adventure, and suspense. Robert E. Howard was a Texan, first and foremost, and in the midst of Texas's greatest time of change, his thoughts and opinions became the building blocks for one of the most significant bodies of work in contemporary literature.

The story of Robert E. Howard is the story of twentieth-century Texas.

Hester Ervin Howard in her Sunday best, circa 1905 (from the collection of Glenn Lord, courtesy of Leo Grin).

ISAAC AND HESTER

> Had not cholera struck the camp of William Benjamin Howard and his band of '49ers on the Arkansas River, reducing their number from nineteen to seven, and weakening their leader so he was forced to turn back, I, his grandson, would have undoubtedly been born in California instead of Texas.
> **Robert E. Howard to H.P. Lovecraft, June 1931**

When writing, researching, or even reading a biography, it is a common practice to learn first about the subject's parentage and general family history. Insofar as Robert E. Howard's family is concerned, the scant firsthand information that has survived the passage of time cannot be trusted. This is especially true for the Ervin side of the family, as Robert's mother, Hester Howard, was an extremely unreliable source. Unfortunately, Robert got most of his information about his family tree from his mother.

That being said, it's not necessary or even particularly feasible to spell out the last four generations of Robert E. Howard's family. Records are scarce, and they don't really tell the story of who these people were. All anyone has to go on, aside from census statistics and other official records, is the oral history that Robert wrote down and repeated at length.

Despite these obstacles, it is possible to get a sense of who Isaac Howard and Hester Ervin were and how they operated. Robert's parents were of supreme importance to his life and development, and their respective family histories (well, their versions of the family histories, in any case) figure appreciably into his psychology. These histories were bolstered by a number of stories told to Robert during infrequent visits from sundry uncles and aunts. He committed these stories to memory, where they would later emerge in bits and pieces through his fiction.

The readily accepted version of the Howard and the Ervin families' history that Robert cheerfully spun out for friends and acquaintances is far more colorful and interesting than the truth. Robert may or may not have known some of the white lies and inconsistencies of his parents' background, but that was not going to stop him from telling a great story. He loved to brag on his family tree and was content to view that tree from a safe distance.

Robert E. Howard wrote the following to H.P. Lovecraft in December 1930:

> Some day I'd like to write a chronicle of the Southwest as it appears to me, but I don't suppose I could handle the thing properly. Well, if I never write it, at least people of my blood had a hand in making it—which is infinitely better than

unromantically writing down the deeds of other men. Kinsmen of mine were among the riflemen at King's Mountain, and with Old Hickory at New Orleans; I had three great-uncles in the '49 gold rush—a Howard and two Martins—the Howard settled in Sonora, California, and one of the Martins left his bones on the trail—both my grandfathers rode for four years with Bedford Forrest, and I had a great grandfather in the Confederate Army, too, as well as a number of great-uncles—one died in a nameless skirmish in the Wilderness and another fell in the battle of Macon, Georgia; my grandfather Colonel George Ervin came into Texas when it was wild and raw, and he went into New Mexico, too, long before it was a state, and worked a silver mine—and once he rode like a bat out of Hell for the Texas line with old Geronimo's turbaned Apaches on his trail; an aunt of mine married and went into the Indian Territory to live years before the government ever opened the land for settlers; and one of my uncles, too, settled in what is now Oklahoma, in its wildest days, when it swarmed with half-wild Indians and murderous renegades from half-a-dozen states.

Colonel Ervin once owned a great deal of property in what is now a very prosperous section of Dallas, and might have grown with the town, but for the whippoorwills. They almost drove him crazy with their incessant calling, and though he was a kindly man with beasts and birds, and killed men with less remorse than he killed animals, in a fit of passion one night, he shot three whippoorwills; it was flying in the face of tradition and he quickly regretted it, but the damage was done. According to legend, you know, human life must pay for the blood of a whippoorwill, and soon the Colonel's family began to die, at the average of one a year, exactly as the old black people prophesied. He stuck it out five years and then, with five of his big family dead, he gave it up. No one ever accused him of cowardice; he hacked his way alone through a cordon of Phil Sheridan's cavalry-men; but the whippoorwills licked him. He sold his Dallas property for a song, went west and bought a sheep-ranch.

Several years later, Robert further embellished his family's lore in a missive to August Derleth, January 1934:

One of the main reasons I've always hoped success would come my way, was so I could travel. There are hundreds of places in my own state I've never seen, though I've roamed over a goodly portion of it. I suppose I've done less traveling than any of my family, for hundreds of years back. They were always a race of wanderers, all branches of my various lines, and seldom stayed long in the locality in which they were born. My father was born in southern Arkansas, my mother in eastern Texas; my maternal grandfather in North Carolina, my maternal grandmother in middle Tennessee; my paternal grandfather in Georgia, my paternal grandmother in Alabama, (and they married in Mississippi); my paternal grandmother's father was born in South Carolina, and his father was born on the Atlantic ocean in an emigrant ship, and his father was born in County Galway, Ireland. My great-great-grandfather, the one born on the ocean, was carried ashore at New York, thence southward by his family, and his wife was from the west coast of Ireland, and their son, my great-grandfather, born in South Carolina, married a Georgia woman whose father was born in Denmark. I've had aunts, uncles and cousins born in every southern state there is except Kentucky and Florida, and a few in the mid-west. Most of them I've never seen. I have relatives all over East Texas, northern Louisiana, southern and western Arkansas, southern and northern Missouri, and eastern and middle Oklahoma, and very few of them have I ever seen.

While Robert's account makes for interesting reading, many of the particulars of the story were handed down to him from his parents and their kin. As such, it is suspect in that any good piece of family trivia should be taken with a grain of salt. The basic movements of each family tend to match up with the Howard family Bible and allow for a measure of fact checking.

Dr. Isaac Mordecai Howard was born on April 1, 1872, in Holly Springs, Arkansas, the second youngest of six children. His father, William Benjamin Howard, and his mother, Louisa Elizabeth Henry, met on the Henry plantation in Mississippi when William was hired on as a manager by Louisa's parents. William and Louisa were married in 1856 and promptly set to the business of making a large family.

Their life together was a series of ups and downs. William fought in the Civil War for the Confederacy, and after the war ended, struggled alongside his father-in-law James Henry to keep the plantation afloat in the midst of the Reconstruction. Unable to do so, the family relocated to Holly Springs, Arkansas, and James Henry opened a general store. In 1884, when James Henry died, William and Louisa decided to make their fortune in Texas. Before the move could be orchestrated, however, William Benjamin Howard fell ill and died in 1885.

Undaunted by the setback, Louisa moved her six children (many of whom were now grown) to Texas. The women went by train, and Isaac and his older brother David took the family's possessions by covered wagon. They settled on a farm in Limestone County, near Waco.

David assumed responsibility for the family, and proceeded to whip the farm into shape. By 1891, Isaac Howard had determined that he was not cut out to be a farmer. He left the family farm, sold his share in the property to his brother, and decided to practice frontier medicine.

Isaac's medical education—a combination of on-the-job training, apprenticeship to an uncle who was himself a doctor, and attendance at a variety of schools, lectures, and courses—would spread out over the next four decades. His initial training took four or five years, and allowed him to practice medicine as early as 1896. From that time on, Dr. Isaac Howard moved frequently from place to place, venturing as far out as Missouri and back to the family farm in Limestone County again. As a doctor on the frontier, he dealt with everything from delivering babies to influenza, with gunshots and stab wounds thrown in for good measure.

In between these wanderings, Isaac decided to go back to medical school in anticipation of the Texas Board of Medical Examiners' newly passed guidelines for doctors. In 1902, when Dr. Howard was practicing medicine both on the Texas–Oklahoma border and in the small town of Graford in Palo Pinto County (locations separated by a distance of over two hundred miles), he enrolled in the Gate City Medical School in Texarkana, Arkansas. It was while he was attending school there that he met Hester Jane Ervin.

Hester's life began in Dallas, Texas, on July 11, 1870. Her father, George Washington Ervin, was a colonel in the Confederate Army, and her mother, Sarah Jane Martin, gave birth to ten children before dying in 1874.

After the Civil War, George moved his family to Texas, buying farmland in Hill County, a stone's throw away from the not-yet-established Howard farm in Limestone County. Texas in 1866 was still largely unsettled frontier, and George moved around, hustling land and cattle where he could.

After Sarah's death in 1874, George felt that Dallas was bad for his family, and he relocated to Lewisville, Texas. He remarried a year later and his new wife, Alice Wynne, bore him six more children. Thankfully, four-year-old Hester got along well with her stepmother. Hester became the bridge between the two sets of children, doting on her half-siblings and helping with their upbringing as a dutiful older sister.

Another move later, in Lampasas, George Ervin found his business dealings in a slump. In 1887, on the news that New Mexico was rich in silver, he moved his entire family out of state via the newly completed railroad. The move didn't last long; Ervin returned south in 1890, buying a farm and a house in Exeter, Missouri. This split the family in two; Sarah Jane Martin's children stayed in Texas, and Alice Wynne's children went to Missouri. The exception was Hester, who stayed with her father and stepmother.

The idyllic splendor of the Missouri house was short-lived. Some time after Hester arrived, she contracted tuberculosis, the disease which was thought to have contributed to her mother's death.

Tuberculosis was called consumption in the nineteenth century, and was considered a disease of refinement. Poets, authors, and other artists were considered even more in tune with the darker elements of human nature if they were so afflicted. Alexandre Dumas remarked, in his novel *Camille*, "It was the fashion to suffer from the lungs; everybody was consumptive, poets especially; it was good form to spit blood after each emotion that was at all sensational, and to die before reaching the age of thirty." In his book *Against Depression*, Peter Kramer called tuberculosis "a disease of recklessness, longing, sensuality, serenity, decadence, sensitivity, glamour, resignation, instinct, and instinctual renunciation, that is to say, of passion or passion repressed, but in any case a disease of emotionally emphasized or refined creatures." During the first decade of the twentieth century, more than 4,000 deaths a year in Texas were attributed to pulmonary tuberculosis. Hester Ervin, the put-upon child in the middle of two families, already inured to tragedy and with an eye toward performance, embraced this diagnosis. It became her identity.

Hester left the plantation house and traveled to Oklahoma in 1894 to live with one of her older sisters, inside the Indian Territory of Muskogee, more a dumping ground for the U.S. Army to place uprooted and relocated tribes like the Creek and Seminole. There she remained until 1900, when her father died in Missouri. George Ervin left the estate to Alice Wynne, and for whatever reason, Hester decided to go forward rather than back. She returned to Texas, settling in Mineral Wells to help some of her siblings who had also contracted tuberculosis. It was there that she met the dashing and charismatic country doctor, Isaac Howard.

The details of their courtship are sketchy at best, and most were delivered near the end of Hester's life, after years of built-up resentment. According to Hester, she was being pursued by another admirer, a well-to-do gentleman from Goldthwaite, when Isaac Howard came along and swept her off her feet. She was so taken with his attentions that she turned her back on the other suitor and married Isaac Howard in 1904. She was thirty-four. He was thirty-two.

It's hard for modern readers to imagine how unusual it was that two people should wait so long to get married. Most of Isaac's and Hester's brothers and sisters married between the ages of eighteen and twenty-five. Hester was considered an "old maid" at the time of her marriage. It was less strange for a man to remain unmarried, particularly one who, like Isaac Howard, had not yet made his mark on the frontier. That Isaac chose a woman two years his elder is interesting, considering that he grew up with such a strong-willed woman for his mother.

Hester was gracious and charming. Isaac was forceful and magnetic. She was maternal and caring. He was dashing and intense. It is not difficult to imagine that Hester saw much of her father in Isaac, just as Isaac saw characteristics of his mother in Hester. Both came from large, roaming families, but they lacked the desire to settle down and cultivate a large family themselves. In this, they were very much kindred spirits.

The couple had a home built for them on Dark Valley Creek in Palo Pinto County, near Graford, Texas. As newlyweds, they doted on one another. "Hessie" and "Howie" were always smiling and laughing, despite the early signs of Hester's disease. Dr. Howard continued with his courses at Gate City Medical School while he practiced medicine in the Graford area. He graduated from the school in 1905 and was licensed by the state of Texas two years later. Long after getting the nod to practice by the Medical Examiners Board, Dr. Howard would continue to take courses, attend seminars, and try to stay current with the medical industry. Later in his life, Isaac's gullibility (or perhaps merely indefatigable optimism) would lead to his offering and endorsing quack remedies like magnetized water in an effort to keep up with the latest advances.

Isaac and Hester both thought that she was too old and too sick to conceive. Nevertheless, the urge (or possibly duty) to raise a child was such that Isaac contacted his older brother, David, about possibly adopting his youngest son, Wallace. But before the deal went down, Hester found out that she was, in fact, with child.

The dangers to a pregnant woman in the wilderness were bad enough if the woman was healthy. For women with tuberculosis, the complications were understandably multiplied. The couple relocated to the nearby town of Peaster to be closer to adequate medical facilities, as a precaution. Despite her outward appearance of smiles and laughter, Hester accompanied Isaac wherever he went. Whether it was her idea or his, both of them were more worried than they showed.

With very little fanfare, Robert Ervin Howard was born on January 22, 1906. According to Robert's birth record, Hester was now miraculously five years younger than Isaac. Robert's birth record also gives his birthday as January 24. While there is no discernable reason for the former incorrect date, the latter discrepancy on the birth record, filled out by a Dr. Williams, was made on February 1, eight days after the birth. Dr. Williams may have simply forgotten Robert's actual birth date. Thus Robert E. Howard's life would begin with a small fiction, a white lie. It would not be the last.

Dr. Isaac Mordecai Howard in his later years (from the collection of Glenn Lord, courtesy of Leo Grin).

The Traveling Howards

I was born in Peaster, Texas, a small town not far from Weatherford, in January, 1906, at an early age. I was named Robert Ervin Howard after my great-grandfather, Robert Ervin. I was also named after George Washington, but not for him. After a few trips, moves, and other adventures which I will pass over as I was too small to take much notice of them, I found myself at Seminole, Texas, just forty miles this side of the New Mexico Border. This was prairie country—extremely so. Water was scarce there; too scarce, so we moved to Bagwell, Texas, which is between Texarkana and Paris. That part of the country where we lived used to be part of Arkansas. It is all piney woods there, and every time I smell the pine scent I get homesick, although I have been away from there for years. If we had too little water at Seminole, we had too much at Bagwell. It rained for weeks at a time; rained until the ground turned green; rained until fish swam around in the roads. I went to my first school there. After a while, I developed a bad case of nasal catarrh. The swampy country was bad for it, so we went to central west Texas.
Robert E. Howard, November 29, 1921 (age 15)

The autobiography above was part of a school assignment, and the young Robert Howard got an "A" on the paper. While he makes light of his family's inclination to roam, he still paints a telling picture about his earliest years.

The Howard family lived in the house on Dark Valley Creek until 1907. During that time, Isaac practiced medicine as a country doctor could, which meant being gone for long hours visiting patients, and sometimes staying overnight. Hester stayed home, kept their house, and cared for their infant boy. She nursed Robert, according to one unverified source, until he was two years old, and as she was tubercular, there is a high probability that Robert was sick as a baby. He cried often, and his harried mother would sometimes bounce him on the family bed for hours at a time until she exhausted herself. Sometimes, Hester would crawl under the bed and push the springs up from below to allow herself a chance to rest. It was during this period that Hester suffered a miscarriage. Robert was no more than a year and a half old.

If Robert knew about this piece of family history, he never told anyone about it. However, the implications of this event had a strong bearing on the adult Robert's life. While unmistakably a tragedy, it is certainly no different from any other hardship of growing up in rural Texas at the turn of the century. Such a thing, though, can weigh heavily on a nervous mother, particularly one as prone to dramatics as Hester. The miscarriage may very well have been the beginning of Hester's retreat from her marriage, and also may have fueled her major depression which she carried with her the rest of her life.

As far as anyone knows, Isaac and Hester never tried again to get pregnant. Certainly Hester's age and her illness played into the decision. After all, their first baby had been a happy accident. So Robert, for better or worse, would be their only child. And Hester, like any mother who had lost a child, would cling to and protect her only son with a fervor.

What happened next is based mostly on the few recorded details from various censuses, newspapers, and county records, along with clues dropped by Robert and his father in letters. After their brief triumph and tragedy on the banks of Dark Valley Creek, the Howard family hit the road. From Robert's descriptions in his letters (no two of which are exactly alike), the family was a pack of nomads. Here's an excerpt from a letter to H.P. Lovecraft, circa October 1930:

> Why, by the time I was nine years old I'd lived in the Palo Pinto hills of Central Texas; in a small town only fifty miles from the Coast; on a ranch in Atascosa County; in San Antonio; on the South Plains close to the New Mexican line; in the Wichita Falls country up next to Oklahoma; and in the piney woods of Red River over next to Arkansas, if you'll glance at a map of Texas you'll note that covers considerable distance, altogether, and I didn't mention a few short stays in Missouri and Oklahoma. I've lived in land boom towns, railroad boom towns, oil boom towns, where life was raw and primitive, and all I can say is: Texas is just too big for me to grasp.

Robert makes no mention of the reasons why the family kept moving, but it's safe to say that Isaac orchestrated all of their moves. Isaac either thought that a boomtown would help him practice his particular brand of medicine, or he thought that he, like his family and Hester's family, could take advantage of the boom and make some shrewd investments. There was nothing that would have prevented him from practicing his trade and getting rich on the side, especially in the early, unsettled days of Texas. It was to his advantage as a rough-and-tumble sort of character, and part of a recurring tendency to speculate and scheme his entire adult life. In fact, Isaac Howard did so much moving around that it's impossible to say where he did and didn't go with one hundred percent certainty. For example, the phrase in Robert's composition, "in a small town only fifty miles from the Coast," has never been authenticated or identified as a place where the Howard family actually lived. As such, we don't know if it was added to the list to further illustrate the vastness of the state to Lovecraft, or if the Howards really did live near the coast.

The family pulled up stakes from Dark Valley Creek and headed west, to Seminole, in Gaines County, in 1908. Seminole was a tiny cattle and ranching town until the Texas Legislature offered land lots for a dollar apiece. Farming and ranching expanded the town to include a new school, the county courthouse, a jail, churches, and other trappings of an infrastructure. While Seminole was a thriving cow town, it was also extremely hot and dry. The climate may have even been beneficial to Hester's health, but the family did not live there very long.

In 1909, the doctor hung his shingle in Coke County, in the town of Bronte, named after the author Charlotte Brontë. (Coke County also boasted a town called Tennyson, named after the English poet.) The entire county was in the middle of a cotton boom at the time of the family's arrival. The railroad tracks were laid in 1907, but the first train didn't run until 1909. This too would be a short-lived stay.

While they lived in Bronte, Isaac Howard had the occasion to visit his older sister, Willie McClung, and her part-Indian husband Oscar in Zavala County, just outside of the tiny town of Crystal City. Robert recalled one eventful visit in a letter to H.P. Lovecraft from August 1931:

> I remember, very faintly, the fall of a meteorite in South Texas, many years ago. I was about four years old at the time, and was at the house of an uncle, in a little town about forty miles from the Mexican Border; a town which had recently sprung up like a mushroom from the wilderness and was still pretty tough. I remember waking suddenly and sitting up in bed, seeing everything bathed in a weird blue light, and hearing a terrific detonation. My uncle—an Indian—had enemies of desperate character, and in the excitement it was thought they had dynamited the house. There was a general leaping and snatching of guns, but nothing further occurred. Next day it was learned that a meteorite had fallen. People who saw it described it as being about the size and shape of a barrel, and averred it burst twice before striking the ground, making a loud explosion and shedding that strange blue light over everything. No trace of it was ever found.

The family was living in Atascosa County in early 1910. According to a letter written by Isaac Howard late in his lifetime, the family spent the summer in Poteet, thirty miles from San Antonio, and the winter months in San Antonio proper. This was the largest city that the family had ever lived in, and their stay was also brief. Years later, Robert would return many times to San Antonio; he considered it one of his favorite cities.

The years 1911 and 1912 are somewhat confusing. Howard mentions in the 1930 letter above that he lived in the Wichita Falls area up next to Oklahoma. He wrote to H.P. Lovecraft, in October 1930:

> But of all lousy lands, the Wichita Falls country takes the cake

to my mind. There the plains are of white alkali and the glare nearly blinds you. The climate is treacherous. You ride out in the morning in your shirt sleeves, admiring the dreamy slumber of the plains, with the birds singing in the one tree the county boasts, and the heat waves shimmering in the distance; you see a coyote loping along with his tongue hanging out in the heat—and then by noon, maybe, a blue blizzard comes howling over the prairie and freezes your gizzard. Before they got gas wells in that country they burned corn cobs; I've seen stacks ten feet high in people's back yards. Before they could ship corn in or raise it, cowpunchers burned dried cattle dung and before them the hunters and traders and Indians burned buffalo chips.

Would a six-year-old Robert E. Howard have remembered such details, or was he merely spinning a yarn for greater effect? His estimation of the climate is pretty accurate, in any case.

The evidence suggests that Isaac pulled the family out to the burgeoning Burkburnett oil field to see if it suited him. When oil was struck in 1912, the town became swamped as a torrent of people invaded the area in what had become the usual boomtown fashion. This could not have been a positive thing for the Howard family, even if it gave Isaac plenty of practice at setting bones, treating industrial wounds, and the like.

In 1912, Hester Howard (and most likely Robert) was receiving mail in Oran, back in Palo Pinto County. Oran is five miles from Graford, Isaac's old stomping grounds, and about fifteen miles from Mineral Wells, where Hester's sister lived. The Howard family had come full circle to regroup and figure out their next move. Whether Isaac was around at this time, trying to work some sort of oil deal in Burkburnett, or doing something else entirely is a matter of sheer speculation.

In any case, the family next moved to Red River County, to the not-quite-booming town of Bagwell, deep in the Piney Woods of East Texas. The Howards would live there for two years. Bagwell was enjoying economic prosperity as cotton farmers moved into the area, bringing a slow but steady increase in the population.

Dr. Howard may have been invited to practice in Bagwell by a colleague from his tenure at the Gate City Medical School, Dr. Willis Stephens. Dr. Stephens's father, another doctor, had recently left town, and it's possible that Dr. Howard was invited to take up the slack. The Howard family moved into what was known as "the old Baker House," and either as a benefit of the position or through the vagaries of Isaac's financial situation, they were able to hire some help for the house.

Bagwell was extremely important to young Robert, despite the rainy weather and his nasal condition. In his autobiography at the age of fifteen, he mentioned that the smell of pine made him homesick. Robert also received a dose of childhood inspiration in the form of his "Aunt" Mary

Bohannan. Howard wrote at length about her in a letter to H.P. Lovecraft, dated September 1930:

> The one to whom I listened most was the cook, old Aunt Mary Bohannon, who was nearly white—about one sixteenth negro, I should say. Mistreatment of slaves is, and has been somewhat exaggerated, but old Aunt Mary had had the misfortune, in her youth, to belong to a man whose wife was a fiend from Hell. The young slave women were fine young animals, and barbarically handsome; her mistress was frenziedly jealous. You understand. Aunt Mary told tales of torture and unmistakable sadism that sickens me to this day when I think of them. Thank God the slaves on my ancestors' plantations were never so misused. And Aunt Mary told how one day, when the black people were in the fields, a hot wind swept over them and they knew that "ol' Misses Bohannon" was dead. Returning to the manor house they found that it was so and the slaves danced and shouted with joy. Aunt Mary said that when a good spirit passes, a breath of cool air follows; but when an evil spirit goes by a blast from the open doors of Hell follows it.

Clearly, this tale-spinning woman, who was in some capacity looking after the Howard house to the point that she was cooking for Robert, had a huge effect on him. Aunt Mary's tale showed up again later in Robert's life, as did the Piney Woods, after Robert had turned his hand to crafting fiction. Another woman in Bagwell fascinated Robert for a similar reason, as he later attested in the same letter to Lovecraft:

> And there was one Arabella Davis, I remember, whom I used to see, when a child, going placidly about town collecting washing—I mean when I was a kid, not Arabella. She was a black philosopher, if there was ever one. Her little granddaughter tagged after her, everywhere she went, carrying Arabella's pipe, matches and tobacco with as much pomposity as a courtier ever carried the train of a queen.
>
> Arabella was born in slavery, but her memories were of a later date. She often told of her conversion, when the spirit of the Lord was so strong upon her that she went for ten days and nights without eating or sleeping. She went into a trance, she said, and for days the fiends of Hell pursued her through the black mountains and the red mountains. For four days she hung in the cobwebs on the gates of Hell, and the hounds of Hell bayed at her. Is that not a splendid sweep of imagination? And the strangest part is, it was so true and realistic to her, that she would have been amazed had anyone questioned her veracity.

This grisly visual told to young Robert went right into the mental hopper of his imagination, where it would emerge years later in the form of poems and prose, many of which were delivered with the same authentic feel as the original tellers of the tales.

It was in Bagwell that Robert first entered elementary school at the age of eight (which was when school started at that time). He was already a precocious reader, having been taught by his mother during the many days and nights that they spent together, alone, while Isaac was out delivering a baby or tending to a farmer that had been kicked by a mule. Hester read stories and recited poetry to Robert, and they amused each other with stories and games. On the rare occasions when Isaac was home, he joined in the games and poetry recitations.

With seven moves, encompassing thousands of miles, in roughly nine years, the only constant in young Robert's life was his mother. When Isaac wasn't doctoring, he was speculating, or at least making the attempt. Regardless of whether or not the moves were particularly traumatic, the fact is that Robert, as an adult, referred to the family's wandering on several occasions, and never in a positive manner. While Robert never complained about moving, he never really had nice things to say about where he lived—and with good reason.

Texas was in a state of upheaval, more so than at any time since 1880. The social order was changing, and small Texas towns were quickly growing into metropolitan centers in the wake of oil, land, and cattle booms. New settlers were pouring into the state from the North and East, many of whom were trying to start fresh, which was the customary reason for anyone moving to Texas in those days. Others were sent by corporations to secure resources, buy what they could, and turn those holdings into lucrative cash reserves.

From 1906 to 1912, the Progressive Party broke under its own strain, as the question of race came up in Texas politics. Texas, lagging behind the rest of the Southern states, had to deal with questions long settled in other parts of the country. When the "People's Party" tried to band the black sharecroppers together with the white sharecroppers, the movement splintered. White men in 1906 were unwilling to admit that they occupied the same social caste as black men. In 1910, when the black heavyweight boxer from Galveston, Jack Johnson, won the title from Jim Jefferies, riots broke out in East Texas. Black farmers and white farmers may have worked neighboring shares of the land, but there the civility ended. Cotton was still the primary cash crop, and most of the Old South attitudes were woefully intact. T.R. Fehrenbach said it best in his seminal history of Texas, *Lone Star*: "The black belt was never to spread successfully much beyond the old cotton line. White—and unseen but equally important, Mexican—hostility kept it out."

In addition to the political situation, the oil boom was in full swing. Boomtowns and boomtown conditions would be the norm for the next thirty years; in Texas in the early teens and twenties, that meant fistfights, gunplay, dangerous animals, and criminal activity. Bootleggers, gamblers, whores, pimps, con men of all sizes, and garden-variety thugs all flocked to the boomtowns to ply their trades openly in the sure absence of the law.

Robert was only a child, and even though he may have stayed at home until the family moved to Bagwell and he had to attend school, he did recall in many of his letters the amount of violence he witnessed in his youth. He was the son of the local doctor, the man folks went to see if they'd been gunshot, stabbed, bludgeoned, or worse, never mind the number of industrial accidents that regularly occurred in oil fields. There was, by Robert's estimation, daily exposure to such wounds and the evidence of such violence.

Rural farm life has its share of horrible accidents, too, and while Texans at the time were extremely pragmatic about such things, Robert got a good deal more gore and mayhem than the average frontier kid. His parents were extremely protective of him, his mother more so than his father, but they both tried very hard to ensure that he was well looked after. It's not clear how socially active Robert was at this time, but it's not surprising that he later never wrote of any childhood friends from these early moves, save perhaps for visits from various cousins. With the average span of one year spent in a town, it would have been difficult to make any friends, much less keep them. Add to that the fact that Isaac and his family usually arrived during the various booms, which may have only added to a community's polite distance. Thus, the Howard family kept to themselves.

Of course this had an effect on Robert. Of course this violence would show up later in his work. How could it not have found its way into the singular means of Howard's self-expression?

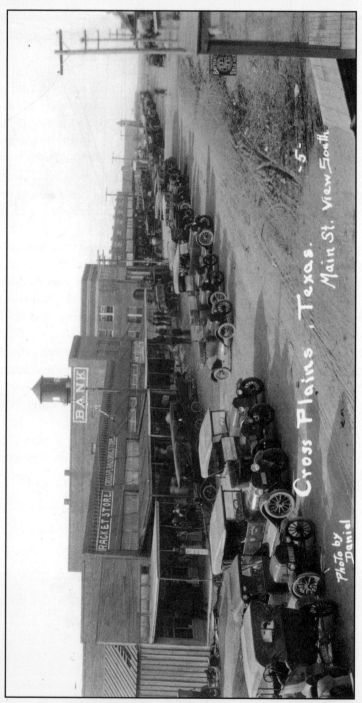

Cross Plains during their monthly Trade Days, when the neighboring communities would gather to buy, sell, and trade goods and services, circa 1922 (photo courtesy Margaret McNeel).

Post Oak Country

> One objection I have heard voiced to works of this kind—dealing with Texas—is the amount of gore spilled across the pages. It can not be otherwise. In order to write a realistic and true history of any part of the Southwest, one must narrate such things, even at the risk of monotony.
>
> **Robert E. Howard to August Derleth, March 1933**

While Pancho Villa's men harried and pillaged the Texas–Mexico border, occupying Chihuahua "on behalf of the people," the Burkburnett oil field opened up and gave roughnecks in East Texas an excuse to head north. Villa's relationship with Texas would sour in a few short years to the point that he would actually attack El Paso in 1916. On the heels of this came the widely publicized but now forgotten "Plan of San Diego," which called for the formation of a "liberating army of races and peoples"—meaning the Mexican, Black, and Japanese—which would seize control of Texas, New Mexico, Arizona, and California, and then form its own nation. It was heady, rhetorical stuff, but the mostly white population of Texas took it very seriously. With border violence occurring daily, the Plan of San Diego seemed more than feasible. In the end, the spillover from the Mexican Revolution, coupled with the unstable conditions on the border and the bloodthirsty zeal with which the various uprisings were quelled by both the army and the Texas Rangers, yielded a death toll estimated in the tens of thousands.

If the Japanese people seem out of place in the above revolutionary screed, it's worth noting that the Japanese warship *Asama* was wrecked off the coast of San Diego in February 1915 and stayed on the coast for months while it underwent repairs, fueling national rumors that a Japanese Navy base had been secretly established in Mexico.

Soon after, America found itself caught up in the Great War, and many sons of Texas served their country with pride. Texas, already isolationist in theory if not in practice, now found itself in two wars—the one along the border and the one overseas. And yet the farmers and ranchers who grew cotton, owned oil leases, and raised cattle benefited greatly from World War I, as the U.S. government bought all of their surplus goods for the war effort. Cotton, in particular, was used in great quantities for both medical supplies and uniforms.

The *Cross Plains Review* carried a small one-line note in their community notices in the January 29, 1915 issue: "Dr. Howard, of Putnam, has moved to Cross Cut." There's no telling how long the Howard family had been living in Putnam, in Callahan County. It's possible that the family visited the town so that Hester Howard could take advantage of the hot springs health resort that had opened in 1910. The snippet above is the only evidence that the Howard family ever stayed in Putnam.

When the family moved to Cross Cut in 1915, they settled into a small, close-knit rural community in the area of West Central Texas. Within the four adjacent counties of Callahan, Brown, Eastland, and Coleman, the Howard family would make friends with people who would know them the rest of their lives. Within these communities, Isaac Howard would become one of the most prominent local citizens, known and respected by all. Robert and Hester would forge relationships and friendships with people who would remember them fondly (and not so fondly) years later. By staying in small towns near Cross Plains, the Howards became a part of the larger community. Their family would live and die in these four counties.

Isaac Howard was now tending to the communities in a fifteen-mile radius. He made his rounds down the packed earth country roads via horse and buggy. Because of the size of the area, he decided to invest in an automobile, and he became one of the first people in Cross Cut to own a fabled Model T. Isaac hired a local handyman, Ben Gunn, to teach him how to drive. He kept the pair of horses and buggy in reserve, however, in case the weather rendered the roads unusable for the Ford.

Robert had no trouble forming friendships with some of the local boys, many of whom kept in touch with him when they were adults. They later recalled endless games of make-believe wherein Robert directed everyone in their parts, leading the others with narratives borrowed from whatever book he had most recently read. Cowboys and Indians, Rebels and Yankees, and even Pirates and Privateers were all parts of their regular playtimes. They also wrestled, boxed, ran all over the countryside, rode horses, fished, and all of the other things that boys in the country did. Robert's running buddies included Earl Baker, Percy Triplett, Fowler Gafford, and next door neighbor Austin Newton.

For all of the whooping and hollering the boys did, a few of the citizens of Cross Cut remembered a different Robert E. Howard. The son of one of Isaac's colleagues remarked that when the doctor and son came to call, "[Robert] just sat down to read." At a time when literacy wasn't strictly necessary for farming and ranching, this was considered odd behavior. It was one thing to read in school, when you had to, but reading outside of school, because you wanted to, was unheard of. For this reason, Robert was labeled "bookish" and a "sissy boy" by some of the Cross Cut population. Whatever some of the other folks might have thought about Robert, it wasn't enough to detract from long nature hikes, horseback rides, and other outdoor shenanigans with his buddies.

On the other hand, here Robert had to endure the first of many boarders. His cousin, Earl Lee Comer, was staying at the Howard house, most likely to work in the nearby oil fields. Robert was forced to share the sleeping porch with this older man, who came to them through Hester's side of the family. Comer stayed for at least a year, presumably until the work ran out, and then moved on like the rest of the oil field folks. Robert never discussed his cousin with anyone. In later years, when the Howards took in more boarders, Robert would have to share his quarters again with strangers. He only alluded to being put out by these arrangements. No one has ever found out the particulars of these houseguests—how long they stayed, how much (if any) they were charged in rent, and so forth.

Isaac found much acceptance in the community. His closest friend in Cross Cut was another colleague, Dr. Solomon Chambers. The two men shared many of the same interests, including twentieth-century "occultism" and hypnotism. Chambers may have been corresponding with Isaac and may have invited him to move his family yet again. Other families that Isaac made friends with included the Newtons and the Bakers. It's entirely probable that Robert was introduced to the sons of his father's friends. The families later shared many stories about Isaac Howard in letters and interviews with science fiction writer and Howard biographer L. Sprague de Camp, and it is through his efforts that we are able to construct such an accurate picture of the Howard family's time in West Central Texas.

According to friends of Isaac Howard, he and Hester weren't getting along very well. The bloom had definitely fallen off the rose for Hester's striking country doctor; the emphasis was now on the word "country." Isaac was well-liked in the community because he was one of them—a tale-spinner, a front-porch philosopher, and a natural-born leg-puller. He loved to hold court on any number of topics, and frequently at all hours of the day or night. Since the doctor made daily rounds to various patients in different parts of the community, he had a new audience at each stop.

Isaac would frequently call on the Newtons, the Bakers, or elsewhere and take full advantage of the hospitality in the houses he visited. Pioneer custom dictated that one offered to feed the doctor (who was usually on horseback and had ridden for miles to make a house call). The automobile did away with some of that, as did the relative proximity of the citizens of Cross Cut to one another, but old habits died hard, and the doctor dined heartily, as often as he could. After a while, Isaac came to expect food, and if none was immediately proffered, he would demand it. That he was still well-liked by these people is a testament to the force of his personality and the easygoing attitude of his neighbors.

This led to a smattering of gossip about Hester not feeding her family, but these allegations were quickly set aside when the Howards entertained, which they did lavishly, albeit extremely infrequently. Hester, in fact, went so far in the other direction that the Bakers thought she was putting on airs: serving the meals in courses, on the best plates, and so on. Hester even had neighbors over for tea in the afternoon. Earl Baker called her "peculiar," and considering how the rest of the community functioned, she was. In later years, Robert would defend her eccentricities by rattling off his mother's lineage as a "true Southern lady" to explain her mannerisms.

It was during this time that Isaac and Hester started fighting. Money was a constant problem in the house. Many of the doctor's patients paid him in produce, canned goods, or meat. Others paid what they could. Still others were allowed to slide for months at a time. How much money Isaac actually took in will never be known. There is also no way of knowing how much money vanished into various get-rich-quick schemes, wells that never came in, and the like. Robert would remark to H.P. Lovecraft years later, "I've eaten the crusts of poverty all my life, and probably will all the rest of it," and this was stated during his years as a professional writer, when he was making good money by community standards.

Hester felt that Isaac was not a good businessman. She also came to resent the differences between what she perceived as her family's station and Isaac's station. More to the point, she thought she had married beneath her class. Isaac was crude and salty in his speech and brusque in his demeanor. He came from farmers; he knew them well. He sometimes made inappropriate jokes at the dinner table. This mortified Hester, who considered herself a woman of refinement. When visitors came to the house, Hester always greeted them in the fashion of a perfect Southern lady, with formal graciousness and charm. She tried, in vain, to "culture up" her husband; Isaac simply egged her on harder. Hester became more tight-lipped, withdrawing completely, and having people over less and less.

Hester confided to a couple of her friends during her lifetime that she desperately regretted allowing herself to be swept off her feet by Isaac. Her other suitor, the one from Goldthwaite, had apparently done very well for himself and no doubt would have kept her in a manner to which she could quickly become accustomed, she said. When Hester married Isaac, she had no idea that she was signing on for a life in small towns, moving frequently, and being made to feel an outsider. While mean-spirited in delivery, her point is well-made. Isaac moved them constantly, and it's a fair complaint to make for a tubercular woman.

Annie Newton, Austin's older sister, knew both Hester and Isaac, and called them "desperately unhappy." In an interview, she told de Camp, "She had no love for him, and she didn't want the child [Robert] to have anything to do with the father."

Whether Isaac, who may have carried a torch for Annie and frequently told his marital troubles to her, gave Annie that impression, or whether Hester implicitly confessed that she was trying to come between Isaac and Robert, is not particularly important. The fact is, the parents were engaged in a battle of wills and Robert was caught in the middle. The fights were serious enough that Isaac would retreat to Solomon Chambers's house and threaten to "light out," to take off and leave Hester and Robert. Dr. Chambers would routinely steer Isaac back home and smooth things over with Isaac and Hester. Other times, after the raised voices would make their way to the Newton home, Isaac would come out of his house, whistling cheerfully, to make his rounds. He confided to one of his friends, "when you hear me whistling like that, you will know I am one mad son of a bitch." Despite Isaac's later claim that he and Hester tried to keep things of a depressing nature away from Robert, they would not have been able to quarrel in so small a house without Robert knowing about it.

In 1916, Robert acquired a new best friend—his dog, Patches, sometimes referred to as Patch. The dog was a mutt, part Walker foxhound and part collie. Robert raised the dog from a puppy, and the two were inseparable companions for the next twelve years of Robert's life. Together, they ran amok in the fields and over hill and dale in search of boyhood adventure. Isaac reminisced to pulp author E. Hoffmann Price, years later, "[Patch] was often fed from the table as Robert ate, sitting down by Robert's chair. When Robert helped himself, before eating a bite, he helped Patch to food."

Robert also caught and briefly took care of a raccoon, although the animal proved to be more than even an animal lover like him could handle. He told August Derleth, in October 1933, "I used to have a pet coon and he was a damn sight smarter than I was. That may not be saying much, but I'll go further and say that in his way, he had more sense than the average human. He'd fight anything from a prairie dog on up to a grizzly—including me; I carry scars from his talons and teeth to this day. I let him go, finally, and he took to the woods without a backward glance."

In 1917, the family moved to Burkett, Texas, some eight miles away from Cross Cut. This didn't sever any ties with their friends; Isaac continued to make his rounds in both towns. Visiting friends were but a horse or car ride away.

Despite its close proximity to larger towns, Burkett, like Cross Cut, had its own little school, and young Robert did passably well, although he insisted for years that he hated school with a passion. He made good grades in reading and writing, but terrible grades in arithmetic. Robert remarked on several occasions that he hated people telling him what to do, and that may well have been the case, but it should be remembered that Robert was an early reader, well advanced beyond what a country school could offer him in the way of challenges. With a photographic memory, able to glance through a book and get the gist, and to commit to memory lengthy poems with a reading or two, Robert was one of the brightest kids in the county. In 1917, however, he would have been forced to sit and read at what would have been an agonizingly slow pace as the rest of the class murmured recitations into their primers. School bored him to death, and he felt trapped by all of the rules and structure of the classroom. Any other child would have acted out, becoming the class clown or a disciplinary problem, but Howard was raised by a mother who insisted on manners and courtesy at all times. In these early years, his mother's influence would have far outweighed his father's contributions to his personality. Robert, instead of thumping a spitwad across the room, sat on his hands and seethed inwardly as he waited for recess, and the chance to work out his frustrations with a bout of wrestling.

Burkett was very similar to Cross Cut; the same kinds of people, with the same values, shared the same problems of watching the weather, tending to their livestock and crops, and finding their pleasures and happiness wherever they could. While the Howards were not regular churchgoers, Robert was made to go to Sunday school. Whatever their problems were behind closed doors, the family did their best to fit into the community.

Years later, Elsie Burns, the postmistress of Burkett, would recall meeting Robert and Patch on one of their outings in 1915. "I'm Robert Howard," he said. "I'm sorry if we frightened you. Patches and I are out for a morning stroll. We like to come here where there are big rocks and caves so we can play make-believe. Some day I am going to be an author and write stories about pirates and maybe cannibals. Would you like to read them?"

By the age of ten, Robert had made the decision that he wanted to be a writer. He told Lovecraft about the first story he had ever written, "that dealt with the adventures of one 'Boealf' a young Dane Viking. Racial loyalties struggled in me when I chronicled his ravages. Celtic patriotism prevented him from winning all his battles; the Gaels dealt him particular hell and the Welsh held him to a draw. But I turned him on the Saxons with gusto and the way he plundered them was a caution; I finally left him safely ensconced at the court of Canute, one of my child-hood heroes."

When the Howard family took car trips, riding around the countryside for picnics and sightseeing, Robert would cheerfully join in waxing oratorical with his story-telling father and poetry-reciting mother. On occasion, Robert and Isaac would venture forth on the doctor's rounds together, but Hester accompanied them as often as she could—ostensibly to ensure that Isaac couldn't forge as strong an attachment with Robert as she already had.

The Ranger oil field opened up in late 1917, and the news of same was conveyed to all parts of the area by the *Cross Plains Review*, the weekly newspaper that served the cities of Cross Cut and Burkett as well. Thereafter, the *Cross Plains Review* beat the drum particularly hard to try to encourage business, progress, and a little forward thinking for the town. The *Review* ran weekly oil news for Brown, Eastland, Coleman, and Callahan Counties, frequently denoting how far the newest well spudding in was from the Cross Plains city limits. Compared with Burkett and Cross Cut, Cross Plains was "the big city," and certainly the largest town in the immediate area, with a population of around 1,500 by 1920.

Here was Isaac's chance. He was close to a boom, and for the first time, in a position to set himself up before the boom struck—a chance to take advantage early rather than come into town with all of the suckers. His wife and son seemed very happy in this particular area, so another move just a few miles down the road couldn't be too objectionable.

In late 1918, Isaac said goodbye to Solomon Chambers, who was giving up his practice to be closer to his family. The crops had failed due to an infestation of grasshoppers, and Chambers had had enough. His family relocated to Galveston, where he took up truck farming. Isaac had lost his closest friend in the area. With nothing else holding him in place, he began looking for a home in Cross Plains.

> Dr. I. M. Howard and family have moved here from Burkett and are occupying one of the Coffman houses in the old town, which he bought some time ago. He has fixed up a nice office over the Farmer's National Bank. He is preparing to practice his profession in earnest here. We are glad to have him.
> *Cross Plains Review*, October 24, 1919

Cross Plains was so named because of its location close to the edge of two naturally defined areas of Texas, the Cross Timbers and the Lower Plains, or Rolling Plains. The Cross Timbers is a long, narrow swath of forest region that runs from Oklahoma to the center of Texas. Further designated by the East and West Timbers, the land, land quality, and trees in these forests sharply demarcate the divide between East and West Texas. Pioneers and settlers used the Cross Timbers as a natural landmark for navigating the Texas wilderness. The Lower Plains are north and west from Callahan County proper, and defined by layers of clay, sandstone, and gypsum that at one time were a vast undersea bed in the Cretaceous Period.

An example of the terrain can be found seven miles outside of Cross Plains on the Caddo Peaks, a pair of natural formations named after the erstwhile Caddo Indians. They boast elevations of roughly 2,000 feet above sea level, and the soft limestone that comprises the peaks is rife with fossils from the ancient sea bed that one can dig out of the ground with one's bare hands. These peaks fascinated Robert, and he used them as settings in various stories.

With the Cross Timbers to the east and the Lower Plains to the west, and surrounded by clear running streams like Turkey Creek and the Pecan

Bayou to the south, Cross Plains was a paradise to the first settlers in the area, German immigrants who made their homes in 1870. Originally called Schleicher by the residents, this tiny village was little more than a trading post at the edge of the Cross Timbers. The presence of Turkey Creek, a rich supply of farmland, and a small, God-fearing community eventually attracted other amenities like a mill for grinding corn. With the next wave of settlers, the name was changed to Turkey Creek, in honor of the local water supply. By 1877, the post office had established itself and the town was renamed Cross Plains. The township grew gradually until the Texas Central Railroad announced that it would build a line one mile from Turkey Creek. In 1911, the town elected to move all six hundred souls closer to progress, and businesses were bought and established along the rail line. Among the businesses to plant themselves were the Neeb Ice Company, the *Cross Plains Review* offices, the Farmer's Bank, the Cozy Drug Store, and Higginbotham's General Store, which came along in 1915. The newly designated Main Street had filled out nicely. The railroad and the movement of the town doubled the population, but this was a not a boom so much as it was the usual expansion of small towns with the support of the railroad.

Many of the businesses boasted of electricity as early as 1917, but the town proper wasn't fully electrified until 1920, when the Cross Plains Electric Light Company offered day and partial night service for the summer months and, after September 1 of that year, twenty-four hour service. Natural gas lines were running and expanding during this time, as well, and many homes bought new cooking stoves from the Main Street merchants.

The *Cross Plains Review* ran this interesting article on August 4, 1922:

Radio Station Being Installed in Cross Plains

Through the enterprise of Dr. John Rumph and a number of the young men of Cross Plains an up to date radio plant is being installed in the Cozy Drug Store. The wires which will retain the broadcasting waves from all parts of the country are suspended from the roof of the Higginbotham Bros Store to the Cozy Drug Store, and all other parts of the equipment is complete except a suitable battery, which has been ordered and will arrive within a few days. Just think, Cross Plains to hear in on the world. Those interested and promoting the unique project are Dr. John Rumph, Renerick Clark, Russel McGowan, C.S. Boyles, Jr., Budge Baum, Ray Adams, and Robert Howard.

Robert was an early and avid listener to the radio. Culturally, the radio was the first mass communication model, and it linked small towns in Texas to New York City, Chicago, and other major industrial centers across the country. In Texas, it was enough to be able to hear programs from El Paso and San Antonio. Robert listened to much of the popular music of his time, as well as the early dramatic readings and audio dramas produced at local stations. Most important to Robert, however, were sports and politics. He spent hours listening to football games, prizefights, and election returns as the occasion warranted.

Throughout this time of increased activity, the *Cross Plains Review* boosted business and kept close tabs on the large families that had long established themselves as integral to the community, like the McGowans, the Baums, and the Robertsons. Not a week went by that the folks in a thirty-mile radius didn't read, for example, chatty tidbits like these from June 13, 1919:

>Mrs. Broad Baum of Stamford is visiting relatives here.
>
>*
>
>Miss Lorain Graves, daughter of Dr. Mary L. Graves, left last week for Canyon, where she will spend the summer in school.
>
>*
>
>Miss Olive McGowan and Mrs. Murman McGowan left on Sunday for Fort Worth, where they go to meet Murman, who is due to be there the first of the week from New York. Murman is in the 142nd Infantry in the 36th.
>
>*
>
>Mose Baum, who has been with Uncle Sam doing border duty, has received his discharge and is now at his old job carrying mail for the same august personage, U.S., on Route 2, relieving his sister, Miss Rivers Lamar, who was his substitute. We are glad to have him back.

L.P. Henslee, who had owned and operated the *Cross Plains Review* since 1914, sold his business in 1921 to one of the most well-connected movers and shakers in the local oil business, Tom Bryant, together with S.F. Bond, the banker, ginner, and owner of the Cross Plains Electric Light Company, and Tom Anderson, the manager of Higginbotham's, the largest general store in town. Not surprisingly, they picked up right where Henslee had left off, and it was the *Cross Plains Review* that first called for a local Chamber of Commerce, civic improvements, and other concerns of the local businesses. Oil news continued to dominate the pages.

While the *Cross Plains Review* cheered the oil industry on, it also dutifully reported with the same bland enthusiasm every disaster, local or otherwise, every death, every mishap and accident, and any other misfortune that befell people, usually right on the front page. Children run over by wagons, people losing arms and legs in mill accidents, and deaths from influenza were all covered (usually in pieces submitted by grief-stricken friends or relatives that began, "The angel of death has collected another beautiful soul..."). As the oil boom descended, crimes and misdemeanors of all sorts were fair game, and shared space with a barrage of classified ads placed by local businesses reminding the citizens to pay their lines of credit on time or risk the suspension of ice deliveries and sundries.

This is not an indictment of the paper so much as it is an illustration of typical country life. That a bigger deal wasn't made about violence and death is simply part of the character of the early Texans. During this time, many of the pioneers who had settled Schleicher in 1879 were still around. Several of the "old timers" could remember the last days of the Indian wars on the open ranges of Texas. Progressive, maybe. Civilized? Not yet.

The *Cross Plains Review* also occasionally ran serialized fiction in its pages, to the delight and indifference of many. A half-page recounting of Paul Bunyan's adventures occupied page four of the May 27, 1921 edition. "Bulldog Drummond" by Henry Cyril McNeile ran for several weeks in 1921. In later years, the *Review* ran "Desert Gold" by Zane Gray and, appropriately, "Drums of the Sunset" by Robert E. Howard.

The houses on or near the banks of Turkey Creek became known as "Old Town," and it was there that Isaac found the family their home. It was an easy half-mile walk to town down Highway 206, which would eventually become Highway 36. Isaac made renovations to the modest one-bedroom house, updating it with indoor plumbing, electricity, and natural gas, in addition to making some modifications to turn the back porch into a bedroom and adding a "sleeping porch" as well. The former back-porch window between the master bedroom and what would eventually become Robert's room was never sealed up. Now the house could comfortably sleep six people. The kitchen was large and roomy, and there was a dining room and a sitting room. Out back was a large, open field, and off to the side, a free-standing garage and pen that would hold a horse and buggy (or a car) and a few farm animals. From his porch, Robert could see the Caddo Peaks. No more well water. No more outhouses. A gas stove for cooking. Electricity for nighttime reading. The Howard family was set.

Isaac bought the house with a cash down payment and a note for the balance later. The extensive renovations, too, cost money. Considering that the home was outfitted for the most modern of conveniences, such as electricity (the house was one of only fifty houses wired for current at the time), this new home may have been a peace offering to Hester. It was no Southern plantation of old, but it was extremely nice by community standards.

That Isaac rented an office in town was another sign of his putting roots down, but he still made rounds in his Model T and spent long hours away from the house, even staying overnight from time to time. Isaac advertised his services in the *Cross Plains Review* two weeks after the family's arrival. In no time, he had clients galore and had made friends with the rest of the local doctors, including John Tyson.

Isaac introduced Robert to Dr. Tyson's son, Lindsey, and the two became fast friends. Tom Ray Wilson and LeeRoy Butler, the older boy who lived next door to the Howards, also became Robert's friends. Robert kept up with Earl Baker and Austin Newton in Cross Cut, as well. The boys traveled by horseback, hitching rides in cars if they could, and continued to run around, have adventures, box, and play games. Lindsey Tyson would remain friends with Robert into adulthood, while Austin Newton, Tom Wilson, and LeeRoy Butler would eventually drift away, as childhood friends are wont to do.

Hester continued to put on airs, but she maintained an on-and-off friendship with Mrs. Butler next door. By now, Hester had lived with tuberculosis for twenty-five years and it was beginning to take its toll. Hester was bedridden more frequently, tired more often, and more sick in general. If Isaac noticed, he didn't appreciably change his routine, and he continued to eat multiple meals a day, stay gone for long periods of time, and pick fights when he was home. The Butler children remembered that Isaac was always whistling when he came out of the house.

The Howard family partook of the annual town picnic in 1920. A tradition started in 1890 by the citizens of Cross Plains to pull the outlying communities together for trade and fellowship, the picnic had grown into a monstrous tradition that included a large country carnival, prizefights, and traveling hucksters. By this time, things were moving pretty fast. Activity in the oil fields meant that more people were coming into town every day. The volunteer fire department staged prizefights to raise money, and it is a certainty that Robert watched the matches eagerly.

All of that, though, would soon take a backseat to the big news. The shallow wells that had been surreptitiously spudded in around town started to come in. By 1921, the boom was on. Cross Plains pulled together and used the influx of oil and people to make civic improvements to the town. A new school, an ice manufacturing plant, more hotels, more general business (the town had three tailors and four drugstores at one time) all sprang up within four years of the first oil boom. What also came into town with the oil boom was increased crime.

Headlines such as "Night Thieves Steal Clothing From Line," "Arrested On Charge of Giving Bad Check," "Thieves Steal $65.00 From Uncle Jim Coffman's Home," and "Woman First Inmate Cross Plains Lockup" were the order of the day, and the paper couldn't keep up with all of the fights, petty theft, gambling, and related activity that went on under the noses of the overworked authorities.

That latter headline from May 19, 1922, is a telling indicator of the character of the town, now booming from oil, and of the general reactions of the citizenry:

> The first person to occupy the new city bastille, or iron cage

thereof, behind locked doors was a woman. Two young women whose home may be designated as Nowhere, their manners left at the same place and routed for Anywhere, visited the dance hall in Cross Plains where the dance was in progress last Saturday night. They soon engaged in butter-fly antics and manners that were shocking to the other attendants and contrary to the rules of the Cross Plains dance hall. They were called to the attention of City Marshall Pinkston, and it did not require a very lengthy investigation for him to decide that they were loaded with something besides red paint and face powder, commonly known in Bootleggerdom as white mule whiskey. In fact one of them was so loaded and "het up" with the stuff that it took two full hours to cool her off in Pink's open air cage—it having just been imported from the county seat, placed on the jail site and not yet enclosed by walls or roof. After the brief cooling process, and a donation covering a fine and costs of $11.75 each they bade Pink and Cross Plains farewell and proceeded on their route to Anywhere.

The most interesting criminal activity reported at this time showed up first in the September 16, 1921 edition under the headline, "Daughter of S.L. Teague Victim of Highwaymen":

Thursday evening of last week while Mrs. Will Boyd, daughter of Mr. and Mrs. S.L. Teague, of Cross Plains, was coming over from Brownwood alone in a small car to visit with her parents she was held up by two men at the Red River Causeway, which extends along side of the Bayou at a place about thirteen miles from Cross Plains, and robbed of the small of cash which she had in her purse, a fraction over eight dollars. She had stopped the car on the causeway with the intention of filling the radiator with water when the two men suddenly approached her with presented revolver and few words indicated their intention of robbery. The purse containing the money was lying on the seat beside her and without speaking a word one of the hold-ups picked up the purse and shook the cash from it into his hand, returning the purse to the seat, after which they immediately disappeared and Mrs. Boyd proceeded on her way to this place. Mrs. Boyd doubts if she could identify the parties, but states that they were of youthful appearances and seemed to be greatly excited.

Years later, Robert would recount the rough details of the incident to an incredulous Novalyne Price as one of the reasons why he kept a gun in his car. At the time, years after the booms had come and gone, Price didn't quite know what to think about his story. Other biographers and friends, in canonizing and eulogizing the dead author, were quick to point out Robert's paranoia over such imagined dangers.

It's important to remember that Cross Plains was a comparatively small Oil Boom town. That is to say, Cross Plains only bloomed from 1,500 to 10,000 (or more) in a matter of months. Even though the size of the boom was small compared with Ranger and nearby towns like Desdemona (originally called "Hogstown" because the number of people crammed into so small a place was not unlike that of hogs at a feeding trough), Cross Plains had to deal with exactly the same set of circumstances: overcrowding, criminal activity, roads ruined by rain and an endless parade of traffic that turned the streets into a quagmire (wooden planks were laid across the streets to help pedestrians navigate from place to place), noise and clamor, violence, and a complete sense of instability that spread through the whole town.

Many folks got rich overnight as the wells they leased came in. Others speculated heavily on their own rigs and went broke. The men working on the rigs and assigned to various crews showed up with money in their pockets in tremendous excess to their meager needs and spent it wantonly on any available vice. Very few of these transients stayed after the business fell off. Only the businessmen who preceded the boom stuck around, and even then, not so many as before.

Local businessmen was quick to respond, and new hotels, new restaurants, and other amenities were erected with great haste, along with a new jail, a new civic center, and a host of new organizations to encourage prosperity and community. With all of the economic progress and civic improvements being made in Cross Plains, there was one bastion of civilization that failed to materialize: a library. That innovation would not arrive in town until 1978. This too is not surprising; in the decade of the 1940s, less than 2% of all of the books published in the United States were purchased in Texas. Considering that Robert, who bought books whenever he could in places like Brownwood, owned over three hundred books and countless magazines at the time of his death, it draws a sharp contrast between Robert and the rest of the town.

For a child living in a boomtown, it was a strange mixture of excitement and hardship. Children were told to stay out of the way of the oil field workers, but it was difficult not to admire certain oil field bullies that cut a heroic figure among the regular townsfolk. They were not unlike the cowboys and other pioneers who had come to Texas fifty or more years before to tame the land. Indeed, many of the roughnecks were failed cowboys, raised on farms and good for nothing else but strong-arm work.

Robert couldn't help but interact with the oil boom in Cross Plains; there was no way to avoid it. By now his hatred of this sense of progress was clearly defined. He saw the hypocrisies of the boom clearly, an ironic state of affairs that allowed for "progress" and "civilization" to come with their own predators and brigands. He watched as a quiet, God-fearing town suddenly became a wild and lawless place. He watched as the backdrop of his early childhood descended on an area of the country he had come to know, and he saw the effect it had on people his family knew very well. The boom changed everything. It was as if Robert had moved again, only this time, his family wasn't moving away from it.

Isaac Howard was doing very well; here were his old frontier days coming back to him, but with a difference. He sewed up various wounds on the oil field workers, and then walked the streets with people smiling and waving and saying, "Hello Doc!" as he promenaded past. It was that combination of respectability and prominence, coupled with the energy and excitement of the boomtown, that appealed to Isaac. He was happy with his practice, if not his wife.

Hester, in an effort to protect Robert from some aspects of the boom, hovered over him even more. Robert was forbidden to play football and any other team sport deemed too violent. At home, with friends, he continued to pursue boxing. But it wasn't the same as football, where the real road to glory lay in Texas.

Robert continued to make his mark at Cross Plains High School, which only went up to the tenth grade at the time. In his spare time, he continued to read and, now, to write. Robert was addicted to the printed word. Whenever the family went to a large city, Robert got to spend time in the library. Cross Plains didn't have one, although one of the drugstores had made an abortive effort to lend used books, or swap out books from the few readers in town. As he got older, Robert bought books from bookstores when he found them, and solicited mail order business from places like Von Blonn's in Waco, Texas. For the interminable stretches of time when Robert had neither car nor access to books, his only choice of reading material was magazines.

Robert read widely, without any guidance, and let his tastes develop naturally. He didn't have the luxury of a library, where someone might have tried to steer him in a particular literary direction. Any book he would have been forced to read in school would have been quickly dismissed— anything Robert didn't take in of his own free will would have been met with resentment. What Robert craved was action, excitement, and intrigue. That which interested him would have been met with favor, be it Shakespeare or the various authors who regularly contributed to *Adventure* magazine.

Robert purchased his first copy of *Adventure* at the age of fifteen from the Cozy Drug Store, which ran large print ads in the *Review* in the June 24, 1921 edition, touting their magazine rack. In addition to the usual listing of "slicks," such as the *Saturday Evening Post* and *Cosmopolitan*, the Cozy Drug Store carried a number of pulps, the list of which is a veritable who's who of Robert's early influences in the writing markets, including *Argosy All-Story*, *Police Gazette*, *Blue Book*, *Adventure*, *Top-Notch*, *Western*

Story, and *Detective Story*.

Here's what Robert said about his purchase, in a 1933 letter to H.P. Lovecraft:

> Magazines were even more scarce than books. It was after I moved into "town" (speaking comparatively) that I began to buy magazines. I well remember the first I ever bought. I was fifteen years old; I bought it one summer night when a wild restlessness in me would not let me keep still, and I had exhausted all the reading material on the place. I'll never forget the thrill it gave me. Somehow it never had occurred to me before that I could buy a magazine. It was an Adventure. I still have the copy. After that I bought Adventure for many years, though at times it cramped my resources to pay the price. It came out three times a month, then.... I skimped and saved from one magazine to the next; I'd buy one copy and have it charged, and when the next issue was out, I'd pay for the one for which I owed, and have the other one charged, and so on. So I generally owed for one, but only one.

Adventure magazine was one of the biggest influences on Robert E. Howard's work, if only for the sheer number of writers to which he was exposed; Harold Lamb and Talbot Mundy leap immediately to mind as authors that Robert eagerly devoured, and whose influences would later be glimpsed in his own work. Robert wrote to H.P. Lovecraft in July 1933, "I wrote my first story when I was fifteen, and sent it—to Adventure, I believe. Three years later I managed to break into Weird Tales. Three years of writing without selling a blasted line. (I never have been able to sell to Adventure; guess my first attempt cooked me with them for ever!)"

The story, "Bill Smalley and the Power of the Human Eye," is a tale of two hunters in Canada and the trouble they get into in trying to construct a bear trap. The setup is not handled well, and the payoff is slight. But it is a western story in setting if nothing else, and it is supposed to be a humorous yarn. Moreover, the central theme of the story hinges on exaggeration and unreliable narration. This, then, was the beginning of Robert's signature style. He would end his career in much the same was as he started it: exaggerating for comedic effect.

Despite the usage of what would become his most successful commercial tools, "Bill Smalley and the Power of the Human Eye" isn't a particularly good story. It is no surprise that Robert's first effort was rejected. The small amount of Robert E. Howard's marginalia and juvenilia that has survived bears little resemblance to even the early work at the beginning of his career.

Besides, *Adventure* had a cadre of authors that were ex-military, soldiers of fortune, and even cowboys… and, of course, the less desirable brand of people who could talk a good game and write a better pulp story.

One of their contributors, a flim-flam man named Major Malcolm Wheeler-Nicholson, would later go on to publish the first collections of original art and stories in what would later be called comic books. Another, later contributor, the bombastic L. Ron Hubbard, forged a variety of globe-trotting careers for himself to establish his credibility and sell the equally bombastic fiction he was churning out at the time.

Robert, at the age of fifteen, with only a smattering of worldly experience, couldn't hope to compete against such learned writers and liars, but he dutifully tried for his entire professional career to make it between the covers of *Adventure*. He never succeeded. However, now that he had started writing, he would never again stop.

Part 2

The men sat on the porch, angled in rocking chairs to better catch the capricious breeze that blew intermittently through the afternoon heat. Pipes and cigars were lit, and the wafting smoke was more pleasant than the smell of the crude oil that hung over much of the countryside.

Dr. Howard nodded to Dr. Tyson. "Mighty fine vittles, John."

"Well, thank you," Dr. Tyson said, easily. "Of course, the meat wasn't so much, but with everyone in town, we have to make do with what we can."

This brought a ripple of chuckles; all of the dinner guests had been served a barbecue of seven enormous briskets, and there was plenty of meat left over.

"Oh, I know what you mean," said Dr. Howard. "Why, when I was plying my trade on the Oklahoma Border, we routinely ate steers so big, we used to ride underneath 'em on horseback and tip them over from below before we could shoot 'em."

Dr. Tyson slapped his leg as he chuckled. The rest of the men broke into grins. Dr. Howard continued. "Those were the days," he said, dreamily. "No matter how thin we sliced them steaks, we had to cook the meat out on the open fire, because they were too big to bring back on horseback!"

Everyone laughed. Dr. Howard turned to his left. "Do you remember any of that, Robert?"

Robert smiled, his eyes dancing. "Oh, yes sir. Why, for years, I was kept in a crib about two feet high, which Dad here made by hollowing out one of them cow hooves. I mean," he continued, as the men laughed harder, "these cows were big."

Dr. Howard was about to put up the narrative, when Robert cut him off. "Heck, everything was bigger in those days. We still have saddles that Mom used to put on the chickens for me to practice my riding with."

As the front porch rocked with laughter, Dr. Tyson's son tapped Robert on the arm. "Let's go spar some."

"Suits me," said Robert. "Excuse us, gentlemen. I gotta show Lindsey the proper way to duck into my left hook."

Dr. Howard watched his son walk around the house with Lindsey, his pride shining in his blue eyes.

"Fine boy you got there, Doc," said one of the men. "Hell of a storyteller."

"Chip off the old block," said Dr. Tyson.

Dr. Howard nodded. "Thank you," he said, gruffly. "He takes after his mother."

That brought whoops of laughter from the porch.

Inside the house, in the drawing room, where the rest of the wives sat with their tea and their thoughts, Hester Howard heard the laughter and flinched.

Local roughnecks posing near one of the wooden oil derricks, circa 1920s (photo courtesy Margaret McNeel).

AUTHENTIC LIARS

An authentic liar knows what he is lying about, knows that his listeners—unless they are tenderfeet, greenhorns—know also, and hence makes no pretense of fooling either himself or them. At his best he is as grave as a historian of the Roman Empire; yet what he is after is neither credulity nor the establishment of truth. He does not take himself too seriously, but he does regard himself as an artist and yearns for recognition of his art. He may lie with satiric intent; he may lie in order to take the wind out of some egotistic fellow of his own tribe or to take in some greener; again, without any purpose at all and directed only by his ebullient and companion-loving nature, he may "stretch the blanket" merely because, like the redoubtable Tom Ochiltree, he had "rather lie on credit than tell the truth for cash." His generous nature revolts at the monotony of everyday facts and overflows with the desire to make his company joyful.
J. Frank Dobie

In order to fully understand and appreciate the depth and breadth of Robert E. Howard's writings, it is necessary to examine one of his most overlooked influences. Robert was surrounded by storytellers from birth: his father, a porch-swing raconteur of the first degree; his mother, who lied consciously and unconsciously about everything from her family tree to her age; and nearly all of Robert's aunts, uncles, and grandparents, who filled the boy's head with violent imagery of the Texas frontier. From the time Robert was a boy, he listened eagerly to any of his elders that had a story to tell. As a young man, and even as an adult, Robert collected oral stories from any of the older generation that would care to talk to him at length. Novalyne Price Ellis, Robert's girlfriend from 1934–35, told Rusty Burke many years later, "Bob is responsible for Clyde [Smith, Robert's best friend] going around and interviewing people, because he was so interested in the stories that older people had to tell. He did a lot more of that before he became a full time writer then he did afterwards, when I knew him. There was never a time, though, that Bob wouldn't stop his car or stop whatever he was doing and go to the courthouse in Brownwood or any other place where he could be around old people to get their stories."

Robert absorbed so much storytelling and oral history that it became a significant contributing influence on his writing. Given his keen interest in the subject of tall tales and oral history; the predominance of characters, settings, and events from Texas in his stories; and most importantly, his large body of humorous fiction in the tall tale tradition; it is clear that Robert was not unlike many of the folklorists and historians of his time, including J. Frank Dobie and Mody C. Boatright. However, whereas Dobie, Boatright, and others were content to merely transcribe and comment on the thousands of tall tales, anecdotes, and oral histories so integral to Texas, Robert did them one better and created new, original fiction built entirely on the precepts of Texas folklore.

In a time before mass communication, when newspapers in small towns were weekly occurrences and all letters were written by hand and moved across the country by rail or on horseback, the quickest, most effective means of communication was asking, "How's business?" Story-telling, yarn-spinning, blanket-stretching, and telling "windies" was, in the most desolate places of the frontier, welcome entertainment and highly valued. As the frontier became the open range, and then the oil fields, the stories dutifully changed to reflect the drives and aims of the tellers and the tellees. Cowboys became roughnecks with only a few alterations in costume and setting. The gist of the stories, however, remained unchanged.

Mody C. Boatright, one of the unsung legends of Texas folklore, summed it up very succinctly: "The frontiersman lied in order to satirize his betters; he lied to cure others of the swell-head; he lied in order to initiate recruits to his way of life. He lied to amuse himself and his fellows. He was an artist, and like all true artists he found his chief reward in the exercise of his art, however surcharged that art might be with social or other significance."

Texas was considered the last frontier for America. As such, books and other trappings of civilization were scarce, and space was limited by the need to pack only what was necessary for survival. For most families moving into Texas, the Bible was the only book any of them carried, and they could all share it. It was just as well, anyway, since the men and women who settled Texas—fighting Indians, taming the wild with firearms and sheer determination, and carving the land into something that had never been before—would have been bored stiff by Charles Dickens and Walt Whitman. Boatright said it best when he observed:

> [T]he westward-moving men of action, unhampered by any high-falutin theories of art, created their own literature. The pathos and tragedy of their experience they recorded in their songs; their zest for the hard life of the frontier in their prose tales. Had they lived in a prescientific age, they might have produced an *Odyssey*, or more probably a *Beowulf*. Since, however, the age of the serious folk epic had passed, and they were essentially realists, their heroic literature took a comic turn; and in keeping with nineteenth-century ideals, their comedy was the comedy of exaggeration. In the tall tale, they developed one of America's few indigenous art forms.

Robert E. Howard came along on the cusp of nineteenth-century values and twentieth-century progress. He watched scientific marvels pile upon themselves, each one going higher, like a technological Tower of Babel, and as he grew older, he prayed for a good, old-fashioned thunderbolt to knock it all down. Robert's worldview was irretrievably altered by this prolonged contact with so many people with strong ties to Texas's colorful history. The tall tale was Robert's birthright, and these precepts appear all throughout his work.

Critics have always commented on Robert E. Howard's natural, flowing prose style, his deft use of language, and, above all, his sense of earnestness; Howard believed implicitly what he was writing. Even his detractors grudgingly admit that his writing has a certain verisimilitude of authenticity not found anywhere else. Some authors and critics have come closer to the truth when they have said that Robert E. Howard actually believed what he wrote, although a pregnant pause at the end of every sentence was usually inserted to drive home the notion that Robert was somehow lacking in the faculties to distinguish reality from fantasy. In fact, Robert merely invested himself in the story in much the same way that a tall liar would earnestly believe the cock-and-bull yarn he was spinning. For oral storytellers, this is the mark of a master, the most difficult skill to acquire. In prose form, it is practically unheard of.

The first instance of being moved by a storyteller that Robert recalled was in his third letter to H.P. Lovecraft, dated September 1930:

> I well remember the tales I listened to and shivered at, when a child in the "piney woods" of East Texas, where Red River marks the Arkansas and Texas boundaries. There were quite a number of old slave darkies still living then. The one to whom I listened most was the cook, old Aunt Mary Bohannon, who was nearly white—about one sixteenth negro, I should say....
>
> She told many tales, one which particularly made my hair rise; it occurred in her youth. A young girl going to the river for water, met, in the dimness of dusk, an old man, long dead, who carried his severed head in one hand. This, said Aunt Mary, occurred on the plantation of her master, and she herself saw the girl come screaming through the dusk, to be whipped for throwing away the water-buckets in her flight.

Howard also remembered his grandmother, Isaac's mother, and the tales she had told, in the same letter:

> But no Negro ghost-story ever gave me the horrors as did the tales told by my grandmother. All the gloominess and dark mysticism of the Gaelic nature was hers, and there was no light and mirth in her. Her tales showed what a strange legion of folk-lore grew up in the Scotch-Irish settlements of the Southwest, where transplanted Celtic myths and fairy-tales met and mingled with a substratum of slave legends. My grandmother was but one generation removed from south Ireland and she knew by heart all the tales and superstitions of the folks, black or white,

about her.

As a child my hair used to stand straight up when she would tell of the wagon that moved down wilderness roads in the dark of the night, with never a horse drawing it—the wagon that was full of severed heads and dismembered limbs; and the yellow horse, the ghastly dream horse that raced up and down the stairs of the grand old plantation house where a wicked woman lay dying; and the ghost-switches that swished against doors when no one dared open those doors lest reason be blasted at what was seen. And in many of her tales, also, appeared the old, deserted plantation mansion, with the weeds growing rank about it and the ghostly pigeons flying up from the rails of the verandah.

That these early storytellers had a lasting effect on Howard is obvious by looking at the number of horror stories he wrote in the 1930s, as well as the subject matter. Howard deftly transposed and combined different aspects of the folklore and invented reasons for the supernatural action, as well as a clever and effective climax.

When Lovecraft replied with remarks in kind, Robert followed up in a letter written in late September 1930:

The tale of the murdered traveler is, as you say, quite common in all sections and reminds me of one, very old, which was once quite prevalent in the Southwest and which must be a garbled version of some legend brought over from Scotland. It deals with three brothers stopping at a lonely cabin high up in the mountains, kept by an evil old woman and her half-idiot sons. In the night they cut the throats of the older brothers, but the younger escapes. Now enters the really fantastic part of the tale. The younger brother flees across the mountains on his fleet horse and the old woman mounts and pursues, carrying a cane held high in her hand. Again and again the boy eludes her, but each time she holds the cane high and sings a sort of incantation:

"Sky-high, caney,
"Where's Toddywell?
"Way over on the Blue-ridgey mountains!
"Haw back!"

Perhaps in the original tale, the answer is given by the cane. Anyway, the cane points out the way the boy has taken and the pursuit is renewed. Eventually the fugitive gains "a pass in the mountains" and escapes. When a youngster I always shuddered at the mental picture that tale brought up—the lean and evil hag with her lank hair flying in the wind, riding hard across the dark mountains under the star-flecked skies, gripping her gory knife and halting on some high ridge to chant her fantastic incantation. But it is but one of the many bloody tales that once flourished in the Scotch-Irish settlements of the Southwest.

Robert was very aware that the folklore of the Old South and Southwest got its start in Europe, the British Isles, and elsewhere before it migrated into a regional American setting. Brought over by immigrants of all nations, the stories were both a badge of the culture and easy currency for the New World, to be spread and redistributed until, like modern Americans, it became difficult to determine where they had originally come from.

Early in Robert's correspondence with Lovecraft, he regaled the New England author with tales of various rattlesnakes he had come across, and like a native Texan entertaining a greenhorn, he tended to stretch the truth about their prowess. Robert later sent Lovecraft the tail section of a rattlesnake with the following prose poem, wherein he gilded the lily more than somewhat:

> Here is the emblem of a lethal form of life for which I have no love, but a definite admiration. The wearer of this emblem is inflexibly individualistic. He mingles not with the herd, nor bows before the thrones of the mighty. Between him and the lords of the earth lies an everlasting feud that shall not be quenched until the last man lies dying and the Conqueror sways in shimmering coils above him.
>
> Lapped in sombre mystery he goes his subtle way, touched by neither pity nor mercy. Realizations of ultimate certitudes are his, when the worm rises and the vulture sinks and the flesh shreds back to the earth that bore it. Other beings may make for Life, but he is consecrated to Death. Promise of ultimate dissolution shimmers in his visible being, and the cold soulless certainty of destruction is in his sibilances. The buzzards mark his path by the pregnant waving of the tall grasses, and the blind worms that gnaw in the dark are glad because of him. The foot of a king can not tread on him with impunity, nor the ignorant hand of innocence bruise him unscathed. The emperor who sits enthroned in gold and purple, with his diadem in the turned-clouds and his sandals on the groaning backs of the nations, let him dare to walk where the rank grass quivers without a wind, and the lethal scent of decay is heavy in the air. Let him dare—and try if his pomp and glory and his lines of steel and gold will awe the coiling death or check the dart of the wedge-shaped head.
>
> For when he sings in the dark it is the voice of Death crackling between fleshless jaw-bones. He reveres not, nor fears, nor sinks his crest for any scruple. He strikes, and the strongest man is carrion for flapping things and crawling things. He is a Lord of the Dark Places, and wise are they whose feet disturb not his meditations.

Robert continued talking about folklore and myths with Lovecraft before they became distracted in their seemingly eternal "barbarism versus civilization" debate. Even afterward, while engaged in heated discourse, Robert couldn't resist sneaking some of the more colorful bits of Texas history or gunfighter lore into the debates. More often than not, he commented on the character of Texans and the general attitudes of his home state to bolster his arguments.

By late 1932, Robert began a correspondence with August Derleth, and their letters gave them both ample opportunity to discuss regional history and swap stories about their respective places of origin. Of particular interest is Robert's admission that he doesn't know much about Pecos Bill, followed immediately by a story of Pecos Bill:

> You mentioned Pecos Bill. I don't know much about that mythical hombre. Likely somebody in the long settled districts of South Texas could tell you more about him. Just now the only legend dealing with his exploits which I call to mind is of obviously recent manufacture. It seems the University of Southern California was going to have a tug-of-war with the University of Oklahoma. The rope was stretched from the campus of one to the campus of the other, and Pecos Bill, who had been imported by the Californians, laid hands on it out on the West Coast and began to heave. He anticipated an easy snap, but lo, and behold, he found himself unable to gain an inch. Amazed, he told the students of U.S.C. to let go and give him full play. He gripped the rope with both hands, planted his feet, and heaved. And at last, inch by inch, the rope came to him. He backed away with it, and it came faster and faster. At last he was wading in the Pacific Ocean up to his waist, and the rope was fairly humming through his hands. Then the people of Colorado began to set up a hell of a yell. The Oklahomans had tied their end of the rope to Pike's Peak, and Pecos Bill had torn the mountain loose from its moorings and was dragging it toward the Pacific Ocean.
>
> But some of the early heroes of the Southwest did feats almost equal to the legendary exploits of the gentleman from the Pecos. There was Jack Hayes, for instance—the first Ranger captain. He went into a thicket where twelve Comanches were lurking, and killed eleven of them in hand-to-hand fighting, and lived to tell the tale, as the saying is. Incidentally the remaining redskin was shot down as he ran, by Jack's Rangers who were stationed around the thicket.

Robert's correspondence with Derleth never reached the heated pitch of his ongoing argument with Lovecraft, but Robert and Derleth batted history and storytelling back and forth until 1936. Robert even corrected errors of folklore for Derleth (who had been given a book of Brown County history written by Robert's friend, Tevis Clyde Smith) in February 1933:

> [S]everal myths and legends, popular thereabouts, were omitted—particularly that concerning Henry Ford, whose writings furnished much of the material for the book, and whose picture you will see opposite page 43. A man of mystery,

though he became the town's leading citizen, there are many old-timers who will swear that Jesse James never died in Saint Jo from Bob Ford's bullet—that he died in Brown County, in 1910, under the name of—Henry Ford. Others maintain that he was Bob Ford, instead of Jesse. The fallacy of these myths is obvious. But who he was, what his real history was, no man knows. One thing is known—that outlaws and bad men fought shy of him, and left him very much alone when they were on the rampage.

Robert's letters demonstrate that he was a capable amateur historian, and would have made an excellent historical authority except for one small quirk: He could not resist tweaking a story, improving on it in some way, or dramatically embellishing to serve his own ends. He told Lovecraft in October 1933, "There is no literary work, to me, half as zestful as rewriting history in the guise of fiction." Robert clearly considered myths and legends a part of history. He lectured his out-of-state correspondents on all aspects of Texas history, even as he rewrote for Derleth the legend of Quanah Parker into a gripping saga of loss, love, and redemption:

> It would take a large volume to tell the full story of Quanah Parker, and of Cynthia Anne Parker, yes, and of Peta Nocona, the last war-chief of the Comanches. It is the classic tale of the Southwest, which has been rewritten scores of times, fictionized and dramatized. I will tell it as briefly as possible.
>
> In the year of 1833 a band of settlers, about thirty-four in number, headed by John Parker, came from Illinois and formed a colony on the Navasota River, in Limestone County, Texas—then, of course, part of Mexico. In 1836, when the Texans were fighting for their freedom, the Comanches were particularly bold in raiding the scattered settlements, and it was in one of those raids that Fort Parker fell. Seven hundred Comanches and Kiowas literally wiped it off the earth, with most of its inhabitants. A handful escaped, through the heart-shaking valor of Falkenberry and his son Evan, both of whom fell a year afterward on the shores of the Trinity in a battle so savage and bloody that the Comanches who survived it retold it as long as they lived. But there Fort Parker passed into oblivion, and among the women and children taken captive were Cynthia Anne Parker, nine years old, and her brother John, a child of six.
>
> They were not held by the same clans. John came to manhood as an Indian, but he never forgot his white blood. The sight of a young Mexican girl, Donna Juanity Espinosa, in captivity among the red men, wakened the slumbering heritage of his blood. He escaped from the tribe, carrying her with him, and they were married. He took up his life again with the people of his own race, joined General Bee's command, fought

with characteristic valor through the Civil War, and afterwards became a well-to-do Texas ranchman.

For Cynthia Anne a different fate was reserved. In 1840 a group of traders found her on the Canadian River with Pahauka's Comanches. They tried to ransom her, but the Indians refused; and then she was seen no more by white men until about 1851. Meanwhile she had grown to womanhood; there were various suitors for her hand, among them Eckitoacup, of whom more later. He was a shrewd fellow, more given to intrigue than to war. But Cynthia Anne became the mate of Peta Nocona, whose fame hung gorily at his scalp-belt, and whose diplomacy was the stroke of a tomahawk. She bore him children, among them a son, Quanah, which means something similar to sweet fragrance. When white men next came into the Comanche camp where Cynthia Anne dwelt, they strove to persuade her to accompany them back to her white relatives. She refused; she had almost forgotten that other life, as she had forgotten her native tongue. Then, in 1860, her Indian life was ended, bloodily, violently, just as her white man's life had ended.

Peta Nocona, apparently kind to her in his way, and possessing all the finer qualities of the red man, was, nevertheless, an unbridled devil along the frontier. His trail was a red one, and many a settler's cabin went up in flames, and many a frontiersman went into the long dark scalpless because of him. When retribution came, it was merciless. On the Pease River his Nemesis overtook him, in the shape of Sul Ross, later governor of the State, and his Rangers. The surprise favored the white men. They were among the tipis shooting and slashing before the Comanches realized what was occurring. They broke and scattered, every man for himself.

Peta Nocona caught up his daughter, a girl of fifteen, and rode away with her. Ross was in full pursuit, knowing his prey. The girl was riding behind her father, and Ross's first shot killed her, and glanced from the shield that hung on Peta Nocona's back. As she fell she pulled the red man off his horse, but he hit on his feet, cat-like, and drove an arrow into the body of Ross's horse. The wounded beast began plunging and Peta Nocona began winging his arrows at the rider in blinding speed. Undoubtedly the erratic motions of the wounded horse caused him to miss his first few shafts, and Ross, firing desperately even while fighting for his seat, struck and shattered the Indian's elbow. Peta Nocona staggered and dropped his bow, and Ross, jerking the trembling horse to a standstill, took good aim and shot his enemy through the body; the Comanche stood as if dazed, then, as another bullet from Ross's pistol tore through his torso, he reeled to a tree near-by, and grasping it for support, began to chant his death-song. Ross approached him, and ordered him to surrender, but his only reply was a ferocious thrust of his lance, which Ross narrowly avoided. Ross shrugged his shoulders, and turned away, making a gesture to his Mexican servant. The crash of a shotgun marked the finish of the last great warchief of the Comanches.

Meanwhile, Lieutenant Kelliheir had ridden down a squaw who was trying to escape on a pony with her papoose. His pistol was cocked and leveled when he saw that she was a white woman. And so Cynthia Anne Parker came again into the lands of her people. The rest is history too obvious to reiterate. She lived with her people, her brother, Colonel Parker, a member of the Legislature, but she was never happy, always mourning for her red mate and children, always seeking to escape back to that wilder life from which she had been brutally torn. In 1864 both she and her baby went into the long dark. And one might question, whether into the Christian Paradise, or the Indian's Happy Hunting Grounds.

This colorful account, written in January 1933, is full of drama, excitement, details that no man could have ever known, and a few historical inaccuracies, but it reads like dynamite. Robert, as a tall tale teller, was most successful when he used those skills and traditions to construct fiction. While the tall tale tradition most obviously appears in Robert's humorous yarns, he also employed it to great effect in his horror, his fantasy, and his historical stories. It's the tall tale tradition that gives Robert's work its unique rhythm, drive, and authenticity.

Mody C. Boatright made a study of the precepts of the tall tale, and of the people who told them. Boatright, along with J. Frank Dobie, did much to popularize and legitimize the study of Texas from a sociohistorical perspective. He roamed all over Southwest Texas, visiting cow-camps, oil fields, and other less savory places, collecting folklore and tall tales from whoever would tell them. Boatright, who did much of his early work in the 1930s, shared a great deal in common with Robert E. Howard. Had the two men ever met (and there's no evidence to say that they didn't), the tarpaulin of balderdash they would have stitched together might still be blanketing the Llano Estacado to this very day.

Boatright laid out the principles of tall tale telling in "The Art of Tall Lying," first published in 1949. These will serve as guideposts through the writings of Robert E. Howard, clear indicators that Robert, as an amateur folklorist, intuitively worked with the precepts that Boatright actively catalogued and studied.

Boatright noted, "Contrary to the conventional analysis of American humor, the folk liar does not depend on mere exaggeration. Exaggeration, he knows, is in itself neither folkish nor funny.... The folk humorist did not say of a hero that he had the strength of ten either because of his pure heart or because of his impure whiskey. He detailed concretely what the hero would do."

Howard's humorous fiction follows this principle in every single story, from some of his earliest humorous sketches to the last funny western he ever wrote. Howard's creations Sailor Steve Costigan and Breckinridge Elkins (and their literary cousins) live in a world of such hyperbole, most often, but not always, in the presence of violence. Such exaggerations are all the more authentic when delivered in a West Texas dialect, as in this excerpt from the chapter "Meet Cap'n Kidd," from the novel *A Gent From Bear Creek*, wherein Breckinridge Elkins tries to tame his infamous horse:

> Well, when Cap'n Kidd recovered his senses and riz up, snorting and war-like, I was on his back. He stood still for a instant like he was trying to figgure out just what the hell was the matter, and then he turned his head and seen me on his back. The next instant I felt like I was astraddle of a ring-tailed cyclone.
>
> I dunno what all he done. He done so many things all at onst I couldn't keep track. I clawed leather. The man which could have stayed onto him without clawing leather ain't been born yet, or else he's a cussed liar. Sometimes my feet was in the stirrups and sometimes they warn't, and sometimes they was in the wrong stirrups. I cain't figger out how that could be, but it was so. Part of the time I was in the saddle and part of the time I was behind it on his rump, or on his neck in front of it. He kept reching back trying to snap my laig and onst he got my thigh between his teeth and would ondoubtedly of tore the muscle out if I hadn't shook him loose by beating him over the head with my fist.

Boatright went on to explain about comedic timing and the construction of the tall tale: "The folk liar had no metaphysic of humor, but he knew that he need not expect much response from his hearers if he merely said that his hero was forty feet tall. He knows that he must provide ludicrous imagery, an ingenious piling up of epithets, a sudden transition, a *non sequitur*—something besides mere exaggeration if his audience was to respond to his tales."

Sailor Steve Costigan, Robert's first real success in the pulp market, was a ham-and-egg prizefighter from Galveston who worked the ports of call in the Asiatic Sea, picking up fights. In many ways Costigan was an ideal version of Robert, and the author used the lighthearted series to perfect his comic timing. Most of the Costigan stories end by a sudden turn of events or a traditional punchline to underscore the plot. This excerpt from "Texas Fists," appropriately delivered by a ranch hand, details some specifics of the fight between Costigan and a group of cowboys:

> "Golly, Miss Joan," said Slim, kinda like he was hurt, "if you

got any sympathy to spend, don't go wastin' it on that gorilla. Us boys needs yore sympathy. I winked at the bar-keep for the dope when I ordered the drinks, and, when I poured the sailor's, I put enough of it in his licker to knock out three or four men. It hit him quick, but he was wise to it and started sluggin'. With all them knockout drops in him, he near wrecked the joint! Lookit this welt on my chin—when he socked me I looked right down my own spine for a second. He busted Red's nose flat, and you oughta see it this mornin'. Pete lammed him over the bean so hard he bent the barrel of his forty-five, but all it done was make Costigan mad. Pete's still sick at his stummick from the sock the sailor give him. I tell you, Miss Joan, us boys oughta have medals pinned on us; we took our lives in our hands, though we didn't know it at the start, and, if it hadn't been for the dope, Costigan would have destroyed us all. If yore dad ever fires me, I'm goin' to git a job with a circus, capturin' tigers and things. After that ruckus, it oughta be a cinch."

Boatright's next principle is perhaps the most important: "Again, contrary to most academic analyses, the folk artist knew the value of understatement and used it skillfully in his boasts and in his narratives of fact and fiction." Boatright is referring to what most people would consider "the way most Texans talk," a strange kind of laconic verbosity that is both dry and outlandish at the same time. The example Boatright gives is a statement from W.S. James, discoursing on the decline of cattle rustling circa 1890:

It is now getting to a point, has been for several years, that jurists and judges are getting so incredulous that the boys [who steal cattle] have been having considerable trouble to explain their mistakes, and the consequence is that many of them have been sent east to work under the supervision of the state; this is invariably done under protest, and nearly every one who signs a state contract is innocent; and if you don't believe it, you may be convinced by going to Rusk, Texas [where the penitentiary was located] and asking them, or to the court records, and almost without exception you find a plea of "not guilty."

Any quick perusal of Robert's letters to Lovecraft will show that this is how Robert "talked" in his letters. Since Robert frequently spoke (some would say shouted) his stories aloud as he spoke, his fiction naturally carries the cadence of his voice, however consciously or unconsciously. Listen, then, to Robert's description of the town picnic, August 9, 1932:

Well, the picnic came and went, and no violence. That's the forty-ninth picnic of its kind to be held in this town, and if there ever was another one that didn't have a few fights, I never heard of it. Certainly I never saw one before so peaceful. But a lot of the old-time toughs were missing—some having left the country, some having previously stopped bullets, some in jail. Even at the boxing matches the crowd seemed to consist largely of youngsters, certainly less pugnacious than those of the previous generation. We stood packed like sardines in the outdoor make-shift arena and I don't believe the fighters suffered much more than the crowd did. One boy had a tough time—somebody kept appropriating the chair on which he was supposed to sit between rounds, and his seconds kept having to dispossess the occupant, who generally put up a resistance. And then somebody stole the kid's shirt which he'd hung up outside the ring for lack of a proper dressing room. The main bout was a flop. They brought a slugger from Fort Worth with a blare of trumpets and a ruffle of drums to fight a local boy called Kid Pancake—I don't know if that's his real name or what he is. He came from Oklahoma, originally, I think, and he looks more like an Italian than anything else. His real name may be something like Panciata. Scarcely had the fight started when the Kid leaped across the ring like the panther he is, shooting a murderous left hook to his adversary's jaw. The city boy went down like a butchered steer, his head lolling over the lower rope; he was carried out, his eyes shut, his limbs trailing limply. He was so unconscious he snored; I've seen many a man knocked stiff, but I never saw one snore before. I've heard of it, but never saw it until then. It was another triumph for the post-oak country over the more civilized portion of the state!

Despite the exaggerations and other forms of misconduct, J. Frank Dobie said, "The authentic liar knows what he is lying about." Boatright added to that the tall liar's art "is essentially realistic. His burlesque, like all good burlesque, rests on a solid foundation of truth." Again we turn to Robert's fictional sailor, Steve Costigan. While it's true that Robert never sailed the Asiatic Seas, he did box, and frequently with the same kinds of rough characters that crossed gloves with his fictional counterpart. Robert knew boxing intimately; he was a lifelong fan. The Costigan stories bristle with boxing lore and technique, from the technical execution of a proper hook to how to defeat a left-handed boxer. Moreover, Robert's fictional boxers all inhabit the real world of boxing. Robert established that his funny sailor, Steve Costigan, lived in the same world as his serious boxer, Iron Mike Costigan, who lived in the same world as Dempsey, Firpo, Joe Grimm, and, not coincidentally, Robert E. Howard himself.

In the Breckinridge Elkins stories, Robert successfully satirized the things he knew best: small towns and Texans, feuds and crooks. Elkins himself is another fun-house reflection of the author—naïve to the point of simplicity, quick to anger, and bristling with loyalty and honor toward family, the opposite sex, and his horse. The time period of the Elkins stories predates the automobile, but that gave Robert a chance to dip backward into his idealized "Good Old Days" and give it a proper skewering.

Boatright brought up an important point about making the story believable: "The folk artist knows the value of circumstantial detail: perhaps just a little prefatory rambling to fix the date—yes, it was '87, the year Roaring Springs went dry; short notes on characters—this was the same Bill Weber who took a fancy to a fine new saddle in Peter Cowan's shop and bought it, although he had a pretty good elum-fork, and he had to sell his only horse to pay for it; definite references to place—it was over on Brushy Creek, where Bob Ware was killed by the Comanches. There would be enough detail of this sort to establish poetic faith, but not enough to clog the action: the main point was never lost sight of."

E. Hoffmann Price, pulp writer and himself a world traveler, remarked on Sailor Steve Costigan in a letter to L. Sprague de Camp, "His China Coast stuff is phony as a three dollar bill—how a writer of his many talents could have rattled off such tripe about China is beyond my imagining." Price was a good friend and colleague to Robert, but he really never understood some of the fundamentals that made Robert's work so interesting. Many a humorous Robert E. Howard yarn opens with the mere sketch of a setting. Why not? It's enough. Costigan is in Zanzibar before his prizefight; that's all one needs to know to enjoy the tale. The details of the setting did little more than fix the backdrop of the story in the minds of the readers. Robert spent more time and energy crafting the things that mattered—the characters and the prizefighting.

This technique shows up in plenty of Robert's serious fiction as well, usually in the disguise of an economy of words, or often misattributed to a poetical suggestion of a scene. In truth, the reader is getting exactly as much information as is needed to get on with the story. Anything else relevant to the story will be either explained or filled in on the fly. That Robert could paint such vivid word-pictures is partially because of his skill at poetry, but also because of the tall tale tradition that encourages such brevity.

Boatright's last principle dealt with the structure of the story itself. "For the tallest of tall tales, as distinguished from mere tall talk, had a logic and a structure. The tall tale is logical in all points but one." Here Robert was able to deviate from the folk tale tradition and work within the realm of fictional precepts. In crafting the ending to any given story, Robert had a wider set of options by way of fiction writing. In fact, his stories were required to make sense all the way through, and so Robert didn't use tall tale endings very often, even in his humorous work. One exception is what Boatright called the "less-than-to-be-expected" ending, whereby after a series of disasters and buildups, the tale-teller seemed close to certain doom, or to absolute redemption, when in fact the result was neither good nor bad, but somewhere in the middle.

These endings show up in both the Elkins and Costigan stories, most frequently after the hapless hero has been battered senseless in the name of true love. Inevitably, however, the woman is nowhere to be found, having run off with the man she really loves. More often as not, these types of endings were worked into the narrative and Robert had the luxury of adding an additional "stinger" at the end of the story for good measure. This is the ending to "Sailor Costigan and the Destiny Gorilla," after Costigan has endured a ferocious fight with a rival for a girl's affections and a battle royale against the thugs who swore vengeance for a perceived transgression. While tending to his wounds, Costigan's rival receives a letter:

> Big Bill grabbed it, tore it open, glared at it, then give a terrible scream. He waved it wildly at me, strangling so he was black in the face. I grabbed it and read:
>
>> Dear Bill:
>> I guess this will teach you that you can't make a girl by beating up all her admirers. When Costigan knocked Gorilla Baker through the wall of my dressing room, I knew Providence had sent me a tool to work with. I played up to the Sailor and ribbed him up into challenging you for a fight, just to get you out of the way long enough for me to marry the boy I've been nuts about all the time—Jimmy Richards, the boy who played the saxophone down at the All Night Inn. The poor boy was so scared of you he didn't dare come about me while you were around. So I fixed it up this way, and by the time you read this, we'll be married and on our way. It was a dirty trick to play on the Sailor, but a weak woman has to use her wits when she's up against gorillas like you. So long, and I hope you break a leg!
>> Love,
>> Teddy
>
> "Married! A saxophone player! Teddy!" moaned Elkins, and laying his head on my shoulder, he bawled like a bull with the belly ache. "She has scornt my love!" he wept. "She has handed me the gaff! I'm a rooint man. I'm scorned and deserted. Oh, Death, where is thy stingaree?"
>
> I was too paralyzed to say anything; a saxophone player! When she could have had me.
>
> "When you get through soakin' my shirt with tears," I said at last, "lemme know. I craves to go forth and drown my unrequited love in blood and cauliflower ears. This is all Gorilla

Baker's fault. If it hadn't been for him, I'd never have got into this mess. He can't make a monkey outta me this way. When I get through with him, I bet he'll be careful whose wall he falls through the next time I sock him."

Robert E. Howard was an intuitive storyteller. He never shied away from the opportunity to tell, or retell, any narrative of interest to him. This poses an interesting challenge for anyone reading and thinking about Robert E. Howard: finding the balance between Boatright's "solid foundation of truth" and Howard's personal goal of "rewriting history in the guise of fiction." As Robert matured into a man, and as he transitioned his early attempts at writing into an enviable professional career, the line between truth and fiction became more blurred and distorted. Boatright concluded his article with this telling observation:

It may be noted, however, that since the pioneer, instead of writing books, told his tales orally as occasion arose, he did not feel a need for unification around a single character. When he told his narratives of ingenious escapes and hair-raising adventure, he might invent the name of the hero on the spot; he might ascribe the feats of daring to some local character; but he was more likely to appropriate the honors himself.

The best yarns are in the first person.

Robert E. Howard in his Senior Year, Brownwood High School, 1923 (photo courtesy of Leo Grin).

The Tattler

Robert Howard, Short Story Writer
Have you been reading Robert Howard's short stories in The Tattler for several issues back? If you haven't you are missing a treat. His Christmas story received commendation from the editor of the Brownwood Bulletin and his later stories are just as good.

We are fortunate in having such a good writer here in our school and we hope he will keep up his contributions. The stories are mostly written in the style of O'Henry, Bret Harte, and Mark Twain, and are just as interesting as their stories. His stories have plenty of action and are spicy with near-cuss words and slang. If for nothing else The Tattler is worth a dime and over if it has a story by Robert Howard.
The Tattler, **March 15, 1923**

In 1922, the Cross Plains School District only covered the tenth grade. While this was plenty of schooling for most children, anyone going on to college had to transfer to Brownwood to complete their eleventh grade. Many of the Cross Plains children moved to Brownwood, lived in boarding houses, and in general started their college experience a year early. Robert spoke often in later years about how much he hated school, and it is likely that his parents expected him, or even pressured him, to go to college. He was, after all, the son of a doctor. Maybe it was an assumption on the part of his parents and family friends that Robert would follow in his father's footsteps.

Hester decided to move to Brownwood to keep house for her son. Isaac thought this was a bad idea, another plot to keep Robert tied to his mother's apron and further distance him from his father. Whether Hester put her foot down or not is unknown, but Isaac decided to rent a room for his wife and son. And so Robert, at the age of sixteen, transferred to Brownwood High School, accompanied by his mother. Isaac drove to Brownwood on the weekends for family time.

Brownwood, about thirty-five miles east and south from Cross Plains, was the largest city in Brown County, and the closest city to Cross Plains. With two colleges in town at the time, Daniel Baker College and Howard Payne College, the town also had bookstores, where Robert bought as many books as he could afford, along with other luxury items not found at Higginbotham's general store. Brownwood was the county seat and the jewel of Brown County in the early twentieth century, made prosperous by cotton farming, several railroad lines, and, of course, oil.

Brownwood High School was where Robert would meet two of the most important people in his life. The high school brought in students from all of the neighboring communities who wished to attend college, and with the rapidly growing population of Brownwood in the 1920s, the school was very overcrowded.

The graduating class of Brownwood High School would eventually include doctors and lawyers, members of the clergy, successful businessmen, a journalist, a teacher, and other middle- to upper-class respectable jobholders. Robert's classmates had already been assimilated into the workforce; they got jobs in town, or started working for the family business. Many went back to the farm. Many more couldn't stand the thought of farming and signed on with the oil field crew. Everyone got busy getting on with their lives.

Not Robert. He had made his choice; he was going to be a writer. To this end, he threw himself into the torturous process of trying to figure out how to write. The problem was, he still had a year of school to contend with. Robert took science as his elective, a strange choice considering that he had already decided that he wanted to craft fiction for a living. Just as improbably, it was his best subject. Students in his senior class included Austin Newton, from Cross Cut, and Lindsey Tyson, and Robert made a new friend: Truett Vinson.

Vinson, a fellow senior, was deeply interested in literature, philosophy, and writing, and, like Robert, harbored literary ambitions. He and Robert became fast friends. Vinson was a Brownwood resident and knew more of the students than Robert, and it was most likely Vinson who introduced Robert to the staff of *The Tattler*, the Brownwood High School newspaper. An unremarkable and thoroughly average student endeavor, it was nevertheless the forum for the earliest work of Robert E. Howard.

The December 1922 issue of *The Tattler* included two stories by Robert, both prize-winning compositions, which earned him a ten-dollar gold piece and a five-dollar gold piece for first and second place, respectively.

"Golden Hope Christmas," the first place story, is a sentimental, gently told tale that revels in its Bret Harte-ness. The ending is predictable and telegraphs itself after the first three paragraphs. Perhaps the judges were swayed by the close proximity of the holidays.

"West is West," on the other hand, contains a glimmer of what would become Robert's signature style. This story is the genesis of Robert's career as a Southwestern humorist, and it is easy to see in it the earliest strands of what would one day become Sailor Steve Costigan and Breckinridge Elkins. The story opens with a telling passage of dialogue:

> "Get me," I told the foreman of the ranch where I was spending my vacation, "a tame and peaceful bronc for I would fain fare forth among the hills to pursue the elusive bovine and, as thou knowest I have naught of riding skill, therefore I wish a quiet

steed and if it be aged I care not."

The foreman gazed at me thoughtfully.

"I have just the cayuse for you," he said.

"Hi Alkali! Bring forth Whirlwind!"

"Nay, nay!" I said hastily, "for doubtless he is a veritable whirlwind and such I will not mount."

"Not so," quoth the foreman, "he is named thus in delicate sarcasm for he is as lazy as a tenderfoot and as gentle as a kitten."

Of course, Whirlwind is anything but. After the horse is saddled and the unnamed narrator (evidently a city slicker from Robert's use of dialect) mounts the beast, Whirlwind comes to life:

I thought at first that a cyclone had hit me but it was only the kittenish pranks of my gallant charger. He bucked. He pitched. He sun-fished. He swapped ends. He rose on his hind legs and danced. He stood on his front legs and capered. He placed his hind and fore feet together and spun around and around with such rapidity that I was dizzy. He leaped high in the air and came down stifflegged with a force that jolted my very intellect. He seemed to be changing the whole landscape.

How did I stay on? There was a reason. Not my fault that I stayed on. I wanted off as bad as he wanted me off. I felt as if all my bones were falling apart. I could scarcely hear the delighted yells of the cowpunchers. Yet I stayed. Even when my steed dashed at full speed under a tree limb which just cleared the saddle horn. I remained but the branch did not. I remained even when my frolicsome charger laid down and rolled on the ground in spite of my protesting screams. He arose and began to do some entirely new tricks when something snapped. It was the two girths breaking simultaneously. I described a parabola and landed on my head some twenty yards away with the heavy saddle on top of me. My erstwhile steed emitted a paean of victory, danced a scalp-dance on my prostrate frame and galloped away over the horizon.

Robert is clearly working in a tall tale style; understatement, clearly stated, and exaggeration, cleverly executed. The anecdote ends with the big reveal, "my gun belt got hung over the saddle horn and the lasso came loose and tangled me up so I was tied to the saddle and couldn't get off to save my life till the saddle came too."

Robert's stories were popular and he continued to run his short, humorous sketches for several issues throughout 1923. These bouts of bombastic humor were a contrast to how the rest of the students saw Robert; a quiet, reserved young man. His high school photo from this time period bears their impression out.

About his school days, Robert later wrote, "I hated school as I hate the memory of school. It wasn't the work I minded; I had no trouble learning the tripe they dished out in the way of lessons—except arithmetic, and I might have learned that if I'd gone to the trouble of studying it. I wasn't at the head of my classes—except in history—but I wasn't at the foot either. I generally did just enough work to keep from flunking the courses, and I don't regret the loafing I did. But what I hated was the confinement—the clock-like regularity of everything; the regulation of my speech and actions; most of all the idea that someone considered himself or herself in authority over me, with the right to question my actions and interfere with my thoughts." This diatribe speaks volumes about the difference between the façade that Robert showed his classmates and his true feelings. All of that pent-up frustration had to go somewhere. Robert funneled it neatly into his fiction writing.

Truett Vinson was responsible for the introduction of another of the friends that would become Robert's inner circle. Tevis Clyde Smith, Jr. was two years younger than Robert and Truett, but he had the same literary ambitions and interests—in fact, Smith owned a small printing press. He and Vinson were talking one day when Smith asked if Vinson knew Robert Howard. Vinson replied, "Yes, there he is now." He brought Robert over and made introductions to Smith, who, many years later, recalled this meeting with Robert: "We shook hands, if it could be called that, for Bob extended a limp palm and executed what was known as a 'dishrag shake.' I hadn't wanted him to break the bones in my hand, but I was a bit surprised at such a greeting, though I soon found that he was warmhearted, and we became good friends before the school term ended."

For the first time in his life, Robert now had not one, but two friends with whom he could talk about the books he had read, discuss prose and poetry, and in general wax philosophic about any number of subjects. Robert thought of Smith and Vinson as his "intellectual" friends, even though he boxed with Smith and took nature walks and made road trips with both of them.

Robert's friendship with Smith is doubly important for the number of letters they exchanged, an ample correspondence filled with local events, musings and ramblings of all sorts, and personal jokes. Robert also deluged Smith with a huge quantity of poems, sketches, and ballads that reveal much about his own personality. Robert talked with Smith about stories he'd recently placed, and his comments about his own work also show a side of Robert not found anywhere else. His later correspondence with various authors, editors, and fans highlights other aspects of Robert's complicated personality, but through the letters to Smith, one can observe a casual, relaxed Robert E. Howard.

Smith and Robert decided to do some writing together through Smith's amateur newspaper, the *All-Around Magazine*. Because he owned the printing press, Smith was the editor, typesetter, publisher, and distributor.

The first issue of the *All-Around Magazine* featured a story by Smith and Robert, titled "Under the Great Tiger." In what may have been the most economical usage of words in Robert's career, the unnamed hero of the stories dispatches three opponents in the span of three hundred words—over the course of two issues. The tale was unfinished, and publication of *All-Around Magazine* suspended, no doubt due to the vagaries of publishing a small independent newspaper for an indifferent eleventh grade class. But Robert's and Smith's writing careers were just getting started.

From 1922 to 1923, Robert wrote several short stories and submitted them to various magazines, with the same results; all were rejected. While certainly longer than Robert's pieces in *The Tattler*, they still show the earmarks of his inexperience with crafting a story. There are inspirational flashes of greatness, but not enough to hold these early efforts together.

While Robert sent manuscripts to various magazines, *The Tattler* continued to publish his short stories, which, given the rejection letters he was receiving from magazines, was still some encouragement. The stories ran until Robert's graduation, but two years later, when Smith became the editor, another short piece appeared, called "The Ideal Girl."

Robert graduated high school in May 1923. Isaac soon thereafter moved the family back to Cross Plains. Robert was ready to start earning a living as a writer, but his parents wanted him to go to college. Isaac still held some hope that Robert would follow in his father's footsteps, but Robert wasn't having any of that. During the summer, he continued to write short stories and worked in Cross Plains for his spending money.

One of Robert's earliest markets was *Weird Tales* magazine. Widely considered one of the greatest pulp magazines of all time, it started on rocky financial ground and never quite made itself profitable. It first saw print in 1923 and quickly went into debt, as it was unable to find its audience. When a Shakespearean scholar named Farnsworth Wright took the editorial reins in late 1924, he heralded the Golden Age of *Weird Tales* by introducing the small but dedicated readership to some of the most important fantasy writers of the twentieth century. At the time that Robert was trying to drum up work, *Weird Tales* was merely one of the ever-increasing number of pulp magazines that filled the newsstands. The Cozy Drug Store carried a small but varied spread of pulp magazines, in addition to various slicks like *The Saturday Evening Post*. Robert knew, as did every engaged reader of the time, that there was a perceived difference in quality between the stories in *Top-Notch* and the stories in *Cosmopolitan*. Laying aside the chasm between the subject matter of the pulps and slicks, Robert knew he had a better chance of breaking in with the pulps. Besides, they were publishing more of the things that Robert wanted to read—and write.

Robert began his mail correspondence with Clyde Smith shortly after returning to Cross Plains. These chatty, informal letters reveal much about the young man's state of mind from the ages of seventeen to eighteen. Like most of his letters to Smith, these epistles are rife with in-jokes, poems both parodic and sincere, and little sketches, anecdotes, and stories to amuse Smith. June of 1923 found Robert in Marlin, presumably staying there while Hester received treatment for tuberculosis. He wrote to Smith:

> I have got whooping-cough, curse it, and I'll bet two rupees that "Robin Hood" comes to Brownwood while I am laid up with it.... Did you see my "What the Nation Owes to the South" in the Bulletin? That's what I won the U.D.C. medal on, you know. I didn't know they had published it until just the other day.... I got a letter from the assistant editor of "The Campus," S.M.U. He said he saw my poem "The Sea" in the "Baylor United Statements" and he asked me to contribute to "The Campus." I sent him a poem.

Robert wasn't resting on his laurels. He sent out other essays and poems in an effort to build up some professional credits, get some feedback, and maybe get paid. By the end of July, Robert was back in Cross Plains, typing letters and, presumably, short stories, while he cast about for a job. He wrote to Smith:

> Rome spread her empire across the world. Then she became dissolute, debauched and—the barbarians drove in. The tribesmen of Genseric, of Attila, of Alaric, raided, looted, in the very streets of Rome.
>
> Cathay was the mightiest nation of Asia. Then she forgot her skill in war for debauchery—and the Mongols swarmed across the Great Wall and Genghis Khan rode his horse into the palace of the emperor.
>
> The nations of Central Asia had become effeminate and rich and proud. The Tartars came from the northern steppes and Tamerlane built his mighty empire over their ruins.
>
> When India turns from war to trade and becomes debauched the wild tribesmen of Afghanistan come down the Khyber Pass with torch and sword.
>
> When a nation forgets her skill in war, when her religion becomes a mockery, when the whole nation becomes a nation of money-grabbers, then the wild tribes, the barbarians drive in... Who will our invaders be? From whence will they come? Where but from Asia? Can a nation ally the Tartars, the Mongols, the Indians; the tribes of Asia?

This is the earliest appearance of Robert's viewpoint on history; the notion that a given civilization battled its way to a cultural pinnacle, and then backslid into moral decay and degeneracy, just in time to be conquered by another group of people on the upswing. This is one of the most frequently recurring plots in Robert E. Howard's canon, one that appeared in every kind of story and genre in which Robert wrote. Certainly, every one of Howard's most important stories is either laid out on the ruins of the past or features institutions and people in the process of becoming those ruins. This ultimately pessimistic outlook on world history was obviously applied to Robert's then-current worldview.

Robert's next letter on August 4, 1923 includes the following statement: "I shall write a story entitled 'The Last Man' as a warning to the white races. If the West falls before the East, it won't be because I haven't warned the white races."

Now is as good a time as any to discuss one of the hot topics that surrounds any serious study (and, in these politically correct times, any casual reading) of Robert's fiction: Was Robert E. Howard a racist? If the above statement is anything to go on, then of course he was. But, like most of us, Robert's beliefs were complex and thoroughly shaped by the time and place in which he lived.

At the age of eighteen, Robert was as racist as he was ever going to be. Clyde Smith's family had fought in the Civil War for the South, as had Robert's. Lovers of history that they both were, it was inevitable that they would discuss such things. Also consider where and when Robert was living: Texas was socially conservative, predominantly Baptist, but most certainly Christian, and phrases like "civil rights" were decades away.

Texas was borne out of violence, and its history bears that out—but it's the nature of the violence that is worth noting. All of the major wars fought in and around Texas were cultural clashes—white settlers versus Native Americans. Or white versus Hispanic. Or Native American versus Native American. The last of the Indian wars with the Comanche were still told and retold in Robert's time—many of the famed Indian fighters were still alive.

The Ku Klux Klan had re-formed in West Central Texas, and while the Klan claimed that their goals were noble, Governor Ferguson attacked Klan leadership until they again went underground. The Mexican Revolution had been over for only three years. Pancho Villa had just been assassinated in his villa. A decade of border violence had drawn to an uneasy close, and the veterans from the Great War had come back with horror stories of the trench warfare with the Huns.

Robert and Clyde were kids. They knew nothing of the world. Their positions on the subject of racial superiority were in keeping with the vast majority of the population of Texas and, truthfully, of the United States. They had both grown up hearing the words "nigger," "wetback," and "redskin" used to describe various peoples of color. There was no other word in casual conversation. The "polite" term was "Negro" or "Colored." Clyde Smith was one of the first friends that Robert could talk to about writing, history, and other topics of mutual interest. If Clyde wanted to bring up racial superiority, Robert, eager to fit in with his new friends, would have cheerfully obliged him.

A theoretical "science" in vogue at the time was eugenics, a term first used in 1883 by Sir Francis Galton to describe the intentional breeding of people with desirable traits to produce genetically superior offspring. The science has since been completely discredited, but in Robert's day, it went hand in hand with the idea of an Aryan race that was naturally superior due to its somehow undiluted bloodline. There was no Aryan race, of course, by anthropological standards, but the idea was quickly seized upon by politicians and scientists. By the 1930s, this quackery was already on its way out the door, but the ensuing events of World War II have made this topic a perennially hot one. It's interesting to point out that Robert himself often tinkered with these conceits, and in two different stories, "Skull Face" and "The Moon of Skulls," when he has occasion to look back to the time when Atlantis was thriving and viable, he points out that the white Europeans are the cave-dwelling savages and that his Atlanteans are brown-skinned.

As Robert matured, his viewpoint on other cultures matured, as well. His love for the underdog of any nation or race, his admiration of black boxer Jack Johnson, and his early exposure to black storytellers in East Texas all softened the hard-nosed sentiments of his youth. Most notably, Robert's viewpoint developed into a one-on-one kind of outlook that goes hand in hand with Texan pragmatism; in other words, every man has the chance to be a stand-up guy until he proves himself otherwise. In his later fiction, Robert used "Negro" and "black" interchangeably to describe African-Americans, many of whom were portrayed sympathetically as the story dictated. Black and Jewish characters became more frequently employed, and for a wider variety of character roles.

Robert's heroes are usually Irish, or a mix of other white cultural strains. His supporting characters enjoyed a more robust palette, as did his villains. However, it is worth pointing out that while Robert was proud of his "Black Irish" heritage, not everyone shared his affection for the Irish, themselves considered as a "mongrel horde" in the nineteenth century when millions of them poured into America's melting pot to escape untenable living conditions in their own country. Robert knew this, too. In his self-identification, and in his heroes' conscious choice of origin, Robert aligned himself with the unwanted cultural underdog.

When Robert utilized ethnic characters, he did so with the pulp market in mind, but he deviated frequently from type to employ his own brand of Texas pragmatism—that is, that a man is proven by his deeds and his words. That pragmatism allowed thousands of Chinese immigrants to thrive in places like San Antonio and El Paso. Often, lone people or families from overseas were cheerfully accepted into a small town, provided they were good farmers and went to church every Sunday. Such broad-minded attitudes were really a phenomenon of exceptions to the rule rather than a policy of benevolent inclusion, but this was a trait of the pioneers, with whom Robert was clearly enamored.

Examples of the suspension of cultural bias on account of the character's deeds and words include Ace Jessel, the protagonist in "The Spirit of Tom Molyneaux" (obviously modeled on Jack Johnson); N'Longa, the witch doctor who helps Solomon Kane and acts as a guide to the supernatural world of Africa; and many of the Middle Eastern characters in the Crusades and El Borak stories. What is generally overlooked by most scholars and diehard fans is that the majority of villains, rogues, and despicable characters in Robert's stories—the westerns, tales of Solomon Kane, Conan, and Kull, his humorous stories, and more—are the white Europeans or their cultural equivalents.

Robert did not tackle racism so much as he waxed literary on clashes of cultures. His point-of-view character is always depicted as being unreasoning or prideful of cultural heritage; Conan hates the Picts because his people, the Cimmerians, have always fought with them. The same is true of King Kull. Since the Picts in Robert's work always represent "the other" in his stories, Conan speaks of them in dehumanizing terms. That type of rhetoric has always been a necessary part of combat and war; if the enemy isn't human, but rather some kind of animal (and particularly dangerous, at that), it's a lot easier to kill them.

It is easy to assume that Robert is prejudiced against the Native Americans if all one ever reads is the Conan story, "Beyond the Black River," but in truth, Robert's letters show that he sympathized with the plight of the Native Americans and frequently expressed sympathy for the Comanche, even as he recounted their sanguinary exploits. In Robert's unfinished story, "The Thunder-Rider," he took the point of view of a Comanche fighting a sorcerer who once ruled the "civilized" Aztecs. As his point-of-view character in "The Thunder-Rider" points out, he finds the barbaric Comanche way of life more fulfilling than modern civilization. Coming from a writer whose mother hated Indians and tried to instill in Robert a fear of the "red man," it's obvious that Robert made up his own mind on many of these types of topics.

When racial hatreds are invoked, Robert's characters do the talking. In the narrative, Robert is always more respectful and usually refrains from comment beyond moving the plot forward or explaining character action. Robert wrote in his letters about racial practices in his county and in Texas in general, but he didn't seem to think very much of them. By his own admission, Robert didn't live in an area of Texas with a large percentage of black and Hispanic people. He formed his early opinions, on this topic as on everything else, out of what he had read. Later, as he moved around more and saw other communities, he lightened or changed his stances.

Then there's the town of Cross Plains to consider—almost completely white and very typical of small Texas towns in the twentieth century. Robert's language was well within societal standards, especially for Texas. "Nigger" was what everyone called people of color, and just as common as "Chinaman" or "Spic." Texas was settled by a wide spread of Europeans, and the number of exotic accents present during the days of the oil booms is impossible to count.

Mexican and Hispanic characters get the short end of the stick with Robert. They are conspicuous by their absence in his work, and the few times that they do ride up, it's to play the lecherous bandit or the lazy peasant; they are always referred to as "greaser" or "Mex," but again, this was not outside the bounds of 1920s Texas. One notable exception is found in his later story, "The Horror From the Mound." The Mexican sharecropper in the story is treated sympathetically, perhaps in deference to Robert's maturing viewpoint. Many of Robert's opinions about race, and in particular Mexicans, were tied up in the political rhetoric of the Mexican Revolution. Robert's prejudice against Hispanics was also extremely polarized, like most of Texas, in that he "loved the culture, but couldn't say the same about the people."

Were Robert a racist by modern definitions, he would have shied completely away from people of color, as his contemporary H.P. Lovecraft usually did, or he would have consistently used his stories to illustrate the inherent superiority of the white Anglo-Saxon Protestant or the deviant nature of the "other races," again as Lovecraft usually did. Also consider that had Robert really been writing of his time and place, the Hyborian Age would have been entirely European in origin.

Robert didn't have to use different cultures in his stories, but he did. A racist might have achieved the same results by writing about the battle of Agincourt and other "white on white" skirmishes throughout history, or he would have written about the heroic British soldiers taming and controlling the Indians because that was their sacred charge. Neither message interested Robert, whose primary concern, it must always be remembered, was the rising up of the barbarians to overthrow the decadent civilization. Considering how many different ways, and from how many different viewpoints, that he chose to depict that conflict, skin color was a secondary consideration. Robert's barbarians were of all races and cultures.

On the other hand, there is something inherently polemical in Robert's "rise of the barbarians" plot. Sometimes the barbarians won. Sometimes they lost. Sometimes Robert focused on the winner, and sometimes he concentrated on the loser. But Robert's eye was always on the conflict. He believed that no matter who won, it was always a temporary victory. Typically overlooked when Bran summons throwbacks from the earth to overwhelm the Romans, or when Baibers raids indiscriminately in the Middle East, it suddenly becomes blatantly offensive in the 1935 horror story, "Black Canaan."

Robert's treatment of Southern black culture is discussed mostly from the point of view of "Pigeons From Hell" and "Black Canaan." Howard fans have a hard time defending the latter against postmodern critical interpretation. But viewed within the context of Robert's canon, it's hard to condemn the story outright, even as it's easy to judge or misjudge it.

Set at the turn of the century in Louisiana, "Black Canaan" concerns itself with an uprising—the "swamp niggers" are being banded together by a conjure man named Saul Stark, a strong, tall, good-looking and charismatic leader who aims to take back the country for his own people. Needless to say, the Howard hero, Kirby Buckner, opposes this plan. He races through the swamps, encountering Saul Stark's voodoo magic at every turn, with plenty of people along the way to help emphasize the differences between whites and blacks. In the end, it must be noted, the barbarians do not triumph, and things return more or less to normal, until the next uprising.

When Robert disingenuously set his "rise of the barbarians" plot in the Reconstruction-era South, he came closer than he may have intended to some deep-seated resentment on both sides of the color line. It's tempting to focus on Robert's stereotypical portrayals of both black women and culture, but these characterizations were actually milder depictions at the time the story was written. Robert tells the story provocatively, almost begging the reader for a reaction, and loads the narrative and plot with ambiguous situations. One of the harbingers of evil in the story is a half-black, half-white woman of such "barbaric fascination," called the Bride of Damballah. Robert emphatically pronounces her to be alien, almost not of this world. He also ties Saul Stark back to the shores of Africa, making the black versus white conflict in the plot into an Africa versus America plot. It almost seems as though Robert is trying to pick a fight with the reader.

The hero Buckner, to his credit, never engages in torture or sadism, nor does he say anything in "Black Canaan" to make the reader think he is as ignorant as his neighbors. Buckner seems to be struggling with the situation, unable to acknowledge that things are unfair, and also unable to effect any kind of change.

"Black Canaan" was one of the last stories that Robert wrote about race. It's part of what makes it so hard to pin down his beliefs regarding racial topics, because he always seemed to keep his own counsel on such matters. In the poem, "The Day that I Die," written in the mid-to-late 1920s when Robert was churning out poetry by the ream, he says:

> The day that I die shall the sky be clear

> And the east sea-wind blow free,
> Sweeping along with its rover's song
> To bear my soul to sea.
> They will carry me out of the bamboo hut
> To the driftwood piled on the lea,
> And ye that name me in after years,
> This shall ye say of me:
> ...
> That I lived to a straight and simple creed
> The whole of my wordly span
> White or black or yellow I dealt
> Foursquare with my fellow man.

As a writer who used race to denote everything from physical characteristics to character motivation, Robert's work is tinged with the very words and ideas that make modern readers uncomfortable. This was not Robert's intention; it was a matter of fictional brevity, nothing more. In his descriptions and narratives, Robert is careful to employ the acceptable language of his day. Vernacular, colorful words, and the like are almost always reserved for dialogue and the occasional time that such things show up in first person. Sailor Steve Costigan constantly complains that the "Chinee can't take a punch," and there is nothing historical to indicate that a glass jaw was ever a stereotype of Asians. Most likely, such a declaration came from one of his frequent trips to San Antonio, where Robert would have had contact with a large-scale population of Chinese immigrants and Chinese-Americans, and where he likewise would have run across some local expression at the prizefights he attended.

In the twenty-first century, postmodern studies have made it possible for anyone to read any kind of subtext into any popular medium. However, it is incredibly naïve to throw a twenty-first-century value judgment onto people who were living a hundred years ago. For every instance of racism found in Robert's work, a compelling counterargument can be found elsewhere. As in most areas of Howard studies, there is no clear answer one way or the other. Each reader brings his or her own experiences to Robert's texts and either finds or refutes what they are looking for. This is a large part of what makes Robert's work both timeless and cyclical. Postmodern racism studies on the uncountable amount of pulp fiction serve no purpose, mainly because every single one of the academics and scholars who flippantly decries the field as full of "racist and/or misogynistic stereotypes" has never read more than a handful of pulps that either make or disprove his or her case.

Robert wrote "The Last White Man" and sent it off to *Weird Tales*. The story isn't very good, and not just because of the subject matter. Set in the far-flung future of 2000, the Negro population has reached six hundred million in number and has risen up to overthrow the fat, complacent white race. While the theme is instantly recognizable as Robert's enduring worldview, the narrative jumps around in several places and the characters spend more time discussing what happened in the time between 1920 and 2000 than actually doing anything productive. However, the white man who opposes the black horde is himself a kind of throwback, more like a six-foot Viking than the effeminate modern men (circa 2000, that is). This man shares more in common with his adversaries than size and strength. Even though he is defeated, the story leaves little doubt that someone will come along and dethrone the black race before they slide back down the ladder of civilization into the pit of barbarism.

Not surprisingly, "The Last White Man" was rejected. Robert filed the story away. It wasn't the first rejection he had gotten, nor would it be the last. But the emotional thrust of that story would return, again and again, in later works.

Robert sent another letter to Smith on August 24, 1923:

> I'm trying to get a job in the post-office. I doubt if I get it, though.... As for that girl-stuff; there are five girls in my neighborhood and I am the only boy, besides the brother of the prettiest one.
>
> One lives across the street, one just across the fence, and the others fairly near. They are all nice girls and very good looking.
>
> I have lived here for four years and so far I have gone my way, unhampered by any girlish attentions. And so far as I know I will continue so.
>
> ... No, I'm not a girl-hater. I have the highest respect for the feminine sex. I just prefer other amusements as a general rule. I'm no lady's man.

Robert was shy around girls, according to many of his classmates, but he was also one of the smartest boys in his class, even if his grades didn't show it. He had an incredible focus on his writing and a characteristic drive to see himself succeed at it. At a time when other fellows his age were wondering who to take to the school social, Robert was wondering how to break into "the writing game." Any time he wasn't writing or working, he was reading, absorbing authors, intuitively looking at techniques, trying to decipher the mechanics of fiction. He was as mentally far away from the rest of his graduating class as a person could be. Robert continues in the letter:

> Do you know a woman brought about the down-fall of Britain? Vortigern, king of the Britons, married Rowena who was, I think either the sister or cousin of Hengist, who led the Jutes. Hengist, by the way, wasn't a Jute but a Dane, so I've heard. Horsa, I think, was a Jute.
>
> So when Vortigern would have hurled his Roman-trained armies against the invaders, Rowena would plead with the king

and persuade him to grant more concessions to the Jutes. So at
last the Britons were driven into Wales and Scotland.

So much the histories know. They do not know that
Vortigern's cousin, Uther, would have driven Vortigern and
Rowena from the throne, seized it himself, and driven the
barbarians into the North Sea. But Uther was slain in battle with
the Jutes.

I know, for then I was a soldier in Vortigern's army. The
army was dissatisfied with the king and had Uther raised the
banner of revolt, far over half the army would have gone over
to him. So it was that a woman helped conquer Britain.

This is another extremely important passage, as it demonstrates that either through force of imagination or an unconscious creative exertion, Robert felt that he was connected to a larger part of history. This vividness would show up in later works and in later letters. Robert talked with many friends and acquaintances about "racial memories." As late as 1935, he was still keenly interested in them.

Robert finally found employment with one of the local tailors, as he related to Smith in September 1923:

I've been busy; start work early in the morning and work until
nearly night.

I walk from five to fifteen miles a day, no exaggeration,
soliciting clothes and delivering them and when I'm not doing
that I wash and clean clothes. Not an overly pleasant occupation,
but I like it all right. I work on commission and ought to make
about $40 per month, some months more.

I've been offered a job at a gin for fifty dollars a month, but
don't think I'll accept as the extra work I'd have to do would
be more than the ten dollars difference, and besides I'd have to
work until late at night and would get paid only at the end of the
month whereas now I get my money every Saturday night.

Later, when Robert looked back on this job at the tailor's job, he offered this opinion of the work to H.P. Lovecraft in December 1930:

When I was a kid I worked in the tailoring business just as one
terrific boom was dwindling out, and harlots used to give me
dresses to be cleaned—sometimes they'd be in a mess from
the wearer having been drunk and in the gutter. Beautiful silk
and lace, delicate of texture and workmanship, but disgustingly
soiled—such dresses always symbolized boom days and nights,
to me—shimmering, tantalizing, alluring things, bright as
dreams, but stained with nameless filth.

There was never a time when Robert didn't hate the oil boom, and this loathing of vice and graft in the garb of progress would, in time, become married to his worldview of the rise and fall of civilization.

The cotton came in by October 1923, and the Cross Plains cotton gin was running day and night. In a letter to Smith written at this time, Robert said:

> I'm writing a book which doubtless would make you tired and would sound like a lot of fool stuff to most folks, but as I am writing it for my own amusement, the opinion of other people about it don't interest me, as I know of.
>
> The book takes in lots of territory and a lot of characters. Some of the characters are, Ammon the Amalekite who was a famous swordsman, Swift-Foot the tree-man, Tostig the Mighty, a viking and something of a villain, Hakon, a Norseman and crafty as a fox, Bran Mak Morn who was the greatest chief the Picts ever had and many others too numerous to mention.

This story Robert was talking about became one of the many unfinished fragments that would survive his life and career, and it's interesting for two reasons. One, this is the first "racial memory" story that Robert had ever sat down and attempted. Each of the above characters were incarnations of the narrator from different time periods. The second point of interest was the name of the last character: Bran Mak Morn.

Robert claims that he came across a reference to the historical Picts during a visit to the New Orleans library when his father was attending a specialization course for his medical practice. Robert was instantly taken with the idea of a savage, warlike race that migrated, conquered, and was eventually beat down into savagery and then nothing by the onward march of civilization. The Picts became Robert's fictional underdogs, and he would reconfigure them over and over and insert them into nearly every one of his fantasy series. Eventually, the Picts would take on the qualities of the Native Americans. Interestingly, they never won their struggle against Progress. Robert could have given them a happy ending, as was his authorial right, and yet he never did. Robert's Picts were always doomed.

Not all of Robert's letters to Smith are packed with meaning. Much of the correspondence seems to have been an effort to stave off Robert's boredom. Presumably he was writing to Truett Vinson at this time, although no letters are known to exist. A letter written in April of 1924 strikes a more lighthearted tone:

> I'm still working at the tailor trade and I haven't made very much money lately as another shop has been put in and three tailor shops are too many for a town of this size. One could do a good business, especially as the shop moved from Pioneer. This is trade's-day. The town's full of horses and horse traders with the usual amount of drunkenness and crookedness. Or, perhaps, not quite so much, for the present town-marshal is something of a scrapper.

By June of 1924, Robert told Smith that he had lost the job at the tailor's, and had been heaving freight at the train depot, but there was "not much money in it." By then, Robert had either decided or been forced by his parents to take a stenographer's course at the Howard Payne Business School in Brownwood. His mother seemed delighted with the idea, but his father still did not approve of his son's decision. Robert, exhausted by all of the manual labor he'd been doing, was no doubt pleased with his living arrangements in Brownwood; instead of his mother keeping house for him, he would be sharing a room at the boarding house with Lindsey Tyson.

That summer, Robert completed and sent off his latest batch of stories. Included in the bundle was "Spear and Fang," a caveman story that pitted Cro-Magnon against Neanderthal with a beautiful cavewoman as the prize. "Spear and Fang" wasn't literature, nor high art, but it stood out in one important aspect: the story was practically all action, galloping along at a breakneck pace. Robert sent "Spear and Fang" to *Weird Tales* and then made his plans to go back to school.

While Robert toiled away in the Commercial School of Howard Payne, learning shorthand and, at long last, the proper way to type, he and Tyson loafed around, attended football games, practiced sparring, and in general acted like college kids. Robert started exercising in order to keep up with the physically stronger Tyson. Robert's parents gave him a small allowance, a pittance that didn't begin to cover his expenses. He was always broke. His friends stood him to sandwiches and sodas when they went out. Robert wrote small amounts of prose and poetry, mainly as practice to help him master typing.

The week of Thanksgiving 1924, Robert received the news that changed his life: Farnsworth Wright, the editor of *Weird Tales*, wrote to tell Robert that they were accepting "Spear and Fang" and would pay him on publication.

Robert was ecstatic. Lindsey Tyson watched as his friend knelt down by the bed and bowed his head quietly for a few minutes. When he stood up, Robert E. Howard was born.

Teen-aged Robert E. Howard, posing with boxing gloves by the side of his home (photo courtesy of Leo Grin).

SODA JERK

> Thanks very much for the kind things you said about "Wolfshead" and other early attempts. I was eighteen when I wrote "Spear and Fang," "The Lost Race," "The Hyena"; nineteen when I wrote "In the Forest of Villefere" and "Wolfshead." And after that it was two solid years before I sold another line of fiction. I don't like to think about those two years.
> **Robert E. Howard to H.P. Lovecraft, July 1933**

In late 1928, Robert sat down at his typewriter and typed out what may have been his last attempt at a "confessional" story, aimed at the market that wanted more "realistic" fiction, and not mummies or ghouls or knights with swords. The novel that Robert wrote was based on his life, from the ages of eighteen to twenty-one years old. The book was posthumously titled *Post Oaks and Sand Roughs*, in reference to the landscape around Cross Plains.

In any case, the book is fiction, although it is culled from Robert's life experiences, and he cheerfully rearranged events to make for a better narrative. In much the same way that a biographical movie heightens tensions and invents drama, *Post Oaks and Sand Roughs* heavily embellishes and even rewrites Robert's personal history for the sake of storytelling.

Despite these shortcomings, *Post Oaks and Sand Roughs* does illustrate, sometimes graphically, all of the ups and downs of Cross Plains during the time of the second oil boom. While it would be foolish to take the book at face value, for Robert was an instinctive storyteller, certain passages from *Post Oaks and Sand Roughs* contain some grains of truth in them and help to show what kinds of jobs Robert held down, and how he felt about them.

After the Thanksgiving break in 1924, Robert returned to the Howard Payne Business School to finish his courses, still walking on air at having made a sale. Lindsey Tyson had dropped out, and Robert's new roommate was more interested in staging crap games in the dormitory. Without Tyson to distract him, Robert buckled down and worked hard on his final examinations. When the semester was over, he dropped out of the school again. After all, he had what he needed to succeed at writing, now, and there was no need to go through the business school. It would have been a waste of time and money.

When Robert returned to Cross Plains after Christmas, he found another letter waiting for him from Farnsworth Wright. *Weird Tales* had bought another of his stories, "The Hyena," for twenty-five dollars. Furthermore,

Wright had requested some changes to another story, "The Lost Race," before he would accept it for publication. Again, the money was to be paid after the story saw print. Robert didn't care. He was on the way up, or so he thought.

Robert sat down at his typewriter and attacked it, pounding out stories and sending them off to *Weird Tales*, *Adventure*, and other pulp magazines. Each story was rejected, although Wright liked the changes Robert made to "The Lost Race" and accepted it for publication.

"The Lost Race" is one of the most important stories that Robert ever wrote, because it is the first public appearance of his ubiquitous Picts. Robert mentioned to H.P. Lovecraft that his concept of "the Picts" was first conceived during a visit to New Orleans when he was twelve, where he found in a library on Canal Street

> ...a book detailing the pageant of British history, from prehistoric times up to—I believe—the Norman conquest. It was written for school-boys and told in an interesting and romantic style, probably with many historical inaccuracies. But there I first learned of the small dark people which first settled Britain, and they were referred to as Picts. I had always felt a strange interest in the term and the people, and now I felt a driving absorption regarding them. The writer painted the aborigines in no more admirable light than had other historians whose works I had read. His Picts were made to be sly, furtive, unwarlike, and altogether inferior to the races which followed—which was doubtless true. And yet I felt a strong sympathy for this people, and then and there adopted them as a medium of connection with ancient times. I made them a strong, warlike race of barbarians, gave them an honorable history of past glories, and created for them a great king—one Bran Mak Morn.

Over time, Robert would shape and mold his Picts into a combination of Scottish highlanders and Native Americans, and they became his fantastic metaphor for the conqueror and the conquered, the eternal underdogs, the forgotten people. The real Picts may have faded from history, but Robert tried to single-handedly bring them back by inserting them in the strangest of places throughout his varied career.

Wright also included constructive criticism and advice in his rejection letters, which was useful to Robert, even if he didn't always heed it. Over many years, Robert gradually learned how to slant material for particular markets. Not every editor was as giving, but Robert did manage to cultivate a few professional relationships over time. Farnsworth Wright was a capricious editor, often rejecting Robert's (and many others') work, seemingly on a whim. Wright later claimed to have taken Howard under his wing. Whether he really did or didn't is immaterial; despite Wright's rejection letters and his reasons for same, Robert never failed to feel some measure of frustration when a story came back.

On January 7, 1925, after a lengthy prizefighting anecdote, Robert wrote to Clyde Smith that he had sold "The Lost Race" and a third story, "The Hyena," for a total of fifty-five dollars—on publication.

If *Post Oaks and Sand Roughs* is to be believed, Hester was extremely encouraging, and while there is no mention of Robert's father's opinion about this period of time, it's a safe bet that he was waiting to see what kind of money all of this activity would bring in. Robert was working on his craft for twelve to eighteen hours a day, stopping only long enough to eat, sleep, and make trips to the post office to mail large envelopes or pick them up when they were returned.

Meanwhile, over in Brownwood, Tevis Clyde Smith resigned as the editor for *The Tattler* and left school just months before his graduation. Robert chided him in his letters, citing a battle with the superintendent over the freedom of speech. Smith later went back for summer school to complete his courses and collect his diploma, but it's worth noting that Smith was just as hot-headed, quick to anger, and unforgiving in his enmity as Robert. It is little wonder that they got along as well as they did and were very influential to one another, as best friends often are.

As Cross Plains thawed and became warmed to the onset of spring, Robert completed and mailed "In the Forest of Villefere," a traditional werewolf story pulled from the pages of French folklore. On the side, to bolster his utter lack of money, he took a job supplying oil news to the *Cross Plains Review*. This involved talking to a number of people he didn't like, and writing on a subject about which he could not have cared less. But the job paid five dollars a column... and it was writing, though not the sort of thing that Robert wanted to do.

Robert found work with a local oil corporation, leasing out of an office over the Farmer's Bank, and he performed stenographer's duties for them. He wrote fiction and poetry, too, when things were slack at the office, which wasn't very often.

The reason for the increased activity in town was simple: The pipeline in Brown County was finally completed, two years after it had begun, and the oil business was back on again in Cross Plains. An old hand at the boomtown phenomenon by now, Robert invited Clyde Smith and Truett Vinson to come up and give it a look-see. Sometime between March and July of 1925, Robert received word that *Weird Tales* had bought "In the Forest of Villefere." Wright called the story "a real gem." Robert had now sold four stories, and not received so much as a nickel in payment.

In June of that year, Hester was gone from the house, either to visit relatives, or to receive another treatment for her tuberculosis, or possibly both. In any case, this gave Robert a chance to try something he'd become interested in while working among the oilmen: beer. Robert had made a promise to his mother, who knows how long ago, that he would never imbibe alcohol.

Easier said than done in a Texas boomtown. Robert had gotten to know some of the oilmen in the office where he worked, and one evening, after a prosperous day in the fields, a promoter of his acquaintance offered him a bottle of beer. Robert instantly took a liking to it, and really, who could blame him? He liked it so much that he actually obtained the recipe for home-brewing and whipped up the first of several batches for himself and his friends to enjoy, grimacing and gasping as they chugged it down. So much for Prohibition. Any regrets about breaking his promise to his mother were swept aside as he was now able to more readily socialize with his friends and with the oilmen in town. Robert even branched out into hard liquor and wine, but only rarely. He remained a beer drinker for the rest of his life.

In July 1925, at long last, *Weird Tales* hit the stands, featuring "Spear and Fang," and Robert was paid fifteen dollars for the story. He bought several copies and gave them to his friends in town. He was now a published, professional author.

Perhaps because of this, his friends Truett Vinson and Clyde Smith drove up from Brownwood to see him. This time, they brought a friend—Ecla Laxton, a young woman Clyde's age that he had known from their high school days. Vinson and Smith had it in mind to play a joke on Robert while the group tooled around in Smith's car. Ecla had been put up to the task of making a pass at Robert, who had stated in his letters and in person that he had not much use for women.

According to the account written in *Post Oaks and Sand Roughs*, Robert somehow or another gleaned his friends' intentions and turned the tables on them by making a pass at Ecla, instead. Robert and Ecla spent t he day in the backseat, snuggling and kissing. While initially amused, after the group broke up and all the parties were safely back at home, Vinson wrote a letter that accused Robert of taking too many liberties with the situation. Smith, he explained, was in love with Ecla, and had been for some time. Ecla had apparently been running around with an older, faster crowd before dating Smith, and he felt that with Robert being older, the same situation had occurred all over again.

Robert, initially hostile at the pair, quickly capitulated and tendered an apology to Smith. The whole affair was their only acknowledged blow-up in the surviving correspondence, and the trio made no more mention of the incident. However, Robert's apology letter to Smith, written in mid-July 1925, is worth glancing over:

> Truett said my letter was like the product of a soul close to the bottom of its rope. How close, and in what manner, neither of you dream. Clyde, do you remember that phantom that followed

our trail that night? That was no illusion. It was the hand of Destiny and how close it came to claiming me, you shall know. Yes, my soul hovered close to the chasm and there were times when I would have welcomed its plunge....

I sat and my life passed before me in a long chain. The whiskey had cleared from my head and I was perfectly clear-minded. Really, I had not taken a drink that day. I saw myself as I had always been, a failure. Battering against a high steel wall and only pulping my hand; clambering nearly to the top of accomplishment, until the rungs of desire gave way beneath my clutching fingers and hurtled me down again.

And I thought, shall it always be this way? Now I have like a blind fool, outraged friendship and trampled on the souls of the best two friends a man ever had. So I sat and thought and the lights went out over the town. The raucous rabble in the streets sank and vanished. Still I sat and even money-crazed, oil-crazed speculators staggered home to bed.

I sat and thought. My thoughts ran, shall I live and continue to be a failure, to grind my life out and at last pass on, a failure, among failures OR ?

I really never expected to leave that office when I entered it, alive.

I sat and the night passed and cold sweat stood upon my forehead as I fought my silent battle.

Something kept whispering over my shoulder, "Come, take a chance. You're a born failure. You lost the game before you saw it. The cards were stacked against you before you sat in the game. You're a damned fool and shall never be anything else. Now you've probably ruined a girl's life and that of your best friend. A great thing. You'll never win. It's no disgrace to take a flop when you're hung on the ropes and know you're licked. And you know it. You won't admit it but you know it; for the first time you're ready to admit it. What's the use of all this? You shall be mine eventually. You are only dust and dust is your eventual destiny. Why delay? Why drag out a few more years? Come, fool them all and step out of the game. Why stay with this torture of life any longer? Come, you are licked and may as well admit it."

I have no fear of the Hereafter. An orthodox hell could hardly be more torture than my life has been. I got so far along that I was chuckling with a ghastly humor as I thought what a hell of a jolt the man who opened that law office next morning would get.

One thing held me back. No high and noble resolve. No wish to make myself better for that I've tried again and again and failed. One thing. The vicious stubbornness that won't let me admit defeat. To have done what I considered would have been to admit that I was licked. I felt licked alright but stubbornly despised to admit it. And, actually against the whole desire of my soul, that stubbornness won and sent me reeling out of the office just as dawn was breaking. I worked all that day and the next.

... I haven't a real job but I don't give a damn. I've been that way before. I ate breakfast yesterday morning and with the exception of some milk and a saucer of cereal that's all I've eaten since then. The two days before that I ate dinner once. That may give you some idea of how I've been working.

In *Post Oaks and Sand Roughs*, Robert writes that his suicidal thoughts, darkly hinted at, were intended to make Vinson and Smith feel low for putting him through the ringer like that. His alter ego Steve Costigan mailed the letter, and then "laughed long and loudly with the first real enjoyment he had felt during the whole unspeakably sordid affair. Kill himself because of Clive [Clyde] and a fool girl? Hell!" Judging from the letter above, Robert had a flair for the dramatic, if not the melodramatic. And even though *Post Oaks and Sand Roughs* was written with the full benefit of hindsight, there is a viewpoint in the above letter that merits a second glance: "The vicious stubbornness that won't let me admit defeat." Robert may have entertained suicidal thoughts as early as nineteen or twenty years of age, but they took a backseat to his desire to make it as a writer on his own terms. That thought, more than anything, ushered him through the second oil boom in Cross Plains.

There may have been another reason, not delineated in *Post Oaks and Sand Roughs*, for the friends' falling-out. Shortly after the incident with Ecla, Robert learned that she had gotten pregnant by Clyde Smith. Robert, displaying a profound lack of understanding in such matters, drafted a fake document on legal letterhead from the office where he worked, accusing Clyde of rape and ordering that he appear before a court in Brownwood to answer the charges. Smith was in love with Ecla and didn't appreciate the joke in the least. Robert's letter, above, may have been a reply to Clyde's blistering rebuke for the thoughtless joke.

Within two weeks, the incident was over with and forgotten, and Robert and his friends picked up their correspondence. By this time, Robert had been let go at the oil company office and found a job at the local post office. He continued to do stenographer's work on the side, but his heart wasn't in it. Robert worked at the post office for about a month, without pay, expecting the remuneration to be double at the end of the month. When the rate for a single month was offered, Robert quit in disgust.

Much ado has been made over the use of the word "enemies" in Robert's vocabulary. Everyone from out-of-state acquaintances to out-of-state biographers has tried to figure out the expression and come to the erroneous conclusion that Robert made up all of his adversaries. In Texas, an "enemy" is anyone who has ever crossed you, for any reason, and that you don't like. It is the other side of the popular expression, "If you ain't my friend, then you're my...."

When considering the list of jobs that Robert held, and the number of people that he came in contact with during the oil boom, it's important to remember that Robert's parents were still actively controlling his life at a time when he should have been out of the house and on his own. Robert had just graduated from school, where he was told over and over what to read, what to think, and what to say in order to get good grades. Robert's choice of profession was in part based on the autonomy that it afforded; he wouldn't have to take orders nor rely on anyone if he was selling stories regularly. The jobs he took in Cross Plains were especially galling, as he felt that he was above and apart from the rest of the rabble, an attitude that his mother tried very hard to cultivate in him. So anyone who gave Robert a hard time, embarrassed him in public, or barked orders at him was considered his "enemy." Modern-day families who grew up in oil towns still use this expression. An appropriate contemporary translation would be "son-of-a-bitch." Robert was just a little more strident about the term; with the exception of his inner circle of friends, Robert never forgave and he never forgot an insult to his person. While it may sound a little dated in the twenty-first century, it was par for the course in 1920s boomtown Texas.

After Robert quit the post office, he got a job working at the Cross Plains Natural Gas Company. Unfortunately, the plant manager expected subservience from his staff. This job didn't last long, either. The reason given in *Post Oaks and Sand Roughs* was a lack of business, but Steve, Robert's alter ego, is convinced it was because of his insubordination; in the book, he loudly calls his boss a son-of-a-bitch. In a letter written to Talman in September 1931, Howard states, "[I] lost the job because I wouldn't kow-tow to my employer and 'yes' him from morning til night. That's one reason I was never very successful in working for people. So many men think an employee is a kind of servant. I'm good natured and easy going, I detest and shrink from rows of all sort, but there's no use in a man swallowing everything."

Robert picked up another job, hauling a surveyor's rod around for an oil field geologist. This was done in the summer months, when the Texas sun beat down on Robert and his boss, an affable Easterner with the patience of a saint. He explained many times the mechanics of surveying to Robert, whose job it was to walk out to a distant hillside and hold the rod upright while the man made his calculations. Robert, though, never listened. The job paid three dollars a day, and Robert picked up oil news on the side, when he could, to supplement his income.

The job ended when the geologist finished his survey, which suited

Robert just fine. He had collapsed one day in the Texas heat, thinking he was having a heart attack. He was ready for an office job, and soon found himself working for another oil company in town, resuming his stenographer's duties.

While at the office, Robert continued writing when he had the time. Many of the stories written during this period were unsold and lost, but he tried his hand at westerns and boxing stories, and even a factual article sent to *Adventure*. Nothing stuck with the editors, and they all came back to him. Robert also wrote a sequel to "In the Forest of Villefere," which had been published in the August 1925 issue of *Weird Tales*. The eight-dollar check he received for the story helped him buy a brand new Underwood typewriter to replace the secondhand model he'd worn out.

The sequel, "Wolfshead," was the longest and most complicated story that Robert had written to date. A change of locales, a slew of characters, and more of what was becoming Robert's mark of distinction—fast, gripping action—made this story stand out. Robert commented on the tale to Smith, in this letter from October 9, 1925: "After reading it, I'm not altogether sure I went off my noodler when I wrote it. I sure mixed slavers, duelists, harlots, drunkards, maniacs and cannibals reckless. The narrator is a libertine and a Middle ages fop; the leading lady is a harlot, the hero is a lunatic, one of the main characters is a slave trader, one a pervert, one a drunkard, no they're all drunkards, but one is a gambler, one a duelist and one a cannibal slave."

The story was accepted by Wright in the fall of 1925, with no payment forthcoming. By this time, Clyde Smith had enrolled in Daniel Baker College and become the editor of the *Daniel Baker Collegian*, the school newspaper, presumably without the theatrics previously exhibited at Brownwood High School. Smith developed an acute interest in poetry, and Robert responded in kind. The two friends wrote many letters discussing poets and sent poems back and forth for many years. Smith published two of Robert's poems, "Illusion" and "Fables for Little Folk," in the *Daniel Baker Collegian*.

By the beginning of 1926, Wright had written Robert and informed him that "Wolfshead" was intended as the cover feature for the April issue. This was a high honor, indeed, and Robert felt a swell of pride. That feeling soon went away as Wright wrote a letter to Robert and requested the carbon copy of the story, as it had mysteriously disappeared from the editorial office.

Of course, Robert had not used a carbon. Thinking quickly, he telegraphed a reply that he would retype the story. This he did from memory, working through the night, and sent it the next day. Another letter soon followed; Wright had found the story, all save the first page, which he was using from Robert's retyped draft. Wright added ten dollars to the original price of forty dollars, as a thank-you for the trouble. Disaster averted by Robert's incredible memory.

Robert took a trip to Brownwood in late April or early May, and he spent the night with Clyde Smith. That night, Robert had one of his sleepwalking incidents. His terrified scream woke the whole house. Smith, groggy, opened his eyes to find Robert grappling with a large shape and, thinking an intruder was in the house, jumped in to help. Before Smith could do anything, Robert went headlong out the closed window, through the screen. The Smith family found Robert outside, wandering around, apparently dazed. Smith, having been told previously what to do by Robert in the event that a sleepwalking incident happened, talked to Robert until he fell back asleep. Once Robert closed his eyes again, Smith woke his friend up. Robert started. "I'm glad you woke me," he said. "I dreamed I saw a newspaper and the headlines said, 'Axe Murderer Slays Three.'" When Smith told him what had happened, Robert said, "I'm glad you couldn't get to me. I have the strength of a goddamn ape when I'm in the middle of one of these nightmares." Robert suffered cuts on his face and a deep gash on his arm. Smith's mother recalled that Robert had let out the most chilling scream she had ever heard.

Robert's night terrors were a long-standing thing. He mentioned them in *Post Oaks and Sand Roughs*, and his friends knew him to be a sleepwalker, as everyone slept over on road trips and out of town visits. Both sleepwalking and night terrors, particularly in adolescents and adults, are linked to high levels of stress. Children who move to new cities, houses, and the like with great frequency are prone to night terrors. This clearly would have been a source of stress and confusion for Robert as a child, but as a young man, it was an indicator that he was dealing with more than he let on: the desire to succeed in his chosen profession, parental tension, a combination of both, or maybe even neither. Since he never thought to examine his stress to the point that he wrote anything down, we will never know what was pulling at Robert.

When "Wolfshead" showed up in the April 1926 issue of *Weird Tales*, Robert reread the story and, disheartened by the now-perceptible flaws, quit his stenographer's job and took a position at the oldest drugstore in town, the City Drug Store.

Robert's time spent at the drugstore would become his most enduring metaphor for the graft, vice, and bullying that went on every day in a boomtown. He wrote extensively about his drugstore job in *Post Oaks and Sand Roughs*:

> He did not read or write, scarcely had time to answer his correspondence. He had absolutely no time for recreation or even rest. All during the day he would dash back and forth behind the fountain which he had grown to hate, serving drinks

and waiting on customers, doing many things he was not paid to do. At night he staggered home to fall into his bed and sleep the sodden sleep of utter exhaustion. He went to bed fatigued, and he woke up fatigued... worse still was the mental effect of taking orders and occasional insults from the scum of the earth.

Robert's weight dropped, and he caught the flu from the long hours in damp conditions. Eventually, he was promoted to head soda jerk, making eighty dollars a week—great money, but spending it on nothing, as he was too tired from working seven days a week from sunup to sundown.

With a veritable stack of unpublished stories, his nerves worn to a frazzled edge, and feeling physically dead on his feet, Robert sought solace at the Neeb Ice House. At the turn of the century, one of the most important new technologies was the development of refrigeration. Meat and poultry could travel farther down the railroad line if they were kept cold. Economically, farmers and ranchers could sell more because it could be kept fresh longer. Because of its commercial value, most of local industries relied on the icehouse to help in some way with their business. It's no accident that a great many of the icehouses in Texas line up alongside the old railroad tracks for easy loading and offloading of goods and supplies.

Ice was also important to the citizens of any given town. It was a mark of refinement to be able to serve cold drinks in the summer, and the icehouse wagon made the rounds through town, cutting off five- and ten-pound blocks at a time for home use.

One of the things that the icehouses did, on the side, was sell cold drinks. Not surprisingly, you could also buy beer if you didn't like RC Cola. When Prohibition was passed, the barrels of beer just moved further into the back of the icehouse, and tradesmen and laborers would gather at the end of the day to have a drink or just cool off from a hard day's work.

Ironically, such a mark of civilization played host to one of the most traditionally barbaric spectacles in Cross Plains. Robert liked to hang out at the icehouse after work, where he strapped on the gloves and boxed with the roughnecks, with whom he had become acquainted while working at the drugstore. Robert's first icehouse fight is one of the storied events in his life; he wrote about it in his letters to Lovecraft, and he immortalized it in *Post Oaks and Sand Roughs*. The fictional roughneck named Bill Murken has never been accurately identified, but there's a good chance that Robert's opponent was the affable Dave Lee:

> They fought it out, as usual, in a small building which was once used to store ice, but was now empty. There were no windows, only one door, and that did not directly connect with the outer air. It was midsummer, and the heat was terrific. Before they got the gloves fastened, they were both wringing wet with sweat.
>
> A crap game was going on in the main building, and the

losers, as they went broke, drifted over to the building where the two were boxing, until the entire ice crew was present, yelling advice and whooping jubilantly. Somehow Steve felt at home here. These roughnecks were different from those who frequented the drugstore, and whom he knew only as customers. These knew him, and there was no antagonism between them. Moreover, they respected him because Bill [Dave] had whipped every one of them, and Steve [Robert] was able to more than stand up to Bill.

That Robert was finally large enough to box, and hold his own, and win, against the workers, dockhands, and tool dressers in town was a significant event in his life. Finally, he had found an outlet for his pent-up frustration. Coupling this with his writing, Robert was able to effectively slough off some old feelings of rage, helplessness, and anger.

Robert E. Howard (left), in full fighting trim, squares off against Dave Lee (photo courtesy of Jim Keegan).

THE DEAL

> I have progressed beyond the average man to the extent that people's belief is not absolutely necessary to my life and living but not to the point where I am absolutely indifferent to flagrant skepticism. I realize that there is really only one person in the world who really believes that I'll ever amount to a damn at the writing game and that person is myself.
>
> **Robert E. Howard to Tevis Clyde Smith, October 1928**

As the August sun baked Cross Plains with no relief in sight, Robert reached the end of his rope. The drugstore job was killing him, even as he engaged in cathartic boxing matches, and his writing was at a standstill. This would not do. Whether it was Robert's idea or his parents', Robert made a pact with his father: Isaac would pay for Robert to complete the bookkeeping course at Howard Payne Business College. After that, Robert would be given one year, free and clear, with which to make a living as a writer. If at that point he hadn't made good and begun earning money, Robert would seek employment as a bookkeeper in town.

Exhausted by a year and a half of menial jobs, no money, and professional rejections, Robert quickly agreed. He spent a few weeks at home in August, finally free of the drugstore, and prepared to move back to Brownwood, to the mutual delight of Smith and Vinson.

During that time, Robert started another story, entitled "The Shadow Kingdom." Without realizing it, Robert was working on his literary legacy. At the time, though, it was little more than an epic story that was giving him trouble. He set it aside, presumably to finish it later.

September 1926 found Robert back at Howard Payne, taking bookkeeping from the same nice old man who had taught him shorthand and stenography two years prior. It was evident from the start that Robert had little interest in taking the course, as he quickly ignored his studies in favor of spending time with his friends and writing.

Robert and Lindsey Tyson were reunited again in Brownwood at the Powell boarding house, and they killed many an afternoon watching movies, going to see prizefights, and boxing and exercising. Robert saw Vinson and Smith, as well, and the four of them spent countless hours at football games or walking the town at all hours of the night as they discussed life and other weighty topics.

Robert resumed writing short, humorous sketches and stories for the school newspaper; this time, it was *The Yellow Jacket*, the Howard Payne house organ. These contributions were enthusiastically received and appeared throughout 1926 and 1927. While they are similar in size and tone to Robert's earlier humor work, the importance of these early efforts cannot be underestimated. Robert was practicing with the use of modern, colloquial dialogue in all of the sketches. More importantly, he returned to the tall tale form for the three most well-written of the stories: "The Thessalians," "Ye College Days," and "Cupid v. Pollux."

In "The Thessalians," Robert lampoons the local theater company and relates an anecdote involving the troupe, a hornet, and a catapulted cat. While light on the understatement, the story is rife with exaggeration. "Ye College Days" is the reminiscences of an older ex-student, comparing modern college life with that of college life "back in the good old days." Through a healthy dose of hyperbole, college rivalries take on aspects of the gunplay of the old frontier fort days. Robert's use of sudden turns here is well done. "Cupid v. Pollux" is a first person account of an incident involving "Steve" (Robert) and "Spike" (Tyson) and their training for an upcoming boxing match while Spike is in the throes of true love.

This is the earliest surviving boxing story that we have from Howard, although his records indicate he'd been writing them since 1924. The story is noteworthy for the use of first person narration from Robert's (Steve's) point of view, the lampooning of himself and Lindsey Tyson, the colorful and inventive tall tale style of recounting the training and subsequent boxing match, and the punchline ending to the tale. "Cupid v. Pollux" was a trifle when Robert wrote it, but he would later return to this type of story at a time when he would need it the most.

While in school, Robert wrote a large amount of poetry, much of which remains unpublished despite several collections that have appeared in the years following. In the passage of time, several collections of Robert's poetry have emerged, but no one has yet attempted to sort and catalogue the vast amounts of unpublished poems that still exist. The surviving body of poetry numbers in the hundreds.

In the poetry of Robert E. Howard, we see his writing style stripped down to its bare bones—a stark, economical word choice, coupled with concise plotting, and powered by short, sharp verbs. It's the sheer variety of content that makes Robert's poetry so hard to classify. He wrote macabre word pictures, venom-tinged emotional diatribes, and structured narratives featuring his fictional characters, as well as humorous ballads, parodies, and folk songs. While many fans and scholars have diligently tried to separate them into categories, Robert himself tended to lump them all together indiscriminately.

A critical appreciation of Robert's poetry notwithstanding, it is evident that the majority of his poetical work was focused, narrative-driven, and clearly expressive of the viewpoint of the author. There is little guesswork as to what Howard meant when reading his verse. During the time period that Robert was living in Brownwood and going to school, and later as he tried his hand at menial jobs, his poems reflected his mood and temperament. It was a release valve for him, a way to quickly sketch a scene or an emotion with just a few words and underscore a particular point.

Robert was an intuitive poet, having been immersed in the recitation of poetry from birth. It may have been a boast when he replied that he had never spent more than thirty minutes on a poem in his life (he also called his work "doggerel"), but it's hard to argue that he was an ineffective poet. This intuitive approach to language, word choice, and cadence found its way into Robert's fiction as he continued to develop and shape his narrative style.

Robert sent out his poetry to several magazines, but only *Weird Tales* bought any during this period, and with the usual payment arrangements. Robert wrote far more poetry than he submitted, and the full extent of his efforts has yet to be published in any form. Despite his insistence at calling his efforts "doggerel," Robert's poetry is one of the most fascinating aspects of his varied career.

A measles epidemic swept through Brown County in October 1926, an epidemic so severe that the daughter of the Powells, Robert's landlords, caught ill and died. Robert's parents rushed down to pull their son out of school, but he didn't want their help and didn't want to be rescued. He went into the Powells' bathroom and buried his face in the girl's bath towel and drank from her glass.

If his tactic was designed to quarantine himself from his parents, it backfired spectacularly. Robert caught the measles, all right, and Isaac brought him home, where he convalesced for two months. Considering that Robert didn't want to leave Brownwood, he was probably infuriated at the fact that he had ended up under his parents' watchful eye yet again.

The Howard Payne Business School was unsympathetic when Robert petitioned to have his tuition refunded and refused to give any money back. Isaac paid for the bookkeeping course all over again, and in early 1927 Robert went back to Brownwood, again rooming with Lindsey Tyson, and resumed his writing, carousing with friends, and occasional studying.

The January 1927 issue of *Weird Tales* brought another pleasant surprise in the publication of "The Lost Race," and Robert was probably grateful for the thirty-dollar check he received for the story. Encouraged by this, he kept up the stream of submissions, even as *The Yellow Jacket* continued to run his stories and skits, gratis.

Another poem by Robert, "The Song of the Bats," showed up in the May 1927 issue of *Weird Tales*. Despite his inattention to his studies, Robert also managed to pass his exams that May. He told Tyson, "If they think I'm going to tie myself down to some grubby bookkeeping job, they're crazy!" The graduation ceremony wasn't scheduled until August, so Robert and Truett Vinson took off on a much-needed vacation to celebrate their impending graduation. Hopping on the train, they headed down to Galveston to gorge on seafood, tour the Bay by motorboat, and take in the salt air, and also to enjoy the bevy of beauties currently engaged in displaying their ample charms for the judges of the Miss Universe pageant, more formally known as the International Pageant of Pulchritude and Annual Bathing Girl Review. Despite the insanely crowded conditions (for who could possibly resist the displayed calves of women in 1927?), Robert and Vinson had a fine old time, but didn't stick around for the crowning ceremony, hopping the train back to Brownwood instead.

Robert went home to Cross Plains and, while waiting for August and his graduation ceremonies, completed "The Shadow Kingdom." Something about it didn't sit well, however, and he hesitated to send it out to anyone just yet. Robert busied himself writing more poetry, and even completing and mailing two more stories to *Weird Tales*, but "The Shadow Kingdom" refused to let go of his subconscious, and he picked it up in August and rewrote the story, perhaps anticipating the reaction it would bring from an editor.

August found Robert, his immediate family, and several family friends back in Brownwood for the long-awaited graduation. Tellingly, Robert was already contemplating his future when he saw the heavy drapes on the stage wafting gently in the breeze and was so inspired that he dashed out as soon as the ceremonies were over and wrote a poem based on the imagery of the moving drapery.

Before Robert settled down fully to the task of making his fictional mark on the world, he embarked on another, longer trip with Truett Vinson. The pair headed first to San Antonio by bus to watch some prizefights and eat Mexican food, and then took the train to Austin to visit the state capitol and buy books. While in Austin, Vinson arranged to meet an old friend of his, Harold Preece. Vinson and Preece had been in the Lone Scouts (a rural alternative to the Boy Scouts) together, and Vinson arranged the meeting because Preece also had hopes of literary immortality. Preece brought with him another ex-Lone Scout, Booth Mooney, and the four hit it off right away.

While jawing over similarities and waxing intellectual, Preece suggested the young men form a literary circle to encourage and amuse one another. The circle would create a publication that would circulate through each member, adding comments in turn. Booth Mooney was chosen as the editor. Early contributors included Tevis Clyde Smith (of course) and Maxine Ervin, Robert's cousin on his mother's side, whom Preece was acquainted with in Dallas. They named themselves and their literary endeavor *The Junto*, meaning "a cabal," after Ben Franklin's similarly titled paper. The Junto would start to make its rounds in mid-1928.

During this period, Robert and Preece became fast, enthusiastic correspondents, and eventually spent much of their letters discussing all things Celtic. Robert was very enchanted with his heredity, as conferred upon him by his mother. In her later years, Hester took to speaking with a "faith and begorrah"-style Irish brogue, either to encourage her son's belief in his ancestry or to bolster her assertion that she was descended from royalty. Whether or not this attitude is related to Robert's inability to get along with the "common people" of Cross Plains is a matter of pure speculation.

Robert's letters to Preece are interesting; they are not as relaxed as his letters to Clyde Smith, nor as formal as his later letters to H.P. Lovecraft, but they are chock-full of anecdotes about boxing, history, and his ruminations on life in a more bleak and savage tone than found in his letters to Smith. This may have been an intentional slant to play up his "dark Irish heritage" to a fellow Celtophile, or it may have been an aspect of Robert's personality that he couldn't share very often with Smith or Vinson.

Robert, Harold Preece, and others came into their "Irish-ness" at a time when the dialogue of race was changing fundamentally in America. Prior to World War I, the world divided itself using British Imperial designations, stating namely that there was a distinct difference racially between the Anglo-Saxon and everyone else, from the Irish, the Scottish, the German, the Indian, and so on. After World War I, a simplified distinction of skin color—White, Brown, Yellow, and Black, the four "colors" so prominent in America—was gradually adopted. This way of thinking was embraced globally as America came into economic power and forced out the older (and just as wrong-headed) way of thinking that actual physiological differences existed between the Irish and the Anglo-Saxons. Prior to the mid-1920s, the Irish population in America had been grouped economically and sociologically with African-Americans. After the Great War, Irish leaders began to claim "white race" status even as they trumpeted their own cultural traits, holdovers from the previous nomenclature. When the Irish broke free of their maligned minority status, pro-Irish Nationalism sentiment in America was all the rage.

However, it's worth noting that this older mode of thinking was still around in the history and sociology books of the time—books that Robert would have had access to. This notion of every single cultural group having distinct characteristics that they alone possessed was all part and parcel of Robert's later creation, the Hyborian Age. The idea figures tangentially into his historical stories, too. Robert chose the race of each of his protagonists with deliberate care, emphasizing their cultural traits in doing so.

Robert finally returned to Cross Plains in late August of 1927, as his correspondence with Clyde Smith resumed. Once more, he found "The Shadow Kingdom" staring up at him from the pile of manuscripts by his typewriter. Robert picked the story up, read through it, and rewrote it again.

Finally, at long last, he sent it to *Weird Tales* in September 1927.

What was it about "The Shadow Kingdom" that was so hard for Robert to get down on paper, though? We really don't know, as Robert was always quick to remark that his King Kull stories sprang to life with very little effort on his part. Considering how often he rewrote the story, that's an outright lie. It may have been that Robert was consciously wrestling with the content of what would ultimately become the first sword-and-sorcery story ever written.

In writing "The Shadow Kingdom," Robert went out on a limb, fully into the realm of his imagination, to craft a story set in ancient Valusia, a land that existed long ago, long before the recognized epochs of history. To further cement how old the tale was, Robert made Kull an Atlantean in exile and, further, a barbarian at that. Before Atlantis was a super-developed civilization, before the sea swallowed her, Kull stalked the land. Atlantis was a hot topic in the 1920s, fueled by the boom of archeology as well as an excitement from various world explorers slowly but surely filling in all of the blank spots on the globe.

Also making an appearance are Robert's fully-developed Picts, cast as a rival barbarian nation, the enemies of Atlantis, but allies with Valusia. The time period is set thousands of years before the time of Bran Mak Morn, but clearly, Robert had charted his fictitious Picts' development from barbarism to extinction. Years later, in the stories of Conan, Atlantis would be referred to as doomed and ancient. By the time Robert returned to modern tales of horror, the Picts had become little more than monsters.

"The Shadow Kingdom" opens with Kull, newly crowned warrior-king of Valusia, watching a parade in his honor. Having successfully won the crown, Kull has uneasily assumed the duties of kingship. He later meets an emissary of the Pict Nation, bearing a request by Ka-nu, the ambassador of the Picts, to dine with him outside the walls of the castle.

Kull warily accepts, and Ka-nu later warns Kull that he has the potential to be the greatest king of Valusia, but that he is caught in a web of conspiracy and intrigue. Ka-nu pairs Kull with Brule, the Spear-Slayer, a Pictish warrior who shows Kull the dangers that lie all around him: his court is infested with shape-changing prehuman serpent men, whose goal is to infiltrate and overthrow human society.

In a bloody night's work, Kull and Brule slay two serpent men, both clearly bent on assassinating the king. Kull discovers that his palace is honeycombed with secret passages, and he finds a room wherein the ghost of a long-dead king resides, silent and alone; the serpent men imprison the souls of the men they kill. Kull and Brule make a pact, putting aside old tribal feuds, to aid each other against the serpent men.

Shaken by these revelations, Kull attempts to govern his people, but now finds himself doubting their reality. While holding court, he is surprised to find his council rise as one and move toward him. Brule appears, shouting the phrase, "ka nama kaa lajerama," which reveals the councilmen for who they are—all serpent men.

Kull and Brule battle side by side, slaying them all while taking a score of wounds. After the last serpent man falls, Kull realizes that the room he is standing in isn't his council chamber but the cursed room of last night's grim business. Brule quickly leads Kull to his real council chamber, and Kull's blood freezes to hear his own voice coming from within. The real Kull leaps for the doppelganger and slays him, and as the King's guards close in, Brule and Ka-nu appear before the council, declaring the plot foiled. They lead the bewildered councilmen back to the cursed chamber, where they are stunned by the sight of the corpses of the serpent men. Kull takes his sword and drives it into the wood, sealing the door shut. He proclaims himself an enemy of the serpent men and then collapses due to his fatigue and loss of blood. Brule, Kull's former enemy of old, delivers the final pronouncement in the story:

> Valka, Ka-nu, but here is such a man as I knew not existed in these degenerate days. He will be in the saddle in a few scant days and then may the serpent-men of the world beware of Kull of Valusia. Valka! but that will be a rare hunt! Ah, I see long years of prosperity for the world with such a king upon the throne of Valusia.

The few paragraphs above don't begin to cover the language of Robert's stirring prose, from Kull's sense of cosmic wonderment at the ancient mysteries he beholds, to the deftly sketched battle sequences and swordplay. Robert had found his stride with "The Shadow Kingdom." Writing a story in this fashion gave him a chance to work allegorically with some of the concepts he and his friends had always debated.

There are other points of interest in this first King Kull story to consider, as well. Robert makes the point early in the story that Kull is an outcast of Atlantis, driven from his homeland by the urge to succeed. When the mercenaries of no land pass by Kull in the parade, they stare at the king boldly, giving no salute. Robert writes, "And Kull gave back a like stare. He granted much to brave men, and there were no braver in all the world, not even among the wild tribesmen who now disowned him." Soon thereafter, Kull reins his stallion and makes for the castle, his commanders following him, and the crowd whispers their admiration, mixed in with their loathing for the barbarian king. Robert writes, "Little did Kull heed. Heavy-handed he had seized the decaying throne of ancient Valusia and with a heavier hand did he hold it, a man against a nation."

Cross Plains in 1927 was changing, reverting slowly back to its former state. The oil had mostly gone away. The drifters had drifted. The oil boom had left money, new buildings, better roads, and a sense of progress in its wake. Cross Plains had a new school, many civic improvements, and likely a sense of relief that the criminals and heathens had finally left.

Robert, then, entered a period of seclusion at a time when most people would wonder where he'd gotten off to, and why he wasn't working in town somewhere. Robert knew he was different in that he didn't have a steady job like his school friends. He also knew that he was patently incapable of taking orders from anyone, save maybe his family. His few attempts at working in town no doubt were passed around as front porch gossip, quite possibly embellished for effect. *If Bob wasn't out working, then what was he doing? Sitting at home, typing. Huh. Well, that's the craziest thing I ever heard.* And to the man running the local mill, or the woman working in the diner, each of whom was barely literate and could never conceive of needing or using a typewriter for anything, this surely seemed odd. Robert either sensed that his place in the community had already been established, or was predicting what that place would become.

Later still, when the conspiracy of the serpent men is revealed to Kull, he realizes that there is no one in his kingdom or court that he can trust, save the fellow barbarian and enemy of the Valusians, Brule, the Spear-Slayer. Many of Robert's underdog characters frequently aligned themselves with fellow underdogs. And speaking of barbarians, Robert slips this passage into one of Kull's silent soliloquies early in the story: "Kull reflected long upon the strange state of affairs that made him ally of ancient foes and foe of ancient friends.... Chains of friendship, tribe and tradition he had broken to satisfy his ambition, and by Valka, god of the sea and the land, he had realized that ambition! He was king of Valusia—a fading, degenerate Valusia, a Valusia living mostly in dreams of bygone glory, but still a mighty land and the greatest of the seven empires."

Here was the decaying civilization and the rise of the barbarians, or rather, the barbarian. Future Kull stories would feature the king battling constant intrigue, unending plots to overthrow him, and the tangled skeins of law that he breaks—literally, with an axe—in his desire to become the sole authority. Kull spends a lot of time lost in thought, trying to puzzle out his identity in relation to his surroundings. These thoughts closely mirror Robert's own thoughts about similar subjects. In a letter written to Clyde Smith on August 26, 1925, Robert says:

> I've been thinking. What is reality and what is illusion? One cannot say that our thoughts are abstract and our actions concrete, for then we are reduced to the level of thoughtless machines. Do our thoughts, as soon as born, assume some unseeable, intangible, yet concrete substance? Or, are your thoughts really born? Or is it that they merely enter your mind from the outside? Is man no more than a vessel for formless, yet tangible, thoughts? Is it that we do not really think and control ourselves by our thoughts, but that some outside influence

controls us? The Hindus, as you know, believe that all things are without beginning. That thoughts are but symbols, concrete evidence of past lives, wandering through space, anon taking up their abode for a time in the human mind. But are thoughts either the creation of the mind, or substances without beginning, lasting forever, or, are they influences of some higher, intangible outside power? What if we were but puppets, dancing on the strings of Destiny?

Ask yourself the question and answer it honestly, how much of your life stands clear and distinct, unclouded by the haze of illusion and uncertainty? Can you truly say of yourself, "This is thus, and this is thus; this much is truth and this is false; here lies concrete fact and here the fabric of illusion; this is hazy and this is clear."?

Then, is anything impossible? Strongly I doubt it. Perhaps training the mind to think is merely training it to become more open to suggestion; in strengthening ourselves, we enslave ourselves.

The subconscious mind controls us more than we think. It is vague, illusive, hazy, yet powerful....

It is controlled by, and yet controls, the conscious mind. It is the part of the mind which can never be destroyed, which retains vanished thoughts and impressions.

... Primitive instincts are stronger in us. A child's strongest, most lasting impressions are received in his earliest years. So with the race. The impressions received in the early, primitive days remain with us longer.

... In my former lives I must have been a man of peace and study. The great fighters now have been fighters in other lives.

Some later age, in some other body, I, too, will be a fighter. For that I am now building the foundation. What some have by subconscious instinct, I am gaining by hard work and study. I duck, guard, jab, parry and spar mechanically and one might say instinctively, but it is not that. It is the act of trained muscle, rather than trained mind, and mind and muscle do not work in unison. But the instincts imparted to the mind in this life will go down the ages. And a thousand years from now, I, clothed in another form, may hear the cheering crowd acclaim my name— the name of a new champion.

Robert followed those thoughts with more of the same, just two days later:

I've been thinking. Did you ever stop and consider that we may be surrounded by things far outside the pale of our thoughts?

We know there are sounds which we cannot hear; they are pitched either too high or too low for our ear, attuned to ordinary noises. There are creatures too small for us to see with the mere eye. Why might there not be things neither too small nor too large, too low, nor too high, too light or too loud, for us to distinguish, but attuned to an invisible, soundless pitch, as far as our senses are concerned? Our senses are deceptive. We can never look at anything and be sure that we see it as it is exactly, or listen to music or any sound and be sure that we catch the exact timbre. In fact, we seldom ever do.

Are there thoughts so high, so magnificent that they escape the mind? If a man could attune all his senses to the whole Universe, he would rule it.

… My soul, if soul I have, is tugged two ways by the idealist and by the materialist in me. The more I learn, the less I know; the more capable I become of forming opinions, the more loath I am to form one. There is so much of the true and the false in all things. Sometimes I believe that the whole is a monstrous joke and human accomplishment and human knowledge, gathered slowly and with incredible labor through the ages, are but shifting, drifting wraiths on the sands of Time, the sands that shall some day devour me. Will it be the changing of bodies, the discarding of this form for perhaps a lighter, more beautiful one, or will it be merely the merging of dust to dust? Who knows?

Kull's thoughts are not so different in "The Shadow Kingdom":

And what, mused Kull, were the realities of life? Ambition, power, pride? The friendship of man, the love of woman—which Kull had never known—battle, plunder, what? Was it the real Kull who sat upon the throne or was it the real Kull who had scaled the hills of Altantis, harried the far isles of the sunset, and laughed upon the green roaring tides of the Atlantean sea? How could a man be so many different men in a lifetime?

Kull, within himself, fights a constant battle between his "civilized" self, in the role of king, and what is his ultimate solution, the swift application of violence and direct action, or his "barbaric" or natural self. Brule and Kull occupy opposite sides of the coin, but it is currency easily flipped, and Brule always brings Kull around to his way of thinking.

The Kull stories are the most introspective of Robert E. Howard's canon. They were written at a time when the author was endeavoring to examine himself and the thought processes of others. Robert told Clyde Smith just one month after he sent "The Shadow Kingdom" to *Weird Tales*, "The subject of psychology is the one I am mainly interested in these days." Needless to say, aside from his circle of friends and maybe his father, Robert was alone in this pursuit in such a practical town as Cross Plains.

Some of these mystical aspects may have come directly from his father's library. Isaac, in his never-ending quest to stay abreast of medical developments, reached far and wide into yoga and mysticism for information and enlightenment. Isaac and his friend, Solomon Chambers, discussed reincarnation often. Along these particular fringes, the topic of Atlantis was then very much in vogue. Robert's theories on what had happened to Atlantis fall right in line with the thinking of the time, but in his Kull stories, he fully remade the living Atlantis into his own image.

Farnsworth Wright offered Robert one hundred dollars for "The Shadow Kingdom," more money than he'd ever been offered before, and equal to two and a half times what he would be making if he were working at the post office. Robert started working on more stories of King Kull. He may have written as many as six stories, but Wright accepted only one, "The Mirrors of Tuzun Thune." Kull, weary of the burdens of kingship, seeks amusement and diversion when he hears of a wizard named Tuzun Thune who may have the answers he is looking for.

What Tuzun Thune has is a variety of mirrors, as the title indicates. In each looking glass, Kull sees different things: his past, running free in the hills; his future, dead and forgotten in the press of time. One mirror in particular fascinates him in that it seems to show him only himself.

For days, Kull tarries at the mirror, losing himself in his thoughts, when he is saved by Brule, the Spear-Slayer. The Pict smashes the mirrors and kills the wizard, telling the king that Tuzan Thune's diversion was a plot to destroy him. Kull, however, looks at the shards of glass and wonders how close he was to absolute truth. In the end, Kull is left to wonder how the conspiracy could have happened and what could have caused Tuzun Thune to help with the plot. Brule admonishes him: "Gold, power, and position... the sooner you learn that men are men whether wizard, king, or thrall, the better you will rule, Kull."

Robert tried a few more Kull stories, but Farnsworth Wright apparently wasn't as enchanted with them. The majority of the Kull stories would remain unpublished until years after Howard's death. The exception, "By This Axe I Rule!" would later become, in a way, the most famous Kull story to have never been printed.

At the time, Robert was busy writing another story, a longer story, more suited to the likes of *Argosy*. After all, *Weird Tales* was paying on publication, not acceptance. It was time to branch out. The story Robert wrote next, "Solomon Kane," thanks to the machinations of Farnsworth Wright's offices, would become the general public's first view of "sword and sorcery," or heroic fantasy.

Unlike in the Kull tales, the setting was historical, albeit the more recent sixteenth century (and less fantastic than Robert's imagined Atlantis), and the character relied on swordplay. Also present in the plot was the threat of magic, both useful and destructive. The mixing of historical romance (even if, in the case of Kull, the history was speculative) with weird or horrific elements (even something as mundane as ghosts and witches) is what defines heroic fantasy.

In "Solomon Kane," we first meet the Puritan swordsman, cursed with wanderlust, who travels the globe, righting wrongs and punishing the guilty. This is clearly imparted to the reader in the first few paragraphs, when Kane comes upon a ransacked and burning village. He finds a single survivor, a young woman near death, who gasps out the story of the village's attack and her rape by outlaws. She dies in Kane's arms, and his pronouncement is the stuff of Howardian legend: "Men shall die for this."

Cut to the brigand's lair, a year later, to find the remnants of the villain Le Loup's gang, harried and worn to a frazzle from their constant pursuit by Solomon Kane. As the pirates dither, Kane appears and slays wantonly with his rapier, and Le Loup once again escapes the retribution assigned to him.

Kane tracks Le Loup to Africa, and follows the pirate into the jungle, where Kane is ambushed and taken prisoner. Le Loup, it seems, has become a leader of a tribe of natives who worship the Black God. Here Kane meets N'Longa the witch doctor, who offers to help Kane dispatch Le Loup.

The action piles up as N'Longa's spirit animates a recently slain native, who attacks the chieftain. All havoc breaks loose, and Kane is once again free to pursue Le Loup into the jungle. This time, Le Loup takes a stand, and they fight a duel in the clearing. Kane is battered, but of course he triumphs over Le Loup.

It's a long story, covering an amazing amount of ground, and the editor at *Argosy* must have thought so too, because he sent it back in February 1928 with an encouraging letter. Robert had been sending stories faithfully to *Argosy* and other pulps as the material suggested, but had so far been unsuccessful in cracking the market. He read the letter, pleased to be getting feedback of any kind. However, Robert sent "Solomon Kane" on to Farnsworth Wright without making any of the suggested changes. A month later, Wright accepted the tale, provided that Robert come up with a catchier title. The redubbed "Red Shadows" wouldn't see print until August of 1928, only five months after Wright accepted it. The eighty-dollar check no doubt helped, as did the smaller checks that rolled in from *Weird Tales* that year, payment for stories and poems that had been purchased up to nine months previously.

Solomon Kane has been compared to Robert E. Howard, and many of Howard's friends and critics have said that Kane was the most like the author himself. If Patrice Louinet's theory that each one of Howard's major characters represents an emotional viewpoint that changed as he got older can be accepted at face value, then there is certainly some of Robert in Solomon Kane. The metaphor of oilmen becoming raping and pillaging pirates is pretty easy to translate, as is Kane's need to punish the seemingly unpunishable.

That Kane is a puritan is also quickly revealed in the first story, but Kane is less a scripture-quoting pacifist and more a sword-wielding angel of vengeance. He mentions several times that he does the Will of God. Dressed all in black, dark-haired and with eyes like blue ice, somber in demeanor and gruff in appearance, it seems very likely that Solomon Kane is based, in part, on Robert's father, Isaac Howard.

It's probably not a coincidence that Solomon's first name is the same as Isaac's best friend in Cross Cut, Solomon Chambers. Kane's idea of divinity seems tied to the Old Testament and wrath, and his pronouncements of justice are akin to Isaac Howard's shouts of "I'd like to take my knife and slash their innards!" when discussing local politicos or ne'er-do-wells, or people who had gotten on the doctor's bad side... in other words, any of Doc Howard's enemies. Kane was conceived when Robert was sixteen, according to one letter. Whether he was committed to paper then is not known, but this creation coincides directly with the oil boom of 1922. Finally, and most obviously, Kane is a wanderer, constantly drifting, seeking out dens of iniquity to destroy and bad men to punish. Listen to some of Kane's dialogue, and imagine it delivered with a slow West Texas drawl: "It has fallen upon me, now and again in my sojourns through the world, to ease various evil men of their lives."

Robert eventually developed Kane to be more open to "heathen religions," accepting help again from N'Longa, the witch doctor, who makes a present of a Ju-Ju Staff, a magic weapon that Kane uses more than once in his travels. In the end, Kane spends most of his time in Africa, protecting the innocent and punishing the wicked, as his missionary zeal dictates. Kane comes to sympathize with the tribesmen, often placing himself between the people he has sworn to protect and the schemes of fellow Europeans.

As a genre, something like this had never been attempted before. It was a new thing when Farnsworth Wright bought these early stories from Robert. There were, of course, tales aplenty of heroes defeating monsters in song and story, mostly coming from the mythic traditions of Europe. And it's true that witches and monsters had plagued mankind in stories and poems for as long as the printing press had turned out pamphlets and newspapers. What had never been tried before, though, was the crystallization of the two worlds, anchored in place by a single, heroic protagonist.

To further nuance the definition, Robert's characters in this genre are all commoners, outlanders, barbarians, and proletarians, who rise up and fight their way into kingship. Nothing is handed to them, and they have to battle for all that they own. This is an extremely American viewpoint, what Hoover mistakenly called "Rugged Individualism." As ill-conceived as the term intended for working-class Americans was, it is very apropos for Robert's heroes; they are as self-reliant as they come.

Finally, these sword-and-sorcery stories, with few exceptions ("Red Shadows" being one of them), occur in a relatively short time frame. The quest, so prominent in *Le Morte D'Arthur* and Jason and the Argonauts, is virtually absent in Howard's stories. If one of Howard's heroes is riding to a distant location, it's usually to finish the fight. There are exceptions to this idea, for Howard wrote hundreds of stories, but by and large, the above are constants in the stories of Kull, Bran Mak Morn, Solomon Kane, Conan, and most of Robert's secondary characters as well.

Farnsworth Wright was right to snap up the stories that Robert was sending him. They were imaginative, had great narration, and made most of the other contributors to "The Unique Magazine" seem like pikers. The real problem with *Weird Tales*, with respect to Robert E. Howard, was that they were behind from the start. Because Wright was going on his gut feeling, the magazine never really had a distinct focus, not like other pulps of the time. This gave Robert the freedom to experiment, to try new things—and as a last resort, to place stories that he couldn't sell anywhere else, his thinking being, *it's better to get paid later for the story than not at all.*

By September of 1928, Robert had received a total of eight checks from *Weird Tales*, including the large check for "Red Shadows." With more checks on the way, Robert could stop worrying about having to get another job. He started in on new markets, trying to crash a title that paid on acceptance.

Robert spent most of the year gunning for *Argosy All-Story*, one of the better-paying, legendary pulp magazines. *Argosy* was a general interest pulp magazine, with a wide variety of adventure stories set in a multitude of genres. He also sent several stories to *Ghost Stories*, a second-string "confessional" pulp. A new pulp magazine appeared in 1928 called *Fight Stories*, and Robert spent the rest of the year trying to sell them a story, with no success. Of course, Robert was also writing poetry, sending it out in stacks. Some poems stuck, but most of them came back to him unsold.

In the spring of 1928, Robert and Fowler Gafford, his childhood friend from Cross Cut, entered into an arrangement. Gafford had dreams of literary immortality, too, and he had written a western novel that had failed to sell. Robert undertook the task of rewriting *West of the Rio Grande*, with the intention of bringing some action to the story and tightening up the prose. What seemed like a good idea at the time turned into drudgery for Robert. The rewrite took months to complete, and the novel never sold. Gafford went back to his job, selling real estate in Cross Plains.

Robert also put together a collection of poetry with the intention of selling to a publisher. The proposed "Singer in the Shadows" would also fail to find a home. It was to be the first of several proposed collections of poetry that never quite made it to print in Robert's lifetime, either through inaction or lack of interest.

At the chiding of his friends, Robert tried his hand at several "realistic" stories, none of which would be published until after his death. Two of the stories written at this time are significant and worth a closer look. "Spanish Gold on Devil Horse" was Robert's first attempt to transfigure the community of Cross Plains into fiction. Using the nearby geography of the Caddo Peaks, Robert wrote himself into a story of buried treasure and bootlegging and, of course, a damsel in distress. As a then-contemporary western, it's not Robert's best work.

The name of Robert's fictional self was Mike Costigan. Howard describes him early in the story:

> He was a tall young man, leanly but powerfully built with massive shoulders and long muscular arms. He had an open, whimsical Irish face, set off by expressive grey eyes and very black hair. His age was somewhere in the late twenties, though he appeared younger.
>
> "Really, I scarcely know. I have a lot of good friends here though, and then—you know my first book and practically all my later stories were laid in this country, based on material I got out of the oil fields."
>
> "Yes, but the boom's gone on and Lost Plains is drowsier than it was before they struck oil here. You're mighty young to be a writer."
>
> "This is the age of youth," grinned Mike. "I'm not many years away from thirty."

This exchange and others like it throughout the story are sheer wishful thinking on Robert's part. Maybe Robert already thought of himself as a successful writer (and by any definition of the word "successful," he was), but the people of Lost—er, Cross Plains weren't quite buying it yet. "Spanish Gold on Devil Horse" does have some trademark Howard action, but unless one is specifically looking for biographical sketches in Robert E. Howard's work, this story merits a pass.

Post Oaks and Sand Roughs isn't much better in terms of quality, but it does a far better job as a fictional allegory to the author's life. Written at the end of 1928, this novel may very well be Robert's *Tom Sawyer* for its darkly idyllic and fantastic autobiographical scope. The novel is full of mean-spirited observations and high-handed moral rebukes, covered in a patina of righteous indignation. While many of the basic facts hold up under cross-checking, a number of the scenes, in particular Steve's [Robert's] confrontations with authority, smack of wish fulfillment and power fantasy. It's an uncomfortable book to read, but Robert seems to have needed to write it. Within, he is critical and judgmental, even of his friends Vinson, Smith, and Tyson.

While the chronology of the events in the book differs somewhat from Robert's life, the emotional intensity is a one-dimensional hatred for his surroundings. Here Robert's battle between barbarism and civilization, which seems to morph slightly to fit his particular needs, resurfaces yet again:

> A slow black fury was beginning to burn sluggishly in Steve's brain. Who was this swine to seek to govern his actions? The man with his watch and his sneer, his huge belly and his flabby flesh seemed to symbolize all that was hateful in civilization—commerce holding a watch on all dreamers. A cruel and dangerous contempt blazed through Steve's growing wrath.

The book deviates sharply from reality in its conclusion. Steve Costigan, tired of the writing game, selling stories and getting nowhere, tries one final time to get a job. The boss, the flabby-bellied man in the above paragraph, goads Steve into beating him up in his own office. Steve stalks out, but only after being thanked by one of the fat man's subordinates. Steve next holds forth in a chapter-long soliloquy on what's wrong with his friends, the town, and life—to his friends, before hopping on the bus. He intends to become a drifter, a hobo tramp, picking up money by prizefighting.

It is just as well that Robert quit trying to fictionalize his own life; he really wasn't very good at looking at himself objectively and head-on. What he was good at, however, was looking at himself out of the corner of his eye and wryly inserting himself into his work, obliquely, in the form of idealized or satirized characters. His direct gaze, his reporter's eye for detail, he reserved for the world around him. The backdrop of his life formed the building blocks for some of his greatest fiction. After 1929, Robert largely kept his personal life in his letters, where he could speak plainly (well, as plainly as a born storyteller like him could, in any case) about jobs, growing up in boomtowns, friends, prizefights, and the like.

The tone of *Post Oaks and Sand Roughs* is not unlike the tone of some of Robert's letters from this time. This missive to Clyde Smith, circa November 1928, indicates that Robert may have been having trouble with the citizens of Cross Plains:

> I can think of no more Hellish form of existence than to live in a common sense world, run entirely for the good of the pipple [people]. I admit that I will probably never get a chance to wallow in the gilt and the glitter, but damitell, I can dream about it, and in a drab world of logic and discipline, not even dreams would be left.... God damn their souls to Hell, God damn their souls to Hell, I'd rather be a wild palomino and die in the wilderness with no saddle marks on me than to live out my days as a respectable and fully fed plough horse, damn their souls. They never can chain such men as you and I, damn their souls.

> Capitalists and laboring men, I say to them, God damn you all.... Damn the son of a bitch who prefers the sledge hammer to the rapier. Damn the blasted fool who boasts about his grimy hands and struts over the earth singing the praises of common sense labor. He is the bastard who would uproot a rose to plant a squash, the slanting skulled, narrow templed, bulbous bellied, rusty rumped, louse brained, swine souled braggart who would tear the leaves from the Alexandrian library to start a fire going under a one horse power engine in a cheese factory. He is the scut who would break up the finest statue in the world to pave the whore town streets, and had rather listen to the squall of a iron foundry whistle than to a mocking bird.

Robert clearly needed to vent. He claimed that the people of Cross Plains didn't understand him, and it's not hard to see why. To the average citizen, Robert wasn't working. There wasn't a model or a precedent for what he was doing. And Cross Plains was just small enough to care about what the son of one of their most prominent citizens was doing, or not doing, with his time.

The comments Robert had to endure may have been completely innocent, along the lines of "I thought you were working at the drugstore," or "Say, Bob, the lumber yard is looking for a new bean-counter." These comments didn't necessarily have to be vicious to get on Robert's nerves, or those of his mother, who severed ties with the Butlers next door because Mrs. Butler complained about Robert's constant singing, banging on the typewriter, and nearly-shouted narration as he typed at all hours of the day.

Maybe in response to, or in spite of, these alleged comments, Robert sold a long western, "Drums of the Sunset," to the *Cross Plains Review* for the handsome figure of twenty dollars. The story ran over nine weeks, into January 1929. This was material that the people of Cross Plains knew and understood: cowboys, Indians, lost mines of gold, gunfights, damsels in distress, and clenched fists. "Drums of the Sunset" is a standard western of the time, showing no real hint of the dark, brooding westerns of his later writing, but again it must be noted that the action sequences are superbly handled and far outweigh the cornball dialogue between the hero, Steve Harmer, and the heroine *du jour*, Joan Farrel. Whether or not the citizens of Cross Plains even noticed that Robert's story was running in the paper remains unknown.

Robert wrote to Smith in February 1929:
> I have been harried for years by people who wanted to know what magazines published my hokum. Up to a short time ago I would always reply apologetically, Only Weird Tales. Now, having the Celtic ability to lie without telling a false hood, I reply as you may have noticed: Weird Tales, Ghost Story, The

Poets' Scroll, The Ring, and various news papers. Most of that means nothing to the average gazoot anyway. Were I pressed for details, I should truthfully give the following statistics: Weird Tales, 13 stories, 13 rhymes; Ghost Story, 1 story; The Poets' Scroll, 2 sonnets; The Ring, 1 rhyme. Newspapers: The Baylor College paper once published 1 rhyme; Cross Plains Review, 1 serial; an Oklahoma paper once published 1 story, reprint from The Tattler. Not forgetting The Junto. And the Bulletin Brownwood, 1 article, i.e. prize winning essay. The Cross Plains Review, 1 rhyme.... The fact that a lot of this stuff brought no money is nobody's business.

By the end of November, Robert received more good news: He had finally placed a story in *Ghost Stories Magazine*. They paid on acceptance. He got ninety-five dollars a few days after the acceptance letter. No more was mentioned about Robert earning a living as a bookkeeper. Isaac began to brag on his writerly son, buying up several copies of the pulps as they appeared on the stands to encourage Robert. He may have given some of them to various friends and acquaintances, but the rest went straight to the house.

The people of Cross Plains, if they cared, simply went about their business, and grew accustomed to seeing Robert walking down the street on his way to the post office, his brow creased in thought, his eyes glaring but seeing nothing. Maybe his former bosses saw him and gave a rueful chuckle and a shake of their head, thinking that his parents must have an awful time with him. Maybe his classmates felt a bite of contempt because Robert didn't seem to work, but had money to buy magazines, newspapers, and go to the picture shows. The townspeople that knew the family, knew Dr. Howard, and Hester, and even Robert, knew them to be nice people, but that wouldn't have kept them from thinking Robert a little odd. And it was definitely odd to see Robert, easily as large as the town rowdies, running around with his friends, Lindsey Tyson and Dave Lee, but not doing what they considered work. Robert was nice and polite when spoken to, and with folks that he had a relationship with, he was pleasant and joking. But those people were few and far between.

Robert, then, dropped out of regular view to pursue his career at roughly the same time that the second oil boom came to an end. Cross Plains, flush with money, spent wisely and invested in new pieces of infrastructure, like schools and other civic improvements. Robert, if he noticed, never seemed to comment on these improvements; in fact, he maintained for the rest of his life that things were bad and getting worse. He had grown up in the presence of daily violence, greed, and turmoil. He was used to looking for trouble. Any perceived slight was pounced upon by Robert as an example that bolstered his already low opinion of things. Cross Plains, on the other hand, couldn't wait to get back to a sense of normalcy, and did so with due expediency. This formed a social disconnect between Robert and the rest of the town. He started to toughen himself at a time when roughnecks were moving away. Robert made his own way in the world and created a buffer to shield himself from what he felt were its worst elements.

Thus the two would part ways and, with rare exceptions, would never quite see eye-to-eye again.

Part 3

The icehouse's lights shone through the windows, cutting the darkness into strange squares. Despite the street lights, Cross Plains was dark and somber. Robert walked quickly, his blood up, his breath coming quickly. The Howard house receded behind him, along with the raised voices, the strangers in their midst. He couldn't write, anyway. Mother didn't want him to go, but he didn't listen.

The back docks were wide open, spilling warm light across the railroad tracks. A group of men stood, beers in their hands, their attention drawn to something inside the icehouse.

"Hey," Robert called out to them, "is that no-good chicken thief Dave Lee in there?"

The men turned around. "Hey, Bob," they called out.

Robert hoisted himself up on the docks, ignoring their offered hands. "How ya'll doin'?" he asked.

"Same old shit," said another man. "Got another shipment in today."

Robert smiled. He knew the dock worker wasn't talking about ice. "I'll take some off your hands, if you're willing."

"Sure thing," said the man. He retreated to an icebox and returned with a bottle of beer. "Here you go," he said.

Robert pulled the roll of bills out of his pocket and selected a dollar. "Keep 'em coming," he said.

The third man's eyes widened as the money disappeared into Robert's pocket. "I guess you sold one of them stories again, huh?" he asked.

Robert stared at the man, trying to decide if he was impressed or making a joke at his expense. The other men looked away, uncomfortable. Just then, another roughneck bounded over, covered in sweat. He pounded Robert on the back.

"Hey Bob," said the roughneck.

"Hey Dave," said Robert.

"We got a new guy this week, from Wichita Falls. Want to try him out?"

Robert grinned and took off his shirt. "You boxed him yet?"

"He's fast, but he's got no starch."

Robert drained his beer bottle. "Bring him on," he said. Dave Lee ran off to set up the fight. Robert followed at a more leisurely pace, shouting in a loud, booming voice, "I was under the general impression that Wichita Falls only bred the shy and retiring types, such as you find in church choirs and fields of daisies. How they found a roughneck to send to Cross Plains is more than I can see!"

The new guy, in the process of lacing up his gloves, took a look at the six-foot-tall man, grinning mirthlessly at him with piercing eyes. His chest was deep, his shoulders broad, and his arms thick and muscled. His face was youthful, but his body was a solid mass of muscle.

"Who the hell is that son-of-a-bitch?" the newcomer asked.

"That's Bob Howard," Dave answered easily.

"What's he do?"

"He's a writer. Stories and such."

The newcomer looked Robert up and down again. "A writer, huh? This oughtta be easy."

Dave chuckled. "Yeah, you ain't the first guy that's said that, neither."

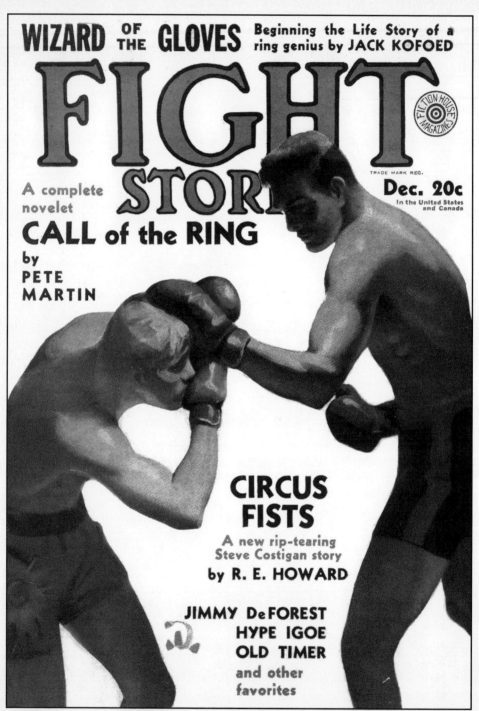

Fight Stories, December, 1931: Robert E. Howard's Sailor Steve Costigan stories were regularly featured on the cover of this successful (if specialized) pulp magazine (from the collection of Dennis McHaney).

THE FIGHTING COSTIGANS

The other night I had about the best time I've had here in a long time. Cross Plains had an American Legion Convention (give 'em three cheers, damn 'em) and a wrestling match with boxing prelims. Kid Dula from Brownwood and Dick Bowers, a tough kid from Breckenridge. There was a tough gang over from Breckenridge and it looked like for awhile things were going to be merry but I was with a tough gang, and kid, I don't mean maybe. Most of the gang was betting strong on Dula and they began to yell fresh remarks at Bowers the minute he climbed in the ring. Now I don't go in for ragging a boxer myself but when the Breckenridge boys began to throw remarks at Dula I let go a few wise cracks and first thing you know the two gangs were exchanging courtesies such as you seldom hear in a drawing room. Especially when Bowers hit Dula on the break away and one of the gang I was with arose and requested the referee to throw Bowers out of the ring. A Breckenridge man made a crack as to the effect of that being Dula's job and I took it on myself to assure him of Dula's entire ability to perform aforesaid job and all of us let fall a few remarks as regards the general manners, customs, facial characteristics and morality of all inhabitants of Breckenridge in general and present company in particular. The flower of Breckenridge were sitting just in front of us and several times they made motions toward rising but nothing came of it. I was the mildest appearing one of the gang and I don't guess I looked like a drawing room product for I was clad in rather rough clothes and was sporting a beautiful blue-and-black eye and a skinned place on my cheek as a result of a four round bout I had in the same stadium some nights before.
Robert E. Howard to Tevis Clyde Smith, circa September 1927

In 1928, William Kofoed, an editor for Fiction House—a publisher of variable-quality pulp magazines—convinced the moneymen to produce an all-boxing pulp title. His twin brother, Jack Kofoed, was a sports writer for the *New York Evening Post*, and knew all of the other sportscasters in New York, so content wouldn't be a problem. But Kofoed had a different idea for his magazine; instead of an all-fiction title, like Street & Smith's *Sport Story Magazine* (a staple since 1923), he wanted to mix in articles and essays, like in *The Ring*, the premiere boxing magazine of its time.

The new title, *Fight Stories*, bore the subtitle, "fiction and fact of the ring." It debuted in 1928 and quickly became a strong-selling title for Fiction

House. If that sounds odd, it's important to remember that boxing was one of the most popular sports of the time, vying for dominance alongside baseball and horse racing. Football was still something that was played in college. The first sports broadcast over the radio was a prizefight—the Jack Dempsey–Jess Willard fight, at that. *Mutt and Jeff*, the popular comic strip, was named after heavyweight Jim Jeffries. Boxing was big, and *Fight Stories* rode that wave with ease.

It's not known when in 1928 that Robert became aware of *Fight Stories* magazine, but it's very likely he bought every issue he came across. In addition to being a new source of information and entertainment about one of his favorite subjects, a new pulp magazine on the newsstands meant a new market had opened up for him to crack. Robert had been reading *The Ring* since 1922, and had steeped himself in the legend and lore of boxing. He attended prizefights locally and as far away as San Antonio. Most importantly, Robert underwent a rigorous exercise program to bulk himself up and stepped into the legendary "squared circle" of combat for himself. Robert boxed at the nearby icehouse, bare-knuckled and with gloves, and he was no slouch. That a man as sensitive, intelligent, and artistic as Robert E. Howard could also bloody noses and blacken eyes and, later, write some of the most amazing boxing fiction ever, is one of the more fascinating aspects of his life.

As early as 1916, Robert was interested in boxing. He and Austin Newton sparred back in Cross Cut. The way Austin told it, "[Robert] read everything he could find about boxing, and was pretty well informed on the subject. We didn't have any boxing gloves, but we spent a lot of time sparring. I ran into a left jab which hit me in the Adams Apple and knocked me down. That ended the sparring for that day. But sparring continued to be one of our main pastimes." It is possible that Robert picked up the boxing bug in one of his earlier homes, most likely Bagwell, since the school would have afforded Robert a good chance to mix with children from different backgrounds.

As Robert grew in size, so did his boxing interest. An early influence on his life and work was Jack London, who wrote several boxing stories in addition to covering prizefights for the *New York Herald* and other newspapers. The topic of interest in London's day was the controversial Jack Johnson, and finding a Great White Hope to reclaim the heavyweight championship for the "white race." London, too, was a product of his time.

As Robert grew from a stocky boy to a young man, his mass redistributed and he became a skinny, if somewhat tall, teenager. During his time in Cross Plains and later Brownwood, Robert continued to box with his friends Lindsey Tyson and Tevis Clyde Smith. After Robert graduated high school and moved back to Cross Plains to pursue writing, he decided to make a change.

Larry McDonough, one of Robert's neighbors, recalled the daily exercise regimen that Robert put himself through:

> He contracted with somebody there to go out there... on the west side of town, and cut down oak trees and bring 'em in as logs, out there in the back yard between that house and where the garage was.... And he would go out there in the afternoon with pants on a little below his knee and a T-shirt and they have a pile of these logs and he would take the spike driving axe and sledge hammers and spikes and split those oak trees up, muscle himself and get over there and do some pull up and down on his outside chinning bars, split all this up and give it to people for firewood. Every damn day!

Isaac noticed this activity, as well. He later wrote to E. Hoffmann Price, while reminiscing about his son, "After a long series of bag punching, bar lifting, and spring exercises of his hands, and general muscle training, I asked him one day, 'Robert, what's this all about?' He replied: 'Dad, when I was in school, I had to take a lot because I was alone and no one to take my part. I entered in to build my body until when a scoundrel crosses me up, I can with my bare hands tear him to pieces, double him up, and break his back with my hands alone.'"

Robert's alleged bullies have been a hotly debated topic by everyone connected to Howard studies. For decades it was asserted by L. Sprague de Camp that Robert E. Howard was bullied as a child, and that the torments he endured made him into a physical powerhouse and inspired him to write tales of wholesale slaughter. While it's true that Robert did mention being bullied in his letters and to his girlfriend Novalyne Price, it's very hard to know to what extent Robert was bullied. Did some older boys take his cap and play keepaway with it? Did Robert receive daily beatings? Were they isolated incidents, or were they habitual? Was his older cousin, Earl Lee Comer, a tormentor in addition to being an oil field roughneck? Nobody knows. Robert never talked specifically about it. What Robert did talk about was getting beaned with a baseball during the town picnic by some roughneck, and getting into a fight with an older kid who fairly trounced him. In later years, Robert took pride in listing off the various injuries accorded him while boxing. But there's no evidence of ritual torture by sadistic bullies, and it's worth remembering that even as Robert was skinny in high school, he was almost six feet tall and didn't mind boxing or wrestling with friends and acquaintances.

Growing up in boomtowns and always on the move, Robert may have endured some fairly typical hazing as the "new kid," but nothing that anyone else wouldn't have had to deal with. That Robert made friends fairly quickly is an indicator that he wasn't as socially maladjusted as he has been portrayed previously. Robert also witnessed a lot of fights during the booms, and may have caught a cuff on the ear by a roughneck or two, or maybe been pushed around by the town's harder elements. Prizefights were regularly held in Cross Plains, initially put on by the Cross Plains Volunteer Fire Department as fundraisers. Later, various athletic clubs sprung up as interest and population peaked. Robert would have surely tried to buy or sneak his way in among the tool dressers and ranch hands to see the fights. All of the violence that may have been done to Robert is entirely speculative, since he never wrote any details about it, nor has anyone been able to confirm any bullying from his school days. In fact, his friends all say the opposite—that he was either well-liked and got along with people, or just that he was quiet and kept to himself.

The bodybuilding that Robert put himself through from 1922 to 1925 may have been an attempt to protect himself from possible further bullying, since the boom had returned to Cross Plains. More likely than not, the strength and endurance training was to help Robert when he boxed. Through an increase of his mother's cooking, regular sparring with Tyson, and his workouts at home, Robert's weight shot up from 160 pounds to 195—all muscle. Robert developed his right hand, and his strength was formidable.

If *Post Oaks and Sand Roughs* can be trusted, Robert was boxing at the icehouse as early as 1926. We know for certain that he was mixing it up in 1927, as he wrote about several fights to Clyde Smith and Harold Preece. He even did some local promoting for the American Legion, rounding up willing fighters, but the work wasn't to his satisfaction. Robert continued to box up through late 1930 or early 1931 before he suddenly quit, no doubt due to the increased demand for his fiction. Robert kept up his exercise routine even after he stopped boxing.

Boxing was the most therapeutic thing Robert could have done for himself. His fistic activity in 1928 came at a time when he was issued a challenge by his father to make good with his writing or get an actual job; he felt an increasing pressure from the community to blend in and become one of them by getting a "real job"; and he was still dealing with the vagaries of writing for the pulps. Most importantly, Robert was coping with the death of his dog, Patch. The account of what happened comes from Isaac's letter to E. Hoffmann Price, circa June 1944:

> [W]hen the dog was 12 years old, he sickened to die. Robert knew his dog was going to die. He packed his grip, opened the gate, walked out, and said 'Mama, I am going.' He went to Brownwood and stayed until his dog died, which was two or three days. But each morning he phoned and asked his mother if Patch (that was the dog's name) was still alive; finally on the third or fourth morning, his mother told him she thought the dog would not last longer than 12 o'clock. He always spoke thus: 'Mama, how are you?' When his mother would reply, he would

say: 'How is Patch?' After the fourth day when his mother told him the dog was going, he never inquired any more; he knew the dog would soon die. Therefore he never spoke of him again. I had the dog buried in a deep grave in the back lot, then had the lot plowed deeply and then had them take a big harrow and harrow it deeply all over to destroy every trace of the grave, so sensitive was he to the loss of the dog. And only once did he ever allude to the death of his dog again. He said to his mother one day: 'Mother, did you bury Patch under the mesquite tree in the corner of the lot on the east side?' She said yes, and the matter was never mentioned by any of us again.

Patch's death was a major blow to Robert, obviously, and it also speaks volumes about the continuing efforts of Robert's parents to keep him from having to deal with painful, albeit inevitable, situations. Robert was twenty-two years old, and he had grown up around death and violence. Yet the loss of his dog was too much for him to deal with, so much so that he willingly took himself out of his dog's life. Robert's letters to Smith in October and November of 1928 are despondent, angry, and bitter. Robert was lashing out at anyone, anything, trying to find a place for his grief.

Robert often lamented that were it not for his weak heart (it tended to race under stress), he would have preferred to become a prizefighter than a writer. Boxing was of major importance to him as a belief system, a social activity, and even as a source of inspiration. Robert attacked the pulp markets of his profession with a boxer's intensity, determined to never be knocked down. His frequent trips to the icehouse, drinking beer, trading lies, and throwing jabs with Dave Lee, Lindsey Tyson, and others, were important enough to him that he mentioned them often to his epistolary correspondents. Later, the fights that he saw and participated in (and very likely the opponents he faced) found their way into his boxing fiction.

Boxing also became an emotional outlet, easily as important as his writing. He could punch out his frustrations with the pulp markets, his anger at the townspeople, and his pent-up resentment of his home situation on the icehouse regulars much more effectively than he could write about them. It was a more immediate way to shake off a bad day.

Robert was interested enough in boxing to submit a poem, "Kid Lavigne is Dead," to *The Ring* magazine, as well as to write laudatory letters to the *Brownwood Bulletin* about local fighter Arthur "Kid" Dula, and a fan letter to *The Ring* wherein he ranked the best heavyweight fighters of all time (a common topic among *The Ring*'s readership). In Robert's letter to *The Ring*, he favored fighters who were known as Iron Men—fighters with the ability to take inhuman amounts of punishment and remain standing.

Robert started, but never completed, an essay called "Men of Iron." "What freak of nature makes an Iron Man?" Howard muses in his opening paragraph. "We know that the human skull is well built to withstand violence, and that the body muscles may be developed into a steel-like toughness. But this alone will not explain the strange and incredible mortal known to the ring and its followers as an Iron Man." The essay recounts the exploits of several Iron Men: Joe Grim, Battling Nelson, Tom Sharkey, Mike Boden, and Joe Goddard. Howard shows that these second-stringers managed to exhaust and frustrate the champions they were matched against by refusing to be knocked out.

The Iron Man is a perfect metaphor for Robert at this time, determined to make it as a pulp writer, no matter what he had to do: alienate himself in the community, endure constant parental pressures at home, and so forth. Robert was the embodiment of such a boxer. He attacked the pulp markets like he fought, relentless, unyielding. When a story didn't sell, he sent it to another publisher and kept plugging away. Robert found out what worked by trial and error, he learned from his mistakes, and he played to his strengths. And, when he needed to broaden his markets, he turned to the one thing he knew best: boxing.

Robert wrote at least three boxing stories in 1928 in response to the appearance of *Fight Stories*: "The Spirit of Tom Molyneaux," "The Right Hook," and "The Weepin' Willow." All three stories met with initial rejection, and Robert dutifully submitted them elsewhere, as there were other magazines publishing the occasional boxing story. When "The Right Hook" and "The Weepin' Willow" failed to place anywhere, Robert went back to the drawing board. But oh, what a drawing board it was. Only "The Spirit of Tom Molyneaux" would find a home at *Ghost Stories* magazine.

The story focuses on a black boxer, "Ace" Jessel, and the heavyweight fight of his life against "Man-Killer" Gomez, another black boxer who is "the very spirit of that morass of barbarism from which mankind has so torturously climbed, and toward which men look with so much suspicion." Ace Jessel, on the other hand, is affable and easygoing—based on former heavyweight champion Jack Johnson. In the story's final confrontation, Gomez has handed Jessel a terrible beating and is about to win, when Jessel sees a ghost in the ring: legendary black Irish boxer Tom Molyneaux, Jessel's idol. Inspired by the appearance of his hero, Jessel rallies one last time to win the fight.

Ghost Stories was a pulp "confessional magazine"; all of their stories were purported to be true, firsthand accounts of the supernatural. Someone on the staff liked Robert's story, and bought it for ninety-five dollars, but then they rewrote the tale in the third person, told from the point of view of Jessel's handler, John Taverel. The renamed "The Apparition in the Prize Ring" was published a few months later. More to the point, Robert got paid, and well, shortly after *Ghost Stories* bought the tale. This was more like the way the other pulps ran their business, and Robert was excited to get paid at the time of a sale, rather than months afterward.

"The Spirit of Tom Molyneaux" illustrates Robert's method of "splashing the field," as he came to call it. Robert would write a story that utilized the genre or subject matter of the market he wanted to crash, but also involving elements that he was comfortable with. The example above would be a prizefight story, something that was still new to him, combined with the supernatural, which he was an old hand at manipulating. Robert did this throughout his writing career, bridging the gap between one genre and another like stepping stones. It is one of the reasons why so much of his fiction is hard to classify by genre. Robert was making his career up as he went. There was no formal training to be a pulp writer, and if there was, Robert would doubtless have never taken it.

Robert wrote a follow-up to the story, called "Double Cross," but there is no evidence to suggest that he sent it out. He was clearly trying to create a series, something that he could write at length and make steady money with. He was still trying to figure out what would work for *Fight Stories*; many of his surviving papers indicate that he was experimenting with style and character.

The other two boxing submissions that were rejected by *Fight Stories* are particularly intriguing. "The Right Hook" is a serious boxing story concerning one former sailor, Steve Harmer, a Battling Nelson (or Robert E. Howard) type of boxer with a punishing right hand. Over his last few fights, Harmer has picked up a glass jaw, and has decided he needs to quit the game. Then his old flame, Gloria, explains that her younger, dumber brother took money from the bank where he was working to bet heavy on the upcoming prizefight. Steve tells Gloria the fix is in, and when Steve hears that Gloria's dumb brother is about to bet on the boxer taking the dive, Steve decides to help out.

He goes to the arena, knocks out the crooked fighter, and steps into the ring as a last-minute substitute. Robert makes no attempt to disguise the real-life inspiration of Steve's opponent, one Battling Rourke:

> Rourke was blond, on the other hand; one seldom finds a blond who is extraordinarily rugged, but there are exceptions. He looked rough—caveman-like. His coarse hair, light and almost colorless, fell about his low forehead, adding to his ferocious appearance; his features were practically expressionless.
>
> Both were squarely and solidly built, with heavy limbs and muscles like knots of iron. Both were short for heavyweights—unusually so for this day and time. Harmer stood five feet and nine inches and weighed 185 pounds. Rourke was an inch shorter and seven pounds heavier.
>
> As they squared off, the old-timers commented on the remarkable resemblance Rourke bore to the great Sharkey, the battling sailor of other days, and on the shortness of the men. If any man doubts that fighters of today are taller than those of

yesterday, a glance at the relative measurements will prove the point.

If Rourke resembled Sharkey in build, he also resembled him in style, for at the first tap of the gong, he rushed in, swinging savagely with both arms.

In the end, of course, Sailor Steve prevails by sheer dogged determination (and, of course, his amazing right hook!), and he ends up in the hospital with his girl, Gloria, hovering over him, with the two about to discuss a different kind of ring—a wedding ring.

"The Right Hook" has elements of Robert's later boxing prose in it, as well as a few unformed building blocks of his later saga. For now, though, it would end up in Robert's trunk. However, "The Right Hook" would eventually be completely cannibalized by Robert, stripped as bare as a Comanche might strip a buffalo carcass.

The other story, "The Weepin' Willow," is the polar opposite of "The Right Hook," as Robert tried a different direction entirely. The narrator, Monk Costigan, is a trainer and promoter of second-string fighters. He finds an awkward-looking dub named Ambrose Willow who weeps as soon as he crosses gloves with somebody. Weirdly, this sad sack is also an Iron Man, very difficult to knock out. But the crying in the ring is unnerving to his opponents, and that usually gives Willow the advantage. Costigan says of his new fighter, "The public always pays out their kale to see freaks, and here was one which would make Joe Grim look like a conventional businessman!"

Sure enough, the Weeping Willow starts to pack the crowds in. His antics wow both the crowds and Costigan, and Willow is given the chance to fight Sailor Flynn. Flynn's manager, Nelson, tells Costigan why he doesn't want Sailor Flynn to fight Willow:

> That dub of yours would make a fool out of Dempsey. He's all wrong, get me. How can a man fight his best with that Adam's apple of his wigglin' in front of him? The mat gets plumb slippery from his weeps and he soaks up the back of his opponent's trunks by cryin' over their shoulders. His sobs would shake the nerves of a brass monkey and his face would give a nervous man the nightmares. He ain't a fighter, he's a blight.

Nelson continues in this vein:

> Your dub couldn't whip nobody if he didn't make nervous wrecks out of 'em by his cruel and unusual tactics. He's a ivory skull if they ever was one. I meet him only once and then I tell him a joke to cheer him up, see, and he merely stares at me in his dumb manner. I walk out on him and as I leave, I hear him bust into shrieks of laughter as the point finally comes home to him. The horse-faced dub."

Yet fight they do, and the Willow is getting creamed by Sailor Flynn when Costigan gets an idea and tells Willow a joke. He leaves the corner with a strange look of concentration on his face instead of his usual morose behavior. Sailor Flynn is spooked by the change of tactics, especially when Willow finally gets the joke and laughs uproariously in the ring. Flynn drops his guard and Willow knocks him out.

Charmingly told in a vernacular first person voice, "The Weepin' Willow" telegraphs its ending, but it was one step closer to the kind of story that Robert was eventually looking for. Monk Costigan could be the narrator for every story, but that point of view would only last so long for Robert. He needed to emotionally connect with his characters to give them real life. He needed to see the story through his own eyes.

"The Apparition in the Prize Ring" was published in April 1929. By that time, Robert had been dealing with a story he had submitted to *Argosy*, one that they had finally accepted. "Crowd-Horror," an interesting little psychological piece, is about a boxer named Slade Costigan, a six-foot-tall, dark-haired Irish fighter who boxes technically very well in training camp, but becomes maddened by the roar of the crowd and turns into a wild-swinging brawler. *Argosy* wanted Robert to cut the length of the tale from 13,000 words to 6,000 words, a substantial revision. Robert did what he could and got the length down to 8,000 words. *Argosy* accepted the new, shorter story and told him that it was still too long, but that they would make the necessary cuts themselves. They soon sent him a check for one hundred dollars.

Even as Robert was cashing that check, he got the news that *Fight Stories* had accepted a story, "The Pit of the Serpent." Set in an Asiatic port of call, the story dealt with one Sailor Steve Costigan, able-bodied mariner and champion boxer of the *Sea Girl*, a tramp freighter. Costigan and a fellow sailor from a rival ship get cross over a woman in a bar, and Costigan, three sheets to the wind, agrees to fight in the eponymous pit, a ten-foot square concrete hole in the ground. What sounds grim and awful becomes hilarious in Robert's hands as Steve and Bat beat the stuffing out of one another, and then present themselves to the woman again. She dismisses them both, pointing to her current paramour. Unspoken, the sailors lay him out with a single punch and head to the bar to drown their woes. In the end, Costigan tries to collect on the bet he made with his opponent and is almost waylaid again for his troubles.

What makes "The Pit of the Serpent" so remarkable is the ingenious use of slapstick in the tall tale tradition, and were the subject matter about punching cows instead of people, it would be classified as regional humor. In the first paragraph of the story, Robert lets the reader know what he is in for:

> The minute I stepped ashore from the Sea *Girl*, merchantman,
> I had a hunch that there would be trouble. This hunch was

caused by seeing some of the crew of the *Dauntless*. The men on the *Dauntless* have disliked the *Sea Girl's* crew ever since our skipper took their captain to a cleaning on the wharfs of Zanzibar—them being narrow-minded that way. They claimed that the old man had a knuckle-duster on his right, which is ridiculous and a dirty lie. He had it on his left.

This is pure tall lying, and it's no accident that Robert was using a first person narrator, and an unreliable one at that, to tell the story. Robert's fictional voice was very similar to his own, as most of his friends and acquaintances later attested. These stories closely mimic the way the Robert talked when he was spinning yarns for his buddies. In the persona of Steve Costigan, Robert gave his sense of humor a full, rich voice, all while playing with the sport that was close to his heart. For the first time in his professional career, Robert was writing what he knew.

Both "Crowd Horror" and "The Pit of the Serpent" were published in July 1929. Robert had already been working on other Steve Costigan stories; he knew he had a hit, and soon, so did *Fight Stories*. Robert wrote to Clyde Smith in July 1929, "My story The Pit of the Serpent came out in Fight Stories this month. Get a copy and read it. It will give you a good idea about how to write sport stories. The style and form are not much, but the mechanics are perfect. Writing is a lot like architecture. The whole structure has to suit—each piece has to be in place. A master of the game, like Kipling, for instance, or Jack London, always places the pieces right. A dub like me stumbles on to the right combination once in every five hundred stories he writes."

Robert didn't hesitate to develop a series for Steve Costigan. He had tried a couple of different approaches, including the first Costigan story, the rejected "Blue River Blues," which also featured a wrestler. While funny in its own right, the story is missing something: Sailor Steve needed a sidekick.

The second published Steve Costigan story, "The Bull Dog Breed," completed what "Pit of the Serpent" had started in character development. The story introduced Steve's boon companion, Mike the bulldog. Together, the pair was a complete, comedic whole, with Mike playing the role of straight man. The story is light on humor, but completely makes up for it by providing an amazing, brutal fight between Steve and a clearly superior opponent, the champion of the French Navy. Outclassed in every way, Steve is near death when he gets an inspiring bark from Mike, whose honor he is defending, and the bark is a reminder that Steve never gave up on a fight. The French Naval champion punches himself out on Steve's hard head, and the big, dumb sailor wins the fight.

Robert had finally created an Iron Man of his own. Based in equal parts on himself (and on Patch, of course, who became the fictional Mike) and on other real boxers like Sailor Tom Sharkey and Jack Dempsey, Steve Costigan was a way for Robert to satirize himself, his surroundings, and his friends, all within the real world of contemporary boxing. Robert kept the sailor angle—he could move his fighter around, throwing up different backdrops for the pugilistic spectacles—and he kept the first person point of view from "The Weepin' Willow," all the more to make Steve Costigan an unreliable narrator. This was essential to Robert's style of humor writing. He also pulled the tall tale structure from "The Weepin' Willow." Costigan is obviously a burlesque exaggeration of himself, and as the series progressed, the stories and comic-turn endings underscored that even more.

These stories are just as important as the many fantasy and horror stories that Robert E. Howard wrote, because they shine a revealing light on the author's sense of humor. Robert wrote humorous fiction professionally starting in 1929, and those stories continued to be published for almost a year after his death in 1936. Many times in his career, Robert would suddenly stop writing a character, usually because he had said all he could say from that specific character's viewpoint. That Robert never stopped writing humorous characters, even through his most trying times, has to be taken into account by anyone wishing to build a complete picture of the author. These funny boxers and later funny cowboys were as valid a means of self-expression as his poetry or his grim, epic fantasy tales. Robert was able to look at his own personality and lampoon what he felt were character flaws and weaknesses—impulsiveness, gullibility, a fondness for food and drink—as well as loyalty, a sense of humor, and politeness. It's all there in Steve Costigan, though the mirror may be distorted.

That Robert spent so much time aligning himself with a fictional presence is interesting. Including the Costigan series, the later Breckinridge Elkins series, *Post Oaks and Sand Roughs*, and "Spanish Gold on Devil Horse," Robert spent most of his career writing from a personal, occasionally cartoonish, viewpoint, either emphasizing his size and strength or romanticizing his physical description for his more serious characters. It's tempting to suggest that Robert was trying to manifest a new reality for himself, but the real reason may be simpler than that. Robert underwent a startling transformation in just a few short years. The first of these kinds of pseudo-autobiographical stories takes place after Robert had transformed himself into, for lack of a better description, a roughneck; the mirror image of the oil field bullies he so despised.

Simultaneously, Robert had turned to the intellectual pursuit of fiction writing as his chosen profession. This seemingly incongruous combination did not sit well with him, and he vacillated back and forth between the two extremes for the rest of his life, striking whichever pose would be of the most use to him at the time—and not infrequently, with the express purpose of being contrary or antagonistic.

Robert was happy to have cracked *Fight Stories*. He talked about his sales and tales constantly in his letters to Clyde Smith. Sometimes, he was just excited, as in this letter from February 1930: "Fiction House—Fight Stories—took another Steve Costigan story for $100. Also they finally located Iron Men and accepted it for $200. This is by far the best fight story I ever wrote. In many ways the best story of any kind I ever wrote. I guess my destiny is tied up with the Costigan family. I've never sold Fight Stories a story that didn't deal with them. The central figure of Iron Men isn't a Costigan, but both Steve and his brother Iron Mike figure in the story. This tale isn't humorous like the others. It's harsh and brutal; I don't know whether the readers will like it or not."

Other times, as in this letter to Smith from May 1931, Robert vented about the business: "I got a laugh out of my story which appeared this month in Action Stories. They changed the name of the character—McClarney—to Steve Costigan, though the style of the tale was nothing at all like Steve. And they capped the story 'by the author of "The TNT. Punch."' I never wrote a story by that title in my life."

The aforementioned "Iron Men" was built on the unused bones of "The Right Hook." The Iron Man in question is Mike Brennan, and this time, our hero is fighting to put a nice young girl through school. Brennan has all the characteristics of the fabled Iron Man, but just to be sure, Robert uses parts of the story to reference the actual boxers to further illustrate his point. The more Brennan fights, the more battered he becomes. He is on the verge of death when Marjory, the object of his affection, dopes his tea to get him to take a fall. Love conquers all, in the end.

Published in June 1930 and now retitled "The Iron Man," Robert's story had a whopping ten thousand words cut out of it. Even in its abridged form, "The Iron Man" is one of his best boxing stories, and one of the most important, serving as the crux of Robert's fictional boxing universe as he set it out, and showing that his boxing stories were premeditated and structured. Mike Brennan ends up fighting with Sailor Slade, Kid Allison, and Iron Mike Costigan, deemed Steve's brother by Robert in the above letter. This story is set in the same, real world as his Iron Man boxers and, incidentally, the author as well. By writing the fictitious boxers in among the real boxers, he lent credibility to his stories and made his characters more fully realized.

Fight Stories editor Jack Byrne was apparently just as capricious as Farnsworth Wright; he randomly rejected stories that didn't suit some unspoken, internal barometer for quality. Certain stories that Byrne went so far as to suggest to Robert would then be rejected. Byrne also routinely changed character's names and cut and rewrote Robert's stories, seemingly at random. While the practice frustrated Robert, *Fight Stories* was his bread and butter, and they paid him regularly and well for his efforts. Byrne was certainly no different from the scores of editors in the pulp industry who did the same things; it was, at the time, the nature of the business. Despite a heavy editorial hand, Byrne was a fan of Robert's work, and seemed to take a genuine interest in his career, offering praise, corrections, and advice in his letters to Robert.

Byrne wasn't acting alone, either. *Fight Stories* readers were very pleased with the Sailor Steve Costigan stories. Robert was one of the magazine's best fiction writers, no two ways about it. Other writers tried light, humorous pieces, but nothing came close to the level of quality of the Costigan series. Robert never knew that the folks reading his stuff at the office were legendary sports writers like Jack Kofoed and Hype Igoe; guys who followed Jack Dempsey around on his world tour and covered every major boxing match in New York City. He must have recognized some of their names, as many of them were veterans of *The Ring* magazine, as well.

Street & Smith's *Sport Story Magazine*, well-established since 1923, was a general interest sports pulp that ran stories about all manner of sports; though baseball and boxing ruled the roost in general, they occasionally ran pulp tales featuring handball, lacrosse, and even polo, the least likely sport to be enjoyed by the average pulp reader. Noticing either the circulation of *Fight Stories* or the quality of Robert's work, the editors of *Sport Story* contacted him in February 1931, requesting that Robert move Steve Costigan over to their magazine. Robert coolly replied that *Fight Stories* was happy with Costigan, but that he would be glad to create a new boxing series exclusively for their magazine. After some hemming and hawing, they agreed, and Robert set to the task of writing Kid Allison.

Another Texan, Kid Allison was a semiprofessional boxer with a manager who had just about as much dumb luck and lack of sense as Steve Costigan. As fictional constructs go, they are closely related, inhabit the same world, and are similarly told but ultimately different characters in execution. Street & Smith apparently thought so, too, as they published only three of the ten stories that Robert wrote. He accepted this as part of the writing game, even as he was griping about the situation to Clyde Smith in April 1932:

> Hear ye the tale of "Fighting Nerves". I wrote this story—a Kid Allison yarn—as a complete novelet for Sport Story. I wrote it, I think, three times, before I sent it off. Back it came with the request to cut out the saloon atmosphere and reduce the length. I re-wrote it and returned it to the same magazine. It came back with the statement that they were all stocked up with fight stories—requested me to keep it several months and return it, with a letter reminding them of it. Not wanting to wait that long if I could help it—a natural desire of a penniless adventurer

like myself—I rewrote most of it, changing the names of the characters, and sent it to Fight Stories. Back it came with the request to cut it down in length. I rewrote it and sent it back. Back it came, with the remark that it was acceptable, but that they couldn't find a place for it just then. I should keep it a month or so, and then they'd like to see it some more. So I sent it to Sport Stories, with a letter reminding them of what they had said. It was returned with no explanation—merely a rejection slip.

Robert hadn't forgotten his other markets in 1929, and especially not *Weird Tales*. One of Robert's most famous stories, "Skull-Face," was serialized starting in October of that year. It, too, is another example of one of Robert's most enduring themes. Rescuing the racial uprising theme from "The Last White Man," Robert recast the villain as an ancient Atlantean mummy who rose from the dead to unite the various factions of Asia and Africa. Skull-Face, a.k.a. Kathulos, plans his toppling of the world, starting with London, but the mad mummy doesn't count on... Steve Costigan.

Neither humorous nor autobiographical, this tale's Steve Costigan is a World War I soldier hooked on opium. His cravings are purged by the mysterious Skull-Face, who demands total subservience in return. Costigan goes along with the game at first, but balks when he's ordered to murder a British investigator bent on stopping Skull-Face. The investigator and Costigan team up to confront the evil that is Skull-Face, reveal his plot, and seemingly destroy him.

Skull-Face has been accused of being a Sax Rohmer riff, a poor man's Fu Manchu, but in reality, he is another metaphor for civilization versus barbarism, cloaked in Orientalist rhetoric this time. Tellingly, Skull-Face's ravings and goals don't seem much different from the Plan of San Diego's call to arms, which was bandied about during the Mexican Revolution to incite Texans to make war on Mexico.

Of greater significance is the emergence of the aberration in Robert's fiction, someone who is bigger, stronger, and faster than anyone around him. Steve Costigan in "Skull-Face" is called a barbarian by Kathulos for his size and great strength. This type of character appears at most of the flashpoints of history that Robert wrote about; on one side of the conflict or the other was an aberrant alpha male, a born leader, who either led the charge or opposed it. Whether or not the scenario was successful depended entirely on the point of view from which Howard wrote the story.

Between the money made by Robert for his prizefighting fiction and the three hundred dollars that *Weird Tales* paid him for "Skull-Face," Robert was sitting pretty in 1929. However, his home life was in a turmoil; the Howards had taken in lodgers again, and the house was filled to capacity. Robert, then, decided to go to Brownwood for six months. No records indicate why he did so, but he left sometime in July 1929, and returned to Cross Plains in December 1929. What Robert did in Brownwood and who he stayed with are unknown. Considering that his parents' marriage had broken down to the point of partial estrangement, it is possible that Robert just needed a change of scenery from his mother's cold silence and hostility his father's loud complaining about his wife's lack of attention and bouts of pretension. Isaac Howard was out of the house more and more; during the first part of 1929, he went to Spur, Texas, either to test the waters and see if he could set up a practice there, or to get away from Hester, or maybe both. Robert, then, may have moved away to force his father to come home and take care of Hester. No one can say for sure what maneuverings took place at the end of 1929, nor what prompted them. After returning from his six month furlough in December 1929, Robert wrote to Smith, "Here I am doing business at the old stand or trying to. I don't know if I'll be able to write worth a damn here or not." Apparently, things hadn't settled down at home just yet.

Throughout 1928 to 1930, *The Junto* was appearing regularly, more or less, circulated throughout the group, one at a time, and passed on to the next with handwritten comments enclosed. Most of the pieces published were poetry, short essays and rants, and small, humorous sketches. Ostensibly a like-minded cabal of iconoclasts, the *Junto* writers would put forth their particular viewpoints on race, religion, and women in every issue.

One particular instance seemed to have been engineered to get a rise out of Robert. Clyde Smith entreated Harold Preece to write a denouncement of women and run it in *The Junto* in an effort to draw Robert out. "Women: A Diatribe" went on to assert that there was no such thing as an intellectual woman. Robert, instead of agreeing with Preece, fired a return volley, extolling the virtues of everyone from Sappho of Greek antiquity to the early Gnostics with their pro-feminist slant. Robert, while holding a quaint set of Texan ideals about how to treat a lady, was surprisingly egalitarian when it came to women.

This round-robin effort was of great value socially to Robert, who benefited from hearing what other young intellectuals thought in other parts of the country. Regarding *The Junto*, Harold Preece wrote to Glenn Lord, years later, "I feel that it gave Bob a specialized, intimate, if small, sort of audience that he needed. Most of its readers were rebellious young intellectuals in that epoch of the depression. Bob's fire and spirit symbolized all sorts of protests—expressed and inchoate—that we felt, though, only in a very limited sense was he any kind of political rebel nor at all any sort of slogan shouter or cliché monger."

Robert also widened his correspondence to include several members of *The Junto*, including most notably Harold Preece, with whom he bonded over their mutual interest in all things Celtic. Robert's letters to Preece are a trove of Celtic lore, Celtic linguistics, and, periodically, Robert's "black Celtic" moods. The two men encouraged each other's Irish-ness, and this, coupled with Hester's fake Irish brogue, launched Robert's foray into full-fledged Celtic mania. He began creating Irish characters and half-Irish characters, some intended for long series. Irish surnames, always present in his work, became more dominant as well. Robert even signed letters to Clyde Smith with "Fear Dun" (the dark man). He called Smith "Fear Finn" (the pale man).

Robert's friendship with Preece and the rest of *The Junto* crowd ran its course sometime in 1931, after the publication ceased its circulation. By that time, Robert had found a new literary group; another circle of friends who would catapult Robert to his greatest fame.

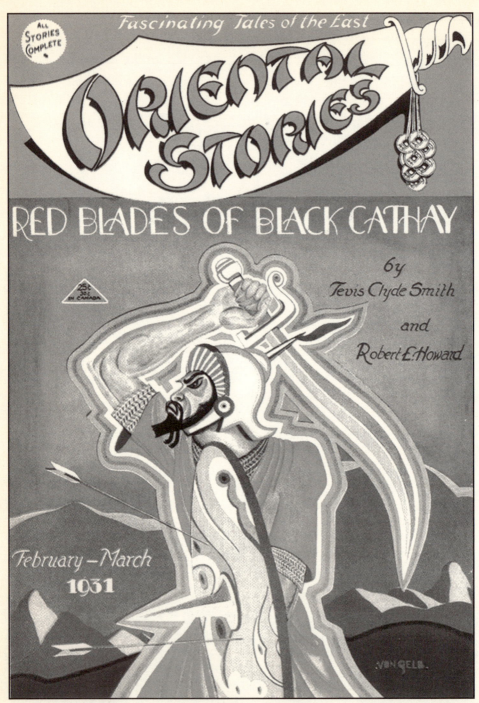

The Spring 1931 issue of *Oriental Stories*, featuring the story Robert co-wrote with Tevis Clyde Smith, "Red Blades of Black Cathay" (from the collection of Dennis McHaney).

LOVECRAFT

> You are right economics will have to revolutionize entirely if the nation is to continue, and the choice seems to lie between fascism and communism—both of which I utterly detest. And doubtless the world will eventually, as you say, sink back into barbarism—if any humans are left alive after the next war. And since the inevitable goal of all civilization seems to be decadence, it seems hardly worth while to struggle up the long road from barbarism in the first place.
> **Robert E. Howard to H.P. Lovecraft, December 1930**

At the same time Robert was writing his rollicking prizefighting stories, he was approached by Farnsworth Wright to contribute to a companion title for *Weird Tales*. The new magazine, *Oriental Stories*, would focus on locales in Asia and the Middle East. In particular, Wright wanted "historical tales—tales of the Crusades, of Genghis Khan, of Tamerlane, and the wars between Islam and Hindooism." This was right up Robert's alley. By the end of the month, Robert had placed "The Voice of El-Lil," a modern weird menace tale of ancient Sumeria, in the premiere issue.

Thereafter, whenever Robert wasn't waxing fistic for the fight fans, he was writing deadly earnest historical fiction. While he wrote only eleven historicals during the time that *Oriental Stories* limped along, they showcase Robert E. Howard in his preferred element. Specifically, all of Robert's historical Oriental stories take place around the Crusades, either before or after, in a dramatic underscoring of his enduring theme of civilization backsliding into barbarism. No one in these stories is a hero; they are motivated by conflict and hatred, by shame and power. Flashes of nobility arise only in the wake of an example of exemplary combat skill, or a refusal to compromise on principles. Otherwise, the stories are richly bleak with the decadence of ancient religious zeal.

The heroes of Robert's Crusades stories were usually half-Dane or half-Frank giants, conspicuously out of place in the Middle East with their red hair, pale skin, and dour demeanor. These knights-errant all projected the same sense of fatalism about their lives and their places in history as they watched the see-saw between the Christians and the Muslims slaying each other over and over for the same strips of land. Their involvements in the crusades were borne less of idealism and more from wanderlust, revenge, or profit. Robert may have had certain historical groups in mind as he wrote about his giant outlanders, but they are nevertheless fictional, even though in his tales they are present at actual historical battles. Robert was able to skillfully insert his protagonists into the creases of these chaotic end times and write convincingly of their involvement.

It took Robert a while to find his stride on these stories. His first story set in the Crusades that sold, "Red Blades of Black Cathay," was cowritten by Tevis Clyde Smith. They presumably split the money, and Robert thereafter became a regular contributor to *Oriental Stories*. His work was considered by the readers to be the best of the lot. Wright agreed, since he bought nearly all of the stories that Robert sent him. In "The Souk," the letter column for the magazine, Wright expounded at length upon his own knowledge of this time period, in detail equal to Robert's. They were, on this particular subject, kindred spirits.

Robert's first character to wade through the gore of the Crusades was Cormac Fitzgeoffrey, a half-Irish mercenary who cast a literary shadow very similar to the later Conan the Cimmerian. Himself the subject of only two stories and an incomplete fragment, Fitzgeoffrey is nevertheless one of the most important characters Robert ever created. It has been easy to dismiss the Fitzgeoffrey stories as merely the forerunners of Conan, but that in and of itself is a significant statement when one considers Conan's worldwide appeal.

The first story, "Hawks of Outremer," appeared in the April 1931 issue of *Oriental Stories*, and it immediately laid a few premises out for the reader; these Crusades weren't romantic, nor particularly worthwhile, and the people involved in them were no more pious than in any other period of history—in fact, many were decidedly less so. Cormac Fitzgeoffrey rides out to avenge the treacherous death of a comrade at the end of the first chapter, and spends the remainder of the story hacking his way ever closer to his foe. This bloody trail of vengeance is a familiar plot device in Robert's canon, but through the historical veil of the Crusades, it garners a new twist. Seconds before Cormac and the villain, El Ghor, cross steel, they are interrupted by a contingent of men led by Saladin, the Lion of Islam, who likewise accuses El Ghor of treachery to the Saracens. Cormac and El Ghor resume their hostilities, with predictable results. Cormac then turns to Saladin and awaits the killing stroke from one of his men. To his surprise, Saladin lets him go, citing Cormac's sense of loyalty to his friend:

> Cormac sheathed his sword ungraciously. A grudging admiration for this weary-faced Moslem was born in him and it angered him. Dimly he realized at last that this attitude of fairness, justice and kindliness, even to foes, was not a crafty pose of Saladin's, not a manner of guile, but a natural nobility of the Kurd's nature. He saw suddenly embodied in the Sultan, the ideals of chivalry and high honor so much talked of—and so little practiced—by the Frankish knights... he suddenly realized his own barbarism and was ashamed.

The follow-up story, "The Blood of Belshazzar," is a wonderful exercise in paranoia, as a host of interests from various nations vie for possession of a large ruby under the roof of a bandit's stronghold in the Taurus Mountains. Everyone is out to get everyone, and is far less interested in the ruby than just living through the night. Greed ignites old grudges, and turns the stronghold into a slaughterhouse.

When the next issue of *Oriental Stories* hit the stands, "The Souk" ran a letter from a fan:

> Wow! What a story that 'The Blood of Belshazzar' by Robert E. Howard in the Autumn issue of Oriental Stories. If I am any judge of good fiction, this is one of the best stories printed this year in any magazine. It is what we readers want. Let us have more of Howard's stuff.
>
> Jack Scott, Editor, *Cross Plains Review*, Texas

At least one person in Cross Plains was reading Robert's work aside from his family and friends. The motives behind Jack Scott writing this letter may have been nothing more than a genuine attempt to boost Robert's efforts. Robert never mentioned it, nor did he count Jack Scott as one of his intimates. The two of them worked together during the second oil boom, as Robert sold oil field gossip by the column inch, and Jack also bought "Drums of the Sunset" to run in the *Cross Plains Review*. They were certainly cordial, if not friendly.

Robert started, but never completed, a third story. Instead, he decided to explore the other Crusades, and from a variety of angles. All of his successive efforts for *Oriental Stories*, "The Sowers of Thunder," "Lord of Samarcand," "The Lion of Tiberias," and "Shadow of the Vulture," feature stand-alone characters, but unlike any that Robert had previously set to paper. These ex-crusaders and ex-mercenaries are grim, hazy men with indistinct edges. Sometimes they are good, and other times, they are bad. Robert called his historical fiction "realistic," and from his point of view, it was. He had introduced shades of gray into the black and white morality of the pulps.

"Shadow of the Vulture" introduced another Germanic campaigner of old, Gottfried von Kalmbach, and the object of his affection, Red Sonya of Rogatino—yes, *that* Red Sonya. When Robert introduced his "She-Devil with a Sword," his Sonya bore little resemblance to what would later become "Red Sonja," an invention of comic book creators Roy Thomas and Barry Windsor-Smith. While they freely admit that Sonya was the model for Sonja, the apple fell very far from the tree.

Robert wrote Sonya as a voluptuous creature, feminine and strong, able to charm with her antics and deal death with a single swing of her sword arm. She may come off to modern readers as a bit of wish fulfillment in the 1930s, but that doesn't keep her from nearly stealing the show from Gottfried, such is her appeal.

Robert wrote this about his character to H.P. Lovecraft, March 6, 1933:

> I'm curious to know how the readers will like Gottfried von Kalmbach, one of the main characters in a long historical yarn I sold Wright, concerning Suleyman the Magnificent's attack on Vienna. A more dissolute vagabond than Gottfried never weaved his drunken way across the pages of a popular magazine: wastrel, drunkard, gambler, whore-monger, renegade, mercenary, plunderer, thief, rogue, rascal—I never created a character whose creation I enjoyed more. They may not seem real to the readers; but Gottfried and his mistress Red Sonya seem more real to me than any other character I've ever drawn.

Kalmbach sounds a lot like some of the roughnecks that Robert was familiar with and spoke about in his many letters. He was taking steps to integrate character history, literally, into his fiction. While none of his prior characters were squeaky-clean to begin with, Robert took great delight in using an actual historical setting in which to depict his morally ambiguous characters.

Unfortunately, the market for *Oriental Stories* was never that strong and, coupled with the fallout from the Great Depression, the magazine (retitled *Magic Carpet*) folded in early 1934, leaving Robert with five unsold stories written specifically for that market. Considering his 100% rejection rate from *Adventure*, it is little wonder that he didn't resubmit them. By that time, Robert was on to bigger and better things.

In June of 1930, Robert wrote a letter that would forever alter the course of his life. He sent it to Farnsworth Wright, saying, in part:

> I have long looked forward to reading Mr. Lovecraft's "The Rats in the Walls" and it certainly comes up to all expectations. I was amazed by the sweep of his imagination—not so much because of the extent of his reachings into the realms of imagination, which though cosmic enough in this story, he has exceeded in other tales, to my mind, but because of the strange and unthinkable by-path into which he has wandered in this tale....
>
> The climax of the story alone puts Mr. Lovecraft in a class by himself; undoubtedly, he must have the most unusual and wonderfully constructed brain of any man in the world.... As to the climax, the maunderings of the maddened victim is like a sweep of horror down the eons, dwindling back and back to be finally lost in those grisly mists of world-birth where the mind of man refuses to follow. And I note from the fact that Mr. Lovecraft has his character speaking Gaelic instead of Cymric, in denoting the Age of the Druids, that he holds to Lhuyd's theory as to the settling of Britain by the Celts.

> This theory is not generally agreed to, but I scarcely think that it has ever been disproved, and it was upon this that my story "The Lost Race" was based—that the Gaelic tribes preceded the Cymric peoples into Britain, by way of Ireland, and were later driven out by them....

Farnsworth Wright dutifully forwarded the letter to H.P. Lovecraft. The rest was history. Lovecraft, tickled that someone had called him out for his hasty linguistic substitution, decided to write Robert a letter, answering the points the author had raised. Thus began one of the most famous epistolary correspondences in the history of modern fantasy.

Howard Phillips Lovecraft (1890–1937) was in many ways like Robert E. Howard: a precocious reader, largely self-educated, extremely literate and opinionated, and emotionally crippled by his family situation. In his youth, Lovecraft suffered from a nervous breakdown, brought on by the decimation of his family fortune. In later years, his frugality with money necessitated some strange eating habits that contributed to his poor health. Initially drawn into amateur journalism during a period of convalescence, Lovecraft began experimenting with fiction as early as 1905. When *Weird Tales* premiered in 1923, Lovecraft was among its earliest contributors, whereupon the foundation of his reputation started.

By 1930, Lovecraft had become one of *Weird Tales*'s star authors, gotten married and divorced, and was living with his two elderly aunts in Providence, Rhode Island. Lovecraft's ancestors had been among the first families to settle in the area and were well-thought-of throughout the state. He was living as a pauper, drawing money from the principal of a dwindling family inheritance, and making sporadic money doing revisions for would-be writers (his most famous clients included the magician Harry Houdini). Lovecraft traveled as often as he could, living cleverly and frugally to make his journeys go farther. When not crafting the occasional short story, Lovecraft wrote letters to other writers, professional and otherwise.

Lovecraft's correspondence is legendary, encompassing upwards of 100,000 letters to hundreds of people, and covering the widest possible array of topics. In addition to writing Robert E. Howard, Lovecraft wrote to a number of pulp authors and fans who later became legends in their own right: Clark Ashton Smith (the three would later be known as "the Three Musketeers" of *Weird Tales*, not in deference to their friendship so much as it was a mark of the quality of their writing), August Derleth, Frank Belknap Long, E. Hoffmann Price, Robert Bloch, Robert Barlow, Julius Schwartz, Donald A. Wollheim, Fritz Leiber, Henry Kuttner, and countless others. Lovecraft was seen by most of his pen pals as a kind of mentor, and he played up the role of Elder Statesman in his exchanges. Notably, he kept a distinct voice and demeanor with each of his friends, employing various nicknames and personal idioms particular to each person he wrote.

Today, Lovecraft has transcended the genre ghetto to become one of the most influential horror and science fiction writers of the twentieth century, a much-touted influence on virtually every modern genre author. His "Cthulhu Mythos" stories and their countless knockoffs by lesser writers have achieved a ubiquity in pop culture the likes of which can be compared to characters such as Sherlock Holmes and, of course, Conan the Barbarian. Despite the widespread success of Lovecraft's work, the ideas behind tales like "The Call of Cthulhu" and "Dreams in the Witch House" usually carry more weight with modern audiences than does his literary style, a stilted and verbose throwback to his preferred eighteenth-century aesthetic.

In the pages of *Weird Tales*, Lovecraft was one of the few real practitioners of the magazine's namesake and something of a contemporary legend amongst the readers. Robert was extremely flattered when Lovecraft's letter came to him, along with compliments of his own work; it seemed Lovecraft had noticed him, too. Robert quickly replied to Lovecraft, and also shot a letter off to Clyde Smith, saying:

> I got a long letter from Lovecraft. That boy is plenty smart. And well read too. He starts out by saying that most of my arguments seem logical enough and that he is about on the point of accepting my views—and then follows with about three or four closely written pages with which he rips practically all my theories to shreds…. I think I'll ask him a lot of questions about things when I write him, instead of presenting my own views. That don't mean, understand, that he's convinced me to his way of thinking. Not at all; I still think I'm right. But I want to find out some of the things I'll bet he knows—obscure phases of history and forgotten cultures, and mystic cults and all that. He says his young friend Frank Belknap Long, and Clark Ashton Smith have often praised my junk. Well, I'm very glad of it, naturally.

Robert may have been initially intimidated by Lovecraft, but not so much that he neglected to keep up the correspondence. Their missives would fly back and forth across the country until the end of Robert's life, and they are the most famous exchanges of all the Lovecraft letters. They represent the largest amount of nonfiction and biographical writing that Howard generated. Howard's letters to Lovecraft are full of Southwestern lore, Texas history, and anecdotes about Howard's life and surroundings. Taken with a grain of salt, for Howard was a veteran yarn-spinner at this point, they reveal much about Howard's character.

Through this correspondence, Robert was introduced to August Derleth, Clark Ashton Smith, and many others in Lovecraft's various circles. Through Lovecraft, Robert was asked to contribute to amateur publishing efforts like *The Fantasy Fan*. Robert exchanged folklore and anecdotes with August Derleth, and discussed the mechanics of writing with Clark Ashton Smith, whom he admired greatly. Robert found a wider exposure in some unusual places through his association with Lovecraft's friends; among them, Wilfred Talman, who published a nonfiction article, "The Ghost of Camp Colorado," in the *Texaco-Star*, a Texas-based publication printed by the eponymous oil company. Lovecraft, it seemed, knew everybody.

This nationwide group of fans, sycophants, and actual writers was a larger, less formal version of *The Junto*. Hearing from places as far away as Northern California, Wisconsin, and Rhode Island gave Robert an opportunity to see a great deal more of the world outside of Cross Plains, Texas. Through it all, however, Lovecraft was the orchestrating presence that kept the various groups together and cross-pollinating.

Initially, Robert and Lovecraft discussed ancient history and the true origins of Lovecraft's made-up mythology, the Cthulhu Mythos. Lovecraft admitted that the whole thing was "a synthetic concoction of my own, like the populous and varied pantheon of Lord Dunsany's *Pegana*." Lovecraft detailed what amounted to a running joke in his own work, as well as that of Clark Ashton Smith. Robert wrote another letter to Clyde Smith in September 1930, saying:

> I'm going to ask Lovecraft if I can use his mythology in my own junk—allusions, you understand. You know, there's a scholarly bunch of men writing for Weird Tales—myself excepted, of course. Well, I have a smattering of various bits of knowledge, and a facile and deceptive mind, that should gain me admittance in various circles. I suppose a person meeting me for the first time would get the erroneous idea that I am well read, for if I do say so, I have a knack of discussing things I know nothing about. Closer acquaintance discloses the fact that my erudition is all superficial—reckon that's why intellectual people lose interest in me so damn quick.

This self-effacing attitude of Robert's was the primer for what would become the most significant aspect of his relationship with Lovecraft, a long-running debate on barbarism versus civilization. Robert felt that civilization was inherently corrupt, a worldview permanently dyed by his constant exposure to boomtown politics. Lovecraft, a product of the Northeast and the comforts of city living, felt that civilization was the best and only way for mankind to achieve its goals. This topic ran through five years' worth of correspondence between the two men. Rarely did it take over the entire theme of any one letter; instead, it was compartmentalized into a scant few paragraphs tucked in between recent road trips, historical observations, or even local political happenings. It wasn't the most learned of debates, either, since both men spent multiple pages per letter expounding on largely discredited theories of racial types and racial origins. Robert's racial viewpoints softened over time, due to contact with the more strident Lovecraft, as well as his own naturally maturing viewpoint. Robert's time and place kept him from reading the most recent books and articles on the subject, and Texas was as behind the times as most of the South in the 1930s. Lovecraft, on the other hand, had no such excuse and continued to voice his support of Hitler and Mussolini until just before his death in 1937.

Reading over their letters, this debate was a natural and inevitable occurrence. For all of their similarities, Robert and Lovecraft were drawn, as Robert pointed out, to opposing sides of the battle lines. Early letters show both men talking about themselves and their backgrounds (and it is in these letters that we find out much about Robert's life), their likes and dislikes, and their writing careers, past and present. They discussed literature, politics, the rise of the Machine Age, crop failures, mythology, folklore, genealogy, fascism (which Lovecraft favored, in spite of voting for Roosevelt), and dozens of other topics. They also bombarded one another with pictures and postcards of each other and the places they'd been to, traded manuscripts and poetry to read, passed off extra copies of magazines, and sent drawings and, in Robert's case, a set of rattlesnake rattles with a prose poem enclosed. Between all of this, they fought like brothers about everything else.

Lovecraft had never lived in a rural environment, much less in the fluctuating frontier boomtowns of Texas. His brief residence in New York left him practically xenophobic and rattled by the size and bustle of the city. Providence, though, was staid and settled, with paved streets, policemen, and all of the amenities accorded a modern city circa 1930. Robert, by contrast, chopped wood, milked goats, hauled hay, and rode horses. His visits to big cities were to places like El Paso and San Antonio, where the population was large, but no less or more sophisticated than he. Culturally, the two men were as different as night and day.

When Robert extolled the virtues of boxing and football, Lovecraft said that he had no use for games of any arbitrary nature. Robert said that such things were useful and that it was okay to be physically fit, as he needed his strength for country living. Lovecraft said that the intellect was more important than the physical, since progress and knowledge came from the brain—and intellect was used to direct physical labor. Robert replied that he tended to not trust the establishment because they were all crooks and thieves, and that he preferred to keep his own counsel like his forefathers. Lovecraft chided him that without laws and government, there would be chaos and madness. Robert said he didn't want anyone telling him what to do; that's what was so great about frontier living. Lovecraft wondered vociferously what possible freedoms could modern radicals want that they didn't enjoy now? And so on, and so on, and so on.

By 1933, Robert tried to jump out of the debate in a long letter written in early March. He started out with an apology, then followed up with a summation of his points of view:

> But before I take up any other matter, I think it's time we reached a true understanding concerning the "mental–physical" argument. This continual debating is as unnecessary as it is fruitless. My position on the matter is much the same as yours, modified on my part only by a greater interest in physical things than you possess.... In other words, you assume that I worship brawn to the exclusion of all else. To put it bluntly, this assumption is absolutely unwarranted. Throughout our discussion of the matter, I have tried to emphasize the fact <u>that I did not glorify the physical above the mental</u>.... The fact that I, for my own amusement, had rather watch a battle of brawn than a battle of wits, does not, as I seem to have said before, mean that I underrate a keen wit....
>
> You are certainly wrong in thinking I possess an inordinate pride in my physical development. I have no reason under the sun for feeling any pride in my muscles, which are very ordinary indeed.... Apparently you got the idea that I was proud of my ability to unload a wagon of feed. If I were proud of so trivial a thing, I would be the biggest fool that ever went down the pike. I mentioned that fact, not because I was proud of it, God knows, but simply as a way of pointing out that a goodly proportion of life, in this country at least, was physical, requiring physical exertion. And that statement is true. Unloading that wagon wasn't a matter of pride, but necessity....
>
> ... You should realize that I live in a sphere entirely different from that in which you live. The fact that I make my living with my typewriter certainly doesn't mean I have no other work to do. I don't live on a farm, but it's almost like one. Specifically, I milk cows, clean out pig-pens and stalls, dig ditches, behead chickens, and unload feed wagons when necessary, just as I help butcher hogs and load calves. Nor is it a matter of pride or choice, but necessity. If I didn't do it, somebody'd have to be hired to do it, and money is not so damned plentiful nowadays that I can afford to keep my hands clean at the expense of my pocket book.... Why, God knows, I'm not ashamed of any work I ever did, but if I felt any emotion regarding it, it was simply gratification that I was healthy and strong enough to do it, and didn't have to be out money hiring it done. I hardly think that feeling justifies your assumption that I place my chief pride in the work I do in the cow-stalls and pig-pens.
>
> ... The point I was trying to make, was the same I am trying to make now:—that not all men can for ever avoid physical exertion, and that the stronger and more fit such men are, the

easier their work is. That was—and is—the whole gist of my argument, and it goes without saying that anyone will agree to that. I am one of those men. I know my needs and necessities. I know that one of my necessities is a strong physique—much stronger than I possess at present...

...

You remark that it is more honor to be able to write "The Black Stone" than to have unloaded a wagon of feed. The question of honor is entirely beside the point. I wrote the story because I needed the money; I unloaded the wagon because it was necessary to do it in order to save money. Exactly the same motive was behind both endeavors.

...

I see no reason for our argument on this matter, since it is evident we hold practically the same opinion. As I understand it, you believe in the idea of a sound mind in a sound body, with the body subordinated to the mind. That is exactly what I believe. Simmered down, the real difference between our opinions is: you are interested wholly in the fruits of the mind, and I divide my interest between the fruits of the mind, and the exertions of the body. (As for subordinating the mental to the physical, I never heard of anyone advocating such a fantastic thing.)

When you thought I was exalting the body above the mind, I was merely remarking on the advantageand occasionally the absolute necessity of a strong body. That the body should be guided by a mind developed as highly as possible, goes without saying. The fact that the greatest instinctive thrill I ever got in my life was obtained in a slugging-match rather than through some purely mental process, does not in the least affect what I have just said. That was purely personal, natural, and instinctive, with no question of the relative merits of physical or mental pride, or intrinsic values. When I box, wrestle or lift weights, it is again an entirely personal matter, and it should not be taken that I despise people who don't do these things. At the same time I deny the right of these people to despise me, because I do. But that again, is beside the point. The point is: I recognize the superiority of the mentality, but I can not afford to neglect my physical side. As you do not ask me to neglect it, there is no cause for debate.

...

... Lord Byron was fond of boxing; Poe was a runner and a swimmer in his youth; Rupert Brooke was fond of diving and hiking; de Castro tells us Bierce was very proud of his skill at knife-throwing; de Castro himself found it necessary to put in a year at muscle-building; Jack London loved to box, fence and wrestle; Frank Harris was once a prizefighter, and so was Jim Tully; even the superior Mr. Shaw was once a clever boxer. I don't suppose anybody ever accused these men of glorifying the physical at the expense of the mental. My attitude is much like theirs, and it strikes me it's just a damned sight broader and more reasonable than that of the "anti-physicalist."

...

To sum it up: you advocate a sound mind in a sound body, but your personal interests lean toward the mental. I advocate a sound mind in a sound body, but some of my personal interests lean toward the physical. I do not deny a keen—perhaps passionate—interest in sports and athletics. This needs no apology. There are few other things in which I'm as passionately interested as athletics. I do not deny that I had rather been an athlete than a writer; if things had run right, I'd have probably been both, I do not deny that I would like to have the physique of a wrestler or a prize-fighter. I do deny that I glorify the physical to despise the mental. I simply do not subordinate the physical to the mental as much as you do. I do deny—and flatly deny—that I take, or have any reason for taking, any such childish pride and vanity in my mediocre muscular powers as you would seem to think.

... So with my usual rambling way, I have taken up a lot of paper in order to show that the differences between our opinions on the matter is too trivial to argue about, consisting entirely in the fact that I have to do more physical work than the average writer does, and that I am more interested in athletics than the average writer is.

This letter never brought up the chief reason for Robert's interest in bodybuilding—namely, to fit in with the roughnecks and farm hands in Cross Plains. In the course of trying to end the argument, Robert obviously emphasized his point to an extreme degree; of course he was proud of his physique, just as he was proud of his proficiency in boxing and wrestling. In Cross Plains, those things were valued; indeed, they were part of the working definition of manhood. Robert had to be physically fit, and he had to be able to handle himself. It was the only way he was going to get a measure of peace in the community. Lovecraft was from landed gentry, and he couldn't understand, or wouldn't understand, that the two of them were from different sides of the world.

Lovecraft acknowledged Robert's lengthy letter with a recitation of his own position:

> In reading over your summary of your side of our debate I am impressed with the fact that we are beginning to understand more of each other's positions. After all, the major differences are purely matters of different emotions—as fortuitously determined by temperament and environmental accident. If I were to make a similar summary of my own position, I suppose, it would run something like this:
>
> 1. I value aesthetic and intellectual activities highly

        because they are beyond doubt an expression of the most thoroughly evolved part of the human personality.

II. I value civilization above barbarism because I feel that it utilizes human personality to the full instead of involving a waste of man's most highly evolved faculties.

III. I think that the most precious possession of a highly evolved man is his freedom of thought and expression; and that conversely the worst hardship he can suffer is the curtailment of that freedom through overt censorship or through the obligation of writing insincere materials to suit commercial editors.

While this is an interesting summation on Lovecraft's part, he did little to appease Robert's call for peace in his very next letter, throwing out statements like, "To say to a man 'your belief is foolish' is *not in any way* akin to saying 'you're a damn fool.'" Lovecraft just liked to argue. He never conceded any point to Robert, backing up just enough to assure Robert that he meant no offense when he said what he said, or praising Robert for finally getting into the spirit of the verbal imbroglio of which he seemed so fond.

Because Lovecraft refused to let the debate drop, whatever reverence Robert had for his pen pal rapidly dwindled, though his appreciation of Lovecraft's creative talent never waned. Both Robert and Lovecraft were universally supportive of each other's efforts, and in between the constant flow of Roman versus Pict banter they indulged in, they kibitzed about sales to magazines (or the lack thereof) and lavished praise on one another's latest literary efforts.

Having a professional to talk to, and in particular one who was less motivated by sales and more emphatic about creative quality, was of real use to Robert. While he sometimes struck the pose of a "working hack" or "a dub" in the pulp writing game, Robert toiled over his stories, often writing detailed synopses of plots, and many times going through multiple drafts of a story before it was sent to an editor. Robert also used many of the philosophical ideas that he and Lovecraft were kicking around in his stories. That Robert's writing took a turn for the better after Lovecraft entered his life is undeniable.

Lovecraft, too, was influenced by Robert's involvement with his life. Lovecraft flung Robert's contributions to the Cthulhu Mythos far and wide, using them in many of his own stories, and praising them loudly to fellow members of the Circle. Lovecraft even picked up a couple of tricks, throwing more movement and action into one of his best stories, "The Shadow Over Innsmouth." Certain key sequences in the story, such as the chase through the village and the protagonist's fight against the monstrous villagers, are positively Howardian. These fictional bouts of physical action would be the only concessions Lovecraft would make toward

Robert's views. Not until after Robert's death, in his heartfelt memorial to his friend, would Lovecraft concede the debate by painting the portrait of Robert as he presented himself, rather than as Lovecraft saw him.

Robert's contributions to the Cthulhu Mythos included the fictitious book, *Nameless Cults*—a blasphemous tome on a par with Lovecraft's invented *Necronomicon*—and the mad poet Justin Geoffrey. As trappings, they were just as good as anything Robert Bloch and Clark Ashton Smith came up with, if not better. By the end of 1930, Robert had already sold what would be his foothold in the door of the Cthulhu Mythos with "The Black Stone," the best of his Lovecraftian stories. Both Robert and Clark Ashton Smith managed to do what no one else was able to do with the Cthulhu Mythos: bend the ideas into their own particular needs and shapes. Robert kept right on with his themes of racial memories, forgotten races of men, and slides into barbarism, but he also went back to some of the authors that influenced Lovecraft to further draw out his ancient horror. Arthur Machen, in particular, was an influence that both Robert and Lovecraft shared, and Robert's Cthulhu Mythos stories hearken back to several specific Machen stories for their eldritch terrors.

Robert was considered by many to be the best of the Lovecraft Circle writers because he didn't regurgitate the formula of "strange book plus unpronounceable monster equals gibbering terror." Robert worked on his own plots, while using the sensibilities that Lovecraft engineered. This is what makes "The Black Stone" so frightening, and still one of the best Cthulhu Mythos stories by any other author. Using dream imagery *à la* racial memories, the narrator in "The Black Stone" is a silent witness to an unspeakable act, unable to react without having to resort to such hackneyed devices as "fear holding him in place" or the like. Only after waking from his dream does the narrator comprehend the connections between the random chance that started him on his quest and the larger universe. Robert lets us be scared without telling us to do it ourselves. It's not surprising at all that the story makes use of folklore and deftly illustrates Robert's ideas about how myths and legends begin and end: "Time has a curiously foreshortening effect on folklore, and just as tales of the Picts became intertwined with legends of an older, Mongoloid race, so that eventually the Picts were ascribed the repulsive appearance of the squat primitives, whose individuality merged, in the telling, into Pictish tales, and was forgotten...."

On the point of folklore, at least, Robert and Lovecraft were in accord. After batting various legends back and forth, Robert began working elements of folklore into his stories. Unlike "The Black Stone," which merely invoked folklore in the narrative, one of Robert's most famous stories, "Pigeons From Hell," went one step further and appropriated elements from his own childhood to create one of his most famous and best stories, despite the seemingly innocuous title.

Set in the swampy back country of Louisiana, the tale features two friends from the East Coast, Griswell and Branner, who run afoul of old, ancestral terror in an abandoned plantation mansion. Branner ends up dead, and back to life again, and sends Griswell screaming into the night, where he meets the hard-as-nails sheriff, Buckner, on horseback. In the course of investigating the man's story, and later the murder of Branner, Sheriff Buckner and Griswell get to the bottom of the ancient legends surrounding the old Blassingville manor and what ultimately happened to the family. And believe it or not, even the pigeons are scary in this story.

There's no mystery, though, as to where Robert cribbed the fantastic elements for the story—from his own East Texas childhood and the ghost stories that his "Aunt" Mary Bonahan used to tell him. This is a terrific example of how Robert worked with a story to make it his own.

Robert told this anecdote to Lovecraft in a letter written in September 1930:

> Two or three men—usually negroes—are traveling in a wagon through some isolated district—usually a broad, deserted river-bottom. They come on to the ruins of a once thriving plantation at dusk, and decide to spend the night in the deserted plantation house. This house is always huge, brooding and forbidding, and always, as the men approach the high columned verandah, through the high weeds that surround the house, great numbers of pigeons rise from their roosting places on the railing and fly away. The men sleep in the big front-room with its crumbling fire-place, and in the night are awakened by a jangling of chains, weird noises and groans from upstairs. Sometimes footsteps descend the stairs with no visible cause. Then a terrible apparition appears to the men who flee in terror. This monster, in all the tales I have heard, is invariably a headless giant, naked or clad in shapeless sort of garment, and is sometimes armed with a broad-axe. This motif appears over and over in negro-lore.

To this anecdotal story, Robert added some of his own family history on his mother's side and artfully rearranged events, characters, and situations to better serve the tale he was telling. It plays fair with the reader and sustains its creepy atmosphere all the way through the narrative. Like an intuitive craftsman, Robert produced his share of clunkers and unfinished efforts, but "Pigeons from Hell" is not one of them. The story was anthologized often, and eventually found immortality as one of the more memorable episodes of *Boris Karloff's Thriller* in the 1960s.

During his correspondence with Lovecraft, Robert was revisiting and revising his mythical Picts, perhaps inspired by his ongoing debate with the author. He had crafted the Picts' eventual ending in his Turlogh

O'Brien story, "The Dark Man," but it wasn't until the Bran Mak Morn story, "Worms in the Earth," that Robert was able to delineate the exact fulcrum shift in the fate of his Picts.

"Worms in the Earth" is one of Robert E. Howard's finest stories, succeeding on many different levels. Shades of Lovecraftian influence, the *Weird Tales* marketplace, and Robert's signature derring-do put this story in every Howard fan's top ten list.

In this return to one of the earliest characters that he had created, Robert pulled out all of the stops. Bran, incensed at having to watch one of his people crucified by the Romans, seeks divine vengeance by forging an alliance with a witch who also bears a grudge against Bran's enemies. With the witch's help, Bran summons up the ancient enemies of the Picts, driven underground ages ago: the worms in the Earth, now misshapen and twisted and supernatural in their viciousness. Bran uses the worms to fetch the Roman who ordered the crucifixion, and the ensuing kidnapping drives the civilized Roman insane as he is whisked from below through subterranean tunnels by gibbering fiends. Bran realizes, too late, that his solution to vengeance was akin to letting out the demons in Pandora's Box. He kills the mad Roman, but takes no pleasure in the mercy stroke. With Robert at the typewriter, however, Bran offers no comment on his irrational solution. He has won the battle, but knows that he will lose the war. By invoking the worms, Bran sees his own tribe's eventual fate, relegated to the shrines of folklore. This story is what pushes the Pictish king onto the path that leads readers to "The Dark Man."

Robert's other Bran story, "Kings in the Night," only bears mentioning in that it resurrects King Kull from his literary exile, when Bran summons him to lead an army against Rome. It is interesting to note that with Kull claiming the entire battle is but a dream, the story feels like Robert's earlier self arguing with Robert's later self. Regardless, with "Worms in the Earth," Robert finally got to say all of the things he wanted to say about the Picts; it's as if he finally figured out the fate of his Lost Race. The Picts continued to show up in Robert's work, right up through the Conan stories, but they never again took the spotlight in Robert's fiction. A later, world-famous essay, "The Hyborian Age," brings the Pictish chief Grom into such prominence that one has to remember that this is supposed to be about the Age of Conan. Robert simply couldn't resist putting his Picts into nearly every historical setting.

As 1931 rolled around, things had changed drastically for Robert. The Farmer's National Bank had failed, and it had wiped out his savings. The Great Depression had finally hit, and it had affected everything in Cross Plains, Texas. Robert had changed banks, only to have that one fail as well. He'd finally moved his money to a postal account. Robert, like most Texans, was exceedingly bitter about President Hoover's failed promises that the Depression was temporary. Cotton, the savior crop of Texas, was selling for five cents a pound. Things were not good. Foreclosures were a weekly occurrence. Urban centers like Dallas, Fort Worth, and Houston got by on a combination of charity, private enterprise, and sheer determination. The folks in rural communities weren't so lucky. This severe change of fortunes was what caused the majority of Texans to back Franklin D. Roosevelt for president in 1932, running on his New Deal platform. Texans, ever wary for a chance to be obstreperous, began to split hairs between Democrats and New Dealers. The political machine in Texas seemed to thrive on abject conflict.

Weird Tales went to a bimonthly schedule to try to weather the nationwide financial storm, along with Fiction House and every other pulp publisher. *Fight Stories* first cut its word rates for stories, then went bimonthly, then quarterly, before suspending publication altogether. It was the same story all over. Robert's markets dried up, but *Weird Tales*, never financially solvent, somehow managed to keep afloat. Robert was still receiving some checks for stories and poems he'd placed months prior.

Around the time that Robert started writing his Conan stories, he took a side trip into the Hyborian Age to create another story, much closer to home, and quite possibly another fictional alter ego. The first of his James Allison stories was "Marchers of Valhalla," a historical narrative that he attempted to sell to both *Weird Tales* and *Oriental Stories*, and which was subsequently rejected by both.

The protagonist, James Allison, is different from every other Robert E. Howard character in that he is not physically fit; in fact, he is crippled by a childhood accident that claimed one of his legs, and is forced to use crutches for locomotion. The opening paragraph may give readers some indicator of where the story is set:

> The sky was lurid, gloomy and repellent, of the blue of tarnished steel, streaked with dully crimson banners. Against the muddled red smear lowered the low hills that are the peaks of that barren upland which is a dreary expanse of sand drifts and post-oak thickets, checkered with sterile fields where tenant farmers toil out their hideously barren lives in fruitless labor and bitter want.

It's not the most flattering picture of Cross Plains, Texas, but it is definitely Robert's own backyard. Allison, in the midst of a depression, scales what may have been the Caddo Peaks, and while he is brooding over his miserable existence, a woman appears and calls him Hialmar. Allison finds out that he has lived many past lives, and that this woman knew him from his time marching with an Aesir army through these very lands, thousands of years ago.

What follows is a heady mix of action and intrigue wrapped in historical fiction. In the telling of the tale, through Hialmar's eyes, Allison comments, "I am James Allison and I was Hialmar, but Hialmar was not James Allison; man may look back for ten thousand years, but he can not look forward, even for a second." It's a wise thing to remember when reading from Robert's canon. His characters sometimes behaved in a way, through deed or word, that would not be acceptable in the modern world. In this case, the Aesir engage in much raping and pillaging, like giant Vikings were wont to do. They are brought down, in the end, by the schemes of the civilized men they are engaged to help, and decide to thin their enemy's ranks before they perish. All of this, plus some love interest, make it one of the better Robert E. Howard stories for fans. It contains a nice blend of themes, content, and headlong action.

Robert, undaunted by the rejection of "Marchers of Valhalla," wrote other James Allison stories, including the more popular and widely anthologized "Valley of the Worm." While they make use of one of Robert's favorite speculative subjects—past lives—there is something significant in the James Allison stories that has to be addressed.

There is, of course, the strong resemblance to Jack London's book, *The Star Rover*, in the James Allison tales. London's protagonist, Darrell Standing, is not unlike James Allison in his past-life penchant for violence. Incarcerated for murder, Standing escapes his prison by visiting his other lives, wherein he is a heroic figure, a dealer-of-death, and, most of all, totally free.

The later James Allison stories place him on his deathbed, but even this first Allison story shows him to be a prisoner of his childhood—he is limited in his ability to travel, and because of this, he feels sorry for himself. This is not unlike Robert, who was himself trapped by his circumstances, forced to stay close to home to take care of his sick mother. In the same way that Allison reached backward to his past lives for comfort, and Standing reached out to the stars for freedom, Robert did the same thing with his prodigious imagination. He used his writing to explore the places he would never get to see and to do the things he would never get to experience.

By the fall of 1932, some pulps had recovered from the financial crash, and others, like *Oriental Stories*, were on their last legs. By then, Robert had resumed his regular submissions to *Weird Tales* because he wanted to try something different, and he knew that if worse came to worse, he could always place a story with Farnsworth Wright if it had the right combination of historical interest, fast action, and some supernatural suspense.

Robert was ready to branch out, both creatively and economically. He sought out an agent to help him place stories—and, most likely, found one through the offices of Farnsworth Wright, in a pulp author turned agent, Otis Adelbert Kline. They agreed to do business in the spring of 1933, and Kline immediately encouraged Robert to start trying other things that he could sell—detective stories, spicys, and westerns—as well as his regular weird fiction. And it worked. The two made a pretty good team. Kline opened several doors for Robert. The author found some of the markets not to his liking, but he also found that he was capable of writing beyond the pages of *Weird Tales*. Money once again flowed into the Howard house, and not a minute too soon.

Weird Tales

NOV. 25¢

SHADOWS IN ZAMBOULA
stark horror in the sinister house of Aram Baksh
by
ROBERT E. HOWARD

DOCTOR SATAN
spreads icy terror in Detroit
"THE CONSUMING FLAME"

Paul Ernst
Leslie F. Stone
E. Hoffmann Price

The November 1935 issue of *Weird Tales*, featuring the Conan story, "Shadows in Zamboula." Cover artist Margaret Brundage was an expert in delineating flappers in peril, and this cover was no exception. By the time this issue hit the newsstands, Robert had abandoned the series (from the collection of Dennis McHaney).

CONAN

> I must repeat that it is not my intention to idealize conditions of barbarism—and here let it be noted that I am not speaking of the American frontier, but of the Gauls and Goths. The American frontiersman was not a barbarian; he was simply a highly specialized type. My conception of barbarism does not glitter, particularly.
> **Robert E. Howard to H.P. Lovecraft, circa June 1933**

Robert E. Howard's greatest contribution to the twentieth century was Conan the Cimmerian (or Barbarian, if you prefer the pop culture appellation that Farnsworth Wright initially hung on him). The name "Conan" is now so inextricably tied to the word "barbarian" that it is impossible to separate them on a cultural level. Furthermore, the American *gestalt* has forever linked Arnold Schwarzenegger to the loincloth-wearing hero that made him internationally famous. The star of movies, comics, cartoons, video games, toy lines, and an endless stream of knockoff novels by a horde of writers, Conan has completely overshadowed his own creator, in much the same way that Sherlock Holmes has dwarfed Arthur Conan Doyle and Tarzan has eclipsed Edgar Rice Burroughs.

As a fictional character, Conan has been written about, studied, and scrutinized by a great many people, from the science fiction community of the 1950s to film students in graduate school, and all points in between. He is the entry point for most people into the mind and life of Robert E. Howard and, sadly, usually the exit point as well. In truth, Conan was little more than just another speed bump in Robert's varied career. While popular in his day, the character wasn't as financially successful (excepting the posthumous tidal wave of marketing and merchandising) as some of Robert's other ongoing series. Had Robert lived, Conan would have been considered the author's final statement on the realm of fantasy before turning his literary eye to the history of the Southwest and the open range. In fact, were it not for sheer grit and determination on Robert E. Howard's part, Conan might not have happened at all.

Following an intense period of nearly two uninterrupted years of steady writing, Robert took a vacation to recharge his batteries in early 1932. Like the rest of his family, he had a roving spirit and wandered all over the state by any means at his disposal. In this case, Robert took the bus to San Antonio to kick around for a few days. Robert told a story of his travels to Clyde Smith in late February 1932:

> I reckon you got my postcard from the Valley. I didn't stay there as long as I'd intended; I found the climate delightful,

> but the altitude was unhealthily low—only about sixty-five feet at Mission. Spent awhile there, and then came back to San Antonio for a few days.
>
> I didn't go to Brownsville; only went down the valley from Mission as far as McAllen once, and did the rest of my exploring up the river—west of Mission, in Starr County, which is a striking contrast to the citrus belt, which is very thickly populated, full of blond Yankees, and rich in plants of all kinds. Starr County is a ranching country, a wild, broken terrain, cut by low hill ranges and dry arroyos, and is predominantly Mexican. Rio Grande City and Roma are almost purely spick. The former town has a population of nearly three thousand people, and there are only about twelve civilian white families there, while in Roma, the only whites are the government officials on the international bridge. Of course, Fort Ringgold is at Rio Grande City, and there are lots of white soldiers there. Architecture and everything is Mexican. It's just like being in Old Mexico.

It was in Mission, Texas, that Robert said his fictional character first came to life. "Conan simply grew up in my mind a few years ago when I was stopping in a little border town on the lower Rio Grande," Robert wrote to Clark Ashton Smith in 1935. "I did not create him by any conscious process. He simply stalked full grown out of oblivion and set me at work recording the saga of his adventures." With those few colorful sentences, Robert was indulging in a little personal myth-making. It is unfortunate that the few statements Robert chose to make about Conan were of this type, as they have all been butchered by the haphazard paraphrasing of movie moguls, fellow authors, and uncomprehending critics. In truth, Conan took a full nine months to be born, and it's a miracle that he survived the labor.

After Robert's vacation, he returned to the task of writing, having replenished his mental reservoir. He had a character in mind, someone with a storied past, like the legendary lawmen of Texas. A person who was born a common man, but rose up through his own force of will to become a king; the most basic version of the American Dream as seen through the rhetoric of the Populism movement. Robert had written a variation on this theme earlier in King Kull. His previous barbarian assumed kingship through his own hand, and so would this new character, Conan. But this time, Robert had a different setting in mind for his stories: a hazy period of history lost to the scholarship of mankind, wherein he could set Conan's adventures. Suddenly, ideas and stories were suggesting themselves, various tales of Conan's exploits at certain times in his career. He traveled everywhere, and he did a little bit of everything. Unlike in his previous Crusades stories, Robert would recount the incidents that made up an adventurer's life rather than allude to them in a single story. All Robert needed was a beginning. And so, like any good commercial artist, he took a shortcut.

One of the unsold Kull stories in Robert's pile of rejections was a bombastic piece of work called "By This Axe I Rule!" and it's one of the best Kull stories for sheer power and dynamic, lyrical writing. The story makes a strong declaration of character, and is also a fantastic display of violence. The King's attempt to hold off a dozen armed assassins in his bedchambers is a four-page-long fight scene of grim intensity. Robert went back through the unsold story, changing character names to better fit in his new setting. He took out the romantic subplot of Kull trying to marry a noble and a slave (only to be refuted by the laws of the land), and inserted a supernatural element tied to (King) Conan's destiny. The retitled "The Phoenix on the Sword" shows the contemplative side of Conan, with the bulk of his career behind him. These kinds of themes ran the gamut of the Kull series, but now Robert was only interested in detailing a few King Conan stories; how Conan got to the throne was far more interesting to him.

The next story Robert wrote from scratch, going all the way back to one of Conan's earliest adventures. Patrice Louinet correctly surmised that "The Frost-Giant's Daughter" borrowed heavily on Greek mythology for the plot of the story, with the roles of Apollo and Daphne reversed. Conan, the last of a raiding party of Aesir, is lured deep into the ice and snow by an alluring goddess. Thus ensorcelled, Conan is confronted by two giants, whom the woman calls her brothers. Heroically, the battered and weakened Conan slays them, and is about to ravish the goddess when she is saved by divine intervention. The Aesir find Conan, unconscious, in the snow, and bring him to. He tells his tale, and the men are slow to believe it, until Conan opens his clenched fist and finds "a wisp of gossamer that was never spun by human distaff."

Robert quickly started on the next Conan story, "The God in the Bowl," and it would take three tries to get it right. A still-young Conan is in the big city, operating as a poor thief. When he is found over the body of a dead guard and with a bauble missing from the local museum, the city watch is summoned. What follows is light on action and heavy on conversation as the local authorities attempt to figure out what happened. Only at the end, after blame has been assigned and reassigned, does Conan find and dispatch the true culprit—a malevolent serpent, worshipped by followers of Set.

Robert had just enough of a handle on the new world to draft a long essay, entitled "The Hyborian Age." This is the fundamental document of the Conan series, and it makes concrete Robert's ideas about the fictional world in which he was working. Instead of writing his fantastic stories into history (and thus having to fact-check his work), Robert took a page out of Lovecraft's book and concocted a kind of hoax or, more precisely, a tall tale. This epoch, the Hyborian Age, was a forgotten chapter in our own real history. Robert's essay traces the developments of the major races (we would now call them cultures) of this distant age, traipsing across a map that closely resembles Europe, Africa, and Asia. "The Hyborian Age" postulated that these groups of people, running around over 12,000 years ago, were once the dominant cultures. They were now mostly forgotten, only hinted at in the current culture, through myths and stories, swept aside by—wait for it—the barbarians who eventually overtook them.

Robert, in creating his mythical Hyborian Age, was trying to add folklore to the real world; it was the tall tale tradition at its most elemental. The Hyborian Age, and indeed all of Robert's stories in his darkly fantastic milieu, were intentionally written to be the stories from which our legends have sprung up. Robert knew that there wasn't a basis for most of the legends and lore that he so enjoyed, so he created it from whole cloth. Consider this passage from Robert to Lovecraft, early in their correspondence, in October 1930:

> The legends you cite are extremely interesting, especially the one about the rock which bleeds in the light of the moon. That is a particularly fantastic touch, so strangely fantastic that it must have some basis of fact, though doubtless the fact is far removed in substance from the details of the myth. It seems to me that the more wildly fantastic a tale is, the more likelihood there is for its being grounded in reality one way or another. The average human is so unimaginative that the highest flights of fantasy are beyond his power to create out of nothing.

The "wildly fantastic" Conan tales, then, are the impetus for the projected myths and legends of the culture that came after the Hyborian Age was subsumed by the barbarians. The entire Conan series is a metaphor for this worldview. Robert never draws any attention to the fact, but there is a point in Conan's career where he goes from being a nobody to being a character that more people have heard stories of than not. And of course, Conan's fame spreads even further, the deeds becoming more grandiose in the retelling, as he becomes the king of Aquilonia.

There's no way of knowing how far Robert intended to string his made-up history. He never tried to pass "The Hyborian Age" off as anything other than the background for his Conan stories. Nevertheless, that Robert delved into mythmaking and, in the case of Conan, meta-mythmaking indicates that this was the most sophisticated writing he'd ever attempted. The first three stories, then, are the nucleus of the Conan series. Viewed through the filter of the Hyborian Age, Conan becomes a mythic figure all his own. The intentionally haphazard presentation of the stories echoes the earlier Steve Costigan quirk of being told tales out of sequence, ostensibly while swapping yarns with a fellow drinker or, in Robert's case, from a fellow scribe.

These early stories defined the character for Robert, as well as the types of stories he would choose to tell. "The Phoenix on the Sword" emphasized action and the supernatural, by now Robert's specialty. "The Frost-Giant's Daughter" was an intentional attempt at mythmaking with a supernatural solution. "The God in the Bowl" picked up the threads of Robert's specific axe to grind: the conflict between the barbarians and civilization or, more appropriately, the frontier. By including ghosts in the first story, divine intervention in the second, and strange supernatural deities in all of these stories, Robert further anchored them to the needs of *Weird Tales*.

Undoubtedly excited by his new series, Robert bundled the first three stories off and sent them to Farnsworth Wright. *Weird Tales* had become his proving ground for new ideas; thanks to Wright's lack of editorial structure, Robert was allowed to experiment with stories that wouldn't have otherwise found a home. Wright knew Robert's work, too, and in good faith bought many stories from Robert that the author couldn't place in other markets.

When Robert got the reply from Wright, it wasn't good news. Wright liked "The Phoenix on the Sword," but wanted Robert to make some changes to the manuscript. He passed on "The Frost-Giant's Daughter," telling Robert plainly that he did not care much for it. This was certainly not the first time that Wright had rejected Robert's stories. Several of Robert's characters only have two or three stories finished, either because Robert grew bored with his creations, or because what he'd written had failed to sell.

Thankfully, Robert was too engrossed in the creation of the Hyborian Age and the further tales of Conan to stop writing. Now that he had some feedback, Robert was able to move some of his invented history into the backstory of "The Phoenix on the Sword," dropping broad strokes of color to help fill in the details of his world. His next story, "The Tower of the Elephant," was eagerly bought by Wright, as it had all of the ingredients that made Conan so memorable: supernatural happenings, swashbuckling action, and culture clash, with a dollop of human greed and cruelty for good measure.

"The Tower of the Elephant" works so well because of the surprising turn that takes place in the story. What starts out as a simple heist becomes a tale of retribution and mercy, leaving the young Conan to ponder the size of his worldview. The business surrounding the act of mercy as well as how Yag Kosha achieves vengeance is terrifically strange stuff, the kind of imagery that stays with the reader.

One of the other early Conan rejections, "The God in the Bowl," is considered controversial because it lacks the breakneck pace and taut action sequences of some of the more notorious Conan stories, but it's nevertheless a key story in the development of Conan as a character. Specifically, Robert intended the story to be Conan's introduction to Civilization, or the "vandals parading under the cloak of law." The city guards are crooked, everyone's on the take, and Conan is the only honorable, if not honest, man in the room. Often compared with some of the Continental Op stories of Dashiell Hammett, "The God in the Bowl" does carry those hard-boiled elements in one hand, but it strives to point out that Conan is far more decent a person than the rest of the civilized men who sit in judgment of his abject barbarism.

Equally as memorable was the sixth Conan story, "Queen of the Black Coast." Robert wrote the story in August 1932, before any of the Conan stories had seen print. By that time, he had invested considerable time and energy in his burgeoning series, and this was his longest and most complicated Conan story to date. Conan fights his way out of a civilized port of call and onto a pirate ship, captained by Belit, the aforementioned Queen of the Black Coast. A pirate, she is fierce, feisty, and passionate, and, not surprisingly, the perfect complement to Conan.

"Queen of the Black Coast" is a transitional story for Conan, both in theme and in scale. Conan starts the story as a brigand on the run from the local constabulary and ends up the first mate of a pirate ship. He also gains and loses Belit, herself easily as fascinating a character as Conan. That Robert chose to take her away from Conan was a mark of his growing maturity in creating memorable fiction that contained relevant themes. Robert had control of the series now, and there was nothing he couldn't or wouldn't do with his world. Moreover, Robert was really in control of his character, so much so that he was able to insert some of Conan's philosophy into one of the conversations between him and Belit:

> Let the teachers and priests and philosophers brood over the questions of reality and illusion. I know this: if life is illusion, then I am no less an illusion, and being thus, the illusion is real to me. I live, I burn with life, I love, I slay, and I am content.

Robert went on a tear, writing several more Conan stories—nine of them were written before "The Phoenix on the Sword" first appeared in the December 1932 issue of *Weird Tales*. Robert took a break from Conan to let the buildup of stories see print (and thus generate money). He returned to the series in mid-1933, refocusing his vision of the character. This middle period is defined by a variety of "by the numbers" Conan stories, wherein Conan ends up rescuing some damsel from amid some ruins and being menaced by some overgrown monster. If these middling stories helped contribute to the pop culture *zeitgeist* of Conan, it's the latter Conan stories that carry the most intellectual punch; stories like "The People of the Black Circle" and "Hour of the Dragon," Robert's attempt at a full-length novel, are particularly fine. But nothing can hold a candle to "Beyond the Black

River."

The story was written at the end of the series, when Robert was ready to branch out in a different direction. He decided to do away with what had become something of a cliché in his Conan stories—the setting. Gone were the crumbling ruins and slave girls clad in silk. Instead, Robert relocated Conan to the frontier, literally.

In "Beyond the Black River," Aquilonia, the symbol of civilized power in Howard's Hyborian Age, is expanding its territory into the last patch of untamed wilderness, bordered by two rivers, Black River and Thunder River. The land is peopled by the Picts, painted savages who are also fierce warriors. Throughout the story, the reader walks the knife-edge between the settlers and soldiers in the log fort and the united Pict tribes bent on wiping them out as the settlers encroach on the Pict's lands.

The allusion to the plight of the early Texan settlers couldn't be more obvious, particularly when considering this letter written to H.P. Lovecraft in August 1931:

> A student of early Texas history is struck by the fact that some of the most savage battles with the Indians were fought in the territory between the Brazos and Trinity rivers. A look at the country makes one realize why this was so. After leaving the thickly timbered littoral of East Texas, the westward sweeping pioneers drove the red men across the treeless rolling expanse now called the Fort Worth prairie, with comparative ease. But beyond the Trinity a new kind of country was encountered—bare, rugged hills, thickly timbered valleys, rocky soil that yielded scanty harvest, and was scantily watered. Here the Indians turned ferociously at bay and among those wild bare hills many a desperate war was fought out to a red finish. It took nearly forty years to win that country, and late into the [18]70's it was the scene of swift and bloody raids and forays—leaving their reservations above Red River, and riding like fiends the Comanches would strike the cross-timber hills within twenty-four hours…. Some times they won, and outracing the avengers, splashed across Red River and gained their tipis, where the fires blazed, the drums boomed and the painted, feathered warriors leaped in grotesque dances celebrating their gains in horses and scalps….

This, in essence, is the plot and conflict of "Beyond the Black River," with the titular river disguising the Brazos River, and Thunder River serving as the Trinity. At the story's conclusion, the Picts have won, and although Conan has saved the lives of the settlers, many soldiers have been slaughtered, including the point-of-view character, Balthus. One of the remaining woodsmen asks Conan if Aquilonia will rebuild the decimated fort, and Conan says that "the frontier has been pushed back. Thunder River will be the new border."

After a somber moment, the woodsman tells Conan, "Barbarism is the natural state of mankind. Civilization is unnatural. It is a whim of circumstance. And barbarism must always ultimately triumph."

Texas lent itself well to the creation of the Hyborian Age. From the mist-shrouded view in Fredericksburg, Texas that gave Robert the inspiration for the poem "Cimmeria," to the set pieces for Conan stories, the geography and character of Texas is undeniably present in the Conan stories. Giant snakes abound in Conan's world, much like humongous rattlesnakes roam the landscape of Texas tall tale tellers' imaginations. The cities in the Hyborian Age are of two qualities—wild, lawless places that clearly draw from the pictures of boomtowns, or rich, cosmopolitan melting pots not unlike the exotic blending in places like stately yet exciting San Antonio. Then comes the famous explanation of Robert's character, written to Clark Ashton Smith in July 1935:

> It may sound fantastic to link the term "realism" with Conan; but as a matter of fact—his supernatural adventures aside—he is the most realistic character I ever evolved. He is simply a combination of a number of men I have known, and I think that's why he seemed to step full-grown into my consciousness when I wrote the first yarn of the series. Some mechanism in my sub-consciousness took the dominant characteristics of various prize-fighters, gunmen, bootleggers, oil field bullies, gamblers, and honest workmen I have come in contact with, and combining them all, produced the amalgamation I call Conan the Cimmerian.

Interestingly, as good as that statement above was, Robert refuted it altogether in a different place. When discussing writing with his girlfriend, Novalyne Price, Robert supplied the following advice:

> [I]f somebody asks you where you get your characters... and they're sure to do that... you always say, 'He's a combination of a lot of people I have known.' That way, if your character is a damn fool, nobody will want to identify with him.... To tell the truth, I don't know how a man gets a character for a story, anymore than I know how he falls in love. I don't know if his characters spring full-blown from his head, or if he sees a man walking down the street and recognizes him instantly....
> I doubt any writer knows for sure where his characters come from.

Farnsworth Wright must have sensed that he had a tiger by the tail. As soon as the Conan stories hit the newsstands, fan reaction was overwhelmingly enthusiastic. Robert's Conan stories regularly took top honors in the monthly readers' polls. Fan mail ran in "The Eyrie," the *Weird Tales* letter column, gushing praise Robert's "he-man," or stridently denouncing Conan in favor of Kull or Solomon Kane. Love him or hate him, everyone reading *Weird Tales* was reading Conan.

In the end, Robert sold only seventeen Conan stories in four years. While the number itself isn't particularly impressive, many of the stories were novella length, with one novel as well. Including the stories that Robert didn't sell in his lifetime, only twenty-three Conan stories exist, along with a number of drafts, fragments, and notated ideas. It doesn't seem like much to leave as a literary legacy, but the content of the Conan stories is rich in metaphor, and has been dissected *ad nauseum* by critics and scholars. The sheer amount of discussion alone should prove the stories' merits as serious literature. But what kind of literature was it?

Robert went into unexplored territory when he started working on Conan. Nothing like Conan had ever been crafted in the pulps before, at least not by anyone other than Robert. The tone was hard-boiled (even taking into account Robert's usual poetical economy), dark, and realistic in feel. This didn't always apply to content, of course, and that is part of what makes the stories so compelling and timeless. The Hyborian Age is rife with monsters of all shapes and sizes, not to mention Cthuloid menaces and sorcerers. But Robert's Conan stories were always about more than just the plot points of Barbarian-Meets-Girl, Barbarian-Rescues-Girl-From-Wizard, Barbarian-Kills-Wizard. The realism came from the politics inherent in Conan's situation from story to story. Always the impetus, if not the focus, Conan keeps his own moral compass that allows readers to see things inevitably from Conan's (and by extension, Robert's) point of view. Through Conan, Robert was able to comment openly on aspects of civilization, the law, politicians, and personal honor. The episodic nature of the stories, along with Conan's many career changes, meant that Robert refocused his critical eye often, but rarely from the other side of the debate. Conan is always the agent of change, alone, keeping his own counsel—sometimes the villain, sometimes the hero, but always right by virtue of his success and continued existence. Conan, then, is much closer to the American western tradition than to epic fantasy.

Robert had a good idea of what was selling, and he tailored the Conan stories to fit the market. Wright, too, knew that a little sex couldn't hurt the sales. Many of the stories written by the popular writers of *Weird Tales* featured scantily clad damsels (never just women) in distress, the most egregious employer of whom was Seabury Quinn, with his occult detective, Jules de Grandin. Robert, then, went where the sales were, and Conan began rescuing the damsel *du jour* in each story, albeit with much grumbling and grousing. Early on in the Conan series, Robert threw the bewitching Belit into the mix, only to take her away at the end of the story. Not until the appearance of Yasmina in "The People of the Black Circle" and, later, Valeria in "Red Nails" do some of Robert's more well-rounded and interesting portrayals of women come to light.

Robert ended his Conan series with "Red Nails," easily one of the best stories in the canon, and Robert's final word on the corruption of civilization. He wrote to Clark Ashton Smith in June 1935:

> The last yarn I sold to Weird Tales—and it may be the last fantasy I'll ever write—was a three-part Conan serial which was the bloodiest and most sexy weird story I ever wrote. I have been dissatisfied with my handling of decaying races in stories, for the reason that degeneracy is so prevalent in such races that even in fiction it can not be ignored as a motive and as a fact if the fiction is to have any claim to realism. I have ignored it in other stories, as one of the taboos, but I did not ignore it in this story. Too much raw meat maybe, but I merely portrayed what I honestly believe would be the reactions of certain types of people in the situations on which the plot of the story hung.

There are two reasons why Robert turned away from Conan. The first reason may have been an allusion to the quote above; Robert had said everything he was trying to say with Conan. There's nothing to suggest that he would have come back to Conan. In fact, everything points to Robert creating a new character, should he have returned to fantasy. Seldom did Robert go back to a character that he had already written about.

The second reason was an economic decision, as this letter to Farnsworth Wright from May 1935 illustrates:

> I always hate to write a letter like this, but dire necessity forces me. It is, in short, an urgent plea for money. It is nothing new for me to need money, but the present circumstances are different from those in which I generally found myself in the past.
>
> My expenses for the past months have been great. My mother was forced to have her gall bladder removed, a very serious operation, especially for a woman of her age and state of health. She has been almost an invalid for years. She was in a hospital at Temple for a month, during which time I stayed with her, and was not able to do any writing at all during that time.... Whether my mother ever recovers or not possibly depends on the kind of care and attention I am able to give her, and that in turn depends on the money I am able to earn.
>
> And that brings to me to the matter at hand. For some time now I have been receiving a check regularly each month from Weird Tales—half checks, it is true, but by practicing the most rigid economy I have managed to keep my head above the water; that I was able to do so was largely because of, not the size but the regularity of the checks. I came to depend upon them and to expect them, as I felt justified in so doing.
> ...
> I do not feel that my request is unreasonable. As you know, it has been six months since "The People of the Black Circle" (the story the check for which is now due me) appeared in Weird Tales. Weird Tales owes me over eight hundred dollars

for stories already published and supposed to be paid for on publication—enough to pay all my debts and get me back on my feet again if I could receive it all at once. Perhaps this is impossible. I have no wish to be unreasonable; I know times are hard to everybody. But I don't believe I am being unreasonable in asking you to pay me a check each month until the accounts are squared. Honestly, at the rate we're going now, I'll be an old man before I get paid up! And my need for money now is urgent.

Of course, I sell to other magazines from time to time, but these sales are uncertain; to make markets regularly requires much time and effort, and for years most of my time and effort has been devoted to the stories I have written for Weird Tales. I may not—may never be a great writer, but no writer ever worked with more earnest sincerity than I have worked on the tales that have appeared in Weird Tales. I have grown up in the magazine, so to speak, and it is as much a part of my life as are my hands and arms. But to a poor man the money he makes is his life's blood, and of late when I write of Conan's adventures I have to struggle against the disheartening reflection that if the story is accepted, it may be years before I get paid for it.

Unfortunately, *Weird Tales* continued its trend of not paying Robert, and he soon turned to other paying markets. And who could blame him? But in terms of the kinds of stories he was writing, as well as what he was interested in writing, he was finally moving away from weird and fantastic allegories of the western frontier and trying to just write about the western frontier. Robert's other markets were slowly but surely catching on as his agent Otis Kline threw a barrage of submissions at a variety of editors, with middling results.

Nevertheless, if "Red Nails" was to be the last Robert E. Howard story that the readers of *Weird Tales* would ever see, that would have been a fantastic high note to go out on. Other events would soon transpire to prevent that from happening, though. But as far as Robert was concerned, he wasn't about to send *Weird Tales* another story until they paid him what he was owed.

Part 4

They walked, arm in arm, through the wide doors. The customers glanced up, did a double take, and then quickly buried their looks in their food and drink: Bob Howard had just walked in with a girl on his arm! He had on a suit! She was pretty! Good God All-Mighty.

Robert felt the room looking at him and he swept an angry stare over the patrons. *Sonsabitches*, he thought. Novalyne didn't notice or didn't care. She smiled up at him, and he felt the anger evaporate in the warmth of her company.

They sat down and ordered ice cream sodas and a side order of fries to split. Novalyne was talking about teaching school, and Robert smiled as he imagined the people around them straining to hear their conversation. He locked eyes with Dr. Dillard, a friend of his father's. The doctor nodded and smiled briefly before turning back to his wife. Robert did the same.

Robert listened to Novalyne speaking, but in the back of his mind, he felt detached and dreamlike, as if he were watching the date unfold through someone else's eyes. In the suit and hat, which sat strangely on his head, he didn't recognize himself. Neither did the townspeople. This wasn't ol' Crazy Bob Howard, stomping to and from the post office in a work shirt and cuffed trousers. Now, he looked respectable. More like a writer ought to look.

Robert glanced around quickly, to see if anyone was indeed looking at him and thinking that very thought. The last thing he needed was for Cross Plains to feel that he was a freak and also putting on airs. Novalyne leaned forward, talking eagerly about a book she had read, and he smiled again. They wouldn't understand. No one could possibly know how good it felt to have a conversation about literature in the middle of downtown Cross Plains and not have the other person staring blankly back at you. *Tonight*, Robert decided, *I'm going to kiss her.*

He kept one eye on the Dr Pepper clock on the wall over the counter. He had to get home by ten o'clock. Mother was sick. She needed her medicine. Everyone had stopped staring, now, back in their own worlds of crops, politics, and the weather. For the first time in a long, long, time, Robert felt like he was part of the community.

The hours of the evening stretched and shrank before him, leaving him dizzy and short of breath. This night would last forever. He would see to it.

The Cross Plains High School Faculty, 1935. Superintendent Nat Williams can be seen at the far right in the dark suit. Not pictured amid these pillars of the community: Novalyne Price (photo courtesy Margaret McNeel).

NOVALYNE

> Some people might think that Bob is just loafing around and not working at anything at all. But that's not true. His mind is hard at work. Although he doesn't get too far from home, he drives around over the country, thinking of stories, talking them out loud to himself. He'll stop the car on some little hill, get out and walk around, listening to the wind blowing across the prairies. He says that on the wind he hears the tuneless little whistles the cowboys made as they rode, stretching themselves now and then, throwing a leg over the saddle horn to ride sideways to relieve the strain, being almost unseated when the horse shied at a prairie-dog or a rattle snake. These are the things he wants to write about… someday.
> **Novalyne Price Ellis,** *One Who Walked Alone*

In the spring of 1934, Robert got a visit from a fellow pulp writer, E. Hoffmann Price, and his wife, Wanda. They pair were driving from Oklahoma to California and decided to take a five-hundred-mile detour to spend a couple of days in Cross Plains. Price was a writer of adventure and western stories, just getting started at the time. His career is not so distinguished as his list of friends and intimates; for years, he dined out on his reputation as "the only man to shake both Robert E. Howard's and H.P. Lovecraft's hands." Price and Robert had been corresponding for several years, but they had never met face-to-face before then.

Price transcribed his first meeting with Robert several times over the years, never changing the plot, and only adding details as the events moved further away from him. In his final recounting of the story, in the memoir "Book of the Dead," Price let a few of the more telling observations slip out.

Price and his wife were greeted at the Howard house by Isaac and Hester. Wanda was made comfortable by Hester, and Price was grilled for hours by Isaac regarding the business of the pulp industry: how business was done, pay rates, the timeliness of checks, and so forth. Price, exhausted by hours at the wheel, kept up as best as he could.

The next morning, Robert greeted his visitors, as he had returned home the previous night after they were already asleep. Price's description of Robert matches up with everyone else's: a big man, broad and tall, but with a round, gentle face and a soft, deep, pleasant voice and a magnetic presence. Price spent the rest of his visit with Robert trying to reconcile his internal image of Robert, culled from Conan and Solomon Kane, with the real man whose company he shared.

Price dutifully notes two "idiosyncrasies" in Robert's speech: he pronounced "wound," meaning an injury, so that it rhymed with the word "hound," and he said "sword" with the "w" sound intact. While the word "wound" may have indeed been something he picked up at an early age as a precocious reader, the sword with a "w" sound was not peculiar to Robert, but rather to many West Texans. West Texans also "warsh" their clothes. It's just a quirk of the dialect, nothing more.

While Robert was taking Price to get a haircut, he said, "Ed, I am goddamn proud to have you come and see me."

Price, taken aback, said he thought it should be the other way around. Robert explained: "Nobody in Cross Plains thinks I amount to much. So I am proud to show these sons of bitches that a successful writer drove a thousand miles to hell and gone out of his way to see me."

Exaggerations notwithstanding, it's worth noting that by this time, Robert had been out of public circulation for about five years. He kept mostly to himself, and more and more took care of his mother when his father wasn't around. That was the accepted arrangement and no one said anything about it, at least not to the family's face. After the above exchange, Price dutifully noted:

> This left me gaping and puzzled. Considering the readership he reached, acceptance in what was just another of many nondescript Texas towns was no great matter. Furthermore, the man rated more than he seemed to realize. There were friendly greetings all along the way to the barber shop....

Easier said than done, of course. Robert did care about acceptance; otherwise, why strike so defensive a pose? Price didn't realize that in small Texas towns, you have no choice but to try to get along with everyone. It didn't do for someone to anger the grocery store clerk, or hack off the guy running the newspaper. Doing so limited what one could get, and who one could socialize with on a daily basis. Robert maintained cordial relations with the townspeople; everyone recalls him being very polite and mild-mannered, unless he was talking about politics or aggravated over some slight, perceived or otherwise. But the conduit of information ran both ways; Robert knew if anyone said anything about him. Gossip is always good currency in small towns. Cross Plains, like so many other places, was rich with it.

Price's second great story occurred the next day, when Robert was helping Price get some information on oil drilling rigs for a story he was working on. After the interview, Robert conferred with Price: "Did he tell you everything you wanted to know? Did he cut you off short? If he did, I'll go back and give him hell—none of these bastards can snub my friends and get away with it!"

Of course, Price found this reaction very odd. It's very probable that

Price had no idea how much Robert hated the oil fields, the oil business, and the oilmen who still lingered in town. Otherwise, he would have felt supremely grateful that Robert would walk into his own personal lion's den for him and arrange an interview. It was the proximity to his ever-hated source of irritation that prompted Robert's next question to Price: "Ed, have you got any enemies?"

Price wrote that he told Robert that he had none, much to Robert's puzzlement. When he realized that Robert didn't believe him, Price told a story about a bully that he had once vanquished with a pickax handle. Price then wrote, "Bob felt a lot better after learning that his initial disbelief had been caused by a semantic breakdown."

Back home, the two friends talked shop in Robert's room while the women talked in the parlor. Price praised the western stories—meaning the Breckinridge Elkins funny westerns—at length, citing the strong characterization and convincing dialogue. Robert replied, "That's the way these ignorant bastards out in this part of the country just naturally think and talk and act. They don't know any other way, and I don't, either."

Their conversation carried them well into the evening. When the Prices reconvened, Wanda mentioned that a phone call had interrupted her chat with Hester, who had answered the phone, called a woman by her first name, and then said Robert was out and that she didn't know when he'd be back. This had occurred at the same time that Robert and Price were discussing pulp writing in Robert's room.

The Prices stayed another day before heading out to California. They came back through in 1935 for another visit, though without the drama and theatrics of their first encounter. Price came away with a picture of Robert that he peddled for years: "Bob lived in a dream world peopled by enemies, and by peers and other folks who downgraded him." Price wrote to L. Sprague de Camp in 1977, "Last time I saw Mrs. Howard was October 1935. She seemed entirely OK, normal. The sweet, deadly mother, bitching up Robert's dates, no doubt."

Price never learned who was calling Robert on that day in 1934, but the behavior of Hester then was identical to the treatment she handed out to another young woman, one who would not be put off by such answers. Her name was Novalyne Price.

Tevis Clyde Smith first met Novalyne Price in high school in Brownwood, around 1921. They became friends in the seventh grade, and went through high school and college together, with the exception that Clyde Smith went to Daniel Baker College every year, and Novalyne had to go every other year, teaching in between to earn her tuition money. She dated Smith on and off from 1929 to 1932, until he suddenly disappeared to get married to another woman. Initially hurt, Novalyne soon patched things up with Smith and they resumed their friendship. To Novalyne, the reason was simple: Clyde Smith was a fellow artist, a writer, and one of the few people with whom she could discuss literature and poetry. Novalyne wanted to write fiction, too, and she listened long and often to Clyde Smith singing the praises of his best friend, Bob Howard, the pulp writer.

Novalyne was slim and vivacious, dark-haired and dark-skinned, with smiling eyes and a sense of style. She carried much more personality in her girlish frame than her nice clothes and good manners suggested. Novalyne was a lady, but she was also a Texas lady, reared by a pair of strong, independent women, her mother and her grandmother. Novalyne was passionate, intelligent, quick-witted, and had a mouth like a merchant marine when she was angry. She didn't like anyone telling her what she could or could not do, either. In many ways, she was the best thing that ever happened to Robert E. Howard.

Robert bought his first car, a used green Chevy, in 1932. He paid cash for it, pulling the wad of bills from his pocket, giving the Fort Worth salesman something to tell his buddies that night. On the way back home to Cross Plains, Robert took the wheel and learned how to drive. Now he had his own transportation.

In addition to some much-needed freedom, Robert paradoxically assumed the responsibility of taking his mother to various hospitals and clinics for the rest of her life. In the spring of 1933, Robert took his mother to the clinic in Brownwood, and also stopped in to visit Clyde Smith. While Hester was being worked on at the hospital, Smith took Robert out driving. They stopped off at the Price farm and caught Novalyne studying for her upcoming classes. Smith cockily asked Novalyne if she still wanted to meet Robert. She enthusiastically said yes.

Novalyne was an obsessive journal writer, and she kept meticulous records of her thoughts, feelings, and major events in her life during this time period. Her diaries formed the vast bulk of her memoir, *One Who Walked Alone*, chronicling her friendship with Robert E. Howard. Her book is without a doubt the best picture we have of Robert at the end of his life.

She walked out to the car, and Robert got out to meet her. Novalyne recalled:

> This man was a writer! Him? It was unbelievable. He was not dressed as I thought a writer should dress. His cap was pulled down low on his forehead. He had on a dingy white shirt and some loose-fitting brown pants that only came to his ankles and the top of his high-buttoned shoes. He took off his cap and I saw that his hair was dark brown, short, almost clipped. He ran his hand over his head.... Bob's a big man. Not as tall as Clyde, but at least six feet tall. He looks so much larger than Clyde. He must weigh two hundred pounds. Maybe more.

> We were beside the car now, and I was looking into his eyes and trying to read the expression in them. How do you describe a man's eyes? They were blue. Or gray. Deep. Shadowy. I couldn't tell from their expression whether he was happy or unhappy. He must be terribly shy, I thought. His eyes are so uncertain... filled with questions. I'll always remember his eyes and this meeting.

That day, the trio drove around Brownwood, and Robert saw for the first time a woman who had the same kinds of interests as he and Smith. Novalyne was quick-witted, well-read, and most of all, reverentially respectful of Robert's chosen profession. She, too, understood what it took to sit down for hours, sweating over sentences and characters, plots and dialogue. The day ended uneventfully: Smith and Robert dropped Novalyne off at her house, they shook hands, and that was that.

Except that Novalyne never forgot Bob Howard, the writer from Cross Plains. In the fall of 1934, her cousin Enid Gwathmey, who was head of the English department at Cross Plains High School, recommended the newly graduated Novalyne to the faculty. In the midst of the Depression, the job was a godsend, and Novalyne worked herself sick, literally, to impress her superiors.

Novalyne took a room at the Hemphill's boarding house, all the while thinking about Robert, about becoming a better writer, and about picking up where the two of them had left off. Of course, she wanted to teach, as well, and she was assigned a full schedule of duties. She had a paying job, in her chosen profession, not too far away from her mother and grandmother, and she had a few friends and cousins in Cross Plains. It was the ideal setup.

Novalyne's high spirits wilted under the oppressive sunshine of the Cross Plains school board. During her first faculty meeting, the school board superintendent, Nat Williams, outlined what was expected of the Cross Plains school system faculty: There was to be no smoking, no drinking, no dancing, no Sunday picture shows, or playing bridge, by any of the teachers. Furthermore, they were expected to stay in town on the weekends instead of going home, and they had to attend church regularly. Novalyne recalled:

> I made an inarticulate gurgle in my throat. These rules and regulations were as strict on the teachers as they were on the students! I got control of myself and wondered why I had thought it might be different here in Cross Plains. Because this town harbored a free spirit—a writer—did I imagine it different from other Texas towns I knew about? The same rules and regulations applied everywhere around here—perhaps even in Brownwood.

A few days later, Novalyne, still shell-shocked from the board of trustee's dictum, went with her cousin and her friends to the drugstore after school on a Wednesday. As the teachers settled in for gossip and refreshments, Isaac Howard came out from the back of the drugstore. He tipped his hat to the women and Novalyne asked her companions who the man was. "That's Dr. Howard," said Mrs. Smith. Novalyne asked her if she knew Bob Howard. "I know a Robert Howard," she said. The table grew quiet. Everyone was staring at Novalyne, unbelieving. Finally, one of the girls spoke up. "Well, I think he's kind of a freak."

"Yeah," said another. "I hear he's crazy."

Sensing that Robert was the underdog, Novalyne instantly jumped to his defense. Her comments fell on deaf ears. Finally, she left the table, marched back to the telephone, and called the Howard house.

Hester Howard answered the phone and seemed a little put out when a woman asked to speak to Robert. She told Novalyne that Robert wasn't home. Novalyne asked her to please tell Bob that Novalyne Price had called. Hester assured Novalyne that she would give him the message, and then she hung up. Novalyne rejoined her group at the table, pleased that she had made some effort to contact Robert, and to hell with what anyone else thought.

By the end of the week, Novalyne was beside herself. She'd left several messages for Robert, who was never home, according to his mother, and he hadn't returned any of her calls. Never mind the inappropriateness of a girl calling a boy; when he didn't reply to her inappropriate advances, well, that was just plain rude. When offered a chance to go on an evening joyride with the girls, Novalyne convinced her disapproving cousins, Enid and Jimmie Lou, to drive by the Howard house. "Take me by," Novalyne said. "I'm going to see him. I'll ask him a question about a story if it kills me."

Excited, nervous, and scared, Novalyne strode down the walk and onto the porch. She could hear the sound of a typewriter, and over that, someone talking loudly. Robert was writing and talking at the top of his voice as he typed. Novalyne knocked. After a long interval, Isaac Howard opened the door. "Yeah?" he barked.

Novalyne said, "I'd like to see Bob, please."

"Bob?"

The typing sounds stopped.

Novalyne, more confident, said, "Yes, I want to speak to Bob."

Isaac called out to Hester, "Mamma, there's somebody here to see Robert. She can't see him, can she?"

"Who is it?" asked Hester from the living room.

"I'm Novalyne Price," she called out.

"Well, Robert is busy," Hester said, but just then, Robert appeared over his father's shoulder.

"Hello," Robert smiled. "Come in. I want you to meet my folks."

The ice broken, at least with Isaac, Robert ushered Novalyne into the house. More awkward introductions followed, but Novalyne didn't care. Robert offered to take her home, and she gleefully shooed her cousins off. They talked in the Howards' living room until polite coughing from the other room convinced Robert to offer Novalyne that ride home. Robert went into the other room, explained his plan to his mother, and Novalyne heard Hester say, loudly and clearly, "That's all right, honey. You go right ahead. Forget about me if you can."

Novalyne did a slow burn while Robert escorted her out of the house. After they had left, Isaac turned to Hester and asked, "Mamma, are we going to lose our boy?"

Hester said simply, "No, don't worry about that. We're not going to lose him."

And with that declaration, the battle lines were drawn between Hester and Novalyne.

Robert drove Novalyne around, and they talked at length, both having been starved for intelligent conversation about art, literature, philosophy, and life. After depositing her on the front porch of the Hemphill house, Robert asked to see her again. She eagerly said yes. Tomorrow evening, then. It was a date.

That next day, Novalyne put on her best dress, a hat, and gloves, while her roommate and fellow schoolteacher, Ethel, said, "Oh, my, my," a lot. The doorbell rang. Novalyne got quiet. Mrs. Hemphill came to Novalyne's room to announce her visitor, and became flustered when she saw Novalyne. Walking down the hall, Novalyne understood the reaction; Robert was dressed more or less in his regular work clothes: a white shirt, cropped pants, high-button shoes, and his work cap, rolled up in his big fist.

"Well, I didn't know," Robert said, lamely.

Novalyne was furious, but she gamely shed a few of her accoutrements and accompanied Robert to the car. He apologized, explaining that he hadn't planned on them going to dinner or a picture show, but thought they'd just drive around and talk. Through sheer force of personality and a few well-placed compliments, Robert managed to recover from his gaffe and by the end of the date, the two were carrying on as if nothing had happened. He dropped her off without kissing her or making plans to see her again.

When Robert did ask her out again, it was for a Sunday afternoon movie in Brownwood. This crashed through several of the restrictions imposed on Novalyne by the Cross Plains school board, but she didn't care. She accepted, by return mail, having decided that she would date Robert Howard and that she didn't really care what anyone else thought about it, either.

That Sunday, Novalyne dressed for a picture show date and even as she idly wondered what Bob would be wearing, he showed up and knocked her socks off. Robert wore a dark brown suit, with a vest and tie, and a light brown fedora. He gallantly presented himself at the door and asked, "How's my best gal?"

That date was the beginning of their relationship in earnest. Robert and Novalyne were a couple through the rest of 1934 and into 1935. Robert took breaks from writing and even let some of his correspondence lapse in order to spend time with Novalyne. And why not? This was Robert's first and only girlfriend. He was twenty-eight at the time. To him, Novalyne was an intellectual equal, even though he tried many times to play the part of male chauvinist during their relationship. Novalyne thought often about being married to Robert. They joked about it on dates. They also bickered about politics, teased each other about their personality quirks, and poured their hearts out to one another about their professions.

It's easy to see how Robert could have been attracted to Novalyne. Certainly, she was pretty and intelligent, but her spirit was vital and alive, and not unlike some of Robert's stronger female characters. Just prior to their first meeting in 1933, Robert sold "The Shadow of the Vulture" in late March, a story that was written in late 1932. It's tempting to insinuate that Red Sonya was inspired by Novalyne, but it's more probable that if any character was a response to Robert's new, outspoken girlfriend, that character was Agnes de Chastillon, the Sword Woman.

No one quite knows when Robert wrote "Sword Woman"; it could have been as early as 1932, or as late as 1934. No records exist of any submissions Robert may have made, but he did send a copy of the manuscript to Catherine L. Moore, who cracked the pages of *Weird Tales* with her heroic female character, Jirel of Joiry, in January of 1935. Moore wrote back an enthusiastic letter, praising Robert for his forward thinking, and wondering if Robert had written any more of her adventures. Only two completed stories and a half-finished third still exist.

"Sword Woman" is as surprising as it is well-written. Robert kept a realistic historical setting for the story, moving the time period up into sixteenth-century France. Gone are large groups of mercenaries fighting for strips of land; instead, Robert wrote about a lone young woman with a will to live outside the confines of her station. Agnes escapes her own impending wedding by slaying the ogre of a man who was to marry her. This puts her on the run, defending her honor from every single man she encounters. Always with something to prove, she hacks and slays her way across the countryside until she finds a temporary peace riding alongside a brigand who more or less accepts her as an equal.

Part of what makes "Sword Woman" so compelling is the incendiary

dialogue that Agnes employs, as in the choice and telling excerpt:
> "Ever the man in men! Let a woman know her proper place: let her milk and spin and sew and bear children, not look beyond her threshold or the command of her lord and master! Bah! I spit on you! There is no man alive who can face me with weapons and live, and before I die, I'll prove it to the world. Women! Cows! Slaves! Whimpering, cringing serfs, crouching to blows, revenging themselves by—taking their own lives, as my sister urged me to do. Ha! You deny me a place among men? By God, I'll live as I please and die as God wills, but if I'm not fit to be a man's comrade, at least I'll be no man's mistress. So go yet to hell… and may the devil tear your heart!"

Agnes rebels completely against the massive social order that would keep her in her place. Her casting off of her womanhood (and by the story's end, she proclaims herself no longer a woman) is one of the most fascinating things about Robert E. Howard's writing; his more commercial endeavors were full of women, naïvely rendered, or at least filtered through polite Texas society, to make them more genteel and refined. Yet every so often (and usually with spectacular results), Robert would cast off that Southern Belle ideal and write of women who did the adventuresome work of men without complaint, usually while maintaining their elemental femininity. Wish fulfillment? Maybe on the surface, but when all of these beautiful and deadly creatures rage against their place, the message becomes more clearly delineated; Robert was writing about rebellion and about throwing out the rules of society to make the ideal life for oneself. In that sense, these protofeminist stories are practically autobiographical. It was no accident that "Sword Woman" was written from a first-person perspective.

Regardless of which came first, Novalyne or Dark Agnes, these two women had plenty in common. They were fiery and independent, and wanted to do things their way. They shared a physical description, as well. Novalyne could cuss a blue streak when she was angered. She was also fiercely loyal and did not shy away from a fight. Whether Robert realized it or not, Novalyne was an idealization of some of his more outspoken fictional characters.

Robert was an engaging boyfriend, thoughtful and considerate, if still a little unsure about himself; he had a jealous streak in him that was usually triggered by Novalyne mentioning a favorite student of hers, or Nat Williams, the handsome and affable superintendent. However, Robert was all charm and manners when he met Novalyne's mother and grandmother. "Mammy," as she was called, took an instant shine to Robert, and he listened intently to her stories of her childhood during the Civil War. Novalyne's mother took a more cool assessment of Robert, but thought he was, if nothing else, nice and pleasant.

Likewise, Robert held Novalyne spellbound, rocking in his seat and lunging against the steering wheel while he wove stories about local history, Genghis Khan, and all of his past lives as they drove pell-mell down the dusty highways that crisscrossed the countryside. Novalyne, too, gave as good as she got, reciting poetry from memory, talking at length about her own life experiences, and challenging Robert whenever he made broad sweeping generalizations about the corruption of civilization, his provincial racial attitudes, or his own self-worth and his standing in the community. When angered by something Robert said, she often gave vent to a torrent of salty language. Whenever he was on the receiving end of one of her diatribes, Robert always backed down. Both of them were quick to forgive, recognizing that they had too much in common to alienate one another.

Robert and Novalyne were extremely compatible in many ways, but they were worlds apart in others. Novalyne tried to get Robert to go to social functions with her, convinced that if he wore a suit and acted like he did when they were alone, the townspeople would see him in a different light. Robert dug in his heels and refused. He maintained that civilization was in complete decay and that "the maggots of corruption" were all around them. Novalyne felt that Robert emphasized his eccentricities in defiance of the town's attitude that he should get a "real job." She defended him often as her fellow faculty members laughed at him. Even as she ticked off Robert's good points to her friends and colleagues, she wondered if Robert couldn't try a little harder to fit in with the rest of the Cross Plains citizenry.

Robert and Novalyne considered marriage but, like star-crossed lovers, never at the same time. When Novalyne was ready, Robert wasn't. When Robert finally came around, Novalyne had moved on. But the largest obstacle in their relationship, the one that proved to be the most daunting, was Hester Howard. Many of Novalyne's journal entries grapple with the nature of Mrs. Howard's hold over her son. Novalyne suspected that Hester was playing up her illness to keep Robert close to home. She never understood why Robert, and not Isaac, was Hester's designated caregiver.

Hester actively tried to sabotage her son's relationship with this spirited young teacher. She intercepted phone calls, as she always did when Robert was pounding out a story, and frequently didn't deliver the message. Knowing of her son's interest in frontier history, she intimated that Novalyne was an Indian by virtue of her relatively dark complexion and hair. But these were small efforts that did little to discourage her son. Her preexisting hold on Robert and her own failing health were more than enough to bind Robert to the quiet dysfunction that was the Howard home. Novalyne was sure that Hester had convinced Robert that a wife would handicap him. "Woman puts chains on a man, and in time he'll hate her for it," Robert told her. Novalyne wondered if that statement were true so far as his mother was concerned.

Isaac Howard, on the surface, seemed to warm up to Novalyne. He took care of her when she caught the flu, and always stopped to shoot the breeze with her in the drugstore. He talked to Novalyne about Robert, telling her little stories, some of which were extremely upsetting to her. Novalyne always inquired about Mrs. Howard's health, and Isaac told her the truth, gruffly stating that she was holding her own or doing as well as could be expected.

By mid-1935, Robert received two close calls in a row. In the spring, he took his mother to Temple, Texas, for a gall bladder removal. Hester's poor health and the resulting complications stretched the stay out to a month's time. By Robert's own account, it was a harrowing and difficult procedure. It may have been the first time that he had had to contemplate the idea that his mother was terminally ill. Prior to the trip, Robert spent the day with Novalyne, and she did her best to cheer him up. Novalyne later wrote in her diary:

> He talked now of wanting to live and to come back again. See the Spring come again... see new life begin again. I couldn't understand it. This change was too fast for me. I listened confused, uncertain. He was going to take his mother to Temple for a serious operation. I realized that. Did he plan to leave her there and never come back?
>
> He began to thank me for all the time I'd given him. He said there were very few women whom he had known who let a man talk about his dreams and his work the way I did. He wanted me to know he thought I was a very unusual woman, and he appreciated knowing me. I began to feel nervous, for he sounded as if he'd never see me again!
>
> "Be sure to write me," I said, again hoping to change his mood. "Tell me how your mother gets along; how you're doing too. I'll be looking forward to having you back again."
>
> He sighed, waited a moment, and said very softly that the one bright spot he saw ahead of him was that he'd come back, for he wanted to see me again.

While Robert was in Temple with his mother, Novalyne set her sights on the upcoming one-act play competition in Breckenridge. She worked her students until late at night. Her own health dipped considerably, and she very nearly starved herself to death. When she began to throw up at the play competition, Nat Williams drove her to the hospital. Her normal weight was ninety-nine pounds, but when weighed at the hospital, she found that she weighed barely eighty-five. The doctors stabilized her via an overnight stay, and then Novalyne was driven back to Cross Plains, to a waiting Isaac Howard, along with Novalyne's mother. Dr. Howard took one look at her and admitted her to the hospital in Brownwood.

In the care of her family doctor, Dr. Daugherty, Novalyne spent over a week convalescing. During that time, Robert came home and was told of Novalyne's condition. He drove to Brownwood and asked to see her, but was turned away by the nurse, saying that Novalyne wasn't to have any visitors. This order, Novalyne later learned, came from Dr. Howard himself.

When Novalyne was strong enough to eat solid foods, Dr. Daugherty gave her a stern talking to. "What made you go and do a thing like that?" he demanded.

Novalyne tried to explain her grueling work schedule to Dr. Daugherty, but he brushed that all aside. "What about that young man you're going with—Dr. Howard's son, Robert? Are you in love with him? Are you trying to starve because of him?"

Novalyne told Dr. Daugherty that she was not in love with Robert. She said, "When a girl gets twenty-seven years old and isn't married, all the good men she meets are either married like Nat Williams, or they're jackasses like Bob Howard."

Dr. Daugherty explained that he was worried because he knew the Howard family personally. He liked Dr. Howard a lot, and had talked to Isaac about family problems, of which Robert seemed to be a big part. Then Dr. Daugherty said, "Has Robert ever said to you that he didn't want to live after his mother dies?"

Novalyne waved that thought off. She considered that it was just Robert blowing wind, nothing more. Dr. Daugherty spent some time explaining to Novalyne that he didn't like Robert, and didn't think much of Mrs. Howard, either. He strongly advised Novalyne to end the relationship. Part of his prescription for her health was to start looking elsewhere for a job, preferably out of state. Novalyne promised to look into attending college in Louisiana.

Novalyne went home to the Hemphill house on Sunday. She hadn't been in Cross Plains more than half an hour before she wanted to see Robert. "A thousand silly, romantic thoughts rushed happily over me as I started for the telephone. Bob and I were right for each other. I had lied to Mother and Dr. Daugherty when I said I didn't care for him. I had lied to myself. I loved Bob."

Robert raced over, and they drove around, happy to be in each other's company. Robert hovered over her, protectively, and Novalyne felt important and safe in his care. Despite their happy reunion, Robert was depressed. He was worried about his mother's health. He turned, suddenly, and looked at Novalyne and said, "You know, don't you, that as long as my mother needs me, I'm not free?"

Novalyne didn't reply. She changed the subject, but Robert kept returning to his parents. The two were talking about marriage, but they were also discussing Robert's relationship with his family. Robert said, "I suppose the truth is that as good a man as my father is, he doesn't always appreciate how helpful and good Mother has been to him. If he'd gone to a larger place like Brownwood, he might have been able to be at home more; then Mother and I wouldn't have been left alone so much at night."

It was not the conversation Novalyne wanted to have with Robert. She wanted, needed, to hear Robert say that he loved her. It wasn't going to happen. He dropped her off at the Hemphill house and they made plans to see each other on Friday, but as Robert drove away, Novalyne thought, "I hope the time comes, Bob, when you want me to say 'I love you' as much as I wanted you to say it to me today. But I'll never say it. I hope it hurts as much as I hurt now."

Shortly thereafter, Novalyne began to pull away from Robert. She buckled down and concentrated on finishing school. During one of her weekend trips to Brownwood, she bumped into Truett Vinson at the bookstore. They chatted briefly, no doubt touching bases regarding Clyde Smith and Robert, and then agreed to go out the next day. After all, Novalyne thought, it's not as if she were promised to anyone. Robert was forever mentioning that women tied men down, and that the road he walked, he walked alone.

As Novalyne's romance with Truett heated up, Robert became more amorous, as well. At the end of one date, Robert told Novalyne that there were moments now when he wished he could devote time to being just a common, everyday man of the town. He told her, "Some of the things you've said to me make me believe in myself as I've never believed before." Novalyne wrote:

> He said I had made him believe that it was possible to stand on the street corners and talk with other men about the rains and the crops, and all the ordinary things of life. Maybe talk with people the way Nat Williams does.
>
> He said he thought he might even, he laughed self-consciously, go back to church.
>
> ... I didn't say so, but I thought to myself what an irony it was that he would finally say what he had tonight... just after I'd had a date with Truett.

After school ended in late May, Novalyne headed back to Brownwood. She and Truett were still secretly seeing each other, and while Novalyne wanted desperately to come clean with Robert, she always chickened out at the last minute. Still, she dropped hints, and when Robert went on vacation with Truett in June of that year, he sent Novalyne a couple of postcards. After the men returned, Robert was much cooler toward Novalyne. If Truett didn't tell him while they were on the trip, Robert eventually figured it out all by himself.

Novalyne tried to maintain her friendship with Robert. He sent her a scathing letter in reply, accusing her and Truett of not playing fair with him. Novalyne hit the roof, and composed a go-to-hell letter in return. Her mother told her that, while she didn't really like Robert, and didn't feel that he was the man to marry her daughter, Novalyne shouldn't end the friendship. The letter Novalyne sent by way of reply was much more measured and even-tempered. Robert replied by sending her own letter back in a new envelope. Novalyne washed her hands of the whole thing.

However, thoughts of Robert kept intruding whenever Novalyne spent time with Truett. It's not surprising, since she and Truett talked about the same kinds of things that she and Robert had discussed, except that their thoughts and conclusions were more closely aligned. Still, Novalyne wondered about Robert and his writing.

In the middle of the summer, Robert wrote Novalyne to tell her he would drop by the house. He strode up wearing a large, drooping mustache. Novalyne was aghast. She hated it right away. Robert asked her to a movie, and out of pity, she said yes. After the show, Robert took her to the drugstore for a soda. He sat in the crowed dining area, dressed in his short pants, drooping mustache and all, and loudly rattled off the stories he'd sold in *Weird Tales*, *Action Stories*, and *Top-Notch*. He vividly reconstructed his last Conan story, "Red Nails," for Novalyne and the drugstore patrons.

Novalyne's reactions went from embarrassment, to anger, to pity, as she realized that Robert was bragging on himself, trying to appear carefree and unconcerned with everyone around him. She wrote:

> He didn't know how men and women acted in real life. He was "different" from other people. He was talented, and his mind ran to worlds created on paper. When he was young, he could have learned how to cope with ordinary life situations, but he had been more interested in books than in people.
>
> His mother? She had played a part in this—innocent or not. Had she understood his talent, his genius, or had she only understood his love for books? She knew how to encourage that. If he stayed home and read, he was not out somewhere away from her getting into trouble! She had felt safe to have him at home, reading. He had been safe. What a price he paid for safety!

Robert railed against the town in the confines of the car. It was an old argument; Robert accused Novalyne of caring too much what people thought. Novalyne agreed with him. He declared that he didn't give a goddamn what anyone thought of him. He'd made a living, not a great one, but he paid his bills and put food on his table. Novalyne added, "You've also made it clear that you don't give a damn about—about people."

Back at the Price home, Novalyne turned to Robert on the porch. "I cannot believe this night," she said. Then:

Without warning, he grabbed me in his arms and kissed me as I had never been kissed before by him or any other man. It had all the careless possessiveness of a barbarian who is here for one moment and is gone the next. It had something of the tenderness of a man's love for a woman.

When school started up again, Novalyne returned to Cross Plains to find that Robert had taken to wearing a black sombrero, a red bandana, and black vaquero pants. She bumped into him coming out of the post office and, mortified, she ran for Mrs. Smith's drugstore across the street. There she met Isaac Howard, coming out of the drugstore. "What is he trying to prove?" she asked.

"I don't know. I really don't know," said Isaac, shaking his head.

After that, whenever Robert wore his vaquero getup, Novalyne kept out of sight. If she couldn't avoid him, she pretended to be too busy to talk at that moment. Robert may have gotten the hint. He showed up one day, minus the sombrero and bandana, and asked if Novalyne wanted to ride around. Novalyne was still seeing Truett, but she was glad that Robert seemed to be all right with their friendship again. Robert was more interested in pushing her buttons than in proposing, and Novalyne was seeing another local, Pat Allen, off and on as well. As the small-town gossip kept the school teachers informed of their dates, so too did it keep Robert informed of any unusual happenings when Novalyne went with other men.

They saw each other irregularly through the Christmas holidays, but without the romantic fervor of before. As 1936 rolled around, Robert and Novalyne continued their strained relationship. In late February, Robert showed up after school outside the Hemphill house, wearing his brown suit. Novalyne got a premonition of impending disaster, but it was too late. Robert was in one of his "black moods." His mother had taken a turn for the worse. Things were bad at home. He tried over and over again to talk to Novalyne, who threw a barrage of banter and quips between them. When Robert explained that he was still acting as nurse to his mother, Novalyne challenged him. She said, "You could get a nurse who is trained to do the job better than you can. You've got the money. Your dad makes money, too. He certainly makes enough to take care of your living expenses, and you know it. You keep saving your money. For what? To take her away somewhere? Well, that's fine, but what about you? You've got to save yourself and keep working to pay for nurses to take care of her. My God, Bob, you're not required to give up your whole life for her, your writing and everything."

Robert grabbed her arm. He was raving. "What's work? A man can do any kind of work. Work is not worth a damn, unless you work for somebody you love. All my life I've loved and needed her. I'm losing her.

I know that. Damn it to hell, I know that. I want to live. You hear that? I want to live! I want a woman to love, a woman to share my life and believe in me, to want me and love me. Don't you know that? My God, my God. Can't you see that? I want to live and to love."

Robert's reply left Novalyne miserable and frightened. "Are you in love with Truett?" he asked. "I want to know. I've got to know. If it's Truett you love, say it. Say it, damn it."

Novalyne, half crying, said, "I don't love anybody. Not anybody at all." She told Robert that she had been accepted to Louisiana State University, and that she would be leaving in the summer to attend classes. She had made up her mind to teach. She knew she was good at it, and she wanted to be even better.

Robert slumped down in his seat. "You have a great cause. For life to be worth living, a man—a man or a woman—must have a great love or a great cause. I have neither."

Despite the drama of their relationship, Robert and Novalyne continued to drive around, talking and laughing, although Novalyne confessed that there were many things unsaid between them, and the strain was sometimes uncomfortable. Novalyne kept being cheerful, light, and playful in his company. Robert thought she was making fun of him. They managed a tender farewell when Novalyne went off to college in late May, but Novalyne unwittingly supplied a final slap to Robert's face the day she left town. Her mother, complaining about the amount of stuff to transport, noticed a large book among Novalyne's things. Novalyne explained that was Bob's book. Her mother tried to get Novalyne to return it, and they decided to leave it with Dr. Howard at his office as they were pulling out of town. Robert answered her with a short, cordial note stating that she needn't have returned the book; he wanted her to keep it. And that was the end of their relationship. Novalyne, though, was determined to keep in touch with Robert. She liked him too much, and wanted too much for them to stay on good terms. She vowed to write him as soon as she got settled into the dorms at LSU.

She never wrote to Robert again.

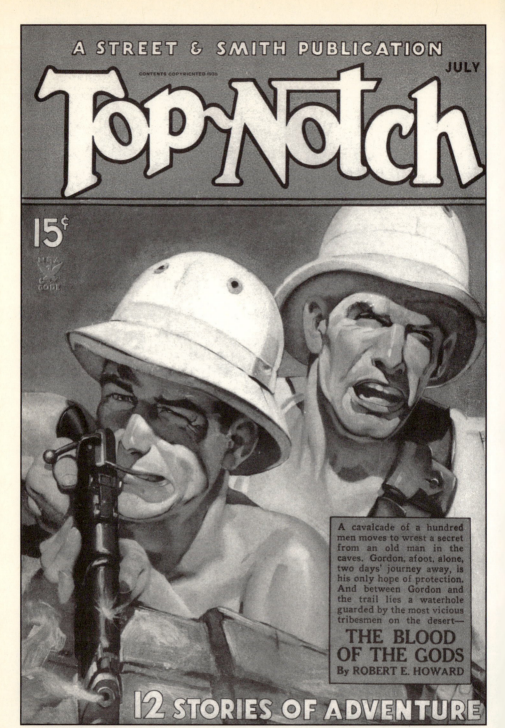

Top Notch magazine, dated July 1936. The cover painting isn't particularly indicative of Francis X. Gordon (a.k.a. "El Borak"), but the pulp was a better paying and better quality magazine than most (from the collection of Dennis McHaney).

Vultures and Grizzlies

> I'm seriously contemplating devoting all my time and efforts to western writing, abandoning all other forms of work entirely; the older I get the more my thoughts and interests are drawn back over the trails of the past; so much has been written; but there is so much that should be written.
> **Robert E. Howard to August Derleth, November 28, 1935**

Robert E. Howard's career began and ended with westerns. His first story, the marginal and juvenile "Bill Smalley and the Power of the Human Eye," was significant only in that Robert chose to make his first literary step a westward one. Throughout his career, Robert would return again and again to westerns and the Southwest as setting, with varied results. Only at the end of his career did he hit his stride both with funny westerns, in the case of Breckinridge Elkins, and with a small but important handful of serious westerns.

Robert tried several times to use Cross Plains and South Central Texas in his stories, but his early efforts were fairly uninspired. In addition to *Post Oaks and Sand Roughs*, Robert also wrote, but never sold, "Spanish Gold on Devil Horse" in 1928. Here we find one Mike Costigan, successful writer of stories and man-about-town, caught up in intrigue, mystery, and a lot of wish fulfillment in the town of Lost Plains. A hidden cache of Spanish treasure and mustachioed bandits crawling all over the disguised Caddo Peaks weren't enough to pull this story out of mediocrity. But it's what Robert did with his character, Mike Costigan, that's so interesting. Costigan is successful, well-liked, known by all in town, and, of course, throws a mean right jab. While it's nothing remarkable in the pulps, which published far worse fare in massive quantities every month, the character rings hollow coming out of Robert's metaphorical mouth. This Costigan is so obviously not a typical Robert E. Howard character that it's difficult to read the story without guffawing.

Yet despite the drawbacks, it's significant that Robert wrote a contemporary western story at a time when ten-gallon hats, six-shooters, and loyal horses ruled the roost. The use of six-shooters in "Spanish Gold on Devil Horse" may seem anachronistic in a story with boardinghouses and pickup trucks, but it is an accurate representation of life in West Texas towns, minus perhaps some of the melodrama. From the perspective of Robert as a regional writer, this was an important first step.

Robert tried other stories set in "Lost Plains" or, sometimes, "Lost Pines," and once, even "Lost Knob." Regardless of the name, the background is unmistakable. These stories are steeped in their environment and include characters that fought the Comanche and died in the Civil War. These characters tend to horses, drink too much and get in fights, and in all other ways, walk and talk like small-town Texans. In fictionalizing his surroundings, Robert borrowed a technique from H.P. Lovecraft, who turned Salem, Massachusetts into Arkham, and so forth. It's no coincidence that several of the Lost Plains stories are in the horror genre.

"Old Garfield's Heart" concerns a man who made a pact with an Indian God for long life, and how that pact is at last fulfilled. *Weird Tales* ran it in December 1933. "For the Love of Barbara Allen," based on the folk song of the same name, dealt with ghostly transference through the ages. It would go unpublished during Robert's lifetime.

Just as Robert fictionalized Cross Plains and Brownwood for his stories, he also drew from modern events. One of his best stories is "Wild Water," a modern western set in the middle of the most dramatic flood ever in Central Texas. The story is one of vengeance, and righting with bullets a wrong done with banking and paper. An old gunfighter, the last of his kind, avenges the wrongful persecution of his kin, only to find that there is a larger menace at work. A disgruntled farmer is threatening to blow up the newly built dam that displaced his family (with authorial asides as to the graft that occurred to build said dam) and flood the town, killing thousands of innocents. With a fantastic thunderstorm playing out around them, in what has to be the grimmest fight Howard ever wrote, the gunfighter pays for his own killing by saving the lives of the people in the town he hates—at a cost of his own life.

More amazing is that the flood Robert wrote about was an actual event in his lifetime. The city of Brownwood had been locked in a struggle with a group of developers attempting to transform the Pecan Bayou into Lake Brownwood, a manmade reservoir intended for recreation and farming, since 1924. The project would take nearly ten years of legal wrangling, court cases, and a generous amount of money thrown around on all sides, but the landowners were eventually paid a settlement and the dam was finally constructed. The average rainfall for the area was calculated and it was estimated that the lake would take two years to fill up. Never bet long odds on Texas weather. On Sunday, July 3, 1932, ferocious flash floods attacked the watershed area, filling both Pecan Bayou and Jim Ned Creek to capacity. The not-quite-completed dam held, and the flooding filled the lake up to 150,000 acre feet of water, over seven thousand acres, in six hours. This event became the set piece for "Wild Water," as this letter to Lovecraft indicates:

> Yesterday I spent most of the day in the flooded district south of here. In that flood, the worst ever experienced in Central West Texas, the devastation to crops and fields has been almost beyond belief.... Fences were torn up for miles and washed

clean out of sight, or left tangled among trees along the banks. I don't know how many cattle and horses were drowned. The most impressive sight, however, was the Brown County lake. I can not describe the sensations of seeing that gigantic body of water where for so many years I have been accustomed to seeing dry-creek beds, or semi-dry creeks, winding among arid post-oak ridges. It has changed the whole aspect of the countryside.... Where bridges and ranch-houses stood, water eighty feet deep ripples instead. It is so strange, seeing a big body of water in the midst of this drouth-haunted country of post-oak hills.... It is but the work of men, who stretched a dam between the hills, yet it seems like a miracle. And more so when one recollects that it literally filled itself over-night. 145 miles of shore-line—and one torrential rain filled and overflowed it. For days the flood-gates have been left wide open, and still all the rivers leading into the lakes are backed up-stream for miles. It is the greatest project ever put forward in this part of the country....

Just now there is a great deal of resentment among the farmers and stockmen who live up the rivers, who consider the dam the main reason for their ruin in the flood, though in reality much of the damage would have been done, dam nor not. But they should be paid for their fields along the rivers, for with the lake full, any kind of a rise will back the water up over these fields again. There is much hard feeling, and talk of guarding the dam against possible dynamiting. Though I hardly think anyone would be mad enough to do such a thing. The town of Brownwood lies directly below the dam, only ten miles away, and should the dam burst, the havoc wrought there could hardly be conceived.

Another of Robert's most memorable westerns was in reality a "weird western," published by *Weird Tales*, of course. After Robert's earlier false starts, it was easier for him to transition from one genre to the next by writing a story that combined the two genres. The best example of Robert's hybrid stories is "The Horror from the Mound." A West Texas rancher hears a tale of Spanish gold buried on his land from the Mexican sharecropper he rents to, and then man's base nature takes over. What he finds, of course, isn't gold, but the aforementioned horror in the form of a Spanish vampire. Lead and fists fly in the dispatching of the monster. "The Horror from the Mound" is a straightforward, ghoulish, action-filled romp that presupposes the splatterpunk movement and Stephen King by fifty years with its cheerful reconfiguring of more traditional monsters, unique setting, and gothic overtones. The readers of *Weird Tales* weren't ready for it; the story was panned in "The Eyrie." Years later, it informed the Weird West trend as one of the first stories ever written in the genre.

In the early 1930s, Robert tried, but failed, to sell several "straight" westerns to various markets. He touched up "Drums of the Sunset" and sent the story to Jack Byrne, who rejected it, saying, "we don't publish stories about Indians." Several of Robert's westerns seem corny, especially when compared to his other, more serious work. These anomalies may have been nothing more than Robert trying to intuitively interpret the formula for the western market at the time. While many of these efforts are full of action and technically well-executed, they are also undistinguished. Robert's serious westerns are entertaining, if not great exemplars of the genre, but only a few stand out as fine examples of his unconventional storytelling.

The best of the lot is, without a doubt, "The Vultures of Wahpeton," written in 1934. It took two years to find a home and, even then, suffered a most unusual publishing event.

Borrowing a theme from an earlier Kull story, "The Shadow Kingdom," Howard returns to a familiar theme of civilized and bureaucratic corruption—in this case, the officers of the law—and the moral man who stands among them to protect the innocent civilians. One of "Vultures'" famous scenes was inspired by a famous gunfight involving Hendry Brown and his efforts to tame the town of Caldwell, Kansas in the early 1880s. Howard wrote, in 1934:

> The way they generally trapped the deputy was to start a commotion in a saloon. Ordinarily, the deputy ran in and saw one drunk—apparently—standing in the center of the saloon and shooting at the ceiling, while a large gang looked on from the bar. When the deputy started to arrest the drunk, the lights suddenly went out, and when they were lit again, there was a deputy with several lead slugs through them. But Brown was wise....
>
> Well, that night in Caldwell, Brown entered the saloon with his long easy stride, unhurried, unruffled. He seemed to be watching the pseudo-drunk staggering about in the center of the saloon; in reality, he was watching the crowd, and the three desperados who crouched back among their fellows with their hands on their guns. Without warning and quick as a striking-rattler, he wheeled and his guns were out and roaring death before the slower-thinking outlaws realized that the new deputy knew their play.

While "Vultures" makes good use of gunfighter lore, it works better as an analogy for paranoia, intrigue, and bureaucratic corruption. The hero of "Vultures," Steve Corcoran, is outnumbered and alone, and doesn't know who to trust. Corcoran is hired to play sheriff by the villains, who think that he won't interfere with the plans and schemes of the gang. Corcoran doesn't like being played, and soon puts himself between the Vultures and the town. This deviation from the traditional western plot was radical at the time, but for Robert, it was just another story from his particular worldview. He wrote similar sentiments to Lovecraft in 1932: "It isn't law-enforcement I resent, but the vandals that parade under the cloak of law.... There are many fine men in Texas ranks of the law; without them chaos and anarchy would result. But surely it is not fanaticism or outlawry to wish to eliminate the worst spots of corruption and injustice."

Even in its day, "Vultures" was recognized as an atypical western, and perhaps Robert sensed it as well. He called it "one of the best stories I've ever written." Perhaps in an effort to stave off the inevitable rejection of the story, Robert wrote two endings: his original, downbeat ending, and a longer, happy ending. When the story ran in the December 1936 issue of *Smashing Novels*, the editor, in his infinite wisdom, decided to run both endings in the magazine, even though he agreed in print that the shorter, darker ending was better.

Many Robert E. Howard critics and scholars, from Don Herron to Steve Tompkins, have written at length about the hard-boiled elements in Robert's stories, and "The Vultures of Wahpeton" is the crown jewel in Robert's dark, grim legacy. Robert's brief experiments with the mystery genre left him cold; the few stories he wrote of that stripe are full of action, intrigue, and little else. Robert later claimed that he hated mysteries and couldn't read them, much less write them. But thematically, Robert has far more in common with Dashiell Hammett and Raymond Chandler than he has with any of his contemporaries in the fantasy or science fiction genres. Writing about the hard-boiled pulps, author and critic John Leland said:

> [T]he hard-boiled hero was a figure of masculinity unbound; big shoulders, strong chin, smart lip, big pistol and a taut gift of gab. As if in answer to Jung, the hero—Phillip Marlowe, Sam Spade, the unnamed Continental Op, Three Gun Terry, Race Williams and others—introduced an all-American style of sex and violence, bordered only by the writers' equally homegrown tools: rhythm, humor, sensationalism, mass production and bald opportunism. The private eye was his own invention, usually an independent operator, unmarried, childless and motherless. He cowed neither to women or work. He did not suffer an employer; in many stories he gained the upper hand by walking away from a check. Similarly, he cut a sexual swath but did not have any attachments or obligations....

With a few exceptions, this write-up could describe the majority of characters in Robert's canon. Elements of realism, cynicism, and even nihilism, coupled with bleak settings and corrupt characters, can be found in almost all of Robert's fiction from King Kull to Francis X. Gordon.

"El Borak," or "the Swift," as he was also known, first appeared in the December 1934 issue of *Top-Notch Magazine*, in "The Daughter of Erlik Khan." The story was written in late 1933, and it took Otis Kline a year to find a home for it. The character, Francis X. Gordon, was another resurrected childhood character from Robert's early writing. In the juvenile fragments, Frank Gordon is merely a world traveler and adventurer who runs about the Orient fomenting unrest. Coincidentally, Gordon sometimes teamed up with Steve Allison, a.k.a. the Sonora Kid, for gunplay and adventure. A decade later, a new and different Gordon walked through the pages of pulp history.

Originally a gunfighter from El Paso, Gordon found his way to the Orient and went native, moving among the desert nomads and bandit chiefs, adopting their ways and customs, but never converting to Islam. Gordon holds no allegiances to the various factions that threaten to plunge Afghanistan into war, preferring to serve his own interests and moral compass instead.

A cursory glance at the El Borak stories and the character might draw comparisons to the works of Talbot Mundy, Harold Lamb, and T.E. Lawrence, with Gordon navigating tribal politics, dueling with swords and rifles, and racing through the desert to ward off treasure hunters and mercenaries. Certain plot elements do carry over, but what is missing from Robert's tales of Oriental adventure is the Jingoistic Imperialism of many of the British writers and soldiers of fortune who sent in nonfiction articles and stories to *Adventure* magazine.

Of Gordon's motivation, Howard scholar Morgan Holmes said this: "There is a hard-bitten cynical side with Howard's approach. It is not about extending British domination; it is about preventing the next would-be Genghis Khan or Tamerlane from emerging in Central Asia." Howard's Gordon stories have as much to do with keeping the region's native resources from being plundered as they do with keeping despots in check—not for any nationalistic reason, but usually because Gordon's friends wind up in the crossfire. It's not hard to see that the conflicts presented in these stories revolve around treachery, the control of resources, or get-rich-quick schemes. Howard wrote this to Lovecraft in June 1933:

> Returning to our discussion of barbarism, you say the trouble with Texas is, she isn't civilized enough. Yet nine tenths of her troubles arise from attempted exploiting of her resources—and her citizens—by individuals and corporations from those very sections which you praise so highly as examples of true civilization. If those individuals and persons of corporations are possessed of the virtues you ascribe to highly civilized people, the actions of many of them have certainly been inconsistent. Please realize that what I say of the state's exploiting by alien individuals does not apply to those good and honest citizens of many other states who have come and settled in Texas and adapted themselves to their new environments and made fine citizens of the state... but there are vandals and vultures who

would bankrupt the state to fill their purses, and practically all of them are from the very sections you speak of as being so highly civilized.

While the El Borak stories aren't westerns by definition, they are certainly westerns in spirit. Richard Slotkin's massive three-volume treatise on the Myth of the Frontier blankets the El Borak stories like the desert sands. Gordon, as written by Robert, fulfills the role of frontier scout, the man who walks the knife-edge between civilization and the frontier. He is too barbaric for the cultured world, and too civilized for the Indians, though they accept him for adopting their ways. If Gordon is the scout, a Texas Natty Bumpo, then the various Afghan tribes are the Native Americans, and the American government wears a British flag. Robert also had intimate knowledge of another bandit-king, one who could rally men to his aid and live like the wolves in the hills for weeks at a time: Pancho Villa. More than one of Robert's villains resembles the charismatic revolutionary in both words and deeds. Robert's Afghanistan was inspired by his wide reading of Middle Eastern history, but its themes and motivations were solidly based on Texas current events.

By relocating the pragmatic Texas gunfighter to the Middle East, Robert was able to write convincingly of the tensions between governments and chieftains, emphasizing his flair for headlong action sequences, intrigue, and a bleak and stark world where no man is all good or all bad, but self-serving. Desert *noir*, perhaps?

Robert created another desert adventurer, Kirby O'Donnell, to place in similar situations. What's missing from these tales of intrigue is the Texas-ness. O'Donnell passes himself off as a tribesman, but he's Irish-American rather than Texan, and is propelled along by the plot, rather than dictating it as Gordon frequently does. The O'Donnell stories are as good as anything else Robert was writing at this time, but they lack that extra veneer of grit and cynicism that the El Borak stories possess. The reason is simple: no hard-boiled gunfighter in the main character's seat.

Robert E. Howard's most famous westerns, however, aren't the serious ones, but just the opposite. Robert's boxing markets, *Fight Stories* and *Sport Story Magazine*, folded temporarily in 1932. Robert cleverly managed to get a little more mileage out of Steve Costigan (literally disguised as Dennis Dorgan) by performing a pseudonymous sleight of hand and placing the fighting sailor in *Magic Carpet* magazine just prior to its cancellation in 1933. By 1934, another short-lived but high quality boxing pulp hit the stands, also started by William Kofoed: *Jack Dempsey's Fight Magazine*. Not surprisingly, Steve Costigan romped through all three issues before the magazine hit the canvas and stayed down.

Robert's humor stories were popular, and he enjoyed writing them for two reasons: they came easily to him, and the markets to which he sold paid promptly. *Action Stories*, Fiction House's answer to *Adventure*, had previously run a few of the Steve Costigan boxing stories, but Robert saw that he could place something else in the magazine's pages with little effort: funny westerns.

Robert had written the first of what would be his longest-running series by July 1933. In keeping with the traditions of tall lying, Robert kept his stories in the first person, the better to write in that humorous style. To make full use of the landscape of his native state's jocularity, Robert set his Texan protagonist down in Bear Creek, Nevada—as thinly disguised a location for Texas as his earlier backdrop of San Antonio doubling for Asiatic ports of call. Dipping into his own autobiography, Robert lampooned himself to an even more outlandish degree, and Breckinridge Elkins was born.

The first Breckinridge Elkins story, "Mountain Man," was in the tall tale tradition that had given birth to Robert E. Howard; it had come full circle. Finally, Robert's real storytelling voice, unfiltered through books and imagined histories, could be heard, and in the medium with which he was most familiar. Elkins is a bear of a man—almost literally, as the first paragraph pointedly illustrates:

> I was robbing a bee tree, when I heard my old man calling: "Breckinridge! Oh, Breckinridge! Where air you? I see you now. You don't need to climb that tree. I ain't goin' to larrup you."

All Pap wants his truculent son to do is pick up a letter from Mississippi that is waiting for him at the post office in town. Maw and Pap have decided that it's time for Elkins to see something of the world. Pap sends him out with some useful advice:

> "Be keerful how you spend that dollar I give you," he said. "Don't gamble. Drink in reason; half a gallon of corn juice is enough for any man. Don't be techy—but don't forgit that yore pap was once the rough-and-tumble champeen of Gonzales County, Texas. And whilst yo're feelin' for the other feller's eye, don't be so keerless and let him chaw yore ear off. And don't resist no officer."

Despite Pap's good intentions, Elkins is quickly stripped of his clothing and possessions by a robber in the night and is forced to hold up a fellow traveler for his duds. Elkins sets the traveler on his mule, Alexander, and the mule takes off. Soon, a gang of men, including the local sheriff, ride up, and Elkins, thinking himself in trouble and not wanting to go against his Pap's instructions, goes along.

The men of Tomahawk stage a boxing match with the nearby town of Gunstock and have wrangled a ringer to do their fighting for them—shades of the earlier Steve Costigan tale, "Texas Fists." Elkins goes along, innocent and trusting, until he's actually in the ring, getting hit. Only then does the truth come out, and Elkins, slow to comprehend, eventually catches up to the plot as the real boxer, Bruiser McGoorty, rides up with a posse of men from Perdition. Once the accusations start flying, things quickly escalate:

> The next instant guns was crashing, knives was gleaming, and men was yelling blue murder. The Gunstock braves turned frothing on the Tomahawk warriors, and the men from Perdition, yelping with glee, pulled their guns and began fanning the crowd indiscriminately, which give back their fire. McGoorty give a howl and fell down on Alexander's neck, gripping around it with both arms, and Alexander departed in a cloud of dust and smoke.

Eventually, Elkins navigates the chaos to pick up the letter for his Pap, and only after fending off looters and bandits does Old Man Braxton at the post office realize he'd misread the letter: "This is for Bill *Elston* that lives between here and Perdition."

The tale ends in a matter similar to how many of the subsequent Elkins stories start: with the setup and execution of the tall tale punchline:

> I want to spike the rumor which says I tried to murder Old Man Braxton and tore his store down for spite. I've done told how he got his leg broke, and the rest was accidental. When I realized that I had went through all that embarrassment for nothing, I was so mad and disgusted I turned and ran out of the back door, and I forgot to open the door and that's how it got tore off its hinges.
>
> I then jumped on Alexander and forgot to untie him from the store. I kicked him in the ribs, and he bolted and tore loose that corner of the building, and that's how come the roof to fall in. Old Man Braxton inside was scared and started yelling bloody murder, and about that time a lot of men come up to investigate the explosion which had stopped the three cornered battle between Perdition, Tomahawk, and Gunstock, and they thought I was the cause of everything, and they all started shooting at me as I took off.
>
> Then was when I got that charge of buckshot in my back.
>
> I went out of Tomahawk and up the hill trail so fast I bet me and Alexander looked like a streak. And I says to myself the next time Pap gets a letter in the post office, he can come after it hisself, because it's evident that civilization ain't no place for a boy which ain't reached his full growth and strength.

Elkins is frequently described as a grizzly in both size and appearance throughout the long-running series. He shares much in personality and temperament with his literary brother, Steve Costigan, but with some notable and not-so-notable differences. Obviously, the settings had changed, and without having to work a boxing match into every story, Robert had a larger canvas on which to depict the mayhem that Elkins frequently stirred up as he trundled through each story.

Elkins's horse, an ill-tempered beast named Cap'n Kidd, makes his first appearance in the second story, "Guns of the Mountains." Cap'n Kidd is the most obstreperous mount to ever knock someone to the ground and step on their head. Only Elkins can ride him, and usually not very well. Ornery, spiteful, and possessing full intelligence, Kidd is to Elkins what Mike the bulldog was to Costigan.

Most of the plots revolve around Elkins having to deal with his family in some fashion: do an errand, keep the peace, or tend to family feuds and concerns. Pap is one of the regular instigators, but Elkins's uncles and aunts also start their share of trouble for the simpleminded hulk. This is significant in that none of Robert's other series characters have parents of any kind, much less any that actively interfere with their offspring's life. Robert may have set the Elkins stories in Nevada, but the cast and characters of these tall tales were all straight out of Cross Plains. These stories are entirely propped up by Howard's use of regional dialect and his penchant for exaggeration and humorous feints. This is the opening paragraph from "The Scalp Hunter":

> The reason I am giving the full facts of this here affair is to refute a lot of rumors which is circulating about me. I am sick and tired of these lies about me terrorizing the town of Grizzly Claw and ruining their wagon-yard just for spite and trying to murder all their leading citizens. They is more'n one side to anything. These folks which is going around telling about me knocking the mayor of Grizzly Claw down a flight of steps with a kitchen stove ain't yet added that the mayor was trying to blast me with a sawed-off shotgun. As for saying that all I done was with malice afore-thought—if I was a hot-headed man like some I know, I could easy lose my temper over this here slander, but being shy and retiring by nature, I keeps my dignity and merely remarks that these gossipers is blamed liars, and I will kick the ears off of them if I catch them.

These funny westerns were easily as popular as the Steve Costigan series and ran for several years in *Action Stories*. They were so popular, in fact, that Robert had created a demand for them; when long-time Fiction House editor Jack Byrne moved to *Argosy* in 1936, he asked Robert to come with him, and specifically asked for funny westerns similar to the Elkins stories. Robert created two additional humorous cowboys, Pike Bearfield of Wolf Mountain, Texas, and Buckner J. Grimes, of Knife River, Texas. They endured similar adventures in the pages of *Argosy* and *Cowboy Stories*, respectively.

It is tempting to compare Elkins to Pecos Bill (and many have done so), but doing this calls a few things into question. Pecos Bill was not a true Texas tall tale legend; he was a manufactured construction, first published in *Century Magazine* in 1923 by Edward O'Reilly, one of those charming dreamers from the Eastern seaboard who wore ten-gallon hats and insisted on being called "Tex." Pecos Bill was first published in 1923 in the October issue of *Century*, with O'Reilly cobbling his folklore together by borrowing heavily from Paul Bunyan and transplanting the character's foibles into a Southwestern setting. Only a small percentage of the original Pecos Bill stories bear any passing resemblance to actual Texas folklore. Even in his day, though, Pecos Bill was considered legitimate folklore, and was initially presented as such. But when someone else wrote a book about Pecos Bill, O'Reilly sued the author for plagiarism, claiming that he had invented Pecos Bill out of whole cloth. While O'Reilly had gone so far as to construct a tall tale from scratch, Robert would do O'Reilly one better and create timeless fiction by employing the traditions of folklore itself. About the only thing that Elkins and Pecos Bill have in common is that they are both fictional. The fundamental difference between the two lies in the fact that Robert recorded in the speech of his characters the "voices" of people around him. Elkins's expressions, plots, and situations are original examples of tall lying as defined by Mody Boatright and other Texas folklorists. They are not copies of other stories, like O'Reilly's Pecos Bill tales. Robert's humorous westerns should be considered as important as any collection of tall lying. His own voice was never more clearly heard than in his humor work. Every one of the Elkins stories can be dissected according to the tenants of Southwestern folklore, and they become indistinguishable from any tale from a cow camp or oil derrick. If Robert wasn't a regional writer, then what was he?

With Otis Kline as his agent, Robert was able to place these and other stories in magazines that he otherwise wouldn't have thought to try. Kline did things much as Robert did them; any manuscript that came back was immediately sent to a different magazine. Kline's agency was persistent and helped Robert to crack a few new markets, leading to more work. Robert also sent Kline stories on his rejection pile, and Kline was able to work them through his contacts and find homes for them. *Weird Tales* was still not paying Robert, and still running Conan stories through their inventory, but Robert was making good money through the Kline agency. In the last year of Robert's life, Otto Binder also represented his work and, as Robert's letter to Novalyne Price from 1936 revealed, William Kofoed acted as an agent, too, though it's unclear whether he represented anything before Robert died.

Indeed, the Kline agency and others associated with it were working diligently on representing Robert in a favorable light to the New York publishers. For being so far away, Robert knew several editors and agents who liked his work and thought enough of it to tell others, or to request more of it for themselves.

Kline also suggested to Robert that he submit some manuscripts to book publishers. One of these manuscripts that Kline tried to find a home for was made up of several reworked Breckinridge Elkins stories, now connected by a tissue of romantic interest in Glory McGraw, a headstrong, plain-talking woman who impels Elkins to action. The book, *A Gent From Bear Creek*, featured a newly written chapter, "Meet Cap'n Kidd," that revealed where Elkins had obtained his famous horse. The manuscript made the rounds, including a trip overseas to the British publisher, Denis Archer, who had turned down a previously submitted collection of Robert's short stories and his Conan novel, *The Hour of the Dragon*. Nothing came of it during Robert's lifetime, however.

In the last two years of his life, Robert was writing the occasional Conan story (albeit with Southwestern flavor in the case of "Beyond the Black River"), the El Borak Middle Eastern adventures, and a slew of regional tall tales. Everyone connected to Robert liked to talk about how much they liked or disliked Conan. It's interesting to note that none of Robert's friends who survived him spoke of Breckinridge Elkins or Francis X. Gordon. Only Conan. Robert never dropped off a Breckinridge Elkins story for Novalyne Price to look through, at least not that we know of. Why? More strange is that Robert seemed more interested in talking about Conan, when his other work was both closer to him personally and also paid good money regularly. Perhaps Robert thought little of Elkins, or felt that his friends wouldn't be interested in reading a story that they were familiar with colloquially on a day-to-day basis. It's also possible that Robert's moneymakers could have been composed of caricatures that were a little too thinly disguised. Maybe Breck Elkins hit a little too close to home for Robert's tastes.

The last six months of Robert's life were difficult for him. His mother's tuberculosis had finally overwhelmed her and she was dying. Robert wrote to Lovecraft in February 1936:

> I've had little opportunity to do any writing of any kind for the past month. In fact this letter is the longest bit of writing I've done since about the 20th of January. After our return from Marlin we stayed at home for about two weeks, and then my mother's pleura filled again, and we took her to a hospital in San Angelo, 105 miles southwest of Cross Plains. After a few days then we put her in a sanatorium about seventeen miles northwest of San Angelo, where she stayed for six weeks, when her condition got so bad we put her back in the hospital at San Angelo. She remained there twelve days, and then we brought her home, since it seemed they had done all they could for her. Her condition is very bad, and she requires frequent aspirations, which are painful, weakening and dangerous. It is wonderful

with what fortitude she endures her afflictions; in every hospital she has been, the doctors and nurses speak of her cheerfulness, her nerve, and her steadiness in the highest terms. But it is only what can be expected in a woman of the old pioneer stock. This has been a bitter winter, and the harshness of the weather has hurt her. First one woman and then another we hired to help wait on her has been taken sick herself, so the job of nursing my mother has been done largely by my father and myself. She is subject to distressing and continual sweats, and naturally has to have constant attention, so I find little, if any time to write, which is why this letter is brief, and possibly so disconnected. Some times we have to be up all night with her. There seems to be little we or anyone can do to help her, though God knows I'd make any sacrifice, including my own life, if it could purchase her any relief.

In his last letter to Lovecraft, in May of 1936, Robert added a few details about his living situation:

Seeing we could expect nothing from specialists or hospitals we brought her home, in the early part of March, and we've been here ever since. We got goats and for weeks she lived mainly on their milk. She seemed to be improving a little when she had an attack of acute pleurisy on her right side, which until then hadn't been affected. My father handled that, and she was definitely on the mend, although the sweats never ceased, when in the early part of April we had the worst dust storm I ever saw in my life, and she developed pneumonia. There seemed no hope for her, yet she managed to live through the attack. Cold weather hung on, and it still isn't as warm as it usually is this time of the year. But comparatively warm weather has brought about a lessening of her sweats and she is much more comfortable than she was; also breath sounds in the affected lung seem to indicate that there is little if any fluid there. I don't know whether she'll live or not. She is very weak and weighs only 109 pounds—150 pounds is her normal weight—and very few kinds of food agree with her; but if she does live, she will owe her life to my father's efforts and his experience gained by nearly forty years of frontier practice. Again and again he saved her when the experts and specialists were helpless. Just an old country doctor, but he has that qualification so many of our smart modern scientists lack—ordinary common sense; the experts themselves have had to admit that. She started sweating in January and it's just the last few days that there has been any appreciable lessening of it. Many a night she had to be changed six or seven times, and that many times a day—sometimes more. Woman after woman we hired, and they quit, either worn out by their work, or unwilling to do it, though my father and I did most of it. Sometimes when we could get a couple of good women we'd get a short breathing spell. Again there were times when we couldn't get anybody, and I not only took care of my mother, while my father handled his wide practice, but did all the housework, washing, and cooking. I've gone for nearly a week at a time without even taking off my shoes, just snatching a nap as I could between times. Things are better now, but anything can happen, and I'm not optimistic. But whatever happens we have such satisfaction that there is in knowing that we've fought the best fight that was in us all the way, without asking quarter from anything or anybody, and doing the best we knew how.

Naturally I haven't been able to do much writing the past few months, but I have managed to sell a few more bubby-twisters to Spicy Adventures, keep the Breckinridge Elkins series going, sell Thrilling Mysteries another blood-curdler, and make new markets in Cowboy Stories and Complete Stories. To say nothing of writing several yarns that haven't clicked yet. I've also taken a short run into Central East Texas (to talk to the surgeon who operated [on] my mother last spring) and one into South Texas (to buy some German wine for my mother from Ludwig Borauer who makes the best in the world); I've learned to mix a dozen or so new drinks, have renewed an old love affair and broken it off again, developed a new set of exercises with sledge-hammers, read several new books, made some more enemies, learned how to take care of milch goats, so altogether the year that brings me into middle age has so far been a rather stormy one. Anyway my health is splendid, my muscles are harder than they've been in years and my literary prospects look good—though of course anything can happen.

Unfortunately for Robert, his time had run out.

The Howard family headstone, in Greenleaf Cemetery. The inscription under their names reads, "They were lovely and pleasant in their lives, and in their death they were not divided" (photo courtesy Rusty Burke).

All Fled, All Done

Whenever Richard Cory went down town,
We people on the pavement looked at him:
He was a gentleman from sole to crown,
Clean favored, and imperially slim.
And he was always quietly arrayed,
And he was always human when he talked;
But still he fluttered pulses when he said,
"Good-morning," and he glittered when he walked.
And he was rich - yes, richer than a king -
And admirably schooled in every grace;
In fine we thought that he was everything
To make us wish that we were in his place.
So on we worked, and waited for the light,
And went without the meat, and cursed the bread;
And Richard Cory, one calm summer night,
Went home and put a bullet through his head.
Edwin Arlington Robinson, "Richard Cory," 1897

Novalyne Price received a telegram on June 15, 1936. It was dated June 11. Pat Allen sent it from Cross Plains The telegram said:
> Bob Howard killed himself this morning. His mother very low.

Novalyne dropped her books. She fumed, swore, and raged. "Why, Bob?" she asked over and over. She thought back on all the things he had said to her, and on all of the times he had obliquely mentioned death, or had had morbid thoughts. "Another picture of Bob flashed across my vision. It was February twenty-fourth. I saw Bob sitting slumped in his car. I could see his eyes, fear-filled, pleading with me. I could hear his words, 'I think I might live if you cared.'" Robert had frequently talked of being in his "sere and yellow leaf," and the phrase always stuck in Novalyne's craw, for she could never remember where she'd heard it before. Earlier that same day in June, at Louisiana State University, she had stumbled across the lines while studying *MacBeth*:

> I have lived long enough: my way of life
> Is fallen into the sear, the yellow leaf;
> And that which should accompany old age,
> As honor, love, obedience, troops of friends,
> I must not look to have....

Novalyne never wrote to Robert from LSU; her life and her schooling got in the way. They never spoke again after their last meeting. Initially devastated by the tragedy, she pulled herself together by sheer force of will and finished her summer school classes. Only then, at the end of the semester, did she allow herself to cry for her dead friend. In her mourning, Novalyne blamed herself for Robert's actions. She thought she could have saved him.

She was wrong.

Robert's suicide has become, literally, the stuff of legend, despite having had a house full of witnesses, from Hester's nurse, to the cook, to Dr. Dill, Isaac's friend and colleague from Rising Star, to Isaac himself. Everyone saw, heard, and eventually believed what he or she wanted to believe.

Robert had kept an all-night vigil at his mother's bedside, drinking coffee with Kate Merryman. Mrs. Green relieved Merryman during the morning, and Robert asked if there was any chance that his mother would regain consciousness. Mrs. Green replied no. Robert got up, went outside and sat in his car. The cook glanced up to see him sitting there. Thinking Robert was making his morning run to the post office, she went back to her morning preparations.

Everyone heard the gunshot. The cook looked up, screamed, and saw Robert slump over the steering wheel. Dr. Dill and Isaac rushed outside. Robert had shot himself above the right ear and the bullet had exited out the left side of his head. The men carried Robert back into house. There was nothing to be done. Incredibly, Robert's body lived for eight hours despite the terrible mortal wound he'd inflicted.

In the chaos and confusion that followed, the cook later remembered that Robert's hands were held aloft, as if he were praying. Jack Scott, the newspaperman for the *Cross Plains Journal*, ran over to cover the tragedy and, after a brief conversation with the justice of the peace, was shown a typed piece of paper that Robert had stuck in his wallet:

> All fled, all done, so lift me on the pyre;
> The feast is over and the lamps expire.

The couplet, once thought to have been paraphrased from an Ernest Dowson poem, has since been identified by Rusty Burke as being cribbed from "The House of Caesar" by Viola Garvin. Scott concluded that it must have been Robert's suicide note. In the *ad nauseum* retelling of the story, the piece of paper in Robert's wallet jumped like a magic bullet into Robert's Underwood typewriter in his room and became something he had typed just prior to walking out to his car. By the time Novalyne was receiving letters of condolences from friends and former students in Cross Plains, Robert's trip to the car had become a litany of prayer as he walked outside, his arms above his head: "Have mercy, God, on my immortal soul. Take me through the valley with you. God, have mercy." By the end of the year, *Weird Tales* was publishing the last story Robert E. Howard had written, intended specifically for Farnsworth Wright. According to Otis Adelbert Kline, Robert had stood up from his typewriter, walked into

Hester's room, and said, "Mother, it's done." When told she would never awaken, Robert walked out of the house... and thus the legend took hold and began to grow.

Hester died the next day without regaining consciousness. Isaac, understandably shattered, was surrounded by friends and colleagues who helped him make preparations for his son's and wife's double funeral. On June 14, 1936, Robert Ervin Howard and Hester Jane Howard were laid to rest in Brownwood's Greenleaf Cemetery, an upscale cemetery where many of the wealthy patrons of Brownwood were laid to rest. It was thought at the time that Robert had chosen Greenleaf because he and his mother didn't like Cross Plains and would have preferred to live in Brownwood. That may be the case, but it didn't stop the town of Cross Plains from mourning Isaac Howard's loss. The story occupied the whole of the *Cross Plains Review* the following Friday, along with one of Robert's last and best funny cowboy stories, "A Man-Eating Jeopard."

The general citizenry packed into the Cross Plains First Baptist Church to witness, in the words of Isaac, one of the four ministers on hand "preaching my boy to hell," in reference to the choice of scripture, I Samuel 31:4: "Then said Saul unto his armor bearer, Draw thy sword, and thrust me through therewith; lest these uncircumcised come and thrust me through, and abuse me. But his armor bearer would not; for he was sore afraid. Therefore Saul took a sword, and fell upon it." After the sermon, the caskets were loaded into the hearse for the drive to Greenleaf Cemetery. Robert's friends and acquaintances, Dave Lee, Lindsey Tyson, Winifred Brigner, Russell McGowen, Earl Baker, and several others, acted as pall bearers.

In the last few weeks of May and the beginning of June, 1936, Robert deliberately planned to take his own life. He wrote to Otis Adelbert Kline, giving him instructions for what to do in the event of his death. He organized his files, making stacks of unsolicited manuscripts with instructions on where they were to be sent. He typed out his last will and testament. He borrowed a Colt .380 pistol from an unsuspecting Lindsey Tyson. He drove out to Brownwood on June 10 and bought a burial plot for the family in Greenleaf Cemetery. The extra effort on Robert's part was due to the fact that his mother had slipped into a coma from which, he was told, she would never awaken. But it was not the first time that Robert had considered taking his own life.

Tevis Clyde Smith mentioned in the notes he wrote for an unwritten biography that Robert had talked of suicide in 1928, when his dog, Patch, was dying and Robert had spent a few days in Brownwood to avoid dealing with it. In the midst of one of his usual letters to Smith, Robert wrote in May 1932:

By the way, there's something I've been intending to speak to you about for some time; in the event of my death, I wish you'd drop a line to each of the following:
Farnsworth Wright, Weird Tales, Chicago, Illinois.
E. Hoffmann Price, 305 Royal Street, New Orleans, La.
H.P. Lovecraft, 10 Barnes Street, Providence, R.I.

Smith also mentioned that Robert was fond of the Edwin Arlington Robinson poem, "Richard Cory," and would recite it often "as proof of the fact that a man who is regarded by his community as having everything actually suffers the same woes and is subject to the same depression as the lesser members of the township."

The earliest mention of Robert's interest in suicide came again from Smith, regarding the death of a fellow classmate of Robert's in the Cross Plains school. Robert wrote to Smith in October 1923: "I see in the papers where Roy Guthrie committed suicide. Why, I wonder? Do you have any idea?" Smith wrote in the essay, "The Magic Name," wherein he confided, "At the period of which I write, Bob was a senior and I was a Sophomore. One of his classmates killed himself a few weeks before graduation. Bob was 17 at the time, and I was 15. The suicide had an impact on him, and, as the years went by, he became more constant in defending the right of self destruction, dropping hints of the value of such an ending."

There were several suicides in Cross Plains and Brownwood in the 1920s, one of whom was Eva Weaver, a sixteen-year-old girl who drank strychnine the year before Robert went to Brownwood to finish his schooling. The *Cross Plains Review* reported, "Soon after going to bed she called the family in and told them of what she had done and that no one was to blame she just wanted to die. The reason not being known for the action it is believed she did it in a despondency." Her suicide appeared on the front page of the *Cross Plains Review*, February 11, 1921, as the banner headline trumpeted across the top, "CROSS PLAINS TO-DAY—WITH A BRIGHT FUTURE."

Other suicides during this time included Don Carlos Keeling, who committed suicide by swallowing acid in 1923; Charlie Greenwood, a driller, who died of a self-inflicted gunshot wound in 1926; and Moses Grady Anderson, who hung himself over a slight that occurred in Sunday School in 1928. At least nine people in the town took their own life between 1922 and 1928. Suicide was not such a rare occurrence, given the amount of sheer violence prevalent throughout the neighboring counties at this time, though it always made for good gossip. All of the suicides listed above received only a fraction of the attention that Robert's did in the *Cross Plains Review*.

Robert's suicidal tendencies were there all along, simmering just underneath the surface for years. His friends knew it, even if many of them didn't believe it. His father knew it, and his mother knew it. Even close friends of the family knew it, mostly from Isaac *kvetching* about his miserable domestic situation. Isaac Howard may have corralled his friends into removing Robert's guns and weapons from the house during the last week of Robert's life, in an effort to thwart his son's plans. Isaac wrote, years later, that he had watched his son go through the preparations to end his life several times during Hester's illnesses, but had never really believed that his son would go through with it. The night before Robert shot himself, Robert asked Isaac if his mother was going to wake up. Isaac said, no, this was it. Robert then asked his father, "Where will you go, Dad?"

Isaac, surprised by the question, thought that Robert meant to travel after the funeral, or possibly move. He said, "Why, wherever you go, Son. I'll go with you."

Robert nodded his head and left the room. It is entirely possible that Robert, thinking he had made his intentions clear throughout the years that he didn't intend to outlive his mother, may have thought that Isaac would follow him down the path of self-destruction.

It seems incongruous that a person whose writing focused excessively on the struggle to survive would have made up his mind at so early an age to take his own life. Many of Robert's letters to friends and colleagues are filled with his determination to make it, to succeed, against all odds, in the fiction writing business. Robert's real-life heroes, the pioneers who settled Texas, and even the conquerors who pillaged on the far side of the world, like Genghis Khan, had a never-say-die attitude. Robert's pugilistic heroes, the various Iron Men of the Golden Age of boxing, kept getting up every time they hit the canvas, refusing to be knocked out and defeated. In the architecture of Robert's influences, he was bolstered on every front by real and fictional characters who exhibited above all other traits the will to survive, to keep going, to never give up. Even Robert's body continued for eight hours after he had fired a bullet into his brain. He was as predisposed to a long life as anyone, maybe even more so. Why, then, did Robert put a gun to his head and end his own life?

Just as there is more than one version of King Saul's death in the Bible, there is also more than one way of looking at the factors that impelled Robert to kill himself. All anyone can do is guess and surmise. In the course of this book, I have tried to show with as little exterior comment as possible what I believe are the events that led to Robert's early and lasting decision to end his own life. It's a complicated situation, and it requires a complicated answer. It should be noted that what follows is based on facts, evidence from various sources, and reading between the lines. Where applicable, quotes are attributed, but in the end, the opinion expressed is just that—my opinion. Ultimately, the only person who will ever know why Robert E. Howard committed suicide is Robert himself.

It begins and ends with Robert's parents. Isaac was absent from his family for extended periods of time, all the while living in small towns and communities that were barely removed from the Texas wilderness. Isaac liked being a doctor for the prestige it offered, and he was a good doctor, by all accounts, if slightly eccentric. Hester admitted on her deathbed that she had married Isaac because he was a doctor; specifically, so that she would be well taken care of regarding her tuberculosis. But after Robert was born, Isaac resumed his practice, staying out all day and coming home at odd hours or not at all if he was too far away from home.

Hester was left to care for Robert in a variety of isolated areas. She was tubercular, and Robert may have even had respiratory problems as a child. He did have an irregular heart as an adult; this condition may have been a holdover from a childhood illness. While living next to Dark Valley Creek, Hester had a miscarriage when Robert was approximately eighteen months old. If Robert knew it, he never discussed the particulars. But it seems obvious to me that Hester became depressed and that she never recovered from the incident. This depression fed into the romantic tragedy of her ailment and forged a shell of quiet, dignified nobility that was in keeping with her Southern upbringing and that leveraged the maximum amount of pity for her condition.

Robert, as a young boy, picked up on this mood of Hester's. The two of them were alone in the house together most of the time, allowing Hester to become dependent on Robert for companionship and vice versa. Robert transferred her depression onto him, taking on the mantle of Hester's "black Irish" heritage, something she encouraged by adopting a staged Irish brogue in her later years. It is possible that she miscarried in October 1907, and Robert, sensing her mood during the autumn months, took it as another aspect of his mother's Gaelic blood. Dark Valley, as recorded in poetry and related in Robert's letters to Lovecraft, is Hester's depression, not Robert's. Even though Robert wrote about the place metaphorically, he was underwhelmed by its appearance when he visited years later.

Hester's miscarriage galvanized her into taking extra care of her only son. She doted on him to an excessive degree. While the dotage included teaching Robert to read and write prior to his entering school in Bagwell at the age of eight, it also allowed Hester to guide and shape her son's tastes in literature. Robert became her audience as she entertained him for hours with poetry recitations and stories read aloud. The situation was exacerbated by the Howard family moving every six to twelve months for the first nine years of Robert's life. Each new town brought a new set of neighbors, a constant shift in town priorities, and, of course, the inherent violence that the boomtowns invariably contained. That Robert mentions no friends his own age until the family moved to Burkett is telling. How could he make friends with local kids if his family was always in motion?

Because of the constant moves to violent towns, Hester controlled Robert to an excessive degree. Maybe she forbade him from certain activities. Maybe she explained her illness to Robert. Regardless of what she said or did, she extracted a promise from Robert during his childhood that he would be her primary caretaker during his father's frequent absences. And since his job was to take care of Hester, he had to take care of himself, too.

Because of Robert's early promises to his mother, he felt chained to his family. Most of Robert's efforts to get away, even get some distance, ended in failure and built up more resentment. His parents seemed particularly unwilling to help their son mature into manhood. Robert rebelled from his mother and father as best as he could, but he could not overcome the guilt of breaking his promise to his mother to take care of her. He felt, rightfully so, that he was not in control of his life.

Robert was a sensitive child, and also much smarter than most of the children he came into contact with. School was particularly maddening for him, since he was held back to the level of the dumbest kid in the room. It's no wonder that he hated it. But to Robert, it was just another mechanism of control that he was forced to endure. Robert was not allowed to go to college for subjects that interested him, as he implied in this letter to Wilford B. Talman in September 1931: "I went to Howard Payne College in Brownwood, Texas, but not to take a literary course, no, no! I studied shorthand and typing, and returning to my hometown, I began my venture in the business world." Whether his father wouldn't pay for a liberal arts education is completely unknown. But Robert resented school in his later years with the same vitriol with which he resented his various menial jobs in Cross Plains.

Robert wanted to belong, to fit in, but that meant playing and roughhousing, and his mother wouldn't let him do that. She held him back in an effort to shelter him from violence, even as Robert was reading about the Crusades, the fall of the Picts, and Genghis Khan. Isaac tried to insert himself into their close-knit circle and alternated between helping Hester to control Robert and doing nothing to dissuade Robert from his various angers and affronts. Over time, these slights would become firmly entrenched in Robert's worldview.

Robert resented his parents' control over him, and as he matured into an adult, he developed an extreme reaction to any kind of authority; he didn't want anyone else telling him what to do, either. Robert's family engineered themselves to shelter him from as many of the realities of life as they could—impossible under normal conditions, and downright foolish in a violent boomtown—and tried to keep negative or unpleasant emotions, however inevitable, away from him. Robert's fear of loss may relate back to him being left alone with his mother for so long as a child. It may have been something that Hester encouraged to help bind her son to his role as her caregiver. Regardless of how it first showed up, Isaac and Hester did nothing to change their son's pattern of thinking, and so loss became taboo for Robert, even as people were tottering up onto his front porch with their bodies mangled from oil field accidents or grudge fights in the street.

Robert, to his credit, did try to pull away—he broke promises to his mother regarding drinking to the point that he actually made his own beer. He participated in boxing matches down at the icehouse, endangering his livelihood by risking his fists. Robert wrote to Lovecraft in November 1932:

> I, myself, was intended by Nature to be an athlete. If events had flowed smoothly and evenly from the time I first entered school, I would at this instant be engaged in some sort of professional athletics, rather than struggling with a profession for which I am not fitted. The chain of circumstances which altered the course of my life is too lengthy and involved to impose upon you. But I will say that I extremely regret those circumstances, and had rather have been a successful athlete than the very minor writer I have become—in honesty I will go further and say that I had rather have been a successful professional athlete than to be a great writer.

This comment suggests that, had he been allowed to pursue a more physical existence from an early age, we might not be discussing the life and art of Robert E. Howard at all. In returning to Howard Payne to complete his education, Robert's attempt to quarantine himself when his parents showed up to fetch him proved a useless gesture. But it's another indicator that he was sick and tired of the ironclad apron strings.

Robert was hemmed in on all sides. His parents provided no direction for his development. While his other friends and acquaintances were leaving the nest, getting married, getting jobs, and in general living the life that was expected by every other person in Cross Plains, Robert was taking a bookkeeping course because it beat getting a job of any kind. We don't know how hard his father pushed for Robert to follow in his footsteps, but regardless, any pressure would have been resented openly by Robert.

Unable to move forward in the manner of his peers, Robert retreated into the one thing that was all his, the one thing that he could control: his writing. Robert fought for his writing career because it was literally all he had left. Writing fiction was his sole means of expression, however oblique. By the time he was twenty-two, he had achieved freedom from the yoke of employment, but he was still living at home. He felt not only that he had to care for his mother, but that his father wouldn't or couldn't do it.

Robert was clinically depressed by any definition applicable, and had been for many years. Whether the cause of the depression was a chemical imbalance, an untenable situation at home, or a combination of the two is not important. Certainly, Robert's thoughts reveal much about his cognitive distortions. When the Howards' cow, Delphi, went off her milk, Robert's first thought was that someone was milking her in secret. It was an automatic thought, with Robert immediately jumping to the conclusion that someone was out to get him. This behavior may have been acquired from his father, who initially browbeat fellow writer E. Hoffmann Price during a visit to the house about why the editors of the magazines were screwing Robert over on payment. Isaac exhibited similar behavior in his belief that everyone was trying to take advantage of him.

Robert also cherished several mistaken assumptions that formed a cognitive triad of self-fulfilling thoughts. He constantly told people that he was a hack, a scribbler, a failure as a writer. Considering the fan mail he received and the correspondences he enjoyed from fellow writers, we know that even during his lifetime, he was well-thought-of as a creator of fiction. Robert made plenty of money writing for the pulps, certainly a comfortable living by his community's standards. Despite a lean period from 1932 to 1934, Robert's career was on an upswing with Jack Byrne moving over to *Argosy*, a market that Robert had longed to crack, and specifically asking him to create a series character for the pulp. Years earlier, Street & Smith, one of the largest names in the pulp industry, had tried to poach Sailor Steve Costigan because of his popularity. These are clear indicators that he was well-regarded, but Robert mentioned to Lovecraft, E. Hoffmann Price, and others that he considered himself a failure, or someone who hadn't made good with his career choice. These thoughts were constantly reinforced by his parents and his perception of the town of Cross Plains. Outside of drugstore gossip, very few people who weren't friends of Robert, Hester, and/or Isaac gave any thought to what Robert did or didn't do. Sure, the tongues wagged, but the bluff persona that Robert created for himself ("I say, to hell with what they think!") meant that he was more troubled by a lack of peer acceptance than he let on. But Robert refused to see himself as successful, despite a body of evidence to the contrary.

Another example can be found in Robert's telling Novalyne that he was haunted by a recurring dream or vision that in his past lives, he would fall in love with a woman, only to be betrayed by his best friend, who would steal the woman away. When Novalyne tried to get close to Robert, he pushed her away because he was incapable of expressing his feelings. When Novalyne later started dating Truett Vinson (because she was hurt and scorned by Robert's rebuffs), Robert was able to fulfill his own prophesy and enhance the feeling that he wasn't in control of his life.

This depression started long before Hester entered the final phase of her illness. Robert may have lived with it, miserable, for long as eight years. We know that Robert had problems as a child and as a teenager. He suffered from sleepwalking and night terrors well past the age that he should have shaken them off, into his late teens and early twenties. Prolonged sleepwalking is indicative of post-traumatic stress, or undue amounts of stress. At that time, Robert had been under stress for many years, both at home in a house of quiet tension, and dealing with his surroundings, in the midst of the oil boom. Add to this the daily violence he was exposed to through his father's trade, and the childhood uncertainty of people and place for the first nine years of his life, all of which was a tremendous influence on Robert's fiction writing. He wrote extensively in his letters about the violence he saw. Even after the family finally dropped anchor in Cross Plains, Robert's father was called upon to take care of the effects of boomtown violence on a daily basis. All of these factors contributed to Robert's mindset and served to establish the cognitive depression that he suffered later in life.

In 1930, Robert went to the Scott and White hospital in Temple, convinced that he had a varicocele (a mass of enlarged veins in the scrotum). He also complained of gas in the stomach and was furthermore convinced that his penis was abnormally small. The doctor's working diagnosis was sexual neurasthenia, a condition characterized by fatigue, weakness, insomnia, and a general disaffection and unhappiness. Modern-day medical thinking links the above symptoms to neurotic depressive disorder. In 1930, the doctor concluded:

> We do not think there is anything wrong with Robert. We can find no varicocele of any consequence, and his organs are normally developed and he tests out good in every respect.
>
> His trouble, in our judgment, is due to his thinking there is something wrong. After he has dispelled this thought from his mind he will be in fine shape.

As anyone who has ever taken antidepressants for clinical depression knows, this is much easier said than done.

Looking at Robert's poetry that he wrote in 1925–1927, it's hard to miss the dark thoughts lurking in his poem about suicide, "The Tempter." While many of these poems are usually offered up as examples of Robert's "black Irish" moods, most of his poetry was written during the period when he toiled at various menial jobs, or was suffering through school. Robert's letters reveal far more about his thoughts, and far more clearly, than his poetry ever could. The following letter is undated, and was most likely written around late 1928 to Clyde Smith. The letter is lengthy, but it summarizes a great deal of Robert's emotional state in a rare bit of candor to his friend:

> I have forgotten whether you or Truett were to write my

biography but at any rate I've decided I don't care to have mine appear in the Junto. There are several reasons, the main one being that as several of my cousins receive it, my mother would be pretty near bound to hear about it and there are a good many things in my life that I don't want her to know about. Another thing, I don't care to have my inner self bared before the readers of the Junto because I have decided that some of them are crumbs. Understand, you have my permission to write anything you want about me in a novel, biography or anything that comes under the title of professional art, and that you will get money for, but I don't wish to drop my mask before the Junto readers as I have dropped it before you and Truett. The more people know about you, the more advantage they have over you. A man weakens himself just that much with every secret nook in his soul that he lays bare. I care not if my real life be made public property when the time comes because the first thing a writer learns is to sacrifice himself on the altar of his art, but I wish someone to profit materially by it, when it is done, and I do not wish my soul to be exposed to the gaze of a lot of immature and amateur gropers, which after all, is what most of them are, when there is no profit in it for you, nor any real publicity in it for me. I am like a high priced harlot, who is not willing to sell her body at a low price or to give it away. I don't mind them knowing what I do but it's none of their business what I think.

No, it don't make much a damn with me. One thing I learned, nobody has any use for a "good" boy. I never made any friends here until I began to drink hard and promiscuous. To Hell with such friends. I'm still a smug brother—the world at large don't know the half of me and if I can help it, they never will. I get a Hell of a kick out of looking honestly into somebody's' eyes and saying, "I have no bad habits. I do not even swear and I don't know the taste of liquor." But strange to say, I do not feel any contempt for the person.

I speak scathingly of vice—bad women, bad liquor and profanity. Hell. Let me dream a silver stream till I sight my vision's gleam, then let me sigh for the days gone when I dreamed of a golden dream.

I am composed of two elements, intellect and animal instinct. Both are above average. My intellect tells, and proves logically that there is nothing to life, that it is a barren and empty bauble to which to cling. My animal instinct commands that I live in spite of Hell and damnation. My intellect sees, knows, and realizes; my instinct gropes blindly in the dark, like a blindfolded giant, seeing nothing, knowing nothing except the tremendous urge to exist. It does not reason, it does not weigh cause and result, nor seek the why and wherefore. All that it

> knows is Life and toward life it grasps and clutches as a tree
> gropes to the light. Deep in my bosom I lock him, the giant that
> grips me to life the floods of Eternity rock him, his talons drip
> red with the strife. He in the shadows is brooding, away from
> the light of my brain, but his hands are forever intruding, he
> anchors my soul with a chain.

As an adult, Robert lived in a house of lies, little, white, and otherwise. His father, the embodiment of a frontier Texan, was, if nothing else, stoic to a fault. Nothing fazed him, though this attitude may have been cultivated to inure him to the horrors of his profession. Robert endeavored to do likewise, but wasn't as successful at pulling it off. He rarely discussed painful subjects and family matters with anyone. That just wasn't how it was done in his house. The one person he bared more of his inner soul to than anyone, Novalyne, stopped seeing him and started dating his best friend. Robert, in his writings, wrote much more than he ever intended to say about himself, his life, and his feelings toward same. His fantastic stories are equal parts wish fulfillment and contemporary commentary, a literary reaction to everything he read, felt, and intuitively understood. Robert's characters do what they want because Robert himself never got to; they are true to themselves because Robert never could be. His literature has that peculiar way of getting under one's skin because it is the author's voice, distilled into images of blood and thunder, of high comedy and black magic.

Robert was a good performer, capable of playing to his audience; the dutiful son to his mother, the rough and ready boxer to the icehouse crew, the poet and author to his Brownwood friends, and the town eccentric to visiting writers. The only place that Robert could be himself was at his typewriter. He wrote about the things that interested him, and the stories that gave him strength, joy, or even, on occasion, monetary reward. But no matter what kind of stories he wrote, Robert had things to say in his fiction that he could not bear to articulate anywhere else. He vented much of his social anger when he was boxing regularly, but after he stopped in 1930 or 1931, he lost a powerful outlet for his frustrations. Robert continued to exercise, and when his writing career took off, he spent more time typing furiously for up to twelve hours at a stretch. He ate meals at the typewriter and went outside to split logs when he couldn't stand sitting down any more. He made the best of things, but it ultimately wasn't what he wanted to do. All of his friends got married, moved away, got jobs, and went about their own business. Not Robert. His eighteen-year-old self found out that his heart's one desire wasn't nearly enough to sustain him. Society told him to leave. The circumstances of his life inveigled him to stay.

This complicated situation is what gave Robert the idea that he would take his own life. Pulling that trigger was the one thing he could do. He could end his life whenever he wanted to. Robert had the ultimate control over that. He simply chose to do it after he had fulfilled his final obligation to his mother.

Robert, then, looked for examples that bolstered his viewpoint of self-destruction. Boxers, he noted, don't get old—they retire after one last fight. They are good only for so long. Men of the frontier, too, also met violent ends, as did soldiers and generals. Robert's choice of literature—from Shakespeare's tragedies to Poe's bleak, romantic ennui—and his choice of role models—like Jack London, who was thought to have killed himself at the time, and Ambrose Bierce, who dictated the circumstances of his own death—reinforced the romantic aspects of self-destruction. Robert's interest in violence, and his long-standing belief that the civilized world was never going to get any better, bolstered his defense of suicide and made his decision seem rational. He wrote to August Derleth on May 9, 1936:

> I am indeed sorry to learn of the deaths in your family. Death to the old is inevitable, and yet somehow I often feel that it is a greater tragedy than death to the young. When a man dies young he misses much suffering, but the old have only life as a possession and somehow to me the tearing of a pitiful remnant from weak old fingers is more tragic than the looting of a life in its full rich prime. I don't want to live to be old. I want to die when my time comes, quickly and suddenly, in the full tide of my strength and health.

Robert wrote a similar sentiment about boxers in November 1933:

> It makes me feel like an old man to watch fighters I knew in their prime, get slapped around by kids. "A fighter's life is short at best, no time to waste, no time to rest; the spot-light shifts, the clock ticks fast, all youth becomes old age at last." Same way with writers, too, some of them.

Robert had made himself ready for suicide several times in his life, usually whenever his mother's health took a turn for the worse. Each time Hester bounced back, so did Robert. Of course, he was affected by his mother's health. For two people who had depended on each other so often in the past, how could her death not upset him? But the events that surround Robert's life are too varied to ascribe so simple and ham-fisted a motivation to so deliberate and calculated an act. Robert's reason overrode his inherent desire to live wide and free, like the pioneers and adventurers on the frontier. Unable to enact his grandest wishes, Robert chose to control his own destiny by opting out of his circumstances permanently. Robert's life was troubled; the anger in his fiction mirrors his own frustrations. And while the anger is there, that spark of life, that vitality, also lives in his larger-than-life characters. Robert's corpus of fiction is alive and vigorous, betraying a passion for living, or at least the desire to live and experience the larger world. Robert escaped his life when he wrote, and took his mind's eye around the world, back in time, and to the distant past, with an intensity that has yet to be matched. Suicide was Robert's final escape. It was the one, the only, thing that he could do, given his circumstances.

Robert's last Conan story, "Red Nails," started running in the July 1936 issue of *Weird Tales*, one month after his death (from the collection of Dennis McHaney).

Mythology

What the ignorant and blundering pens of sensational yellow-backed novel writers failed in doing, the pens of sophisticated arm-chair critics completed.
Robert E. Howard to H.P. Lovecraft, February 1931

Robert E. Howard and Hester Howard were buried together in Greenleaf Cemetery, in Brownwood. Both Robert and his mother liked Brownwood, and Robert's choice to place them there may have been a final snub to the citizens of Cross Plains, or even a final insult to Isaac. Regardless, the old doctor was sufficiently shattered by what happened, but not so much so that he didn't make every effort, in a boomtown squatter's fashion, to secure Robert's legacy and ensure some income for himself in his twilight years.

While attempting to make sense of Robert's papers, Kate Merryman and Isaac came across Robert's typed will, which stated that Robert wished for his literary estate to be given to Lindsey Tyson. Isaac instructed Merryman not to tell anyone about what they had found. On June 16, 1936, Isaac applied to the county court to become the administrator of Robert's estate, which would allow Isaac to keep all of Robert's literary works. He swore to the court that Robert had left no will. Shortly thereafter, after exchanging courtesies and condolences, Isaac began corresponding with Otis Adelbert Kline in an effort to collect monies owed to Robert at the time of his death—monies which would now be paid to Isaac himself. This included, depending on who one talked to, between $800 and $1,300 dollars that *Weird Tales* owed Robert. Kline agreed to continue to act as an agent for Isaac, and now as the collection agency for monies owed Robert at the time of his death, for the same percentages at which he sold Robert's stories.

The Callahan County court proved more daunting for Isaac to navigate. He wrote to Kline in August 31, 1936:

> Twice I have appeared before the county court and asked that they close the estate of Robert E. Howard and release me as Administrator, and also my Bondsmen. Twice they have refused....
>
> Robert's insurance was made to his mother. The Insurance company would not pay it because he died before his mother did; some thirty hours difference in their death. The Insurance company demanded an administration. When this was applied for the court ordered an administration on Robert's business. I have succeeded in closing the estate of his mother, but the court obstinately refuses to close Robert's estate....

> [The judge] informed me that he would not permit moneys coming to this estate to be collected by anyone who had furnished a written contract for same....

The foot-dragging from the judge regarding the closing of Robert's estate may have been due to the fact that it's difficult to keep a secret in a small town. Lindsey Tyson was approached by one of the town's lawyers two days after Robert's death, and was informed as to Robert's wishes regarding his literary estate. Tyson, already badly shaken by the news of his friend's suicide, claimed that he didn't know and furthermore wanted nothing to do with the business. The court delays may have been courtesies extended to Tyson, who never did speak up to challenge Isaac's claim.

Isaac was all business, even as the news traveled out in waves to Robert's friends and correspondents. Editors Byrne and Wright were baffled. Kline was saddened. Lovecraft went into a funk. E. Hoffmann Price was floored. No one had seen it coming. Considering how hard Robert had worked at showing only certain sides of himself to his correspondents, this is hardly surprising. Only Robert's close circle of intimates had ever heard Robert speak of taking his life. But given how hard Robert worked at writing, worked at playing, and tried to enjoy life, no one suspected anything. Only in his writings did the shadows of anger and frustration show up.

Not long afterward, the tributes began pouring out from the pulp community. *Weird Tales* ran a glowing and appreciative article on Robert's talent. Fan letters showed up in an avalanche. The amateur publishing community ran Lovecraft's moving memorial of Robert. In it, he quoted and represented his friend accurately, writing of Robert as he had so often presented himself in their private letters. In this, it may be said that Robert got the final word in their debate, after all. These outpourings of grief and admiration continued for six months.

Lovecraft died in the hospital a year later of cancer. The deaths of both Robert E. Howard and H.P. Lovecraft signaled the end of the Golden Age of *Weird Tales*. Clark Ashton Smith largely abandoned short story writing. The other members of Lovecraft's various epistolary circles consoled each other. They decided, for better or for worse, to pick up where Lovecraft had left off, with the results available in bookstores even to this day. Robert's friends, on the other hand, simply got on with their lives. Dave Lee and Lindsey Tyson stayed in Cross Plains, becoming noteworthy, if not leading, citizens, with many friends and admirers. They are still mentioned fondly by those who knew them.

Only Clyde Smith made good on his promise to make a living as a writer; he wrote for the newspaper, and eventually his articles were collected into books. Later, during the Howard Boom of the 1970s, some of Smith's stories and poems were published as well. Novalyne retreated into teaching, where she found much success and happiness. While she eventually wrote stories and even a radio script, her first book would not be published until after she had retired from her chosen profession.

By July 1936, Isaac and Kline had moved forward in their business arrangements. Isaac had sent two rewritten and unsold manuscripts to Wright, the editor he was most familiar with from Robert's business dealings. With these manuscripts came the sob story that Robert had written his last story for the readers of *Weird Tales*. How could Wright refuse such a sensational bit of abject flattery? Wright bought both stories for a total of $150.00, and with that out of the way, Isaac began hammering on Wright to pay the money he felt he was owed.

The amount was eventually paid, but is it not certain whether Kline collected the money for Isaac or the checks went straight to the doctor. In any case, Isaac had moved on to his next scheme: collecting Robert's stories into book form and releasing them to the general public. He talked Wright into releasing the rights on eight Conan stories with the idea of securing a collection from a publisher. This idea came from the unsold Breckinridge Elkins novel, *A Gent from Bear Creek*, that Kline was unable to place domestically. Isaac also tried to drum up interest in a Steve Costigan collection, without much success.

Isaac sent Robert's books and pulp magazines to the Howard Payne library for cataloging and storage, under the auspices of securing a suitable memorial for his son. When Wright allegedly released the rights on eight Conan stories, Isaac removed a portion of the pulp magazines from the library, so that he and Kline would have the printed stories with which to construct a manuscript. This was just as well, as the librarians weren't doing anything to preserve the pulps in the first place. Over time, this incident would transform into a picture of an outraged, bereaved father, upset at the mistreatment of his boy's literary legacy. The house of white lies could still spin a yarn or two.

Kline continued to act as an agent for Isaac, peddling Robert's fiction, though the sales tapered off by the end of 1937. By then, Herbert Jenkins, a British publisher with whom Robert had long dallied, had published the first book devoted solely to Robert's writing: *A Gent From Bear Creek*. The title didn't sell very well, and a great many of the books were destroyed. It is now the most highly sought-after Robert E. Howard book of all; likely fewer than a dozen copies are known to exist.

Fight Stories began rerunning old Steve Costigan stories, changing the titles and crediting "Mark Adam" or "John Starr," their generic house names used for stories they owned or to disguise multiple contributions by more than one author. The practice wasn't unusual in the pulps; Frederick Faust, a.k.a. Max Brand, published under multiple pseudonyms, sometimes encompassing the entire contents of a single issue. *Weird Tales* continued to offer up stories and poems until late 1939, when Wright published

"Almuric," unfinished when Robert was alive and most likely completed by legendary pulp writer and friend of Otis Kline, Otto Binder. Shortly thereafter, Wright stepped down from the magazine he had made immortal, his Parkinson's disease having overcome him, and he died in 1940.

Isaac Howard, too, had grown old. In his late sixties, his failing health necessitated that he retire from regular practice. He moved out to Ranger, Texas, now a thriving small town that bore little resemblance to the gunfire, mud, and flu-bog that had attracted him to the area so many years before. In Ranger, he helped out at a clinic run by his colleague, Dr. Pere M. Kuykendall, until cataracts robbed him of most of his eyesight. The last two years of his life were spent going to church, living frugally, and writing letters to the few of Robert's friends who maintained contact with him. He died in 1944 at the age of 72, a local legend, one of the more colorful characters in the area. Old-timers still have "Doc Howard" stories to tell to this day.

Many of the pulp magazines began to slowly, quietly die off. Science fiction fans soon crowded out the other genres. These kids were organized, obsessive, and scornful of anything that didn't relate directly to rocketry, mathematics, or the problems inherent to colonizing the moon. By the late 1940s, the fantasy fans had grown quiet, but many of them still remembered the visionary Texas author. Kline's tenure representing Robert E. Howard came to a close. The last deal he helped usher through for the tough old doctor was done with August Derleth, now the owner of a publishing concern called Arkham House, who navigated the waters to put together *Skull-Face and Others*, a commemorative sampler along the lines of the books that Derleth had published to honor H.P. Lovecraft. *Skull-Face and Others* contained remarks by Derleth and the first of what would be several reminiscences about Robert from E. Hoffmann Price. While Price guessed correctly about some things in Robert's life, he also missed the boat on others. After all, during both of Price's visits, the whole family had been on their best behavior. As with all of his correspondents, Robert showed Price exactly what he wished him to see, and nothing more.

Isaac kept up a correspondence with Price, and the two wrote long letters to one another for the last eight years of Isaac's life. Early in the correspondence, Isaac offered to put Price and his wife up for a year if they would just come live in the house (Wanda, Price's wife, was to do the chores). Price declined by not answering and the subject was not mentioned again. But much of what they wrote to one another was centered on Robert. Isaac recounted stories, as best as his ailing memory and yarn-spinning skills would allow, of Robert in his youth. Much of the information that Price divulged in his memoir of Robert came directly from Isaac.

Skull-Face and Others was written up, amazingly, by the *New York Times Book Review*. The reviewer, Hoffman Reynolds Hays, is now most recognized as the first translator for Pablo Neruda's poetry. Hays had just published his first novel, *Stranger on the Highway*, to indifferent reactions. Later, he would become a champion of Latin-American poets and a supporter of the feminist movement. Not surprisingly, his remarks on the Robert E. Howard tribute were less than favorable. The title chosen for Hays's review was "Superman on a Psychotic Bender." Thus began a series of preconceived notions that would mushroom into a full-blown psychotic delusion. Hays wrote:

> The collected stories of Robert E. Howard range from the standard "weird tales" pattern (the monster unloosed and its final destruction, or the destruction of the dabbler in the occult) to a kind of action story in costume set in a prehistoric world of Lemuria and Atlantis invented by the author. Howard used a good deal of the Lovecraft cosmogony and demonology, but his own contribution was a sadistic conqueror who, when cracking heads did not solve his difficulties, had recourse to magic and the aid of Lovecraft's Elder Gods. The stories are written on a competent pulp level (a higher level, by the way, than that of some best sellers) and are allied to the Superman genre which pours forth in countless comic books and radio serials. Since this genre commands an incredibly large audience in the United States and seems to be an American phenomenon, its sociological and psychological significance cannot be lightly brushed away.
>
> E. Hoffmann Price contributes a biographical sketch of Howard which is remarkably revealing. Howard, it seems, spent all of his life in the small town of Cross Plains, Tex. A sensitive boy, he was apparently bullied by his schoolmates. He began writing successfully at a very early age but felt that his profession was looked down upon by his neighbors. When Price met him he carried a loaded revolver wherever he went and talked of nonexistent "enemies." Upon the death of his mother in 1936 he committed suicide with the same revolver.
>
> Howard's heroes were consequently wish-projections of himself. All of the frustrations of his own life were conquered in a dream world of magic and heroic carnage. In exactly the same way Superman compensates for all the bewilderment and frustration in which the semi-literate product of the Industrial age finds himself enmeshed. The problem of evil is solved by an impossibly omnipotent hero.
>
> Now if anything like democracy is to prevail in modern life it means that a heavy burden of responsibility is thrown upon the average citizen. It means that he must take a realistic interest in the difficulties of living. But the prevalence of Superman as reading matter for adults indicates a complete evasion of this responsibility. Howard's life is like a fable illustrating the sad

consequences of this situation. Living in the never-never land of Conan and King Kull, he slaughtered enemies by the dozen. He was fearless, inscrutable, desired by all women. Single-handed he toppled rulers from their thrones and built empires of oriental splendor. Even the menace of the supernatural was vanquished by magic that he alone was able to control. In the real world, however, he had no resources. When he was faced with the loss of maternal protection he took the way of self-destruction.

Thus the hero-literature of the pulps and the comics is symptomatic of a profound contradiction. On the one hand it is testimony to insecurity and apprehension, and on the other it is a degraded echo of the epic. But the ancient hero story was a glorification of significant elements in the culture that produced it. Mr. Howard's heroes project the immature fantasy of a split mind and logically pave the way to schizophrenia.

Already the scanty facts of Robert's biography were being torn out of context and stretched like Silly Putty over the rude shapes of the Freudian psychology that was still fashionable in the late 1940s. Hays was not a fan of Robert's, nor does he seem to have had much affection for the kinds of things that he wrote. That he was able to grudgingly admit that the writing is good despite its many psychological flaws was extremely big of him. However, it is this sort of backhanded compliment that would tinge all biographical information spread about Robert E. Howard for the next fifty years.

It was around this time that L. Sprague de Camp entered the scene. Himself a successful science fiction writer, de Camp found prominence under the guidance of the legendary John W. Campbell, whose editorial reins on *Astounding Stories* forever altered the field of science fiction. What Campbell wanted for his magazines would eventually become known as "hard science fiction." That is, whatever intellectual problem the characters were facing had to be extrapolated from preexisting conditions and technologies. Gone were the days of "death rays," Martian princesses, and heroic muscle-men on Mars—at least, not without a life-support suit. Math, logic, and dire consequences were the order of the day. De Camp was a devoted Campbellite and, like so many of his fellow science fiction writers, thought, acted, and wrote along similar lines; the "space opera" story was on the outs.

De Camp was an engineer by trade, served in the Navy reserve, and wrote a prodigious amount of fiction and historical works. Many of his fellow writers commented frequently on his science fiction stories and, later, on his various nonfiction works, all ruthlessly researched. But what de Camp seemed to really love more than all of that was fantasy. De Camp was an early fan of comic fantasy, and later contributed several novels and short stories in that particular genre. He later claimed that he initially gave Robert's fiction a pass when he came across it in *Weird Tales* all those years ago for some perceived historical inaccuracy. More importantly, de Camp became an advocate of fantasy, boosting the works of Robert E. Howard and others, largely because he really enjoyed them, but also to further his own career.

By 1950, things had changed and a new situation had developed regarding Robert's literary works. Following the deaths of Isaac Howard and Otis Adelbert Kline, Kline's partner, Oscar Friend, continued the agency in their name. Isaac left his estate to Dr. Kuykendall, who had taken Isaac in prior to his death. This included control of Robert's literary legacy; not only the rights to Robert's prose and poetry, but also a large mishmash of unpublished stories, tear sheets, letters, high school themes, fragments, notes, drafts, outlines... all in all, reams of unpublished material. This had already been sorted through by Kline during his stewardship as agent, while looking for other things to sell—things like the unfinished "Almuric" as well as several unpublished Conan stories—anything Kline deemed sellable. He sent the rest back to Isaac, who held onto it for several years. As *Skull-Face and Others* was being assembled, he sent the material to E. Hoffmann Price to paw through in what would become known as "the Trunk." Isaac intended for Price to keep this miscellaneous material, even as Isaac willed his estate to Dr. Kuykendall. This, at least, was done with the full knowledge of all parties concerned. The Trunk eventually ended up in the possession of Oscar Friend.

Sometime in 1949, Martin Greenberg (an early fan, active in several circles and an admirer of Robert from the 1930s), operating as Gnome Press, approached Friend with the idea of doing hardcover collections of Robert E. Howard's stories. Their first effort, *Conan the Conqueror* (in reality *The Hour of the Dragon* renamed), was released in 1950, and sold well enough to proceed with the rest of the volumes. In *Conan the Conqueror*, John D. Clark, who had created with P. Schuyler Miller "A Probable Outline of Conan's Career" back in 1936, contributed the introduction to the first book devoted solely to Conan of Cimmeria. In his introduction, Clark makes a baffling statement: "Don't look for hidden philosophical meanings or intellectual puzzles in these yarns—they aren't there." Even the fans, it seemed, brought different expectations to the table when they read Robert E. Howard. Anyone who missed the underpinnings of Robert's stories hadn't read them closely enough.

De Camp learned of the existence of the unpublished Conan stories when Friend engaged de Camp to edit the stories and prepare them for publication. To ensure that a "saga" would be created, de Camp took the various notes and fragments in Friend's possession and wrote up new Conan stories which he inserted into what he considered the official "timeline" of Conan, as created by Clark and Miller. De Camp found that the work was to his liking; soon he took some of Robert's unsold, non-Conan stories and converted them by means of simple substitution; guns became swords, and so on. These "posthumous collaborations" were then sold to various fantasy and science fiction magazines, now mostly in a digest format.

The Gnome books brought the three unsold Conan stories, "The Frost Giant's Daughter," "The God in the Bowl," and "Vale of the Lost Women," into print for the first time. Several fragments that were finished by de Camp, including "The Snout in the Dark," "The Hall of the Dead," and "Wolves Beyond the Border" were included in the Gnome collections. De Camp also converted a Crusades story, "Hawks over Egypt," and another historical story, "The Road of the Eagles," into Conan stories (renaming the former "Hawks Over Shem" in a stunning burst of creativity). He also converted an El Borak story, "Three Bladed-Doom," into "The Flame Knife," and a Kirby O'Donnell story, "Curse of the Crimson God," into "The Bloodstained God," all now featuring Conan and set in the Hyborian Age. The most famous of these "posthumous collaborations" was "The Black Stranger," an unsold Conan story that Robert rewrote as a Black Vulmea story, "Swords of the Red Brotherhood." De Camp took this rewrite and rewrote it *again*, turning it into "The Treasure of Tranicos." Of this work, de Camp said, "Robert E. Howard's heroes were mostly cut from the same cloth. It was mostly a matter of changing names, eliminating gunpowder, and dragging in a supernatural element." Gnome eventually published seven Conan books from 1950 to 1957. The last Conan novel, *The Return of Conan*, was a whole-cloth pastiche written by a Swedish fan, Bjorn Nyberg, and rewritten by de Camp. The best thing anyone can say about this book was that it had a spectacular cover by comic book artist Wally Wood.

With the reappearance of Conan in the Gnome editions came renewed fan activity. A fanzine known as *Amra* appeared in 1959, the purpose of which was to talk about Robert E. Howard, Conan, and the broader topic of sword and sorcery. Started by de Camp and George Scithers, the fanzine attracted many established writers to its publication, largely on the strength of de Camp's participation. Contributors eventually included Poul Anderson, Fritz Lieber, Michael Moorcock, Jerry Pournelle, Leigh Brackett, Avram Davidson, Marion Zimmer Bradley, and, most importantly, a young Robert E. Howard fan, collector, and Korean War veteran living in Pasadena, Texas, named Glenn Lord.

Many professional artists contributed their time and energy to the 'zine, including Berni Wrightson, Jeff Jones, Frank Frazetta, Gray Morrow, George Barr, Alex Niño, and the artist most closely connected with the project, Roy Krenkel. While the subject matter sometimes veered far away from sword and sorcery (as Fritz Lieber had so named it), *Amra* enjoyed a thirty-three-year run and kept the small flame of devoted fans talking about Robert E. Howard.

It was during this time that information began to spread about Robert's personal life. In an early issue of *Amra*, for example, Glenn Lord stepped up to refute the charge that had appeared in one of the Gnome hardcover introductions that Robert drove thirty miles out into the desert before shooting himself. Lord used the coverage in the *Cross Plains Review* for his source material. De Camp also started sharing his opinions on Robert's life and, more importantly, his suicide, in the pages of *Amra*.

From 1959 to 1963, the copyrights on the original seventeen Conan stories printed in *Weird Tales* expired. De Camp quietly filed copyrights on the stories he had edited, along with the new material he had written, as his basis for control of the character. He later made the claim that "my lawyer advised it, to strengthen my position in my litigation with Greenberg." Shortly before the last Conan book was published by Gnome, de Camp and Greenberg had a falling out over monies owed de Camp. Eventually, de Camp took Greenberg to court to wrest all of the rights away from Gnome, now defunct.

In 1959, P.M. Kuykendall died, and control of the estate passed to his widow, Alla Ray Kuykendall, and his daughter, Alla Ray Morris, jointly. Shortly thereafter, Oscar Friend died, and his daughter, Kittie West, assumed control of the literary agency. West continued to talk to Kuykendall and Morris, paying out whatever small royalties came in, but by 1965, she was ready to close up shop for good. She contacted de Camp to see if he would act as an agent for the Robert E. Howard estate. Fearing a conflict of interest, de Camp refused. Instead, he recommended fan and collector Glenn Lord to the heirs.

Lord had heard about the Trunk owned by E. Hoffmann Price. On his own, he tracked Price down and inquired about purchasing the contents of the Trunk. Price had been an inefficient caretaker; some of the papers had been borrowed and never returned, others were on loan, and the contents were by and large scattered. Lord took it upon himself to secure and recover the contents of the Trunk, which took a great deal of his time, not to mention his money. But the effort was well worth it; the Trunk contained an estimated fifty percent or more of everything that Robert E. Howard had ever written, and at the time of Lord's new appointment, none of it had seen print.

In 1957, Lord made arrangements through Arkham House to publish a collection of Robert E. Howard's poetry, *Always Comes Evening*. He financed the project on his own, using Arkham House's name and mail-order sales to move the print run. Several years later, Lord started *The Howard Collector*, a self-published fanzine showcasing some of his more interesting finds, unpublished stories, and poetry. Lord also published various research discoveries in *The Howard Collector*, which became a highly sought-after collectible among the growing number of Robert E. Howard fans.

De Camp knew about all of these things and felt that Lord would be the perfect person to represent the works of Robert E. Howard. The heirs and Lord quickly reached a decision to do business. De Camp made it clear that he would take care of Conan, and Lord was to do what he could with everything else.

In order to keep the money flowing, de Camp started looking elsewhere to place the Conan stories. The pulps had died out in the 1950s, killed by comic books, television, and the now-burgeoning paperback book market. De Camp started making the rounds. The fourth publisher, Lancer, another small outfit in New York, accepted the deal, provided that de Camp was able to deliver all of the Conan stories without legal complications and build them into a full-blown series, similar to Lancer's line of Edgar Rice Burroughs paperbacks. De Camp delivered, contacting fellow fantasy fan and writer Lin Carter, who collaborated with him and helped fill out additional stories of Conan, including a full-length novel, *Conan the Buccaneer*. Along the way, de Camp took another editorial whack at the stories he had previously "collaborated on," trimming and revising the text even further.

Lancer started publishing as soon as the dust was settled in the de Camp lawsuit. The first Lancer Conan paperback appeared in 1966, containing four Conan tales out of both the publication order and the imposed chronology as set forth by de Camp. None of that mattered when people were staring at the cover, however.

Frank Frazetta is most closely linked with Robert E. Howard, despite successfully depicting the works of Tolkien and Burroughs among others, painting hundreds of book covers and fantastic images, and in all other respects earning the right to be called a living legend in American illustration. Ace had been using Frazetta on their Edgar Rice Burroughs paperbacks, and Lancer editor Larry Shaw thought he seemed like a natural choice for the job of illustrating Conan. When Frazetta read the stories, he too was gripped by Robert's prose style. The cover painting that he turned in blew everyone away. Frazetta had turned a corner. He had found in the works of Robert E. Howard a kindred spirit. It was a perfect match. And it sold millions.

"Conan the Barbarian" became a household name, and right at a time when fantastic literature was enjoying a renaissance. The reissued Edgar Rice Burroughs books, along with paperback editions of J.R.R. Tolkien's *Lord of the Rings* trilogy, were embraced by the counterculture of the day, and even folded into more liberal study groups on university campuses. And nestled right in there with them was Robert E. Howard and his varied characters and stories.

Meanwhile, Glenn Lord had wasted no time in his role as literary agent. He made arrangements with small press publisher Donald Grant to produce a line of hardcover books. The first was a reprint of the Herbert Jenkins *A Gent From Bear Creek*, shot from Lord's own copy. Other volumes quickly followed as the paperback sales of the Lancer Conans drove people to seek out more Robert E. Howard. Lord managed to wedge several non-Conan paperbacks into the Lancer line of books, including *Almuric* and the first collection of King Kull stories.

In 1970, Lord also sold the rights to Marvel Comics to produce *Conan the Barbarian* and, later, *The Savage Sword of Conan*. *Savage Sword* was a black-and-white magazine, not a four-color comic book, and was perceived in the marketplace as a more "mature" title, since it was not bound by the Comics Code Authority. Thus, the stories were more violent, and the artwork more suggestive (but all well within the standards of taste). What really separated *Savage Sword* from the comic was the inclusion of articles by Fred Blosser, Glenn Lord, and even de Camp and Carter on various subjects from the construction of the Hyborian Age to short biographical pieces on Robert E. Howard. Between the Lancer paperbacks and the Conan comics, millions of fans were exposed to the character for the first time.

Anytime de Camp had the opportunity, he wrote introductions or short articles about Robert E. Howard. Increasingly, de Camp became regarded as an expert on the subject, particularly as he worked some biographical facts, and even more biographical opinion, into his remarks. The earliest of these remarks first appear in a book de Camp wrote in 1953 called *The Science Fiction Handbook*, a survey of the science fiction field at the time. In discussing the more recent trends in modern imaginative literature, de Camp wrote:

> Howard's work suffered from careless haste. His barbarian heroes are overgrown juvenile delinquents; his settings are a riot of anachronisms; and his plots overwork the long arm of coincidence. Nevertheless the tales have such zest, speed, vitality, and color that a connoisseur of fantasy will find them well worth reading. The neurotic Howard suffered from Oedipean devotion to his mother and, though a big and powerful man like his heroes, from delusions of persecution. He took to carrying a pistol against his "enemies" and, when his aged mother died, drove out into the desert and blew his brains out.

The number of factual inaccuracies listed above need not be pointed out. However, at the time, it was all anyone had to go on. Glenn Lord did what he could do in the fan press to refute some of the above statements, and de Camp was always grateful for more information and made gracious thanks and apologies when corrected on the facts. By the 1970s, de Camp had finally stopped using the outmoded term "Oedipal" to describe Robert's relationship with his mother. One area that de Camp never backed away from was the idea that Robert was crazy because he committed suicide.

De Camp was not alone in his character assassinations, either. Many of his fellow Campbellites in the science fiction field took it upon themselves to take a few swipes at Robert's creation, and at Robert himself. *In Search of Wonder*, first published in 1967, was a collection of essays, really reviews of books, from Damon Knight, who said this of Robert E. Howard (whom he listed under "the Classics"):

> The Coming of Conan, by Robert E. Howard, is of interest to Howard enthusiasts, who will treasure it no matter what anyone says, and to students who may find it, as I do, an intriguing companion to L. Sprague de Camp's The Tritonian Ring. Howard's tales lack the de Camp verisimilitude—Howard never tried, or never tried intelligently, to give his preposterous saga the ring of truth—but they have something that de Camp's stories lack: a vividness, a color, a dream-dust sparkle, even when they're most insulting to the rational mind.
>
> Howard had the maniac's advantage of believing whatever he wrote; de Camp is too wise to believe wholeheartedly in anything....
>
> All the great fantasies, I suppose, have been written by emotionally crippled men. Howard was a recluse and a man so morbidly attached to his mother that when she died he committed suicide....

Damon Knight, wearing the hairshirt of science fiction critic, took great delight in puncturing every inflated balloon of science fiction cliché while extolling the virtues of his friends' literary efforts and lauding marginalized authors. Knight took such a pessimistic view of science fiction that he would recommend a book he thought was written badly if the theme of the novel was something he felt everyone should experience.

Why Knight didn't like Robert E. Howard is only partially a mystery. Frank Cioffi, in his book *Formula Fiction?: An Anatomy of American Science Fiction*, summed up what was significant about the changes Campbell brought to his magazines:

> [S]cience fiction distinguished itself from other popular genres because it depicted not society in status, but society in flux....
> [S]cience fiction usually works through juxtaposing a picture of contemporary social reality with a vision of some scientifically explicable change in that reality. The interplay between these two components allows science fiction to comment on social structures and institutions associated with change, progress, and development (in addition to those linked to stability, stasis, and stagnation) in ways other popular forms cannot.

However dire the predictions of the Campbellians, they usually occurred in the far-flung future; not the here and now, and certainly never in the past. These self-styled prophets of the apocalypse (Knight included) told their tales with all of the gravitas that only a mathematics professor or model rocketry enthusiast can muster. Yet they were, at their core, optimists—looking forward, safeguarding the future, hoping that their shrill warnings would be heeded before it was too late.

Robert's fiction couldn't have been more diametrically opposed. Robert looked backward, saw that mankind had always been lousy, and didn't think things were getting any better. Antiprogress, anticivilization, and antiauthoritarian. Is it any wonder the science fiction crowd didn't like him? And yet, because of the popularity of Conan, or perhaps because of their confusion over why one of their own (de Camp) would dally with such trash, that didn't stop them from commenting on Robert's work whenever they could. Knight openly admitted in *In Search of Wonder*, "I'm no great fantasy-lover; most of Merritt bores me to tears; so do Howard and Lovecraft...." He wasn't alone. Most of the science fiction crowd to which Knight addressed those remarks was so firmly entrenched in their narrow viewpoint that they were incapable of appreciating anything not directly connected to cigar-shaped rocket ships.

But all was not slings and arrows at this time. With the increased reprinting of Robert E. Howard material, a number of other fan groups and fanzines appeared, all devoted to Howard and his writings. The second most noteworthy after *Amra* was the Robert E. Howard United Press Association (or REHupa), which formed in 1972. An outgrowth of fan clubs and fanzines, the APA, or Amateur Press Association, was designed to serve a small group of dedicated fans, bound together over a common subject. Each member submits a fanzine or a newsletter, with enough copies to mail to every other member, to the Official Editor. The O.E. collates the 'zines received into stacks of one of each member's 'zine, and then mails those bundled packages out to each member. As fan-based activity goes, it's as archaic an enterprise as anything, but many APAs exist to this day, including REHupa.

When REHupa formed, it brought together a hardcore group of enthusiasts who began asking questions about de Camp, Robert E. Howard, Conan, and related subjects. These questions and discussions spilled over into other fanzines, and soon a small but vocal group of fans were calling for the chance to see Robert E. Howard's Conan stories without de Camp's corrections and additions. These "purists," as they would later be known, became openly antagonistic and hostile to de Camp, who at first was puzzled by the reaction, but quickly turned a deaf ear to their entreaties. De Camp's activity in various fanzines began to decrease, partly because of these reactions, but also because he was becoming involved more and more in the business side of managing Conan.

Lancer inexplicably filed for bankruptcy in 1973, but managed to limp along, doing business until 1976. De Camp went back to court, suing Lancer for unpaid royalties. Interestingly, Lord accused de Camp of exactly the same thing, citing that Kuykendall and Morris were entitled to royalties from foreign language editions of Conan books, a deal brokered by de Camp through Lancer. Their gentleman's agreement had fallen completely apart. By this time, de Camp had assumed full control over anything related to Conan, and Lord was dealing exclusively with everything else. They soon settled these affairs; de Camp paid the money owed, and everyone went back to doing business, but now with no further illusions as to who was capable of doing what.

To further protect himself, de Camp initiated the formation of Conan Properties, Inc., in January of 1977. The corporation was a means to channel further inquiries about licensing Conan through a single entity. The early board of directors included both de Camp and Lord. Things moved rapidly after that, as the rights to make a Conan movie were soon bought by film producer Dino de Laurentis. It took years to get the movie made, from multiple drafts of the script to casting a young, then-unknown bodybuilder named Arnold Schwarzenegger in the title role. The director, John Milius—an unstable maverick with a penchant for stubbornness—made only a cursory examination of the source material available to him, instead opting to include as much pseudo-Bushido rhetoric and as many Nietzschean themes as possible, turning Conan into a beefy Ronin who killed even beefier Vikings. Thulsa Doom, a villain plucked from King Kull, was the main bad guy. What the film lacks in authenticity, it makes up for in nudity, swordplay, gore, and garbled dialogue.

The image of Schwarzenegger as Conan, enunciating with marbles in his mouth, resplendent in a furry loincloth, and holding a sword the width of a cricket bat, was seen by hundreds of millions of people around the world. It was just enough for the average person to "get" the idea of Conan. *Conan the Barbarian* remains the most successful sword-and-sorcery movie of all time. A sequel, *Conan the Destroyer*, was released, but whatever marginal vision Milius was able to bring to the first film was absent (as was Milius) from the second, and the movie grossed only a fraction of the first.

Regardless of how well *Conan the Destroyer* did, Conan Properties, Inc. had established themselves as a profitable enterprise. Ace was now publishing the Conan paperbacks, in chronological order, a full twelve-book saga. De Camp and his cowriters were responsible for just over fifty percent of the material in the paperback series. Ace also made a deal with CPI to produce new stories of Conan in novel form, many written by newcomers like Roland Green and Robert Jordan. These novels were churned out by the pound throughout the 1980s and deep into the 90s, well after all of the original Robert E. Howard books were out of print.

As early as 1977, the strident cry to produce Robert E. Howard's Conan stories without the tangential nonsense was gathering momentum. The most vocal opponent of de Camp during this era was fantasy author Karl Edward Wagner, who worked a deal with Glenn Lord to publish the Conan stories thought to be in the public domain (as originally printed in *Weird Tales*) for Berkeley Books, along with clearly worded essays stating that Robert E. Howard's work was just fine all by itself and needed no additional tampering. These books were sought after for a long time by fans for just such a reason.

The fan community was picking up momentum. Literary critic Don Herron locked horns with de Camp with his infamous "Conan vs. Conantics" essay, wherein he showed de Camp and Carter's textual blunders to the rest of the purist Robert E. Howard fans. Herron used de Camp's arguments about what a poor and slipshod writer Robert E. Howard was against de Camp's own Conan contributions. De Camp continued to hang in the margins of fan activity for years, mostly to see what was being said about him. When he eventually quit the scene altogether, it was because, as he put it, no one was saying anything new that they hadn't been saying for twenty years.

Interest in a third Conan movie eventually died down, and so did the demand for sword and sorcery. Years of imitators, bad books, and worse movies had soured the public's interest in anything remotely connected to the genre. In the mid-1980s, the first attempts at serious criticism were begun, again, by L. Sprague de Camp.

The first full-length biography of Robert E. Howard, *Dark Valley Destiny*, was published in 1983 to applause from the science fiction community and howls of outrage from Robert E. Howard fans. The book was essentially a full-blown treatment of *The Miscast Barbarian*, de Camp's lengthy historical sketch of Robert E. Howard published in 1975 by a small fan press. De Camp, his wife Catherine, and a former teacher named Jane Whittington Griffin spent several years compiling interviews from the people that had known Robert who were still living. These interviews are now archived, along with the rest of de Camp's papers, at the Harry Ransom Center at the University of Texas in Austin. De Camp was an indefatigable researcher, but his tireless zeal was tempered by his narrow range of questions. In essence, de Camp's thesis revolved around trying to figure out what made Robert so crazy that he would take his own life. All of de Camp's questions to Robert's friends, acquaintances, and the general populace of Cross Plains who deigned to speak to him were tinged with that sort of bias. De Camp went looking specifically for the pieces of Robert's life that would validate his thesis. All other extraneous information was not used or, worse, not followed up on. Worst of all, de

Camp, who had so long worked in the shadow of Robert's genius, allowed himself to be fooled by the man he thought he knew better than anyone else.

De Camp was a cultured, intelligent, highly educated man, and also what even Robert would have less charitably called a Yankee. In writing *Dark Valley Destiny*, he showed himself to be the perennial greenhorn by allowing himself to be taken in by Robert's tall lying. The arrogance was so total that de Camp was never able to see past the things that Robert said about himself. Most importantly, he discounted completely Robert's larger surroundings. He researched, he recorded, he interviewed, and then he ignored much of what he found. Robert's line of bull was just too compelling. *Dark Valley Destiny* was written on the ironic premise that "if it ain't true, it oughtta be." Maybe de Camp learned more than he realized.

By now, the battle lines were clearly drawn between de Camp and the fans, who now included Glenn Lord, Fritz Leiber, and many others. Two of the most important books of critical study appeared after de Camp's biography. The first was *The Dark Barbarian*, edited by Don Herron, a collection of learned, well-researched, and above all positive essays about Robert's varied literary endeavors. Several years later, *The Starmont Reader's Guide*, a small-press series dedicated to academic discussions of genre subjects and authors, published a book on Robert E. Howard, written by fans and scholars Marc Cerasini and Charles Hoffman. *The Starmont Reader's Guide* represented the first book-length study of Robert's various works with insightful comments and explanations dealing with Robert's style and use of language.

Despite these advances, the imagery that de Camp threw out for the science fiction community for so long was hard to ignore. Moreover, it made for a good story. Harry Harrison accused Conan of being a "crypto-homosexual" in his laughable book, *Great Balls of Fire*, about sex in science fiction. Who was going to dispute that? Well, one person did dispute it, in the pages of *Amra*: Dr. Frederic Wertham, best known as the author of *Seduction of the Innnocent*, the infamous book about comics and juvenile delinquency. Wertham states:

> May I say a few words in Amra in defense of Conan? The article "The Psychological Conan" in V2 #57 reduces Conan to a composite cliché of Freudian terminology. This is not the image Howard created and thousands of readers enjoy. The real Conan is anything but that. He cannot be reduced to such a lifeless formula.... Psychoanalysis of living people and of literary figures requires not the labeling with Freudian terms but an interpretation based on concrete data. This article represents a misunderstanding of both psychoanalysis and Conan. Howard and Conan deserve better.

The last fifteen years have seen the deaths of Catherine and L. Sprague de Camp, the sale of Conan Properties, Inc. not once, but twice, and, most damnably, the disappearance of Robert E. Howard's fiction from bookshelves altogether as the Conan pastiches written by Robert Jordan, Roland Green, and others crowded the shelves and the original stories that spawned the imitations were not reprinted. Several longtime fans, tired of years of inaction, have taken up the charge that Glenn Lord started so many years ago and spearheaded the effort to publish new editions of Robert E. Howard's work. No less than six publishers are now reissuing Robert E. Howard fiction collections—some which are public domain, and others that have been reedited to conform to Robert's original manuscripts—and in a far greater diversity than any other previous effort. Glenn Lord continues to assist with these literary endeavors, sharing his materials and experience with publishers like Wandering Star, Del Rey, Bison Books, and Wildside Press.

Cross Plains, too, has gotten into the act. Project Pride was formed in 1990 to promote the community of Cross Plains. Their first act was to buy the then-vacant Robert E. Howard house with an eye toward establishing a museum for the various Howard fans that have been showing up on the front lawn from the late 1960s on. Over a ten-year period, the house, now listed on the National Register of Historical Places, has become a fantastic literary shrine to Robert's life and work. Every June, the community opens the house and people and fans come to visit from all over the world, to view the tiny room where Robert wrote or to walk the grounds where he exercised. The event has become an informal meeting place and pilgrimage for the members of REHupa, who were early boosters of Project Pride, and who contributed some of the artifacts now found in the Howard House, including a copy of the extremely rare Herbert Jenkins *A Gent from Bear Creek*.

In the centennial year of Robert E. Howard's birth, rumors abound on the Internet about new movies in preproduction. New comics continue to sell like gangbusters. More critical studies have been written, and fanzine activity has returned with a vengeance. Most importantly, Robert's fiction is back on bookshelves. Old fans are calling it "the second Howard Boom," hearkening to the halcyon days of the 1970s when Frazetta and Howard ruled the roost in book and comic stores across the country.

Slowly, by degrees, the muddled half-truths and outright lies and misrepresentations are being replaced by factual information or a truthful "We don't know" regarding Robert's biographical details. As new books continue to be published, and new fans arrive to catch the enthusiasm inherent in Robert's fiction, it is hard to not compare this cyclical development to Robert's own theories about the cycles of history. The myths of Robert E. Howard will, for better or worse, always be there to lend an aspect of forbidden fruit to his fiction.

Even now, seventy years after his death, Robert simply won't let the facts stand in the way of a good story.

Robert E. Howard posing with a little sip of beer. The original caption on the back of this photo says, "Schlitz didn't pay a penny for this endorsement—and probably won't. R.E.H." (Photo courtesy Leo Grin)

AFTERWORD

> I have said that Texas is a state of mind, but I think it is more than that. It is a mystique closely approximating a religion. And this is true to the extent that people either passionately love Texas or passionately hate it and, as in other religions, few people dare to inspect it for fear of losing their bearings in mystery or paradox. But I think there will be little quarrel with my feeling that Texas is one thing. For all its enormous range of space, climate, and physical appearance, and for all the internal squabbles, contentions, and strivings, Texas has a tight cohesiveness perhaps stronger than any other section of America. Rich, poor, Panhandle, Gulf, city, country, Texas is the obsession, the proper study and the passionate possession of all Texans.
>
> **John Steinbeck**, *Travels With Charley*, **1962**

One cannot write about Robert E. Howard without writing about Texas. This is inevitable, and particularly so when discussing any aspect of Howard's biography. To ignore the presence of the Lone Star State in Robert E. Howard's life and writing invites, at the very least, a few wrongheaded conclusions, and at worst, abject character assassination. This doesn't keep people from plunging right in and getting it wrong every time. The popularity of Conan notwithstanding, the average person with a working knowledge of genre authors and subjects will have barely heard of Robert E. Howard at all. Odds are pretty good that what little they have heard revolves around Robert's suicide at the age of thirty, or perhaps an intimation that Robert and his mother were, well, very close to one another. The latter is usually delivered with a raised eyebrow or a knowing nod. The deeply entrenched fan or lay scholar may have heard additional tidbits about Howard: that he was a recluse, that he had no friends, that he was neurotic. Deranged. Just plain crazy.

All of the above is patently false. Just the same, for the past sixty years, nearly everyone involved with Robert E. Howard has been playing fast and loose with the facts in his biography. Some merely repeated bad information, like an out-of-control game of Telephone. Others simply drew a few conclusions based on an opinion or two and presented them as facts. Still others chose to omit information entirely, provided that it suited their needs.

It's hardly surprising that all of Robert E. Howard's biographers, past and present, became frustrated at the amount of information that they didn't know—far more than what is known, despite a wealth of personal correspondences, reminiscences from friends, and firsthand accounts. With so many people now dead, there is no telling what information, secrets, and general family knowledge the Howards took to their graves.

What remains, though, is a literary legacy that has traveled the world many times over, been translated into more than a dozen languages, and inspired generations of writers and artists. The echoes of Robert E. Howard's life can be found in the places where he best lived it—in his copious amount of fiction and verse. And while that is a good place to start forming a complete picture of Howard, eventually the Lone Star State will rear its ungainly head and bellow, "Well, what about me?" You can always take the man out of Texas, but it's impossible to take Texas out of the man. Robert E. Howard was certainly no exception.

As the author of the first full-length biography of Robert E. Howard in over twenty years, it is inevitable that I would have to refute some of the assertions laid down in L. Sprague de Camp's book, *Dark Valley Destiny*. I have tried to do this without undue malice, for de Camp was a Yankee and quite frankly didn't know no better. In many ways, it was because I have such a strong negative reaction to *Dark Valley Destiny* that I chose to write this book the way I did; I tried to think of everything that I didn't like about de Camp's effort, and then I tried very hard not to do that.

Constructing a biography is an inexact science. This book was written with an eye toward correcting the mistakes of the previous efforts (and doubtless making new ones in their place), but no one has ever attempted to incorporate Texas history into the life and times of Robert E. Howard. Doing this gives a different picture than the ones previously offered. As a lifelong Texan myself, it just felt right to do it that way. Give Robert the credit he's due. Show folks what it would have been like for him. Make some of his seemingly random decisions have meaning. Tell Robert's story in front of the backdrop of Texas history. I think Robert would have liked that.

Mark Finn
Austin Texas
May 31, 2006

BIBLIOGRAPHY

Many of the books and articles listed here were of instrumental importance to the completion of this project; others served as inspiration, or a guide, or an influence. All of them contributed to my knowledge and understanding of the life and times of Robert E. Howard, as well as his influences, his working conditions, his friendships, and his obstacles. In the course of the text, I gave citations for quotes pulled from other sources and other authors. All quotes from Robert E. Howard came directly from his letters. Unidentified quotes from Robert were also from various letters, published or unpublished. Quotes from Robert's fiction have also been identified within the body of the work, to keep the reader from flipping back and forth to see where a given passage came from.

Alpers, Hans Joachim. "Loincloth, Double Ax, and Magic: 'Heroic Fantasy' and Related Genres" *Science Fiction Studies* Volume V, part 1, March, 1978.

Amis, Kingsley. *New Maps of Hell: A Survey of Science Fiction*. New York, NY. Harcourt Brace and Co., 1960.

Anderson, Gary Clayton. *The Conquest of Texas: Ethnic Cleansing in the Promised Land, 1820-1875*. Norman, OK. University of Oklahoma Press, 2005.

Bacon, Jonathan. *Runes of Ahrh Eih Eche*. Lamoni, Ia. Jonathan Bacon, 1976.

Bainbridge, John. *The Super Americans: A Picture of Life in the United States as Brought into Focus, Bigger Than Life, in the Land of Millionaires—Texas*. Garden City, NY. Doubleday & Co. 1961.

Blosser, Fred. "When Kull Rode the Range." *The Dark Man #5 The Journal of Robert E. Howard Studies*, Winter 2001. Mind's Eye HyperPublishing/Iron Harp Publications. Rockford, Ill, 2001.

Boatright, Mody C. "The Art of Tall Lying" *The Southwest Review*, Autumn 1949, Dallas, TX. Southern Methodist University, 1949 pp. 357-363.

---. *Folklore of the Oil Industry*. Dallas, TX. Southern Methodist University Press, 1963.

---. "The Myth of Frontier Individualism" *The Southwestern Social Science Quarterly*, June 1941, Vol XXII, No. 1, Austin, TX Southwestern Social Science Association 1941, pp 14-32.

Boatright, Mody C. and William Owens. *Tales From the Derrick Floor: A People's History of the Oil Company*. New York, NY. Doubleday and Co. 1970.

---. *Tall Tales From Texas Cow-Camps*. Dallas, TX. Southwest Press, 1934.

Brown, Mel. *Chinese Heart of Texas: The San Antonio Community, 1875-1975*. Austin, Texas. Lily on the Water Publishing, 2005.

Carter, Paul A. *Another Part of the Fifties*. New York, NY. Columbia University Press, 1983.

Cioffi, Frank. *Formula Fiction? An Anatomy of American Science Fiction, 1930-1940*. Westport, CT. Greenwood Press, 1982.

Cross Plains Review, various issues, 1917-1936, Courtesy of the Texas Tech University Southwestern Collection.

de Camp, L. Sprague and Catherine Crook de Camp. *Dark Valley Destiny: The Life of Robert E. Howard*. New York, NY. Bluejay Books, 1983.

de Camp, L. Sprague. *Science Fiction Handbook: The Writing of Imaginative Fiction*. New York, NY. Hermitage House, 1953.

Dinan, John. *Sports in the Pulp Magazines*. Jefferson, NC. MacFarland and Co. 1998.

Di Tommaso, Lorenzo. "Robert E. Howard's Hyborian Tales and the Question of Race in Fantastic Literature." *Extrapolation*, Vol. 37, No. 2. Kent State University Press, 1996.

Dobie, J. Frank. *The Flavor of Texas*. Dallas, TX. Dealey & Lowe, 1936.

---. *Coronado's Children: Tales of Lost Mines and Buried Treasure of the Southwest*. New York, NY Garden City Publishing, 1930.

Ellis, Novalyne Price and Rusty Burke. *Day of the Stranger: Further Memories of Robert E. Howard*. West Warwick, RI. Necronomicon Press, 1989.

Ellis, Novalyne Price. *One Who Walked Alone: Robert E. Howard, The Final Years* Hampton Falls, NH. Donald M. Grant, 1986.

Ettinger, R.H., Robert L. Crooks, and Jean Stein. *Psychology: Science, Behavior, and Life* (3rd edition). Fort Worth, TX. Harcourt Brace and Company, 1991.

Fehrenbach, T. R. *Lone Star: A History of Texas and the Texans*. New York, NY. American Legacy Press, 1983.

Haaga, David A. F. and Aaron T. Beck. "Perspectives on Depressive Realism: Implications for Cognitive Theory of Depression." *Behaviour Research and Therapy* Volume 33, Issue 1, January 1995, Pages 41-48.

Havins, T.R. *Something About Brown (A History of Brown County, Texas)*. Brownwood, TX. Banner Printing Company, 1958.

Hays, H.R. "Superman on a Psychotic Bender," *New York Times*, Sept 29th, 1946. pg. 67.

Herron, Don, ed. *The Dark Barbarian, The Writings of Robert E. Howard: A Critical Anthology*. Gillette, NJ. Wildside Press, 2000.

---. *The Barbaric Triumph: A Critical Anthology on the Writings of Robert E.

Howard. Gillette, NJ. Wildside Press, 2004.

Howard, Robert E. *Selected Letters: 1923-1930*. West Warwick, R.I. Necronomicon Press, 1989.

Howard, Robert E. *Selected Letters: 1931-1936*. West Warwick, R.I. Necronomicon Press, 1991.

---. *Almuric.* New York, Berkeley Books, 1977.

---. *Beyond the Borders*. New York, NY. Baen Books, 1996.

---. *The Black Stranger and Other American Tales*. Lincoln, NE. University of Nebraska Press, 2005.

---. *The Bloody Crown of Conan (Conan of Cimmeria Book 2)*. New York, NY. Del Rey, 2004.

---. *Boxing Stories*. Lincoln, NE. University of Nebraska Press, 2005.

---. *Bran Mak Morn: The Last King*. New York, NY. Del Rey, 2004.

---. *The Coming of Conan the Cimmerian (Conan of Cimmeria Book 1)*. New York, NY. Del Rey, 2003.

---. *The Complete Action Stories.* Carrollton, Texas. Hermanthis, 2001.

---. *The Conquering Sword of Conan (Conan of Cimmeria Book 3)*. New York, NY. Del Rey, 2005.

---. *Cthulhu: The Mythos and Kindred Horrors*. New York, NY. Baen Books, 1987.

---. *The End of the Trail*. Lincoln, NE. University of Nebraska Press, 2005.

---. *Eons of the Night*. New York, NY. Baen Books, 1996.

---. *A Gent from Bear Creek*. New York, NY. Zebra Books, 1975.

---. *King Kull*. New York, NY. Lancer Books, 1969.

---. *The Last Ride.* New York, NY. Berkeley, 1978.

---. *Lord of Samarcand and Other Adventure Tales of the Old Orient*. Lincoln, NE. University of Nebraska Press, 2005.

---. *The Lost Valley of Iskander.* New York, NY. Zebra, 1976.

---. *Pigeons From Hell*. New York, NY. Ace, 1979.

---. *Post Oaks & Sand Roughs*. Hampton Falls, NH, Donald Grant, 1990.

---. *The Riot at Bucksnort and Other Western Tale* . Lincoln, NE. University of Nebraska Press, 2005..

---. *The Savage Tales of Solomon Kane*. New York, NY. Del Rey, 2003.

---. *Trails in Darkness*. New York, NY. Baen Books, 1996.

---. *The Ultimate Triumph.* London, England: Wandering Star, 1999.

---. *The Vultures of Whapeton.* New York, NY. Zebra, 1975.

---. *Waterfront Fists: the Complete Fight Stories of Robert E. Howard.* Holicong, PA: Wildside Press, 2003.

---. *The Weird Works of Robert E. Howard Volume 1: Shadow Kingdoms.* Holicong, PA. Wildside Press, 2005.

---. *The Weird Works of Robert E. Howard Volume 2: The Moon of Skulls.* Holicong, PA. Wildside Press, 2005.

---. *The Weird Works of Robert E. Howard Volume 3: People of the Dark.* Holicong, PA. Wildside Press, 2005.

---. *West is West.* Rob Roehm and Alex Runions, ed. Morrisville, NC. Lulu Press, 2006.

Jones, Gerard. *Men of Tomorrow: Geeks, Gangsters, and the Birth of the Comic Book.* New York, NY. Basic Books, 2004.

Jones, Robert Kenneth. *The Shudder Pulps: A History of the Weird Menace Magazines of the 1930s.* New York, NY. New American Library, 1978.

Joshi, S.T. *The Weird Tale.* Austin, TX University of Texas Press, 1990.

---. *H.P. Lovecraft: A Life.* West Warwick, RI. Necronomicon Press, 1996.

Kahn, Roger. *A Flame of Pure Fire: Jack Dempsey and the Roaring 20's.* New York, NY. Harcourt, Inc. 1999.

Kennedy, Dane. *The Highly Civilized Man: Richard Burton and the Victorian World.* Cambridge, MA. Harvard University Press, 2005.

Knight, Damon. *In Search of Wonder: Essays on Modern Science Fiction.* Chicago, Il. Advent Publishing, 1967.

Leland, John. *Hip: The History.* New York, NY. HarperCollins, 2004.

Lord, Glenn. *The Last Celt: A Bio-Bibliography of Robert E. Howard.* New York, NY. Berkeley Books, 1976.

Lord, Glenn, ed. *The Howard Collector.* New York, NY. Ace, 1979.

---. *The Book of Robert E. Howard.* New York, NY. Zebra, 1976.

---. *The Second Book of Robert E. Howard.* New York, NY. Zebra, 1977.

Lovecraft, H. P. *Selected Letters Volume 5: 1934-1937.* Derleth, August, and Turner, James, ed. Sauk City, WI. Arkham House, 1976.

Lovecraft, H. P. *Selected Letters Volume 4: 1932-1934.* Derleth, August, and Turner, James, ed. Sauk City, WI. Arkham House, 1976.

Lovecraft, H. P. *Selected Letters Volume 3: 1929-1931.* Derleth, August, and Wandrei, Donald, ed. Sauk City, WI. Arkham House, 1971.

Merrifield, Scott T. "Niggers, all of them…Revisiting the Racial Ideology of Robert E. Howard" *Vector* 217, Berkshire, England, 2001 pp. 8-11.

Morens, David M. "At the Deathbed of Consumptive Art" *Emerging Infectious Diseases*, Vol. 8 No. 11, November 2002 pp. 1353-1358.

Nichols, James W. *On the Banks of Turkey Creek*. Bloomington, IN. First Books Library, 2003.

O'Reilly, Edward. "The Saga of Pecos Bill" *Century Magazine*, October, 1923, pp. 827-833.

Olien, Roger M. and Diana Davids. *Oil in Texas: the Gusher Age, 1895-1945*. Austin, TX. University of Texas Press, 2002.

Olien, Roger M. *Oil Booms: Social Change in Five Texas Towns*. Lincoln, NE. University o Nebraska Press, 1982.

Said, Edward W. *Orientalism*. New York, NY. Vintage Books, 1979.

Schechter, Harold. *Savage Pastimes: A Cultural History of Violent Entertainment*. New York, NY. St. Martin's Press, 2005.

Scheina, Robert L. *Villa: Soldier of the Mexican Revolution*. Dulles, VA. Brassey's, Inc. 2004.

Schweitzer, Darrell, ed. *Exploring Fantasy Worlds*. San Bernardino, CA. Borgo Press, 1985.

Server, Lee. *Danger is my Business: An Illustrated History of the Fabulous Pulp Magazines, 1896-953*. San Francisco, CA. Chronicle Books, 1993.

Smith, Tevis Clyde. *Report on a Writing Man and Other Reminiscences of Robert E. Howard*. West Warwick, RI. Necronomicon Press, 1991.

Smith, Erin A. *Hard-Boiled: Working Class Readers and Pulp Magazines*. Philadelphia, PA. Temple University Press, 2000.

Turner, Hicks A. ed. *Remember Callahan: A History of Callahan County, Texas*. Dallas, Texas. Taylor Publishing Co. 1986.

Van Hise, James (ed). *The Fantastic Worlds of Robert E. Howard*. Yucca Valley, CA. James Van Hise, 1997.

Waggoner, Diana. *The Hills of Faraway: A Guide to Fantasy*. New York, NY. Antheum, 1978.

White, James C. *The Promised Land: A History of Brown County, Texas*. Brownwood, TX. Starns Printing Company, 1995.

INDEX

A
Action Stories 138, 192, 204, 206
Adams, Ray 44
Adventure 50, 92, 98, 148, 202, 204
Africa 81
Allen, Pat 193, 213
Amra 236, 237, 241
Anderson, Moses Grady 216
Anderson, Poul 236
Apollo 167
Argosy 50, 113, 114, 116, 135, 206, 221
Arizona 37
Arkansas 30
  Holly Springs 23
  Texarkana 24
Arkham House 237
Asama (Japanese warship) 37
Astounding Stories 234

B
Bainbridge, John
  The Super-Americans: A Picture of Life in the United States as Brought into Focus, Bigger Than Life, in the Land of Millionaires—Texas 13
Baker, Earl 38, 40, 47, 215
Barlow, Robert 149
Barr, George 236
Baum, Broad 45
Baum, Budge 44
Baum, Mose 45
Beowulf 58
Berkeley Books 243
Bierce, Ambrose 154
Binder, Otto 207, 232
Bison Books 245
Bjorn, Nyberg
  Return of Conan, The. *See* de Camp, L. Sprague
Bloch, Robert 149
Blosser, Fred 239
Blue Book 50
Boatright, Mody C. 58, 65
Boden, Mike 132
Bohannon, Aunt Mary 33, 59, 158
Boris Karloff's Thriller 158
Boyd, Mrs. Will 48
Boyles, C.S., Jr. 44
Brackett, Leigh 236
Bradley, Marion Zimmer 236
Brigner, Winifred 215
Brontë, Charlotte 31
Brooke, Rupert 154
Bunyan, Paul 207
Burns, Elsie 42
Burroughs, Edgar Rice 238
  Tarzan 165
Butler, LeeRoy 47
Byrne, Jack 138, 200, 206, 221, 230
Byron, Lord 154

C
Caddo Indians 43
California 37, 151, 179, 181
  San Diego 37
Campbell, John W. 234
Carter, Lin 238, 239
Century Magazine 207
Cerasini, Marc 244
Chambers, Dr. Solomon 39, 41, 43
Chandler, Raymond 201
Cioffi, Frank
  Formula Fiction?: An Anatomy of American Science Fiction 240
Civil War 23, 24, 79
Clark, John D. 235
  "A Probable Outline of Conan's Career" 235
Clark, Renerick 44
Comanches 171
Comer, Earl Lee 39, 129
Comics Code Authority 239
Conan Properties, Inc. 242. *See also* de Camp, L. Sprague

Conan the Barbarian (film) 242
Conan the Destroyer (film) 242
Coolidge, Calvin 11
Cosmopolitan 50, 77
cotton 160
Cowboy Stories 206, 210
Creek Indians 25
Cretaceous Period 43
Cross Plains
  Cross Plains Natural Gas Company 97

D

Dallas (television series) 13–250
Daphne 167
Daugherty, Doctor 190
Davidson, Avram 236
Davis, Arabella 33
Del Rey 245
Dempsey, Jack 128, 137, 139
Derleth, August 22, 41, 62, 149, 150, 151, 197, 232
Detective Story 51
de Camp, Catherine 243
de Camp, L. Sprague 39, 69, 129, 181, 234–236, 239–249
  "Conan vs. Conantics" 243
  Dark Valley Destiny 243, 244, 250
  Miscast Barbarian, The 243
  Return of Conan, The 236
  Science Fiction Handbook, The 239
de Laurentis, Dino 242
Díaz, Porfirio 11
Dickens, Charles 58
Dill, Dr. 214
Dobie, J. Frank 57, 58, 65
Doyle, Arthur Conan
  Holmes, Sherlock 150, 165
Dula, Arthur "Kid" 131
Dumas, Alexandre
  Camille 25
Dunsany, Lord
  Pegana 151

E

Ervin, George Washington 24
Ervin, Maxine 106
Espinosa, Donna Juanity 63

F

Fantasy Fan, The 151
Faust, Frederick a.k.a. Max Brand 231
Fehrenbach, T.R. 9
  Lone Star 34
Ferguson, Governor 79
Fiction House 127, 138, 204
Fight Stories 116, 127, 128, 132, 133, 136, 138, 139, 160, 203, 231
Franklin, Ben 106
Frazetta, Frank 236, 238
Friend, Oscar 235, 237

G

Gafford, Fowler 38
  West of the Rio Grande 116
Galton, Sir Francis 80
Garvin, Viola
  "The House of Caesar" 214
Gate City Medical School 24, 32
Genghis Khan 188, 202, 217, 219
Germany 11
Ghost Stories 116, 120, 132
Gnome Press. See Greenberg, Martin
Goddard, Joe 132
Grant, Donald 239
Graves, Dr. Mary L. 45
Graves, Lorain 45
Gray, Zane
  "Desert Gold" 46
Great Depression, the 159
Greek mythology 167
Green, Mrs. 214
Green, Roland 242, 245
Greenberg, Martin 235, 237
  Gnome Press 235, 236
Greenwood, Charlie 216
Griffin, Jane Whittington 243
Grim, Joe 132, 134
Gunn, Ben 38
Guthrie, Roy 216
Gwathmey, Enid 183

H

Hammett, Dashiell 201
  Continental Op, the 170

Harris, Frank 154
Harrison, Harry
  Great Balls of Fire 244
Hays, Hoffman Reynolds 232
  "Superman on a Psychotic Bender" 233
  Stranger on the Highway 233
Henry, James 23
Henry, Louisa Elizabeth 23
Henslee, L.P. 45, 15
Herron, Don 201
  Dark Barbarian, The 244
Hoffman, Charles 244
Holmes, Morgan 202
Hoover, Herbert 159
  "Rugged Individualism" 115
Howard, David 23
Howard, Dr. Isaac Mordecai 15, 21, 21–29, 23, 24, 29–37, 53, 73, 105, 120, 179, 184, 189, 190, 193, 214, 217, 218, 229
  death 232
Howard, Hester Ervin 21, 24, 25, 29–37, 73, 93, 107, 120, 179, 184, 188, 214, 218, 229–231
  death 215
  ill health 174, 208
Howard, Robert E.
  "enemies" 96
  "Fear Dun" (the dark man) 142
  "mental-physical" argument with Lovecraft 153–154
  "realistic" stories 117
  adopts strange dress 193
  boxing 101, 128–145
  bullies 129
  characters
    Allison, James 160, 161
    Allison, Kid 139
    Bearfield, Pike 206
    Bran Mak Morn 17, 82, 87, 108, 159
    Buckner, Kirby 83
    Cimmerians, the 81
    Conan 17, 81, 108, 146, 150, 165–177, 207, 208, 231, 238
    Corcoran, Steve 200
    Costigan, Iron Mike 138
    Costigan, Mike 117, 197
    Costigan, Monk 134
    Costigan, Sailor Steve 66, 69, 84, 135, 136, 139
    Costigan, Slade 135
    Costigan, Steve 96, 136, 140, 203, 204, 206, 231
    Dorgan, Dennis 203
    Elkins, Breckinridge 66, 137, 204–206, 208
    Fitzgeoffrey, Cormac 17, 146
    Gordon, Francis X., "El Borak" 17, 201, 208, 236
    Grimes, Buckner J. 206
    Harmer, Steve 133
    Kane, Solomon 17, 81, 114–117, 172
      Le Loup 114–115
      N'Longa 114–117
    Kull 108–113, 166, 172, 200, 201, 239
      Atlantis 18, 108
      Brule, the Spear-Slayer 108–113
      Valusia 108
    O'Brien, Turlogh 159
    O'Donnell, Kirby 203, 236
    Picts, the 81, 87, 92, 108, 158, 171, 219
    Red Sonja 147
    Red Sonya of Rogatino 147
    Slade, Sailor 138
    Stark, Saul 83
    Valeria 173
    von Kalmbach, Gottfried 147
    Yasmina 173
  childhood reading habits 50
  common elements in his heroic stories 115
  contributions to the Cthulhu Mythos 157
  daily exercise regimen 129
  depression 221, 222
  first paycheck 94
  first professional sale 88
  friends 47
  funeral 215

historical stories 145–148
his first car 182
influence of Adventure magazine 51
influence of oral storytelling tradition 57–73
influence of the oil boom on 49
last will and testament 229
measles 105
Patches the dog 41, 130, 215
poetry 105
posthumous collaborations 236. *See also* de Camp, L. Sprague
proto-feminism 141
reason for keeping a gun in car 48
suicide 213
Underwood typewriter 98
viewpoint on history 78
view on races 79–83, 107
writings
"Almuric" 232
"A Man-Eating Jeopard" 215
"Beyond the Black River" 81, 171, 208
"Bill Smalley and the Power of the Human Eye" 51, 197
"Black Canaan" 83
"Blue River Blues" 136
"By This Axe I Rule!" 167
"Cimmeria" 172
"Crowd Horror" 135, 136
"Cupid v. Pollux" 104
"Curse of the Crimson God" 236
"Double Cross" 133
"Drums of the Sunset" 46, 119, 147, 200
"Fables for Little Folk" 98
"Fighting Nerves" 139
"For the Love of Barbara Allen" 198
"Golden Hope Christmas" 74
"Guns of the Mountains" 206
"Hawks of Outremer" 146
"Hawks Over Egypt" 236
"Hawks Over Shem" 236
"Hour of the Dragon" 170
"Illusion" 98
"In the Forest of Villefere" 91, 93, 98
"Iron Men" 138
"Kid Lavigne is Dead" 131
"Kings in the Night" 159
"Lord of Samarcand" 147
"Marchers of Valhalla" 160
"Men of Iron" 131
"Mountain Man" 204
"Old Garfield's Heart" 198
"Pigeons From Hell" 157
"Queen of the Black Coast" 170
"Red Blades of Black Cathay" 146
"Red Nails" 173, 175, 192
"Red Shadows" 116
"Sailor Costigan and the Destiny Gorilla" 70
"Sailor Steve Costigan" 135
"Shadow of the Vulture" 147
"Singer in the Shadows" 116
"Skull-Face" 140
"Solomon Kane" 113
"Spanish Gold on Devil Horse" 117, 137, 197
"Spear and Fang" 88, 91, 94
"Sword Woman" 186
"Texas Fists" 204
"The Apparition in the Prize Ring" 132, 135
"The Black Stone" 157
"The Black Stranger" 236
"The Bloodstained God" 236
"The Blood of Belshazzar" 146
"The Bull Dog Breed" 136
"The Dark Man" 159
"The Daughter of Erlik Khan" 201
"The Day that I Die" 83
"The Flame Knife" 236
"The Frost-Giant's Daughter" 167, 169, 236
"The Ghost of Camp Colorado" 151
"The God in the Bowl" 167, 169, 170, 236
"The Hall of the Dead" 236
"The Horror from the Mound" 82, 199
"The Hyborian Age" 159, 167, 168

"The Hyena" 91, 93
"The Ideal Girl" 77
"The Iron Man" 138
"The Last White Man" 84, 140
"The Lion of Tiberias" 147
"The Lost Race" 91, 92, 93, 105
"The People of the Black Circle" 170, 173, 174
"The Phoenix on the Sword" 169
"The Pit of the Serpent" 135
"The Right Hook" 132, 134, 138
"The Road of the Eagles" 236
"The Shadow Kingdom" 103, 106, 107, 108, 112, 200
"The Shadow of the Vulture" 186
"The Snout in the Dark" 236
"The Song of the Bats" 105
"The Sowers of Thunder" 147
"The Spirit of Tom Molyneaux" 81, 132
"The Tempter" 222
"The Thessalians" 104
"The Thunder-Rider" 81
"The Tower of the Elephant" 169
"The Voice of El-Lil" 145
"The Vultures of Wahpeton" 200, 201
"The Weepin' Willow" 132, 134, 137
"Three Bladed-Doom" 236
"Under the Great Tiger" 77
"Vale of the Lost Women" 236
"Valley of the Worm" 161
"West is West" 74
"Wild Water" 198
"Wolfshead" 91, 98, 99
"Wolves Beyond the Border" 236
"Worms in the Earth" 159
"Ye College Days" 104
Always Comes Evening 237
A Gent From Bear Creek 66, 208, 231, 239
Conan the Conqueror 235
Hour of the Dragon 235
Nameless Cults 157
Post Oaks and Sand Roughs 16, 91, 93, 94, 96, 99, 117, 130, 137, 197

Skull-Face and Others 232, 235
Howard, Wallace 26
Howard, William Benjamin 23
Hubbard, L. Ron 52
Hughes, Howard 12
Hyborian Age 18

I

Igoe, Hype 139
Illinois 63
Industrial Revolution 13

J

Jack Dempsey's Fight Magazine 203
James, W.S. 67
Jason and the Argonauts 116
Jefferies, Jim 34
Jeffries, Jim 128
Jenkins, Herbert 231, 239, 245
Johnson, Jack 34, 81, 128
Jones, Jeff 236
Jordan, Robert 242, 245
Junto, The 106, 141, 151

K

Keeling, Don Carlos 216
Kelliheir, Lieutenant 65
King, Stephen 199
King Kull 17, 81
Kline, Otis Adelbert 161, 201, 207, 208, 214, 215, 229, 231, 232, 235
Knight, Damon
  In Search of Wonder 240, 241
Kofoed, Jack 127, 139
Kofoed, William 127, 203, 207
Kramer, Peter
  Against Depression 25
Krenkel, Roy 236
Kuttner, Henry 149
Kuykendall, Alla Ray 237
Kuykendall, P.M. 235, 237, 242
Ku Klux Klan 10, 79

L

Lamar, Rivers 45
Lamb, Harold 51, 202
Lancer 238, 239, 242

Lawrence, T.E. 202
Laxton, Ecla 94
Lee, Dave 100, 123, 131, 215, 230
Leiber, Fritz 149, 244
Lieber, Fritz 236
London, Jack 128, 154
  Star Rover, The 161
Lone Scouts 106
Long, Frank Belknap 149
Lord, Glenn 236, 237, 239, 244, 245
  Howard Collector, The 237
Louinet, Patrice 167
Louisiana 158
  Louisiana State University 194, 213
Lovecraft, H.P. 17, 21, 30, 31, 40, 42, 51, 59, 60, 67, 82, 91, 92, 100, 107, 145, 148, 149–165, 165, 168, 171, 198, 202, 208, 220, 230, 232
  "Dreams in the Witch House" 150
  "The Call of Cthulhu" 150
  "The Rats in the Walls" 148
  "The Shadow Over Innsmouth" 156
  Cthulhu Mythos 150, 151, 156

M
Machen, Arthur 157
Madero, Francisco 11
Magic Carpet 148, 203
Malory, Sir Thomas
  Le Morte D'Arthur 116
Martin, Sarah Jane 24
Marvel Comics
  Conan the Barbarian 239
  Savage Sword of Conan, The 239
Massachusetts
  Salem 198
McClesky farm, the 14
McClung, Oscar 31
McClung, Willia 31
McDonough, Larry 129
McGowan, Murman 45
McGowan, Olive 45
McGowan, Russel 44
McGowen, Russell 215
McNeile, Henry Cyril
  "Bulldog Drummond" 46

Meichinger, Martin 13
Merryman, Kate 214, 229
Mexico 10, 63
  Civil War 11
  Mexican Revolution 10, 79, 140
Miller, P. Schuyler. *See* Clark, John D.
Missouri 24, 25, 30
  Exeter 24
Miss Universe pageant 106
Mooney, Booth 106
Moorcock, Michael 236
Moore, Catherine L
  Jirel of Joiry 186
Morris, Alla Ray 237, 242
Morrow, Gray 236
Mundy, Talbot 51, 202
music
  East Texas Blues 12
  New Orleans Jazz 12
  Texas swing 12

N
National Register of Historical Places 245
Navasota River, the 63
Nelson, Battling 132, 133
Neruda, Pablo 233
Nevada
  Bear Creek 204
Newton, Austin 38, 47, 74, 128
New Mexico 37
New Orleans 87, 92
New Yorker magazine 13
New York Evening Post 127
New York Herald 128
New York Times Book Review 232
Niño, Alex 236
Nocona, Peta 63

O
"old Baker House, the" 32
O'Reilly, Edward 207
Odyssey 58
Oklahoma 25, 30, 31, 179
Oriental Stories 145, 146, 148, 160, 161

P

"People's Party, the" 34
"Plan of San Diego" 37, 140
Parker, Cynthia Anne 63
Parker, John 63
Parker, Quanah 63
Pecos Bill 62, 206
Pennsylvania 13
Pinkston, City Marshall 48
Police Gazette 50
Pournelle, Jerry 236
Preece, Harold 106, 107, 130, 141
Price, E. Hoffmann 69, 129, 130, 149, 179–181, 230, 232, 235, 237
  "Book of the Dead" 179
Price, Novalyne 48, 57, 129, 172, 177, 179, 207, 208, 213, 221, 224
  One Who Walked Alone 182
Price, Wanda 179
Progressive era, the 11
Progressive movement, the 10
Progressive Party, The 34
pulp magazines 50

Q

Quinn, Seabury
  de Grandin, Jules 173

R

"Rugged Individualism" 11
Ranger Field 14, 16, 42
Reconstruction 23, 83
Red River, The 30
Rhode Island 151
  Providence 149
Ring, The 127, 128, 131, 139
Robert E. Howard United Press Association (REHupa) 241
Robinson, Edwin Arlington
  "Richard Cory" 213, 216
Rohmer, Sax 140
  Fu Manchu 140
Roosevelt, Franklin D. 160
  New Deal 160
Rumph, Dr. John 16, 44

S

Saturday Evening Post 50, 77
Schwartz, Julius 149
Schwarzenegger, Arnold 165, 242
Scithers, George 236
Scott, Jack 147, 214
Seminole Indians 25
Shakespeare, William
  MacBeth 213
Sharkey, Tom 132, 137
Shaw, George Bernard 154
Shaw, Larry 238
Slotkin, Richard 203
Smashing Novels 201
Smith, Clark Ashton 149, 150, 151, 157, 166, 172, 174, 230
Smith, Tevis Clyde, Jr. 57, 62, 76, 93, 94, 96, 98, 103, 106, 107, 110, 118, 127, 128, 130, 138, 141, 146, 150, 151, 165, 181, 191, 215, 222, 230
  All-Around Magazine, the 76
Southland Oil 16
Spicy Adventures 210
Sport Story 139
Sport Story Magazine 127, 139, 203
Starmont Reader's Guide, The 244
Steinbeck, John
  Travels With Charley 249
Stephens, Dr. Willis 32
Street & Smith 127, 139

T

Talman, Wilford B. 219
Talman, Wilfred 151
Tamerlane 202
Teagarden, Weldon "Jack" 12
Teague, S.L. 48
Texaco-Star 151
Texas 9
  Atascosa County 30, 31
  Austin 106
    Harry Ransom Center 243
    University of Texas at Austin 243
  Bagwell 29
  Bandera 9
  Beaumont 13

Breckenridge 189
Bronte 31
Brownsville 166
Brownwood 13, 15, 57, 73, 93, 128, 140, 183, 185, 189, 198
  Brownwood Bulletin 131
  Brownwood High School 73
  The Tattler school newspaper 74–91, 93
  Daniel Baker College 73
  Daniel Baker Collegian school newspaper 98
  Greenleaf Cemetery 215, 229
  Howard Payne Business School 73, 91, 103, 105, 219
  Yellow Jacket school newspaper 103, 105
Brown county 15, 38, 43, 62, 73, 93, 105
Burkburnett 14
Burkett 16, 41
Caddo Peaks 160
Caddo Peaks, the 43
Callahan county 15, 16, 37, 38, 43, 229
Canyon 45
Central West Texas 15
Coleman county 38, 43
Cross Cut 15, 16, 38, 41, 47, 128
Cross Plains 15, 16, 18, 43, 44–53, 73, 82, 93, 103, 109, 120, 123, 128, 141, 151, 155, 160, 177, 180, 230, 243, 245
  cotton gin 86
  Cozy Drug Store, the 44, 50
  Cross Plains Chamber of Commerce 16
  Cross Plains Electric Light Company 44
  Cross Plains High School 16, 50, 183
  Cross Plains Journal 214
  Cross Plains Review 15, 16, 37, 42, 44, 45, 46, 93, 147, 215, 216, 237
  Cross Plains School District 73
  Farmer's Bank, the 44, 93, 159
  first radio station 44
  Higginbotham's general store 15, 44, 73
  Main Street 44
  Neeb Ice Company, the 44, 100
  Project Pride 245
  ross Plains Volunteer Fire Department 130
Cross Timbers, the 43
Crystal City 31
Dallas 9, 10, 24, 160
Dark Valley Creek 26, 29, 30
Desdemona 14, 16, 49
Eastland county 15, 38, 43
El Paso 11, 37, 80, 152, 202
Fort Ringgold 166
Fort Worth 9, 10, 45, 160
Gaines County 31
Galveston 34, 66, 106
Goldthwaite 25, 40
Graford 24, 26, 32
Gulf Coast 13
Highway 206 46
Highway 36 46
Hill County 24
Houston 9, 10, 160
Jim Ned Creek 198
Lampasas 24
Lewisville 24
Limestone county 24, 63
Lower Plains, the 43
McAllen 166
Mission 166
oil industry 12, 12–21
Oran 32
Palo Pinto County 24, 26, 32
Paris 29
Peaster 29
Pecan Bayou 43, 198
Piney Woods 32
Poteet 31
Putnam 37
Ranger 14, 16
Red River County 32
Rio Grande City 166
Roma 166
San Antonio 10, 11, 30, 31, 80, 152,

165
Schleicher 44
Seminole 31
Spindletop 13
Starr County 166
swing music 12
Temple 174, 189
Tennyson 31
Texarkana 29
Turkey Creek 43, 44, 46
Vernon 12
Weatherford 29
Wichita Falls 30, 31, 123
Zavala County 31
Texas Board of Medical Examiners 24
Texas Central Railroad 44
Texas Central Railroad line 15
Texas Pacific Coal and Oil Company 14
Texas Rangers 10, 11, 37
Thomas, Roy 147
Thrilling Mysteries 210
Tolkien, J.R.R.
  Lord of the Rings 18, 238
Tompkins, Steve 201
Top-Notch 50, 77, 192
Top-Notch Magazine 201
Triplett, Percy 38
Tully, Jim 154
Turlogh O'Brien 17
Twain, Mark
  Tom Sawyer 117
Tyson, John 46, 53
Tyson, Lindsey 47, 74, 88, 105, 118, 131, 215, 229, 230

U
United States of America 11

V
Vestal Well, the 16
Villa, Francisco "Pancho" 11, 37, 79, 203

Vinson, Truett 74, 93, 94, 96, 106, 107, 118, 191, 221, 222

W
Wagner, Karl Edward 243
Wandering Star 245
Weaver, Eva 216
Weird Tales 12, 18, 77, 84, 88, 91, 92, 93, 94, 98, 99, 105, 106, 108, 113, 116, 140, 145, 149, 150, 160, 161, 162, 169, 170, 172, 173, 174, 175, 186, 192, 198, 199, 207, 214, 229, 230, 231, 235, 237, 243
  "The Three Musketeers" 149
Wertham, Dr. Frederic 244
  Seduction of the Innocent 244
West, Kittie 237
Western Story 50
Wheeler-Nicholson, Major Malcolm 52
Whitman, Walt 58
Wildside Press 245
Willard, Jess 128
Williams, Dr. 26
Williams, Nat 183
Wills, Bob 12
Wilson, Tom Ray 47
Windsor-Smith, Barry 147
Wisconsin 151
Wollheim, Donald A. 149
Wood, Wally 236
World War I 37, 79
World War II 80
Wright, Farnsworth 12, 77, 88, 91, 92, 113, 116, 145, 148, 149, 161, 169, 174, 214, 230, 231
Wrightson, Berni 236
Wynne, Alice 24

Z
Zanzibar 69